From the archives of the Comptrollerate-General for Scrutiny and Survey

TREASON'S SPRING

Robert Wilton worked in a number of British Government Departments. He was advisor to the Prime Minister of Kosovo in the lead-up to the country's independence, and is now helping to run an international mission in Albania. He's also co-founder of The Ideas Partnership charity working with marginalized children in the Balkans. *Treason's Tide* won the Historical Writers' Association/Goldsboro Crown for best historical debut; in addition to his novels he writes on international intervention and translates a little poetry. He divides his time between Cornwall and the Balkans.

Praise for *Treason's Tide*:

'A sparkling gem of a novel; not only a gripping espionage thriller that has the extra thrill of being grounded in genuine history, but a beautiful, lyrical novel alive with the sheer joy of language... Not since Hilary Mantel's *Wolf Hall* has a novel been so drenched in a sense of time and place' M. C. Scott

'Brilliant invention, the ideal vehicle for a narrative revealing hidden conspiracies behind one of the turning points in British history... a compelling thriller' *Sunday Times*

'Robert Wilton... has discovered a fresh vein of literary gold with this dense, superbly satisfying novel... beautifully written, wonderfully clever, this is another triumph' *Daily Telegraph*

'Bernard Cornwell meets Ken Follett in a Southwark pub and someone gets coshed. That is to say, great, intelligent, fun' *Time Out*

Praise for *Traitor's Field*:

'Brilliantly written, *Traitor's Field* brings the sense of melancholy and paranoia – as well as a page-turning plot – familiar to fans of classic spy fiction' *Birmingham Post*

'Sets a new benchmark for the literary historical thriller' M. C. Scott

'A thoroughly satisfying read... it is done so well that one feels no resentment about being tricked' *Historical Novels Review*

'A wonderful sense mystery' *Falcata Times*

Praise for *The Spider of Sarajevo*:

'A learned, beautifully written, elegant spy thriller.' *The Times*

'Robert Wilton is one of the smartest novelists we have. A touch of Conrad, more than a dash of Buchan... and a daring prose style that can set you blinking and thinking. Simply brilliant.' John Lawton

'Wilton captures a sense of place and time with immense vigour... This is a dense, rewarding beast of a book which makes sense of a tumultuous and critical few months in our history.' Antonia Senior, *The Times* Books of the Year

'[A] very rewarding work of historical spy fiction... intelligent and interesting' Nick Rennison, BBC History

'Fascinating history, exciting narrative and a wonderfully gripping (true) yarn.' The Bookbag

'A fast-paced and fascinating tale which draws the reader into the pre-war spying world... an excellent read' Lovereading

'Bringing this kind of novel to light takes writing skill, and knowledge of how states function (including secret services), of international relations, of the history of Europe... Above all, it takes knowledge, love and respect for the Albanians and their culture.' Daut Dauti, *Telegrafi*

'This is very much a literary thriller with a highly intricate and exciting plot... a brilliant work of fiction... Highly recommended.' Promoting Crime Fiction

Also by Robert Wilton

Treason's Tide

Traitor's Field

The Spider of Sarajevo

From the archives of the Comptrollerate-General for Scrutiny and Survey

TREASON'S SPRING

arranged by

ROBERT WILTON

CORVUS

First published in Great Britain in 2017 by Corvus,
an imprint of Atlantic Books Ltd.

This edition published in 2018

10 9 8 7 6 5 4 3 2 1

A CIP catalogue record for this book is available from the British Library.

Paperback ISBN: 978 1 78239 198 2
E-book ISBN: 978 1 78239 197 5

Printed in Great Britain by CPI Group (UK) Ltd, Croydon CR0 4YY

Corvus
An imprint of Atlantic Books Ltd
Ormond House
26–27 Boswell Street
London
WC1N 3JZ

www.corvus-books.co.uk

For the history teachers of
Stoke Brunswick School,
Whitgift School and
Christ Church, Oxford
The inaccuracies, as ever, are mine;
the inspiration remains theirs.

From the archives of the Comptrollerate-General for Scrutiny and Survey

TREASON'S
SPRING

Introduction

In the Travellers Club in Pall Mall, the bannister rail has the remains of the primitive stair-lift used to hoist the increasingly vast Talleyrand up to the first floor for his luncheon. It reminds us that, after his decades of service to a king, a revolution and an emperor, the legendary French diplomatist found the genteel society of London far more congenial than his own country. (And the fast footwork that had kept him alive through such changes of affiliation was becoming rather harder, especially after luncheon.)

Such were the games of allegiance, played across Europe and three decades. They first became tangled back when Talleyrand was enjoying an earlier sojourn in London, in 1792. The French Revolution controlled but had not executed Louis XVI; France was at war, and Talleyrand was sent to keep the British out of it. Loyalties were blurred and shifting, at a time when British radicals were basking in the new dawn of the Revolution, and French aristocrats and priests were fleeing for their lives in the other direction, and the European nations were trying to decide whether the blood on the cobblestones of Paris and a dozen other cities was a terrifying threat to their own social order or a handy weakening of the French.

The secret archive of the Comptrollerate-General for Scrutiny and Survey, discovered a few years ago under the Ministry of Defence in London, exposes the intrigue and violence in the shadows of the guillotine in 1792, as the Revolution began to break into factions, and the European powers schemed for advantage and watched in shock as their security and their traditions of secret diplomacy were exploded. It illuminates the uncomfortable cohabitation between royalty and revolution in the autumn of 1792; a fraught, feverish phase when it was clear there was a new France, but not clear whether or not there was room in it for the old king; when the revolutionaries were feeling their way towards an understanding of what their revolution would be like; and when, during the first battles between this France and her neighbours, Europe was coming to terms with a new world.

This phase – of pitched battles and backstair intrigues, of idealists and adventurers and spies, of desperate national and personal manoeuvring, plots and gambles and treacheries – is the landscape of *Treason's Spring*. Drawing as usual on the archive of the Comptrollerate-General, it gives a new prominence to two remarkable footnotes in the story of the chaos that was Paris: the spectacular robbery at the Garde-Meuble, and the affair of the Armoire de Fer – a discovery that at the time gripped Europe. These two events are a matter of historical record, but the record had until now not shown what was really behind and between them.

Within the centuries covered by the Comptrollerate-General archive, there are as far as I can tell documents spanning the whole revolutionary period. Some of the figures introduced in this volume reappear in the shadows surrounding Napoleon's attempted invasion of Britain in 1805 (presented in *Treason's Tide*), and there are strands of this story that would only be resolved a generation later, on the field of Waterloo (due to be explored in *Treason's Flood*).

Intriguingly, the Comptrollerate-General seems to have acquired early or unusual drafts of certain significant memoirs that were subsequently published in more anodyne form. Thus for example we have here Mlle Pauline de Tourzel, a royal lady who escaped the Terror and whose published autobiography omits certain details of her adventures which are reproduced here in their unredacted form; and of course we have Talleyrand, European titan, with a perspective on the politics, and hints at his own desperate dance of loyalty, that the public record has never revealed.

Treason's Spring also introduces three of the most extraordinary and elusive figures in the history of European espionage: one a mercurial Briton; one a Prussian; and one a Frenchman whose second greatest triumph was to betray and outlive a series of men of much higher profile and repute, and whose greatest was his enduring anonymity.

The strategic framework of events for this account is common knowledge. The detail is drawn directly from the archives of the Comptrollerate-General for Scrutiny and Survey, along with other relevant sources (specific documents are referenced with the SS prefix or equivalent; references are not given here for the many other documents that have contributed colour and background). The exact play of dialogue and emotion is of course my conjecture, consistent with the data and tending I hope to illuminate rather than distort what happened. If my fictionalization of these incidental elements inspires the reader to their own investigation of the facts, so much the better.

This latest presentation of a narrative drawing on the Comptrollerate-General archive has been written in diverse places: in Cuba, and Canada, and Cornwall and odd corners between. But mostly it's been written on my weekly commute between Tirana and Prishtina. So to the lads of Memi bus, and the fellow passengers who have tolerated my laptop jostling their infants and bags of peppers, thanks always for the ride, and *rrugë të mbarë*.

R.J.W., February 2016

A list of persons prominent in this section of the archive and active in Paris in autumn 1792, who are also the subject of individual files

The French

Georges Danton, Minister of Justice

Jean-Marie Roland, Minister of the Interior

Marie-Jeanne 'Manon' Roland, his wife

Joseph Fouché, member of the National Convention and on the staff of
the Ministry of the Interior

Saint-Jean Guilbert, seconded to the service of M. Fouché and the
ministry

Madame Emma Lavalier

Mademoiselle Lucie Gérard

Antoine-Laurent Lavoisier, natural philosopher

Mademoiselle Pauline de Tourzel

The Comte and Mademoiselle de Charette

Madame Emilie Violet, seamstress

François Gamain, locksmith

The Foreigners

Sir Raphael Benjamin, Bt.

Edward Pinsent, Esq.

Henry Greene

Keith Kinnaird

Hauptberater Karl Arnim, retinue of His Serene Highness the Duke of
Brunswick

Pieter Marinus of Delft

Jonathan Murad, on commission from the Congress of the United
States of America

Rien ne se perd, rien ne se crée, tout se transforme

– after Lavoisier, on combustion

Prologue

The Machine

My dear Kinny,

out of your darkness he brought you forth into light — was that not the line the old hypocrite Simms used to spout at us rascals? — and may his precious God have granted him heaven for hope rather than wisdom. And if I have so surely found the darkness here in France, damn me if I don't secure an equal measure of light.

They're a peevish and miserable sort, these rebels, but — Kinny! — it is a very paradise for a man with an eye for the deal. Their revolution has set every man at the other's throat, and left none to provide a musket or a mouthful of broth but your own Greene. I am in with all the sides in the district — you know me for the most credible rogue there ever was — and come and go as I please and all will buy or sell with me even when with none else.

I need you, Kinny. I need your cold head for the figures, I need your eye for a false man and a true coin, and, so help me, I need your sour visage scowling and preaching at me for it would do me good to see you and I love you for the one honest man in Europe. So stir yourself out of whatever squalid shack you inhabit, and get you to Saint-Denis. At the Tambour they know me.

And believe me as ever,

unfaithfully yours,

H. Greene

[SS K/1/1]

7

And Keith Kinnaird had kept the letter with him all the way from Edinburgh, down the coast and across to France; kept it with certain other documents, in an oilcloth wrap in an inside pocket, as if in its physical presence, in the re-perusal of its words, he could capture a more faithful Henry Greene.

But at the Tambour in St-Denis, the rain beating its tattoo on the drum that swung over the door, they knew no more of Greene than to mumble a direction and check that Kinnaird wasn't pinching the spoons. Greene's rooms were easily found, and Greene had clearly been living there: a patched coat, a wretched sketch of Holyrood, and a variety of books intermittently missing pages that had been called to greater service in the fire or the privy, were as unmistakable an identification as the man's face would have been. But the man was absent, and the landlord was vague about days and ignorant of where he might have gone.

Henry Greene had vanished, and all that was left of his mind and intentions was in that letter; and to Kinnaird, alone and rather foolish, having come to the end of his journey and found himself nowhere, the letter seemed less substantial than ever.

————— ◆ —————

The Place du Carrousel is a pool of mud, swirled with the shit of horses and dogs and humans under thousands of feet, as they shift and try to shuffle forwards. Towards the centre of the square the bodies are packed tight. Hands clench and unclench in reaction to the spectacle, clutch at arms, hover over mouths as if to stifle vomit or a scream, grope, or reach for a pocket. The faces bob and strain for the view, exultant – and alarmed by what their exultation has conjured. There's only a memory of light in the evening sky, and the windows of the buildings around the square twinkle orange in the blaze of the torches.

At the exact centre of the crowd is the machine. The crowd is all movement and uncertainty, emotion and noise. The machine rises erect and exact, a thing of calculation and design, legislation and craftsmanship. At the summit of the machine, high over the faces, metal gleams in the torchlight.

A single shout, and for an instant Europe is silent and holding its breath and watching.

A flash and a thump – and did anyone actually see the movement? – and a great sigh rises out of the belly of the crowd. And the faces stare and gasp and cheer, and look uneasily at each other to measure their emotions; it is not an age, it is not a place, to be the one standing out from the crowd.

Two foreigners watched from a first-floor window, standing instinctively back from the glass. Even behind the glass, even back from it, their voices were murmurs.

'Don't seem poor Colly'll be much use to us now, Raph.'

'Leastways he won't peach.'

A glance. 'You ain't that cold.'

'Quite the contrary.'

'You . . . ' – incredulous – 'you worried, Raph?'

A smile, without warmth. 'The world just changed, d'you see, Ned?' The elegant Englishman gazed out into the chaos, to the ridiculous torso of Louis Collenot d'Angremont, confidential agent for the King, executioners approaching it uneasily as if they too felt the change. 'Like some great weight dropped in the eternal clock.' Near the machine, its second political victim was being dragged down from a cart, white-faced and staring. 'The game is now quite new.'

1

Blood on the Cobbles

In which the arrival of a stranger in Paris is noted by divers
parties, M. Fouché begins to develop his responsibilities
in the revolutionary administration, two Englishmen
undergo certain remarkable adventures, and a criminal
outrage strikes the capital

The Memoirs of Charles Maurice de Talleyrand

(extract from unpublished annex)

---

*My mission of diplomacy in England proceeded with the stately torpor of
one of their puddings through the bowel. When they tired of their efforts
to tempt me to indiscretions political, financial, or amorous, my hosts
in London would beg me for enlightenment about what was happening
in France. They would gather around me, like savages before an oracle,
and if they didn't slaughter anything or offer much gold at least I got a
satisfactory supper or two out of them. In truth, they were as bewildered
and shocked by events in Paris as their primitive ancestors were by the
eclipse.*

*I tried to explain that to comprehend the secret dealings of that feverish
epoch in France — to comprehend, indeed, how a man such as myself,*

a prince, a bishop, a diplomatist, could be the counsellor and chief envoy of three Kings, one Emperor and the Revolution — it was essential first to comprehend the chaos. Or, I should say, for incomprehensibility was its very nature, it was essential first to accept the chaos. This, I fear, is not in the English character.

In the summer of 1792, the chaos was France alone in Europe with an army untrained, unfed and unled — her generals fleeing France with the rest of the nobility — being invaded by Prussia. The Duke of Brunswick with forty thousand men had crossed the frontier into France on the 19. of August. The chaos was not only a new government but a new system of government. In August my erstwhile employer Louis — the Sixteenth of that name, Louis the almost-magnificent, Louis the ditherer, Louis the soi-disant man of the people (who had then so impertinently decided that theirs he was not) — had been ejected from the Palace of the Tuileries by the mob, and then arrested; but the revolutionary regime had not yet abolished the monarchy, and so Louis lingered, and already the revolutionaries were dividing against each other.

Thus the chaos, and those most culpable were least capable. And yet, should the skilled diplomatist come to terms with the chaos, then he immediately finds ways to use it. He finds ways, one may say, to see its parts as so many wheels and levers in the mechanism of a clock or lock. And all the time, the diplomatist holds fast to his aim — he sees it as the pillar of fire in the night — and so he comes through the chaos.

However, the chaos brings in its turbulent train many unfortunate elements of untidiness to trouble the diplomatist. Past indiscretions, if not adequately obscured, return more monstrous and grotesque, so that they appear as great crimes. A letter that when written might have caused the raising of an eyebrow, in the chaos risks the losing of a head.

We are coming to think of wars as fought between two parties, as if they were an arrangement between two contracting merchants. Yet the experience of my age has been rather different. Wars to me were diffuse irruptions of violence in the vast web of relationships that was Europe. Wars were not an expression of enmity, but a means of argument — between parties who had been, and would once again be, in concert.

The American colonies fought Britain for their independence in 1776, and fought again in 1812, and yet in Paris and Vienna it was widely taken for granted that these antagonists' mentalities and their economic interests were so congruent that their natural state would remain the closest harmony. The European monarchies fought against the French revolutionary armies, yet this was but a convenience, a temporary suspension of their wider calculations and contests. The settlement after the Thirty Years War a century before — let us call it a cessation of hostilities, a continental catching of the breath — settled nothing, and I continued to regard Europe as so many pieces moving around the chessboard, now attacking the one point, now reinforcing the other, to be blocked or supported or pushed now here and now there.

Now pray consider the additional complexity when France, seen so wrongly as a unity, began in the 1780s to break down into so many parts. Consider the different factions at court, reformers and compromisers and faint-hearts and defiants and traditionalists; consider the different elements of political France, in and out of the National Assembly and its successors, those who sought genteel adjustments to the system of government and those who sought its utter destruction. Consider everyone writing to everyone, positioning and manoeuvring themselves on that mighty board. Consider every power of note in Europe, desperate for knowledge and influence and advantage. And in the middle of it all, dear Louis. A man so unsure of himself, and accordingly so determined to prove himself. He would insist on maintaining a correspondence with everyone — with all of Europe if he could — and he had his agents maintain correspondence with every faction in France. History has not known so great a spider's web of intrigue.

And pray consider, accordingly, the great alarm — the great potential devastation — across France and across all of Europe, at the merest suggestion that so much correspondence, between so many powerful and sensitive people, might threaten to become at once and uncontrollably public.

[SS G/66/X3 (EXTRACT)]

The abbey of Saint-Germain-des-Prés shelters the remains of the Merovingian kings, France's link to the mystic and the divine and a power greater than her own history. It's also where they buried Descartes, who knew that what you can dream is more powerful than what you can see.

On this September day in 1792, the heat hangs heavy around the spire of the abbey church. It drapes itself over the stalls and streets nearby, stewing the blood of those who loiter in them. The spire seems thin today; anxious. It senses something truculent and feverish in the heat. The capture of Verdun has spread across Paris in whispers and wide eyes. Prussians are over every hill, behind every corner. All that anger, all that violence, will have had a cause after all. The alarm guns have fired. Shops are shutting. The streets are fuller than usual because no one wants to miss a word or a warning. They're recruiting an army in the Champ de Mars. The politics – the talk – have become war; and the war is here in Paris.

Through the heat trudges a line of shuffling people, towards the abbey. Priests mostly – you can see the costumes. No voices, but the shuffling in the dust makes the line groan and wheeze. And it clanks. They're not going to the abbey, but to its prison: priests who've refused to swear the oath to the state.

Somewhere close, unshaded by the spire, one head is seething hotter. The Prussians are getting closer. The Prussians will capture Paris and restore the old order and nothing will have changed after all. These people comfortable in their prison, they're waiting and hoping for the Prussians and when the Prussians arrive they'll come out again and come out on top, and the possibility that something could be better in our shitty little lives will have gone forever.

Paris is a city of craftsmen and workers; Paris is always armed: knives and mallets and chisels and stirring poles and whips and shovels and anything else you can lay your hands on.

And as the line of prisoners trudges forwards and one face glances up towards the sky, with a prayer or the feel of the sun on his face or a faint sound in the distance that might be Prussians coming to save him, something boils over in the watcher. Something will have changed and this will have been worth something after all and I will not wait to be trodden down again and I will not be the first to suffer and he's running forwards towards the line of prisoners with a blade in his fist and he barges into the nearest and clutches at the collar and stabs, and keeps stabbing as the prisoner topples and they're scrabbling in the dust. Around them the line recoils and moans because now even the order and certainty of punishment has gone, and the mob is on them. First the assault is anger, fear, self-protection: a dust cloud of clubbing and stabbing. Then triumph, and the certainty that they cannot go back so they must go on, and it turns out that a dead man is a frustratingly inert reward for all that passion, and they begin to hack at the corpses for something more.

———— ◆ ————

The mêlée: arms scrabbling at him but he's got two hands on the saddle and heaves himself up, a bird soaring, and now he has height and a horse and he plants a glorious kick in the nearest chest and the man goes sprawling; already the horse is skittering and wheeling and he digs his heels in and the beast leaps away.

The night roars in his ears: the wind in his face and the moon flashing through the leaves above and the thunder of the hooves beneath, and his exultation. The grim theatre of the executions in the Place du Carrousel, the massacres of priests and prisoners, this is now France *and a typically Froggie sort of buggers' muddle it is too*, but amidst it all a man of style may yet do something splendid: in the 'tween-world of darkness, in the under-policed countryside north of Paris . . . A suggestion from a friend, a note, a name, and so he's playing a bit of havoc with the petty officials of the Revolution. Another escapade, another escape, and he feels the joy of it in his own gasps at breath, hears it in his heartbeat.

He can afford to slow the horse now, and he begins to enjoy the ride for its own sake: a fresh evening, a man alive and free, a good horse and a straight ride and ahead the promise of wine and beauty.

A quarter-hour later and the house in St-Denis becomes aware of him: hooves rumble in the lane, and then he's a shout and a shadow above the ostler and swirling to the ground and throwing the reins over and striding for the building. The double doors of the salon burst open and he's on the threshold – and for a moment he pauses, bows before the company; then forward again with long steps making straight for his hostess.

She's turned to meet him – everyone has turned – and her hand is outstretched before he reaches it. He kisses the hand, and momentum carries him a few kisses farther up the arm then brings his head up close to hers. He grins, and in the grin there's a growl left over from the energy of the ride.

Her smile is alive, pleasured. He feels warmed by it, acknowledged and admired. Then she starts to frown as she glances down at his clothes. 'What happened to you?'

Again the grin. 'So much elegance: I have to expect a certain jealousy.'

From one of the company: 'There's mud all over your coat, old fellow.'

'And blood all over my blade, Ned. My only consolation is that the other fellows are in rather worse shape.'

There's real concern in his hostess's face. 'What happened? How did you get in this – and how out?'

'I told them, most courteous-like, that I wasn't ready to die this evening; that there was wine undrunk and lips unkissed.' Both points are soon remedied.

Sir Raphael Benjamin has arrived.

———— ◆ ————

Danton, brilliant bull of the Revolution, is strangely guarded tonight. So, at least, thinks Roland, Minister of the Interior. Normally Danton dominates: by strength of voice, by physical bulk, by the generous display of his intellect. Tonight he's quiet; he waits for someone else to speak. *Danton's worried*, Roland thinks.

Roland's office is compact, comfortable. A safe place in the middle of the ministry building, in the middle of Paris. He checks the papers in front of him on his desk.

Having sat, Danton stands abruptly. 'A tempest around the house,' he says, too loudly; everything he says is a rehearsal for a speech. 'And the foundations rotting.' He swoops back down into the chair – it lurches and creaks – and his great head looms at Roland. 'Do we even have foundations?'

'The – ah . . . ' – the glance at his papers, the hesitation, as if Roland has to check the point – 'the people are the foundations.'

Danton thinks that Roland is guarded; but Roland is always guarded. It's one of the things that Danton respects about him.

Danton rolls his eyes, and they pull him up out of the chair again and around the room. 'The people are the tempest!' he roars at Roland and a future audience. 'Part of it, anyway. Their expectation. Their anger. The Pru-' Stop. 'Their justified expectation, and their justified anger,' he adds, remembering the third man in the room.

Fouché listens. Fouché watches. Fouché waits.

Danton continues his tour of the room. 'The Prussians in the Argonne, fifty thousand of them and all coming this way. Nine kinds of danger within Paris, every shade of royalism and every shade of compromise and every shade of treason. And . . . ' – he turns to face them – 'no foundations.' Closer, softer: 'No money.' He leans into Roland. 'The Revolution is penniless. We can't buy a loaf; we certainly can't buy an army.'

Roland leans back. 'Surely that is properly the province of Clavière, as Minister of Finance.'

'No one cares to be taxed by us, and no one cares to buy from us. We don't have any finances. Clavière's irrelevant accordingly.' Back down into the chair. 'Finance has become a matter of security.' His eyes flick between them. 'Of survival.'

Fouché listens. Fouché watches. Fouché waits. *Danton needs something*, he thinks. *Or he knows something*.

Fouché isn't guarded: he's locked tight; he's safe behind the ramparts of his alertness, of his scheming. It's one of the things Danton dislikes about him.

———————◆———————

In the doorway, Raphael Benjamin's hand rests on his hostess's forearm, and rests a moment longer, and then his fingers close around it and his eyes come level with hers.

'Not tonight, Raph,' she says; from her French throat the 'r' is a growl, and the 'f' a whisper mingling with the night breeze.

Benjamin stood a little straighter, regained dignity, smiled down at her. 'We may not have nights to waste, Emma.'

Emma Lavalier ignored the roguery. 'The nights we have, we may have to fight for.'

'Hah. You're becoming wise, Madame Lavalier. I know that face. Sometimes it comes on most inopportunely.'

She saw him suddenly weary – immediately older around his eyes. 'Poor Raph; so few moments of rest, and I fill them with worry.' She laid her hand over his, partly to lift it from her arm. 'Shouldn't we worry a little? These last two days have been . . . atrocious. The mob are dragging prisoners into the streets and slaughtering them. Paris is become an abattoir.'

'The fever will pass.'

'No! It will not.'

He scowled. 'It will not. They've tasted blood, these rebels. Savagery has become normal.'

'And what do your English Government?'

'Nothing they're telling me about.' She slipped her hand under his arm, and began to walk him down the path towards the gate. 'They watch, Emma. We're not at war yet, and the ministry have wound themselves tight as clocks over radicalism at home. They'll do nothing unless they have to.'

'And they don't . . . communicate?'

'Since Gower closed the embassy last month and fled back to London with all the silver, it's rather harder. Greene used to get the occasional message from friends of his in London . . . '

'I haven't seen dear Greene for several days at least.'

Benjamin slowed; his boots crunched on the stones. A grunt. 'Probably turning over the prisons with the rest of his ruffian friends.'

At the gate, a servant handing Benjamin his reins. His lips brushed a kiss on the lady's hands, and then he swung up into the saddle.

'I worry for you, riding around alone at night.' There was little worry in her voice.

'Your Revolution's mighty powerful, Emma. But it hasn't a faster blade or a faster horse than I.'

Emma Lavalier listened to the hoof-beats into the darkness.

------- ◆ -------

In Minister Roland's office in Paris, the candles are still now that Danton has subsided, and they emphasize the silence of night. 'There are some questions,' Fouché says, and Danton and Roland are immediately watching him; 'there is some . . . disquiet.' Fouché doesn't speak without he means to achieve something very precise. He gives out words as if he has a limited stock, and knows what each must buy. 'About the execution of La Porte.'

Roland watches him. Fouché is a very able man.

Danton watches him. Fouché is dangerous.

'I have been . . . listening. Among our supporters.' Danton's holding himself back, rare restraint. *I'll bet you have.* Fouché is counting out his next words. *Did they even know you were there?* 'The essence – They feel that the essence of the Revolution is justice. It were wise – that it were wiser – if the first political deaths had been of more certain opponents.'

Danton watches, ill-restrained. He doesn't know Joseph Fouché, except to dislike him. A young man; a new man. He has the suspicion that Fouché doesn't drink.

'Collenot d'Angremont was the King's provocateur and intermediary for royalist resistance,' Roland says, reassuring himself. Roland creaks and squeaks when he talks; like a door opening for ever. 'La Porte was the King's confidential secretary for all of his most secret dealings. His counter-revolutionary correspondence, his . . .' – hesitation; we're not sure about this word yet – 'his treasons.'

'A message to the royalists,' Danton growls. 'Their world has changed; their games are done.' He swells, boisterous. 'This isn't like you, young Fouché. Usually you're the hungriest of us all.'

He regrets it immediately. A cheap and shallow point, and Fouché will suspect it the more. *Why does this weasel worry me so?*

Fouché remains placid, but his eyes are bright. 'I wonder where all that correspondence of La Porte's has gone.'

Danton stares at him. *You miserable little shit.* So quickly the glorious sweep of the Revolution has become individual, private calculations. *Will I have to kill you?*

⸻ ◆ ⸻

The small hours of the night, the brittle hours; the candles dying, Sir Raphael Benjamin alone in his room and with no distractions to protect him.

What would I not give for one copper-bottomed certainty? For one true man?

He took another gulp of wine.

Pinsent. Dear old Ned.

Greene?

He could feel his head fogging. He could feel his mind drifting.

Emma . . . Ah, what a possibility.

On the chaise longue across the room, a girl was sleeping. Periodically her breaths would catch in her throat, and the sheet would shiver around her shoulders and hips.

In a different France; a different life.

There were times when he could not remember his past, before France; and times when he was able to forget it.

Now is all the time that there is. This . . . is all the man that I am.

The pattern on the wallpaper loomed strange. He took another mouthful of wine.

Greene's odd obsession with papers. The ruffianery he'd been encouraged to in St-Denis. And now the second name from Greene's note; the promise of a hell of an escapade.

He grinned at the shadows on the wall; laughed at them. And downed the wine, held the goblet between finger and thumb for one swaying moment, then let it drop.

⸻ ◆ ⸻

Natural philosophy encounters natural scepticism

Sir, you earlier expressed your interest in the project of the French Academy to measure the meridian from north to south through that portion which is comprised within France and Spain. Confiding that you are concerned lest the French should seek some political advantage from having a more authoritative meridian than Greenwich, or some practical advantage from their scheme to create a new system of measurement, I haste to report that, after a protracted hiatus caused by the persistent upheavals, and by the fluctuating reputations of some of the natural philosophers involved, the project is underway in earnest. The astronomer P. MÉCHAIN is en route southwards from Paris, while J. DELAMBRE works northwards. Your own men will be able to speak better to the reputation and capabilities of these two, but they are reputed diligent and well-equipped.

They remain, however, bedevilled by the instabilities roused by the same movement that has set them on their task. The business of surveying and triangulation naturally requires a deal of equipment, unfamiliar to the ignorant, and repetitive and pedantic technical proceedings of a peculiarity likely to excite curiosity and indeed suspicion among minds conditioned to fear and hostility. We learn that Delambre has been much delayed by angry sceptical peasants near St-Denis. Were they set on by your long hand reaching from London? In any case, his will not be an easy journey.

And yet they will persevere, and they are like to have the authority of the new regime, for its high-priests do idolize science.

E. E.

[SS F/24/141 (DECYPHERED)]

Day now, and the ministry pattering with its regular rhythms. Once he was sure that the Minister of the Interior was alone, Danton found an excuse to visit his office.

'What's young Fouché up to then, eh?'

'Very able man, Fouché.' Minister Roland regathers the papers on his desk. With Danton, there's always the impression he's about to break something, or grab it. 'Most committed to the security of the Revolution.'

'Quite. Very good. Hope he's not wasting his time with pedantries.'

Roland smooths his papers. 'There's a great deal of . . . passion, Danton. Ideals. Powerful wonderful dreams.' His hands shelter his papers from the passion. 'A few of these cooler heads, like Fouché, will help to keep us straight. Keep us effective.' He means: Fouché reassures me in the face of your volatility, Danton. 'He's not a factionalist. I respect that.'

Danton thinks, *Fouché is his own personal faction.* 'Well that's good,' he says. 'So why is he stirring up doubt about Collenot?' He leans over Roland's desk. 'No money, old lad. That's the real threat to the Revolution. No money.'

Roland nods. It doesn't mean that he agrees.

Danton glares down from his height. 'I am meditating on a solution. We may . . . ' – he glances round, as if checking that Fouché really isn't there – 'we may need a more radical solution.'

Roland's eyes widen in concern.

———— ◆ ————

Can it be? Appearing at the top of the stairs across the inn-yard, a man's face, body, and for an instant Lucie knew that it was Greene.

She'd been, as so often in the endless summer afternoons when the heat slumped like wet washing over St-Denis, sitting on a bench in the yard talking to one of the dogs.

And as the dog shifted its head against her stroking, and nibbled at her wrist, she'd looked up to see the outline of a man growing and moving along the walkway and the light catching his face and then he was outside Greene's door.

But it wasn't Greene, of course. Another man: not quite as tall as the Englishman, and thinner; and duller clothes.

Lucie continued to watch from the shadows, her hands absently scratching the dog's throat. The stranger stood in front of Greene's door for a long time. Brown coat. Brown hair. He looked dusty somehow; and maybe the coat and the hair were greyer than brown.

He didn't seem worried, as he stood up there on the walkway. He didn't even seem uncertain. He was just . . . waiting. He was somehow absorbing the scene around him, like he was breathing it – she thought she could see his shoulders rising and falling; she thought she saw his head shift to left and then to right, widening his perspective. *What is he waiting for? What does he do?* Absolutely still. He must be able to hear everything now. Even though he was looking the other way, Lucie Gérard knew that he was absorbing her, too; hearing her breaths from thirty paces away, smelling her, feeling her through his shoulders.

The dog buried his snout in her thighs and snorted, and she took hold of the scruff of its neck and pulled up the head and bent to scold it. When she looked up again, the stranger was looking towards her.

Towards her, then once around the whole inn-yard, head turning at the same even pace, and then he was back at Greene's door and lifting the latch and he was in.

From across the yard Lucie watched the empty doorway for a second, and then stood and hurried away.

———————— ◆ ————————

Roland and Fouché were sitting at the same desk. Fouché finished explaining a report. The minister signed two papers.

'What else, Fouché? What else occupies that lively mind of yours?'

Fouché smiles humility. 'Just trying to keep the papers moving, Minister.'

'Good. Yes.' Roland scratches his nose. 'You seemed . . . exercised by the deaths of La Porte and Collenot.'

Fouché knows that Danton has prompted this. 'I feel my way only, Minister. I mean no disrespect. I like things straight.' Thin smile. 'Everything in order.' Roland winces. He knows Fouché is exploiting his preoccupations. 'As Minister Danton very colourfully and rightly described, we face a set of diverse and powerful threats. External and' – he straightens a paper, and says to it – 'internal.'

It sets Roland worrying. Most things did. 'It's true, Fouché. We know that there are British spies and provocateurs active in Paris. We know that Prussia is likewise active. I fear that too many of those who presently co-operate with us will at any moment prove fickle.'

'Or false.' Fouché looks up into Roland's weary uncomfortable face. 'When Collenot died on the guillotine, his provocations died with him. La Porte's death gives no such certainty. Who can say what messages of sedition are still journeying across Europe, sent from his hand before he died? He was the centre of all intrigue, and' – hesitation; Fouché is rarely fanciful – 'his handwriting lives after him.'

Again he adjusts the paper. A redundant gesture; Roland waits. 'More than what he sent, Minister, I wonder at what he received.' Fouché looks up from the paper; his eyes show life for once.

———————— ◆ ————————

After the stranger had disappeared into Henry Greene's rooms, Lucie Gérard had on instinct walked away from the inn.

Strangers. Men.

Greene.

She turned after fifty paces.

She found Fessy the innkeeper in the kitchen, complaining to the cook. 'Monsieur' – quiet, near his shoulder; sometimes you had to be polite – 'who's the stranger in Greene's rooms?'

Fessy's face was immediately bright behind his tiny glasses. 'Ah, it's the little princesse of the posts and the potions!' His hand, shaking like fever, came up towards her cheek. Her eyes rolled; he wasn't looking at her face anyway. 'What's he want, your father? Money or a bottle?'

With a triumph of daring the innkeeper's fingers touched her cheek, and instantly hurried away. 'Who's the stranger in Greene's rooms?'

'O-ho! Little Lucie wants information.' Fessy's face brightened again, and the round glasses emphasized the calculation; something to sell, something to gain. The face cooled. 'There are many things that I could tell, little Lucie; but I don't know if it would be worth it for me.'

Inward sigh. She stepped closer, pulled out a handkerchief and with great deliberation brushed some flour off Fessy's lapel. Her hand stayed there a moment. 'There are many things that I could tell, Monsieur; tell Madame, or the gendos, and it would not be worth it for you either.' And her eyes came up level with his.

Always the big eyes for the men.

He pushed her hand away; uncertainty; forced smile. 'Another British. A friend of Monsieur Henry Greene.' He overrode the question in her face. 'He has a letter from Greene. Maybe he waits; maybe he leaves a message. He wants to see his friend Greene.'

'We all want that.'

Sniff. 'Maybe he pays Monsieur Greene's rent at last.'

Her eyes narrowed. 'Maybe he already has, eh?' Fessy bridled. Her eyes wide, down; mumbled: 'Thank you for your courtesy, M'sieur.' And she walked out, gut twisting.

———————— ◆ ————————

Into Interior Minister Roland's office slipped a secretary, a leather folder in his hands. The minister beckoned him to the desk. The secretary looked at Fouché, still sitting next to the minister and head down again; he continued to watch Fouché as he came closer to the desk and passed the folder to the minister.

'Thank you, Raviot,' Roland said.

'Yes, thank you Raviot,' Fouché said, and now he looked up, and smiled briefly. The others glanced at him. Raviot left, uneasy.

Roland opened the folder, and the scrawls of police reports began to slither down towards his lap. He caught them, and laid the folder flat, and straightened the papers. A quiet sigh, mind full of France, and of Danton, and unable to discern any distinct words in the script of his police agents.

A little cough. 'You might have a look at these, dear Fouché.' Fouché looks round, interested. 'You seem to like this sort of thing. You have the mind and the patience for it.'

'If I may serve, Minister . . . ' Fouché's eyes are already on the papers.

'I have meetings,' Roland says vaguely, and stands. Fouché is still in the papers.

Roland watches him. 'You're a good man, Fouché,' he says.

Now Fouché is looking up, alert; uncertain.

'This must seem a strange world to you – after Arras, after Nantes.' The minister's uncomfortable apology of a smile. 'No longer the provinces, eh?'

Still Fouché waits. He's never known what to say on these occasions.

'Not yet elected to the National Convention, and already we mark you for your discretion. Your assiduity.'

Careful. 'The minister is most kind. I am . . . not a man of passions, Minister. But I care for what we achieve now.'

'Quite. Quite right.' Roland fidgets, as if trying to remember the way to the door. 'Well done.'

Fouché murmurs something, and bows his head reverentially. Then he resumes his perusal of the police reports. Roland watches him for a last uncomfortable moment. *Damn the man!*

———————◆———————

DEPARTMENT 2

St-Denis, the 6. of September

A stranger is reported in St-Denis. He has been asking for Greene, known to this Department.

He is staying at the Tambour, in the rooms of Greene. Greene has not been seen in the area for a little time.

The stranger speaks to all who come to the Tambour. He has paid money to the owner and is ready to pay money to any who will give him information.

The stranger is an Englishman, of average height, thin frame, pale complexion, by name Quienaire/Quienairde ???

[SS K/1/X1/1 (AUTHOR TRANSLATION)]

26

With this report, Fouché starts a new pile to one side of the desk, aligned with its bevelled edge. He takes a fresh piece of paper and writes on it 'Greene, St-Denis', then 'Quienaire???, St-Denis', and then he turns to the next report.

———————◆———————

Lucie Gérard stopped a step before the open doorway of Greene's rooms at the Tambour.

Lucie: the walking store of messages written and messages murmured; messages of love and threat and speculative investment in the saltpetre trade; things heard and things seen and things never spoken of.

Down to her right, over the rickety balustrade of the walkway, the familiar inn-yard with the dog and the bench and the scattering of straw in the dust. Below her, her dirt-hemmed skirts and the toes of her boots and the boards beneath them, light-cracked. To her left, and just a step ahead, something unknown. A stranger, and a stranger was always a risk and a threat. But she had to know.

She took a step forwards, and turned to the doorway.

It was unsettling; it was alarming. Once again she found herself staring at the stranger's back.

He was standing in the middle of Greene's living-room. Silent, gazing at – she couldn't tell what he was gazing at; she didn't even know if he was gazing. *How long has he been standing here?* Just his shoulders, rising and falling. The hair and the coat were indeed brown, but they seemed as thin as the body under them; faint, somehow.

The shoulders stiffened.

The head shifted to the right a fraction and down; following the movement, Lucie saw how her shadow lay over the table and onto the back wall. *You have a moment to run.*

Slowly, the stranger turned.

Thin face; high forehead; bony.

A skull-face; a skeleton with no flesh on him.

Dark eyes watching her; searching her.

'Bonjour, Mademoiselle.'

'Who are you?' she said too loud. 'M'sieur' as an afterthought.

He frowned, as if he didn't know. She assumed it would be a lie.

'I am a friend of Mr Greene. My name is Kinnaird.'

He spoke French slowly; carefully; knowing limits.

Lucie said: 'We don't know where he is.'

'Mm. Pardon me, Mademoiselle: may I know your name?'

'Lucie Gérard.'

He made a little bow with his head.

His eyes hadn't moved from hers; hadn't travelled down over her breasts and legs.

A strange man.

He stayed silent.

She watched him sullenly.

Silence didn't seem to make him uncomfortable.

'I take messages for him sometimes.'

The face sharpened, tilted slightly. 'Messages?'

'My father is the apothecary, and sometimes he works as a copyist. I take messages – deliveries – for him. I take them for other people too.'

He glanced at her boots, as if to confirm how worn they were. Then up again. She could feel him measuring her poverty. 'Has Henry – Mr Greene – been gone long?'

She shrugged. 'Days. Week maybe?'

'There are no signs that he fled.' His eyes indicated the room around them. 'He didn't say anything? Didn't give you a message?'

She shrugged again. Shook her head. *I have been in this room so often, but now the stranger seems to own it.* Another shrug. 'He was out often. Meeting people.'

'People?'

'People. You an English too?'

The mouth opened in a smile; painful somehow – the skeleton showed through.

'I am Scottish, Mademoiselle.'

———— ◆ ————

Fouché has come through mediaeval Paris to reach the Royal Arsenal. Through streets of cobblestones and shit, through districts where the slums have not been entirely replaced by newer, taller buildings. To the fortress itself, a squat thing of thick walls and no decoration, all grey, all stone. This had been a Paris of defensiveness, of uncertainty; a Paris not yet confident enough of the peace of France, nor of its status in that France, to spread beyond its own walls in elegance and prosperity.

And in the heart of this mediaeval world, he has opened a small wooden door and found himself in a wizard's cave. A wall of shelves holds nothing but jars, and in the jars he can see a hundred different powders and liquids, of every colour from dull lowering greys and browns to vivid yellows and blues that like poisonous reptiles warn of volatility and danger. Below the jars is a line of larger earthenware pots, their contents hidden from him. Every jar and pot is labelled, with fragile scratching script whispering names he cannot understand, the wizard's ominous polysyllabic foreign gods. A board fills half of one wall, an enormous tabulation of abbreviations and endless lines of numbers. On the wooden benches that run along two walls and through the centre of the chamber there are marble slabs and wooden bowls and glass vessels and strange metal apparati. He looks instinctively for animal skulls, for snake skins, stuffed birds, strange herbs, deformities preserved in liquid and pentagrams on the floor.

He doesn't see them. The laboratory of Lavoisier is no cave, but the most modern room in the world. The two vast windows have let in the Enlightenment. Its wizard is humanity's standard-bearer to the future, the most advanced mind of the age.

He's also, Fouché thinks, a swindling money-grabbing remnant of all that was worst about the royal regime: a tax farmer, a chiseller, a profiteer. *He hoped to hide here*, Fouché decides. *Make himself the prophet of the new age, and hope we all forgot that he'd been the high priest of the old.* Lavoisier the gunpowder-improver, Lavoisier the would-be education-reformer. *No chance.* Marat has denounced Lavoisier for watering down tobacco, which is surely the least crime that any man in France is guilty of these days, but it's funny what'll get you into trouble now. And popular hatred of the tax farmers is vicious and unforgetting, and any excuse'll do to kick the complacent man out on his arse.

Fouché walks between the benches cautiously, wondering what clues about the future he's supposed to see; wondering what hints of the old corruption might yet taint him.

'Monsieur?' A servant has appeared in the doorway. 'You asked if there were any more documents, top of what he'd taken with him and what you've already got.' Fouché waits patiently. The servant has something paper in his hand. 'This letter came this morning. Porter didn't know to say the Professor had already gone.'

Fouché takes the letter, and a sheaf of calculations he's found pinned to one of the benches, and a ledger from the back of a drawer. As he leaves, he looks uneasily at the board on the wall, wondering if it could be some sort of code, if he should have the whole thing unscrewed and carried out after him.

———— ◆ ————

'Ready, Ned?'

'Never readier, old lad. Feel the blade at my neck already.'

'Then you'll move the quicker, I fancy.'

Edward Pinsent looked down at the shadow beside the coach, then up at the stone wall beyond, and up, and up as it soared above them in the night.

'This is La Force, by God!'

'I do hope so, otherwise you're not the coachman I need.'

'La Force, Raph! God's sake: this isn't daring; it's madness!'

The shadow seemed to regather itself. 'Brilliance, my dear fellow, though lesser men might easily confuse them,' he said, but it was lost beneath Pinsent's growl of irritation.

'This is one of Hal Greene's insane fancies, isn't it? Something else he's got fresh from London.' Pinsent shook his head. 'Damned easy to be brave when you're boozing and fucking your way along Pall Mall.'

'A bit of politics no doubt,' Benjamin whispered; 'but transformed by style, eh?' He thrust up a piece of paper. 'Take this, would you, old lad? Wouldn't want them finding my *aide memoire*.' Pinsent grabbed it, and stuffed it into his pocket.

Benjamin turned, and for the first time his eyes took the long journey up the wall that Pinsent's had done.

From the Memoirs of Mlle Pauline de Tourzel

(first manuscript version, unpublished)

Of our confinement I can say little more. For my poor dear mother and myself, life was nought but empty hours and fear and the search for sleep — oh, vain hope of oblivion in our trials! The days passed with ghastly monotony — we were cold, and constantly afraid — and we fought to preserve our spirits with memories of little incidents from happier days, and with prayer.

We insisted to each other that we must strive somehow to bear our torment with the dignity that became our station — most particularly my mother's — in the closest intimacy with the royal family and as sometime guardian of their dear children. We recollected moments of His Majesty's magnificent grace during the most tiresome episodes of His oppression at the hands of the upstart bandits, and swore that we would aim in our littler way at His example, and carry ourselves as if we were always in His presence.

The atrocious events of recent months — and, lately, the frightful deaths of persons most close to us — had given me at once a feeling of the greatest fragility — but also a kind of grace. If I could no longer control my fate — and who would claim to control that which the true God has ordained? — I would face it proudly.

With my mother's assistance, I took the greatest care of my appearance, and I likewise assisted her. I found a pride — and the Lord must judge whether it was vanity or gratitude for His mercies — in what I knew to be my physical advantages.

I was determined that our dignity of bearing would grow in exact proportion to the growing indignity of our circumstances. We might with justification suspect that our fate was to be some fraudulent proceeding of their illegitimate law, and then — my poor mother! — murder. We might, as all good Christian souls, fear that infinitely greater judgement that must follow, and approach it with humble faith. But we need show

no fear nor humility before the mob and their tribunes, and we vowed to
prove the falseness of their malformed world by maintaining the virtue of
the greater world.

And yet, for all my attempts at womanly bravery, I confess that I was
not prepared for — indeed, how could I have foreseen? — the surprises of
my last night in that infernal place.

———————◆———————

La Force: the blank soot-scoured prison of Paris since 1780; if the Bastille
was the symbol of the Revolution's hope, La Force was the symbol of its
despair.

La Force was five storeys of stone, and wherever there was a window there
was iron in a tight harsh grille. By this time it was reserved for political
prisoners; at night you could hear the occasional cry from the whores'
prison next door. On 3rd September the mob had attacked. When they'd
attacked the Bastille it had been to release the inhabitants; when they
attacked La Force it was to quicken the inhabitants' punishment. After an
informal tribunal in which she refused to swear for liberty and against the
King, the Princesse de Lamballe – closest companion to Marie Antoinette
– was dragged into the street outside the prison and hacked to death. It
was said that her head was cut off, and then recoiffured by a local barber
and presented on a pike outside the window of the imprisoned Queen.
In the course of a few days, dozens of prisoners from La Force had been
slaughtered in its environs.

At the gate Benjamin turned up his lapel to show the button underneath
it, and the sentry, chin buried in neck and indifferent, nodded him past.

I'm in.

And then, with the hollower sound of his feet on the cobbles under the
vault of the arch, came the realization that this achievement might not be
such a clever thing.

Into the yard, head down into collar but walking steady, into the yard
and immediately left; up three steps. The door opened under his hand. To
the right, and suddenly his footsteps had an echo and he looked up and a

figure was walking towards him.

Benjamin kept going, even pace, and the other figure's head was down into its collar too, and the reflections neared each other and passed and Benjamin wondered if he'd passed right through the other. *Are we all at the same sport this evening?*

An archway in the corridor ahead; an archway where a sentry should wait. He kept onwards, and the arch shrank around his shoulders – and there was no sentry and the arch lifted away behind him. The turn in the corridor was where it was supposed to be, and he followed it without breaking stride. *Confidence. I should be here.* And for a heartbeat his mind found a perspective wider than the dank walls. *I should be here because none else could be.* But now the perspective was blocked: the corridor was interrupted by a table, a man sitting at that table, and every step carried Benjamin closer to that man's question.

Benjamin kept walking. Even pace. Indifferent glance. The unavoidable justice of the Revolution: if a man is in La Force, it is because he should be in La Force. The desk, the man, was five paces away now and he glanced up – and then glanced down again as if he himself were the English intruder; three paces, one, and Benjamin slowed. He murmured the phrase he'd been given, waited, but the man at the desk said nothing, didn't even move his head. *If they do not want to see me then I shall not be seen.* Benjamin swallowed and strode on.

Door after door seemed to open in front of him, pulled silently by hands unseen; his feet seemed to glide. He was untouchable, unstoppable, a spirit of the air, a whisper penetrating the trickiest keyhole.

———————— ◆ ————————

From the Memoirs of Mlle Pauline de Tourzel

(first manuscript version, unpublished)

It was the greatest of shocks: we were drowsy, in the gloom and the despair, and so the more startled by the crack of the latch and the immediate opening of the door and the appearance of a man. For the hundredth time we readied ourselves for the order that would send us to destruction — our hands found each other's — we stared, with what defiance we could summon, towards the intruder.

But the surprise was not to be resolved. This figure was no gaoler known to us from our days in the prison, and nor did he seem dressed for a gaoler: his clothes were of quality — but his face was obscured behind his collar and his hat and what may — the darkness of the corridor was forbidding — have been a mask.

I cannot properly recollect our exchange: it was urgent on his part, and desperate on mine. I must fly with him now — I refused — this was madness — some new trick — but he assured me and my mother insisted that I had no alternative — but I could not conceive of leaving her behind me — unthinkable betrayal of the soul most dear to me, and most vulnerable! — but our spectre insisted that only one could leave at a time — that he would return for my mother — and she urged me with the most desperate pleas to heed him. Mother wrapped a cloak around my shoulders, pulled up the hood, and laid the gentlest of kisses upon my forehead. And with a sob I wrenched myself from her and presented myself to the man at the door.

Our departure from that vile lair was a sickly dream: I scarce knew where I went or how I trod; I seemed to see no one — no thing — but the broad back of the mysterious man leading me. Through a maze of stone and gloom we came at last into the air — I thrilled at the sight of the stars, high and pure above me — and thus miraculously via some unwatched postern into the street. Immediately in front of me was a carriage, the door open, and my deliverer was with a firm word and a brusque hand pushing me up into its darkness. Barely had he joined me than the carriage lurched forwards and away, with the most ferocious speed, and we began to sway and bounce with sickening jolts through the city night.

———————— ◆ ————————

The new ideas of liberty and equality, and some very old ideas of fraternity, were good news for the whores of Paris. The bustle of the House Under

The Clock – a constant ballet of feet on stairs and doors opening and doors closing and abundant curtains swaying and liquid pouring and petticoats glimpsed and flashed and moans – was become routine.

On the top floor, a knock at a door and it opened. But there was no face in the doorway, no smile, no breasts in no bodice and no enticement. The visitor took one uneasy step forwards.

Then the door swung wide and hands grabbed at collar and arm and wrenched him in, and the door closed again. The visitor went stumbling down, scrabbling on hands and knees on the boards and his head squashed into the mattress for which he'd had other plans. As he clambered round to a sitting position the hands were on him again, driving him down against the floor. A pair of masks loomed over him in the gloom, something flashed, and he felt the blade at his throat.

'Where did La Porte put what he was sent?'

Gabbling: 'What? – What are – ' The blade pricked his throat. 'Fore-'

'Where did La Porte put what he was sent?'

'Wha-? I – I don't know!' Again the prick. 'I don't know!'

'What did he do with what you gave him?'

'He just took it! I – I never saw.'

'And if he wanted to send something?'

'He'd hang a cloth in his window – a – a sign. Then a rendezvous by the Luxembourg Gardens.'

The eyes behind the mask behind the blade consider this.

'You must forget it all; you hear me?' Frantic nodding. 'That time has passed. If you ever talk of – '

'I swear it! You can trust me, you must! Tell Dant-'

The knife pushed through the throat, a squawk, and blood, and then nothing. The man behind the mask wiped his blade, then rummaged in the dead man's coat for the purse. The house would be eager to hush up a robbery that had gone too far, and would know how to.

The second man watched the performance wide-eyed behind his own mask, the last words clear in his head. The first turned to him, and the look dared him to speak the syllable.

The second man dropped his eyes, and turned away to check the door. It is not a time to talk. It is not a time to hear.

From the Memoirs of Mlle Pauline de Tourzel

(first manuscript version, unpublished)

The next episode was perhaps the strangest, and it brought me new alarms and mysteries.

We were still in the heart of Paris — I had lost my bearings, but I could see through as the cloth over the window flapped with our brisk progress the houses rattling past, and these were the comfortable buildings of the centre of the capital — and yet the coach stopped. Was this to be some new precaution, or — I could not overcome my fears — was my faint hope at last to be extinguished? My companion stepped over me, his cloak brushing my clamped knees, and opened the door and descended.

He beckoned to me.

I hesitated, not unnaturally I think, and he spat an urgent command. Startled, and not a little affronted, I followed him into the street. I felt that many eyes must be watching me, and I knew that one alone would be my downfall. But mercifully the street was deserted. And I had but moments in the gloom to take in the grease of the cobbles and the impression of unremarkable bourgeois dwellings before my companion had grabbed my upper arm and quite dragged me towards one of them. I writhed at this unnatural treatment, but his fingers were iron in my flesh and I followed bitterly, my legs clumsy in my sadly tattered dress.

He pulled me up the step and in through a doorway that opened in front of him by some unseen power. We were in a dark hallway: it stretched away in front of me, with the suggestion of a candle in the distance adding subtleties to the gloom; beside me was a staircase.

The finger pointed upstairs. Here was I, in a gloomy and unknown house, still the prey of every revolutionary agent in France, with a silent ghost directing me further into peril.

Gathering myself, I mounted the stair. A step creaked halfway up, I remember, and it was as thunder. On instinct I turned to my shadowy companion, and I sensed the greater tension even in him. I resumed my climb. At the top there was a single door, half open. I summoned a deeper breath, and entered. It was a small room, I think, although the very little light from a lamp on a bare table showed little of its dimensions, and it seemed uninhabited. On each side of the table was a chair. I felt as though I had interrupted some secret conversation. I waited on the threshold.

'Sit!' said a voice, and it came from the shadows of the room! I hesitated — for a moment I think I considered escaping down the stair again — and the single word was repeated.

I sat, looking into the gloom for the source of the words.

A figure emerged from the shadows, and sat opposite me. But with a gasp I saw that it was cloaked and masked, and the pitiful lamp gave me no aid.

'You will be safe, Mademoiselle.' In my predicament — hunted through revolutionary Paris, the prisoner of anonymous spirits — it was a laughable statement, and yet the gravity of the voice gave me some confidence.

The words, I should say, were in the English tongue, but I felt that the voice was nonetheless that of a Frenchman.

'But in return you must be of some assistance to your rescuers.'

I believe I said something courteous but without commitment.

'You must trust that we are friends to you, and friends to His Majesty.' I bowed slightly at the name. 'We seek his papers, Mademoiselle. His correspondence. We know that when the mob attacked the Tuileries and the royal family fled, the royal papers were shared among the most trusted of the Queen's women: Madame Campan; no doubt your mother and yourself. Where are these papers?'

'I know no-'

'The papers!'

'I assure you, sir' — I confess a little heat in my reply — 'that in my possession or my mother's there are no such papers.'

---- ◆ ----

The next morning came into Paris on a fresh breeze. Fouché found himself noticing it as he stood by the coach, unwilling to let the postillion haul his box onto the roof unsupervised. A rare treat in the city: ninety-nine days in a hundred the streets were clogged with soot and stench. Today some freak of the climate had made the sky seem clearer and blown away the reek from the gutters and the Seine. A day for a journey, perhaps. Fresher air; the beauties of nature.

Fouché had never seen the point.

His mind was not in the beauties of nature.

Dear Friend,

I hear today from my old pupil Delambre, and I fancy that his experiences may offer you some interest, and even some weary amusement at the nature of our time.

For the project of triangulating the meridian, Delambre is now en route on its trajectory north from Paris, while Méchain ventures in the directly opposite direction, south for the border with Spain and Barcelona beyond. I speak of the route and the trajectory, but in truth of course Delambre's has the essential anarchy of the triangulator's path, yet perceiving within it the perfect arc of the meridian, just as we insignificant astronomers, from our diverse humble stations at the feet of chords dropped from its curve, may observe, note and define the magnificent orbit of a celestial body through the firmament.

Poor Delambre had trouble enough following his star beyond the city walls! For as much as the triangulator's path must be logically eccentric, and practically interrupted by the difficulties of identifying and negotiating appropriate vantage points, so much must it spiritually be hampered by the obligation to navigate the obstacles of ignorance and confusion that lie in the path of all such as we. On the night of the 4. September, near Belle-Assise, he was with his assistants detained overnight by the militia, this after some interruptions and ugly scenes in the darkness when he was accosted by men of the worst sort, their superstitions having been stirred by his activities during the day, so strange to their brute minds, and by the alarming phenomenon of the signal flares he must perforce use to pierce the northern atmosphere. On the 6. he was obliged to secure a certificate of safe passage from the district office at Saint-Denis, after more alarms and incidents, and then to conduct a public lecture impromptu among the peasants on the rudiments of surveying, and still he must return to Saint-D., and be confined to a cupboard while the mob rummaged in his instruments. By now he was beginning to perceive some malice behind his interruptions, one of his assistants having informed him that he had seen, during a scuffle on the evening of the 4., a man of apparent quality among the peasants, stirring them and perhaps even spreading coin.

Such mysterious forces we may choose to perceive as true physical phenomena, or as superstitious projections, the fancies of a tired and junior mind, as insubstantial and obscure as the gods that govern the peasants' crops and the witches that turn their milk. Yet it is sure that Delambre will have slow going through their domain, even though the Convention has now made the two men official emissaries of the Republic, we may say gilding the lily of their original royal appointment.

I hear from other sources that Méchain is making swifter going on his southward journey. He is a more experienced man, and perhaps the peasants of the middle Loire are more phlegmatic, or better-read in trigonometry, than their brothers of Picardy!

Bailly.

116

Such the letter that had not caught Lavoisier before his ejection from his offices at the Arsenal. Fouché knew of the triangulation of the meridian, of course; and now he recalled a police report of disturbances around St-Denis because of the activities of one of the men involved. He felt the usual hungry insistence of a coincidence. But it was followed by its usual hollowness: the disappointing sense that there was not, after all, anything to it; coincidence did not mean significance. One distinguished man of science writing to another, about the most substantial scientific activity of the moment. Why shouldn't natural philosophers gossip as much as shopkeepers, or members of the Legislative Assembly? He wondered what '1/6' meant.

The letter, with the sheaf of notes and the ledger, should have been sent on to Lavoisier. A courtesy would do no harm, even if it involved someone out of favour.

But what about Bailly, the originator? Bailly the astronomer and man of letters; Bailly the former mayor of Paris; Bailly the godfather of the Revolution, the man who had presided at its birth in a Versailles tennis court. Bailly who had ordered the National Guard against protesters in the Champ de Mars, and so fallen from revolutionary grace, and was now fled to Fouché's own Nantes. Did that make the letter more suspicious? Or might Bailly come back to prominence, in which case doing him a courtesy would have been neat work?

Either way, one trod carefully. You try to follow a man upwards, and find too late he's on the steps of the guillotine.

After due consideration, he'd had the notes and the ledger sent on to Lavoisier, *on behalf of Joseph Fouché of the Cabinet of the Minister of the Interior*. But for now he was keeping the letter from Bailly to Lavoisier, one among a small but growing collection of papers that interested him.

The coach to Nantes was a tiresome necessity for Fouché. He was a young man from the provinces, without connections or reputation, particularly not in Paris. Roland would serve to get him a little influence, but he needed a base as well. So back to the provinces he must go – briefly, anyway – to be able to return with more strength. He needed election to the National Convention; and probably a wife, too – for revolutionary France is deeply conservative, and a brief and inconsequential ceremony may transform one of a thousand unknown young men on the make, vulnerable and undependable and unpredictable, into a man of reassuring respectability. They will not notice – they will not worry about – such a Fouché. It's becoming a dangerous time to be noticed, to be worried about.

His box was small – the minimum necessities for a the briefest visit; a new shirt, a token for a bride, and papers to study – and came up easily in his hands and on up to the postillion. He watched it strapped into place.

'Your pardon, M'sieur.'

Fouché turned. A man his own height, close enough that the words had carried in a murmur.

'You are Monsieur Joseph Fouché, I think.'

A screech, and a child raced past chased by another.

For some reason Fouché hesitated; sometimes, in these days, to admit a name is to admit an accusation.

But this is not an official, and surely Fouché is too insignificant for an assassin. He nodded.

'Your pardon, but I seek two minutes' private conversation with you before you depart. There is time before the coach.'

A slight man, apparently – but, on second glance, not at all frail. In the cheeks, in the jaw, in the neck there was a fleshless strength. The mechanisms of this man's body are visible. An active man. Fouché had always mistrusted them.

Something about the voice appealed, though: the quietness, the intensity to match the eyes; *this is a discreet man.*

Again, Fouché nodded. With a second glance up to his box, now secure on the coach roof, he followed the discreet stranger into the shadow of the inn doorway. *What should I – ?*

But the stranger spoke first. 'My name is Saint-Jean Guilbert. I am . . .' – for a moment Fouché felt disappointment, waited for the tale, the beg – 'I am a servant for hire.'

Frown. 'I already ha-'

'Not that kind of servant, Monsieur. A . . . political servant.' Still the frown. Fouché waited. Guilbert took a breath; prepared himself. Not a man of words. 'Monsieur Fouché, these are difficult times. A man of ability – a man of ambition – he wishes to rise. He has some friends. He buys a good coat. He makes some speeches. He gets a reputation in the salons.' The voice was still flat. 'But such a man is in the clouds, Monsieur. He hasn't his boots in the street. He knows nothing of what happens in the street, what is said there. The Paris street, Monsieur, is destroying many a salon reputation.'

Somehow a melancholy man. The low steady voice, the ominous message. Not for the first time, Fouché felt his inexperience in an unfamiliar world.

'Such a man cannot get his boots dirty, Monsieur. He needs a trusted servant to walk the streets for him. He needs the little errands that such a servant may do for him.' Oddly, Guilbert folded his arms together, hands at elbows. 'He needs the information that such a servant may bring.'

Now he unfolded his arms, and as his hands passed each other a knife appeared in his right, short and vicious. It stood erect between his thumb and forefinger, it dropped and disappeared into his fist, and then it reappeared and flicked and flashed finger by finger over his hand and then the arms came together again and it had gone, and Fouché could not be sure he had even seen it.

Guilbert's hands were by his sides again. In the background, another squeal from one of the children.

A witticism to reclaim control: 'And, Monsieur Guilbert, do you make this offer to every passenger on the coaches?'

A tiny private thrill: Fouché knew the answer before it came – hoped it. 'You are . . . you are spoken of, Monsieur.'

Fouché took a breath. He had the sense of being on a threshold.

'I must leave Paris for a few days, to – '

'To Nantes, Monsieur; yes.'

Fouché nodded; wondered a little. 'Yes. I hope to return within the week.' He tried to muster an appropriate formality for the step. 'I would be pleased if you would call on me as soon as I return.'

No more words were required. Guilbert gave a brief nod and stepped back farther into the doorway. Watching him, Fouché noticed a faint scar pulling down the skin next to his left eye.

Not a melancholy man; *a dangerous man*.

'Monsieur Guilbert – ' It was out before he'd thought of what to say. Guilbert waited. 'I am surely not the only man who is . . . spoken of.'

And Saint-Jean Guilbert smiled. The smile did not touch his eyes; it did not touch the scar. *Truly, a dangerous man*.

'Loyalty and service will be repaid, Monsieur Fouché.' Guilbert's eyes were harder still as he spoke; then another nod.

Fouché stepped back quickly into the sunlight. He looked around him, found the coach again, glanced back into the shadowed doorway. He could no longer see Guilbert.

Who has given his soul to whom?

As he stepped up into the coach, Fouché took a last look at the Paris street around him; up the overbalancing house-fronts, from cellars full of filth to attics full of plots. The wind had retreated again, and the stench was filling the street. The air felt warm – fat – pregnant. The Paris climate: a storm forever about to break.

The doorway was still in shadow. He knew that Guilbert was watching him.

I cannot be away from this place for long.

————————◆————————

The relative successes of his father and then himself had left the apothecary Gérard, of St-Denis, a good house and no ability to maintain it.

Lucie Gérard was in the kitchen, on a stool close to the window that gave light for her darning and a hint of life in the view of the chickens pecking indifferently at the dirt.

From the front of the house the bell rang – once, before jamming. 'Lucie!' – her father, muffled through the wall – 'door!'

She trod soft along the passageway. Perhaps if she was soft enough she wouldn't be here at all. Perhaps the floorboards wouldn't give way.

When she opened the door the stranger was gazing into her face again, the man from Greene's rooms; a nightmare she couldn't escape.

Lucie was stone. *Let me not be here. Let this remorseless mad existence not be real.*

The stranger started to speak; stopped, reconsidered. 'Is the master of the house at home, please?'

She stepped back, trying to disappear into the gloom. She nodded to the room where a message might be left or a potion collected.

The world had ceased to hold promise for apothecary Gérard. But a visitor – *good boots*; *tidy coat* – might represent enough for a meal, or at least a drink; and with a meal or a drink another day might pass. Humble bow, thoughtful smile. 'You're most welcome, sir.'

'*Bonjour, maitre.*' The twittered courtesies of welcome, of concern. 'A double interest, *maitre*. A small malady, and I find I might ask your further assistance.' Wariness. 'A persistent headache.' The stranger touched the offending temple. 'Perhaps you have some – ' *But of course!* Apothecary Gérard's movements suddenly perked up, became smooth, and he was turning, clearing a precise space on the marble block at the centre of his desk – the cleanest whitest space in St-Denis – and reaching for a small paper packet and placing it there. *A preparation of bark and certain herbs, most efficacious and quite tasteless in the gentleman's glass of wine . . .* The apothecary waited.

'I'm a stranger here.' *Strangers are dangerous.* The apothecary's face showed polite interest. *Strangers don't know the prices of things.* 'I am here on business, looking for an old acquaintance, but he is not to be found, and knowledge of him would be most helpful for my business.' The apothecary waited. 'I thought perhaps you, as a man of affairs in the town – or even your daughter, who is often out on errands . . . ' The stranger's eyes narrowed. 'Naturally anyone who helped me should properly benefit from my advantage.'

Apothecary Gérard's lips smiled obligingly, as yet another grain of his soul ossified. *A meal, a drink, and life will pass.*

Lucie had stayed in the kitchen, listening. She heard the stranger step out of her father's room, and waited for the front door to open and close.

Soft footsteps in the passage, and at the last moment Lucie understood what they meant and pulled away and the door opened and once again the stranger was gazing at her.

She waited, dumb.

'Pardon me, Mademoiselle. Your father gave me permission to ask for your help.'

It felt like betrayal. 'How much did you give him?'

'I – '

'How much?'

'Ten livres.'

She sniffed. 'For a gold Louis he'd have sold me to you.'

The stranger seemed to consider this.

'But I did not wish to purchase you, Mademoiselle.'

She shrugged. Somehow, bizarrely, she felt insulted.

'May we sit?'

Another shrug.

The stranger in the sunken bursting armchair, the terrier Jacques relegated to a surly consideration of the stranger from the foot of the back door, and Lucie retreated to her stool.

'It is important that I find my friend, Monsieur Greene. For this, it seems I will need more detailed information. More systematic. Perhaps help to talk to other people who knew him.'

Lucie said sulkily: 'You pay me, maybe.'

'I have already – '

'What's spent at the tavern brings no benefit here.'

His face hardened, weary. 'Of course, Mademoiselle.'

With great focus Lucie had picked up her darning and examined it in the light from the kitchen window.

But the stranger had stayed silent, and eventually her eyes came round to his.

His were so dark, and watching her.

Eventually he said, 'My friend Greene asks you to send messages, you say.' She didn't reply. He waited for a moment. 'I need to learn whom he does business with. Perhaps these people know where he is. Perhaps I need to act for him while he is away.'

She shrugged.

'Can you tell me whom he sends messages to?'

She shrugged.

'What sort of people?'

She shrugged, and she saw his face stiffen. 'People of affairs: merchants, bankers. Sometimes writers.' More like a skull than ever.

'And . . . for a share of the benefits, you can name these people and I can contact them also?' She didn't bother shrugging. 'Does he have any particular friends – people he takes a drink with, people he visits?'

'Different people. It's a mixed-up time. St-Denis is a mixed-up place. There is a group of British – British and some others – he passes time with them often.'

He was silent again. She considered him more openly. He sat stiff, which was a challenge in the old sagging chair. Against the fading plaster and old wood, he seemed to blend in.

Her father had told her of a creature that changed its colour to match the place it stood. Or maybe dust just suited this man.

He didn't stop watching her. She felt uncomfortable, and she didn't know . . . Yes, she did know. Most men would have been across the kitchen by now. A stool conveniently close; leaning against the counter. Standing strong, words beginning to drawl.

'Can you please describe the last time you saw him?'

Lucie shrugged.

'The last time you saw him.'

She tried to look more attentive. 'One of the first days of the month.' She forestalled the frown. 'Tuesday maybe; I think it was drying day at the mill.'

'Tuesday?'

'Maybe not.' The stranger took a long breath. 'There was a party that night. At Madame Lavalier's house.'

'Lavalier, you say? That's helpful; thank you. And what . . . what was the conversation? The last time you met him.'

'He asked to meet me. Said he'd have a message. There's a place near the river. But he didn't come.'

'He didn't come?' She shook her head. 'Had that happened before?'

'Sometimes. Your friend . . . he's not always reliable.'

He considered this; nodded.

'So . . .' Still the eyes dark and level. She waited. 'So that wasn't the last time you saw him.'

Lucie scowled. 'Earlier that day, maybe. Day before.'

'Had he said whom he would want the message to go to?'

She considered.

And shook her head. The shortest answer to keep the world out.

She followed the stranger along the passage, to check that this time he really did go.

At the doorway he stopped, and reached up and freed the doorbell. Then he turned, bowed his head to her, and was gone.

———————— ◆ ————————

'You look troubled.'

Pieter Marinus does look troubled. 'I look at you,' he replies.

The object of his consideration sits across the table from him, lifting delicate chunks of goose from plate to mouth with remorseless rhythm. Delicacy ensures that the knife and fork make only the faintest of taps on the plate – not as loud as when an elaborate ring, heavy at the edge of the left hand, happens to touch it. A big man – running a little to fat, but it's more the bones of shoulders and chest that fill him out; and a big face above, high bare forehead and a heavy jaw. It sits over a lace stock and a high coat collar that are rather old-fashioned now. At the centre of this arrangement, and gazing at his guest, the man's eyes are small – and very blue.

'Neither the action nor the sentiment is seemly.'

Karl Arnim touches his napkin to his lips, grandly, precisely. He's near the end of his second plate of goose, and surely a full bottle of wine by now. Every mouthful is small, savoured, and bidden farewell with the deliberate flourish of the napkin.

Marinus says, 'I wonder about you.' He tries to invest it with the warmth, with the admiration, that he feels. 'I worry about you.'

Now his host's cutlery rattles. 'Must we?'

Marinus's face jerks away in frustration.

His arrival was discreet. The room is shuttered. There are no others at table. The servant is trusted, which is nice, and deaf, which is better.

And still Pieter Marinus looks troubled. He's fiddled with his portion of goose, tried it, winced at a succulence he is incapable of appreciating today. He seems to experiment with knife and fork as if introduced to them for the first time.

'They're cutting throats in the street now, mein Herr.' He was born to the subtler languages of the Low Countries, but sometimes – now – the weight and sharpness of German feels right. 'You don't even need to be arrested to be murdered by these criminals. No need even for one of their sham trials.'

'What of it? My cellar is excellent, and Theodor may be induced to venture out and find me the occasional goose, and if time by time you will visit me I shall never go in the street again and yet be content.' The defiance, and the affection, seem without warmth.

'The Duke of Brunswick is advancing on Reims with the Prussian army. France is afraid – Paris . . . Paris boils with this fear – and Prussia is their devil. The object of all their hate. And here, in the centre of Paris – here, drinking wine and discussing chess barely two paces from the gutter and the blood – is a Prussian. Among a million Frenchmen, a single Prussian.'

'Well.' Napkin at lips. 'At least they wouldn't expect it.' And Arnim leans back, satisfied.

Marinus drops his fork onto the plate, another attempt at a mouthful abandoned. 'You'll pardon me, mein Herr, but that's mere bravado.'

Something in Arnim's face changes. It seems to harden. Somehow stone. Somehow brittle.

He seems even taller. The word comes out in a long hiss. 'Naturally.'

Marinus swallows his non-existent mouthful. 'Naturally,' he repeats. 'Forgive me. Forgive me. I – I cannot imagine what it requires to endure as you do. But – '

'But what is the alternative?' Anger now. 'What would you have me do? Fly?' Anger gives each word extra gravity, a pebble become a rock, but they still emerge at even pace and volume. 'Do as precious Louis tried to do? Dress up as a shepherd, or a nursemaid, and swim back across the Rhine and present myself to the Duke and advise him to proceed as he thinks fit in my absence?'

Marinus shakes his head. And it is indeed inconceivable that Karl Arnim could show the weakness – or, frankly, the emotion – necessary for flight. He sits across the table larger than ever.

'No . . . No, now is when we live, my dear friend.' A little smile after the rolling words. 'Not die, you hear me? Now is when we must most live.' With two hands he pushes his plate away, and the hands fold together and rest on the tablecloth. 'These Frenchmen, these clerks and peasants, will forget their fever soon enough.'

'They're fanatics.'

The Prussian's lip twists up in a sneer. 'So much the better. Around a calculating man I am careful; but one who has put his reason second to his obsession does not impress me.' Again the smile. 'And besides, my dear friend, in these difficult times are there not revolutionaries enough who are willing to forget their principles in return for a coin or a promise of friendship?' He shakes his head. 'Their future is as unpredictable as mine; except that I have Brunswick's army at my shoulder.'

Marinus allows himself to relax a little. *And I am so weary of the worry.* 'Your confidence is infectious.'

Arnim spreads his hand towards his guest in show of generosity, and continues the movement to reach for a grape. He holds the pose a moment longer, until their eyes meet. 'But what of the British?'

'You worry about them more than the French?'

'I am ignorant of them more than of the French. The French are desperate, and living from hour to hour, and I may buy any ten of them according to my mood. But the British play a longer game. They would rather we were all equally weak.'

'We monitor some of their communications now. We can bring pressure. You are not satisfied?'

A sniff, and a shake of the head. 'They may fail and fail again behind that sea of theirs, and yet flourish. While we . . . ' The face twists: dissatisfaction rather than discomfort. 'We must press them. We must shake them out. We must learn them and weaken them.'

'You could hardly be more ruthless in that direction than you have already been.'

There's real surprise on Arnim's face. And again the little smile. 'My dear friend: I have not *begun* to be ruthless.'

A goose and a bottle of wine unevenly shared between them, and their business concluded, Arnim escorts his guest to the door. He takes Marinus's hand, as so often: holds it flat between his own palms, not to press but somehow to sense, to draw out.

Pieter Marinus bends forward, vulnerable. And Arnim places a kiss on the top of his forehead; it seems like a benediction, but it is held too long for that.

Marinus lifts his head, breathes in his host's confidence, looks him hard in the eyes. 'If you will permit an impertinence, my friend: depend on your brilliance, not your bravado.'

Arnim considers it soberly, and nods. 'I will live long enough to do my duty, and I will die when I choose.'

Marinus touches the elaborate ring on his host's finger. 'And the bitter drops in here shall be your choice. A hard choice.'

'Not at all. If the moment ever comes, it will be a very simple choice.' His hand lands firm on his guest's shoulder; grand smile. 'I will see Paris fall first.'

———— ◆ ————

Over the mantlepiece in Edward Pinsent's living room – his only room, in truth; it beat calling it the dying room, though it might yet serve for that also – was an ink portrait. A girl of – fifteen, was it? – with a much younger girl – five, say? – perched uncomfortably on her knee. The discomfort was shared between the face of the older girl and the limited skill of the artist.

The knock at the door came hard, and Pinsent was startled; had he been looking at the portrait? Not sure. Lost the thread of . . .

Ned's Angels, Raph called them. Or sometimes Ned's Consciences. *Ha bloody ha.*

Another knock.

Landlord?

Not due. Surprising. Always seemed due.

Pinsent took the pistol from its string on the back of the door, and cocked it. Boot and knee braced to stop it opening more than a crack, he opened the door.

Dark eyes watching him. Dark eyes, bony head. Pale. A fleshless, bloodless head.

'Mr Edward Pinsent?'

'Who are you?' Very dark eyes, the fellow had.

They looked at him. Blank. 'My name is Kinnaird.'

'Jolly good. Now who are you?'

The stranger glanced down and up the minimal gap of the door. 'I'm a friend of Henry Greene.'

'He's not here.'

The stranger frowned. 'I didn't expect so.'

'Right.'

'Could I come in, Mr Pinsent?'

Spur of the moment. Pinsent couldn't think of any reason not.

He stepped back, and the stranger waited a moment and then stepped forwards. He hesitated on the threshold, and looked around the room before coming any further. As he stepped around the door he saw the pistol in Pinsent's hand, and his eyes widened.

'Oh. Beg pardon.' Grin. He uncocked the piece and rehung it on the back of the door.

The stranger's glance followed the pistol onto the door, and then up Pinsent's arm to his face. 'A man must go carefully.'

'Right.' Pinsent threw out a hand to suggest welcome. 'Will you take a drink, Mr . . . ?'

'Kinnaird. Thank you no.'

'Kinnaird; right. Er – a man must go carefully, eh?'

The stranger smiled. The smile was even more unsettling. 'Quite so, Mr Pinsent.'

'You'd better sit.' The stranger – this Kinnaird – took the wooden chair – he looked a fellow for a wooden chair – and Pinsent slumped on the burst sofa.

'Friend of old Greene, you said.'

'Indeed. He invited me to visit him for a while. We worked together in the past. I think he'd an idea we might do so again.' The stranger's voice didn't seem to vary, not in pace or volume.

'What sort of work might that be? Pardon my asking. Curiosity, you know?'

The stranger shrugged slightly. 'Merchantry.'

'Trade, eh?'

The stranger caught the edge in it. His glance sharpened. Then it moved away from Pinsent, and around the room: wooden chair and table, the bed ill-made and the pot beneath it, the torn wall-paper and the solitary item of decoration; two girls looking rather austerely from the mantlepiece onto their threadbare surroundings. Pinsent saw the glance as it travelled. 'Well now! Trade's the thing in these times, eh?'

The stranger's glance came back to Pinsent. 'Perhaps so.'

'Fellow must shift as best he can, eh?'

A briefer glance at the room, and back. 'Indeed.'

Queer, prickly little fellow.

'No one seems to have seen Henry recently. I don't suppose you . . . ' Pinsent shook his head. 'I beg your pardon, Mr Pinsent: do you mean merely that you happen not to have seen him, or would you say that he was . . . missing?'

Pinsent got the distinction, and his face opened in thought. 'Worried for him, are you? Fair enough; fair enough. Odd times these, Mr – er – Kinnaird. Would I say he was missing? I don't rightly know. Week or more. Perhaps.'

'You must pardon my probing. Were you intimates? Would you often see him? To notice him absent, or to hear of his plans?'

Pinsent gave a big shrug. 'We were close enough, you might say. For company, or a bit of sport.' He ran a big hand through his hair; it felt long, and he knew his wig wouldn't sit well. 'He was a close one, though, old Greene.'

The stranger absorbed this. 'Yes. Yes, he could be that. Was he often away?'

Shrug. 'Sometimes. Few days. Hard to say.'

'This long?'

Shrug. The stranger's lip twitched.

Pinsent took a second look at him. Tidy fellow; neat. A tradesman would have to be, of course. Impress the ladies; clean shirt and a bit of affected humility. *Gods, what a life*. Comfy with it, no doubt. Every third penny saved and no excess, *dear me no*; life all buttoned up, spick and span.

But what a damned queer object to wash up in revolutionary Paris. Fellow was lucky he hadn't been turned insides-out half a dozen times on the journey. And now bumbling around asking his questions. Pinsent smiled faintly.

The stranger said: 'It must be a strange life: an Englishman – here – now.'

Pinsent smiled. ''Tis rather.'

The stranger glanced at the room again. 'Lonely, I mean to say.' He nodded to the pistol on its string. 'And insecure. The English community must be pretty close-knit.'

Impertinence. Pinsent's words came with the suggestion of a sneer: 'We have our diversions. And our duties.'

'Did you and Henry Greene – '

A wooden slap and the door swung open, there was a figure in the opening and a hand that reached around for the pistol and swung it down and cocked it and had it pointing, and a voice that said 'Don't shoot!' – and then roared at its own wit.

Pinsent was halfway to his feet and half-reaching for the pistol himself and bewildered. 'Don't – ? Oh, damn you, Raph.' Raphael Benjamin watched his face, and chuckled again.

Now he saw the second man in the room properly. 'You must forgive me, sir. A bit of sport with a friend.' The stranger, stiff in his chair, was still startled. 'You must tell me if I intrude.' Benjamin was already striding the short distance to the cupboard and pulling out a bottle and a glass. He poured and drank, and then looked up. 'Well that ain't right, Ned,' he said softly, and he poured out two more measures – one into the only other glass and the second into a beaker.

'Fellow don't want – ' Pinsent began, but the stranger had stood and it seemed that under the force of Raphael Benjamin's momentum he did want. He sipped, and Benjamin took another swig and considered him carefully.

'Where are my manners?' he said without obvious concern. 'Benjamin. Raphael Benjamin, at your service.'

'Your servant, sir.' Quiet; still a little overwhelmed. 'My name is Kinnaird.'

Benjamin seemed to consider this. 'You must excuse a discourtesy, my dear fellow; but what with revolutionaries cutting every throat they can get their dirty paws on, a fellow gets a little wary around a stranger.'

'Mr – er – Kinnaird is a friend of old Greene's,' Pinsent said. 'He was just asking – '

'I'm sure he was. Asking; yes.' Benjamin grinned, and there was no life in it. 'A friend; of course.'

Pinsent started to speak, but Benjamin's hand was suddenly on his shoulder, and the blue eyes were gazing at the stranger.

The stranger gathered himself. 'Indeed. Very naturally your friend is cautious, Mr Pinsent.' The eyes came up. 'Very naturally. I have a letter from Henry – '

'A letter!' Hard amusement; Benjamin slapped Pinsent on the shoulder. 'Think of that, Ned! A letter.'

Silence. It waited there between them.

The stranger stood.

'Thank you for your hospitality, Mr Pinsent,' he said; but his eyes were on Sir Raphael Benjamin.

'Oh! You off, old fe-? Yes. But – '

But the stranger was out of the door, and it closed silently behind him.

Benjamin started to laugh quietly; after a moment, Pinsent joined in.

But Benjamin's hand was still on his shoulder. 'Careful, Ned.' He looked to the door. 'What a specimen!'

'Fellow's in trade, Raph.' He glanced up. 'So he said, any rate.'

'Trade . . .' Benjamin said quietly. 'But what, Ned? What does he trade? The damnedest things are getting valuable these days.'

———— ◆ ————

After their supper, Marinus and Arnim in the doorway of the latter's lodging. His lodging gives onto a side-street; almost an alley, really – a carriage would fill it. Open to larger streets at both ends: exits; options. Marinus glances around. With evening, the shadows are filling the angles of the street; the grime on the cobbles is dulled.

'I thank you for your company, as ever. It is a treasure to me.' Arnim's words are steady; sincere.

Boisterous laughter from the end of the street; Marinus glances to it, and back. 'I trust that you do not take me for granted.'

Arnim's face is expressionless. The Dutchman wonders if he's gone too far. 'I will ask everything of you that I possibly can,' Arnim says. 'But I will take your refusal on any point as the prudent judgement of an intelligent and not unbrave man.' Pause. Thin smile. 'There. Can you ask more than – '

'Prussians!' Both men freeze. 'You're Prussians!' Three or four men are gathered close by. Arnim turns to face them slowly. Cheap clothes. Workers, or worse. Scum. 'You was speaking German.'

The spokesman is shorter than his comrades. He stands forward, head thrust out, a big nose seeming to sniff at his quarry, while the others shuffle with interested hungry faces. 'You zpeak zee Djar-man!' – a silly parody of the accent.

Marinus sees the distaste in Arnim's eyes, and speaks quickly, and quietly. 'You are mistaken,' he says, turning to the man. 'We spoke Dutch.'

The spokesman looks scornful, but Marinus is unwavering. More shuffling from the companions. Polite smile from Marinus, almost commiseration. A companion jogs the spokesman's arm and they slouch off down the street.

Another smile from the Dutchman, uncomfortable relief. 'French, I think, in the street.' Arnim's lip twists, but he doesn't disagree. He accompanies his companion down the street a few paces. 'No. To answer your question, no, I ask no more than that.'

'It is for you to judge,' Arnim says, speaking stolid correct French.

'It is getting riskier.' Arnim says nothing. 'The revolutionaries grow feverish in their fears. Always new papers, new checks, new impositions.' They're at the end of the street; he glances back. 'Even to be thought a Prussian could kill you. If they knew . . . '

He lets it hang. Arnim's face sours a moment, then recomposes. 'I will play the game as long as I am able.' Formal dismissal: 'Again, my thanks for your company.'

Marinus smiles, turns and walks away into the evening.

'I knew it! You *are* Prussian.' The voice comes from the shadow where the facade of the building projects forward. 'He just said so.'

Karl Arnim scans the street in front of him. A few walkers; one carriage. Dusk is falling.

Now he turns to face the voice. It is the spokesman, from before, alone now. The eyes are wide with excitement. He too looks around, the bully seeking supporters. Arnim smiles. He nods over his shoulder, beckoning the man back into the side street.

'Like to see you all strung up! A stretch from the lantern'd suit you.' Again he looks round for support.

Arnim seems to consider this. 'Mm. If you find friends, you'll have to share your good fortune with them.' The French feels slippery, clumsy in his mouth. He beckons again, and turns and begins to walk back into the side street.

'Hey! You wait for – ' But the man is following now instinctively, and as he stares at Arnim's back he sees a hand appear over the shoulder with a flash of gold in it.

Again Arnim looks ahead down the side-street, to the other street beyond, empty in the gloom. Now he turns, the coin still held high, and he sees the eyes of the beast in front of him following it. And with his other hand he drives the knife up into the man's chest. He catches him as he starts to drop, glances around again, drags the body across to the other side of the alley and lets it fall, then stoops and repositions it in a drunk's slouch.

Up, a last glance around him, and back into his lodgings. His servant has seen nothing and would say nothing in any case. The body will not be found until morning, and it will not be remarked.

———◆———

In the second week of September, while the inhabitants of the prisons waited to see if there would be more informal trials and more informal executions, and while the inhabitants of Paris waited for the Prussians, a curious ripple began to spread from the north of the city. It was the stranger, the man who called himself Kinnaird; and he was willing to sit for many hours in a tavern, or to tramp for many hours through the streets and lanes, in his search.

At first he was felt only in the little circle of the Tambour; felt, and then forgotten, as his presence near the counter became routine. A drink carefully guarded; a simple meal; payment prompt with a satisfactory tip. Sometimes a polite conversation with an old lag, or with a stranger, and always the situation of foreigners in France would come up, and thence by degrees Henry Greene, and Henry Greene's affairs. Fessy, of the Tambour, had found reason not only to tolerate but to facilitate this inoffensive habit.

Then the stranger's presence began to spread: through St-Denis, to its few shops, to the conversations of the serious tradesmen, to the squalid rooms where the pedlars and market-boys drank. Then to the lanes around. He might be a wayside conversation; he might happen to be walking and stop at a farm for a glass of milk. Quiet civilities, and eventually the conversation would take the same turn.

Sometimes the conversation was easy. The stranger was a quiet, vulnerable sort of man, and the tavern men were quick to roll out their prejudices about foreigners, and merchants found it easy to correct his mistakes – about Henry Greene's business, for example. Sometimes the conversation was hard. The stranger was an unwarm, indefinable sort of man, and everyone was alert for spies and police agents. Doors slammed shut. Stones, dung, were thrown. These are the times.

The ripples continued to spread; and at last the stranger, the man who called himself Kinnaird, made his first journey into Paris.

———————— ♦ ————————

Emma Lavalier's coterie this September evening in St-Denis: three Frenchmen of diverse quality and eccentricity; an Italian singer; a beautiful Spanish boy, arguing with an American; her two favourite Englishmen; a Dutchman; the women all French, with the exception of Maria Halász, who was rumoured to have shot her husband back in Buda.

And now her Belgian was here and wanting to pay his respects, bouncing like a bladder at the edge of her vision, and Raph was murmuring something charming and forgettable in her ear and drifting away, and she was beaming at the Belgian and he bounced at her and she let herself enjoy the effusive, elaborate, *not-to-say-madame-exquisite* compliments that made him such an . . . effervescent guest; and then she managed to direct him in some other appealing direction, and off he went and for a blessed breath of a moment Emma Lavalier found herself alone at the centre of her circle; the eye of the storm; her little world.

The door to the front hall ahead of her, guarded by a servant. The certainty of the small door to her private salon behind her.

The salon pleasant; simply elegant; thrift carefully deployed by taste. The transformative power of a curtain; the decoration on one panel of a screen instead of every wall; the mischievous beauty of candles.

Emma Lavalier chose her guests like her decor. There was little money in this room, but there was much style; and for an evening with her these personalities would summon the finery, and the energy, that wouldn't otherwise be used in a week and they would come together and live a little. She wanted brilliance and desperation; she wanted perfect taste and utter abandon. She wanted great lovers, and great betrayers – and one tended naturally to be the other.

She watched them move, and mingle: temptations, and treacheries, and all hers.

This was her playful haven, a gleaming joy safe from the madness of the world outside, its brilliance hidden in the darkness, a highwayman's eye glittering in a mask.

And in this haven such games! Games of hearts and games of souls. Games, both, of loyalties.

In earlier life – in another life – she had travelled once to the south of France, near Spain, and seen the fighting of the bulls in the arena. Supposedly a forbidden spectacle for a genteel woman; an illicit pleasure, an erotic thrill in the thundering beast and the roars of the men. A controlled spectacle; a game with limits. She was in her arena now, pirouetting and dancing, in and away.

Raph, of course. She loved to watch him across a room. He was more resistible at a distance; somehow vulnerable when she could look at him without him breathing close by. But what a magnificent beast, far or near . . . The meat of the man, in his tight-cut elegance, and the movement. Graceful movement; and thrilling because she knew he could do it with a sword, or a horse, or a woman.

With a Severine Vial, for example? A lovely creature, rather too girlish of form for Lavalier's preference – though Raph would think her an easier, fresher challenge. She watched them bobbing and swaying together, corners of eyes and murmuring lips. But Emma could see Vial's eyes, which Raph could not – *does he ever see a woman straight in the eye?* – and knew that she would not be a conquest unless she set out to be most deliberately. Emma watched her a moment longer: the pale slender face, the neck, the suggestion of her breasts, the way she swayed from her waist in the conversation. A shrewd invitation after all: a woman needed her men to have distractions, and sometimes a woman needed a distraction herself.

Ned Pinsent had given up on the other side of La Vial, and was standing stiffly looking at a nearby group.

Poor wrecked Ned. Near him, glancing at him – *it is not only I who sees your solitude, dear Ned* – the Dutchman . . . Marinus. Good to have a serious man – easier to flirt, and much more satisfying, in a discussion about revolution than a gossip about lace. Though it seemed highly unlikely that the Dutchman himself was of the conventional erotic taste.

A glimpsed dream of girls and of unnatural men and then the world seemed to close in on her again: someone had clapped and called for music and someone else had called for a game and the bodies were hurrying into the adjoining room and the servant was walking silently towards her.

Benjamin was following the charming Madame Vial through the doorway when he saw the servant leaning towards his mistress, saw her frown. Benjamin murmured an unheard excuse and stepped back and towards Emma. Pinsent saw this and followed.

'Does either of you,' Lavalier said quietly, 'know a British called Kinnaird?' The vowels were uncomfortable.

Shakes of the head. But then a sort of growl from Pinsent, which meant he was thinking, and the others waited. 'I think . . . yes, I think that was the name – fellow called on me the other day.' His eyes came up. 'You were there, Raph. Fellow you booted out.'

Benjamin nodded slowly, and turned to his hostess. 'Why d'you ask?'

Emma looked towards the hall. 'Because he's calling on me now.'

She commanded a chair, and sat, and faced the door. Benjamin stood at her shoulder; Pinsent was somewhere to the side. This was the view that faced the stranger when he entered.

He stopped, and considered it. Then he stepped forwards, and bowed slightly from the waist.

'I ask pardon for the interruption, Madame,' he began in plodding French. 'If I knew you are with guests – '

'It is endless,' she said in English. 'I cannot seem to keep them away.'

The stranger said stiffly: 'That is surely understandable, Madame.' Three pairs of eyes considered this, albeit from different perspectives.

Sir Raphael Benjamin said quietly: 'And you, dear sir, seem equally hard to keep away.'

Lavalier half-turned to the interruption, then back to the stranger. His eyes were still on her. A plain man in every respect, surely; somehow contained. His eyes very dark and still.

'I am in the district visiting a friend,' he said to her. 'Mr Henry Greene, who I was told was an habitué of your circle, Madame. An acquaintance' – his eyes flicked to Pinsent, who looked uncomfortable – 'suggested that I might pay my respects.'

The eyes moved to Benjamin, then back down to her. 'That is if *you* permit, Madame.' The defiance, the dare, was for Benjamin as well as her, and they both felt it. Emma smiled faintly; no easy triumphs for Raph tonight, neither the lovely Severine nor this implacable visitor.

She lifted her hand slowly towards the stranger. 'I am become the oasis for the lost souls of Britain,' she said. 'I bid you welcome.'

He didn't seem to have seen a Frenchwoman's hand before. He considered it, then her face, then advanced towards it, took the fingers uneasily, and bowed over them. Still in the bow he stared into her face – it unsettled her a moment – *what does he look for? what does he see?* – and then he'd dropped the fingers and stood quickly. 'Keith Kinnaird: your humble servant, Madame.'

'I am glad of it, Mr Kinnaird. You will find music and more lost souls through that door.' She nodded to it, and he looked between it and her, and bowed stiffly again, and walked carefully towards whatever fate lay within.

Emma Lavalier watched him go, and then her eyes moved up to Raph Benjamin and she suppressed a chuckle. 'Your friends, Raph. Such curiosities. Is this the real Revolution?'

'What an object!' Benjamin said. More seriously: 'Ned, did you actually suggest he come here, as he implied?'

Pinsent hesitated, and Benjamin sighed at him. 'Don't recall so,' Pinsent said quickly. 'Anyway, a fellow doesn't invite strangers to ladies' houses; and certainly not strangers like that.'

'Yet here he is,' Emma said to the closed door.

'Next question, Ned: did – '

'Easy with your damned interrogation, Benjamin.'

'Did he ever explain how he came to fix on you as a route to old Henry?'

'He said . . . No. No, he didn't say.'

'I'll bet. And did you mention Emma to him?'

'A lady's name to a stranger?'

Emma was still talking to the space the stranger had left. 'Perhaps he really is just looking for his friend.'

'Dear Emma . . . ' Benjamin was earnest rather than sneering.

'I don't like his being here.' Pinsent, affronted.

Emma Lavalier looked up at him. 'Then you shouldn't have enabled it, Ned.' Again she looked to the closed door. 'Because he's here now.'

———————◆———————

(RECEIVED IN THE DUKE OF BRUNSWICK'S CAMP, NEAR VERDUN, 15. SEPTEMBER 1792)

From No. 1

Your Serene Highness, Paris is chaos. The mob passionate for France and against Prussia, but uncontrollable. Assaults on men of status and privilege have devastated the quality, commitment and morale at the higher levels of the army. Sources report indiscipline and problems of supply: grain and horses scarce. General Dumouriez with his forces is hurrying to attempt to block you, and must struggle to co-operate with Kellermann, isolated with his forces to your east. The new 'National Convention' has yet to meet, and its elected members have neither coherence nor a clear centre. The leaders of the Revolution have their weaknesses (to wit money and legitimacy), their worries (to wit money and legitimacy and you) and their divisions – these even within the so-called Club of the Jacobins, between passionate theorists such as Brissot and Roland, and the calculating mob-stirrers such as Marat, Danton and Robespierre; the attitudes of men like General Dumouriez, necessary to France's survival but surely not revolutionaries in character, must be reckoned different again. But though brittle as a body, they are resolute, ruthless, and in some cases brilliant, and have nothing to lose. They are sustained by the momentum of their madness. Culpable for great treasons, complicit, and trapped in the machinery of their schemes, they can only go forwards – looking sometime sidelong to perceive potential treachery and make sure to inflict it first. Your Serene Highness's instincts on this were of course right. There are some who do seek to reinsure themselves against a fall, and who begin to calculate that private accommodation with Prussia may be a surer path than trusting to the faith of their confederates. At the same time it is rumoured that Dumouriez, with Talleyrand still in London, seeks accommodation with Britain. Your package was passed precisely according to your instructions, and you are promised a satisfactory return. Your Grace's servant closes with gratitude for the honour of serving you.

[Decyphered text in Bundesarkiv Berlin-Lichterfelde, Reserve Collection (author translation)]

The encyphered message slipped into its hiding place, Karl Arnim had gazed at his original draft for a full minute before placing it deliberately in the centre of the fire. He was uncomfortable as the messenger of messages he did not read: the package from the Duke of Brunswick that he had forwarded unopened to his contact, and whatever that remarkable man would want forwarded to the Duke in return. And so for a moment he had considered keeping the unencyphered draft, as sign of his neutral obedience and ignorance should it become necessary. But when the game, if there was a game, went wrong – and if there were a game, it would sooner or later go wrong – this would serve him little.

So into the fire it went, and he watched to see it burn: a possible change of wind in Berlin was merely one among many prudent speculations about the distant future; the revolutionaries could break his door down within the hour and his draft message would get him torn apart.

It writhed and shrivelled black among the flames, and crumbled into ash and dropped through the grate; and he bent and checked that it really was all ash.

He wondered, as every time, if the men he dealt with here in Paris were as careful. As every time, he feared not. So full of games and treacheries, these political men. So proud of their clevernesses.

And their fallen King would be the worst of them, for stupid pride.

So where, now – in this vast Paris, in this chaos – where were his papers?

------◆------

Fouché was back in Paris. He'd not been able to keep away, even in the middle of his election campaign. One was supposed to carry the Revolution to the provinces – even, the good God help us, to Nantes – but getting down from the coach in the capital, taking one's first steps in the street after just a short absence, was to feel like Lazarus brought back to life. The future was being made in the streets of Paris – and in certain private rooms in the city – and anywhere outside its walls was obscurity and oblivion.

The two men considered each other with a kind – with different kinds – of hunger.

Joseph Fouché's was a nervous appetite, as he considered Guilbert; an appetite for the sinful, for forbidden fruit, a prurient enjoyment of something bloody. He checked himself, remembered that it was late, acknowledged that no one would have seen Guilbert slipping through back alleys to this office, glanced instinctively beyond the man to the door. A smile; an open palm. 'Sit.'

Saint-Jean Guilbert's was a workman's appetite, as he considered Fouché; an appetite for the sustenance needed to get through the next half-day. And in this office the nourishment was rich indeed. Prompted by Fouché's concern, he checked over his own shoulder, and closed the door before he sat.

Another thin smile from Fouché. 'The door open again, if you please. I do not wish to seem to have secrets. And I wish to hear the approach of any man who comes to check the point.'

Guilbert's eyes hardened. He stood, opened the door a crack, and sat again.

Fouché had quill and ink and paper poised. 'Begin.'

Guilbert licked his lips. 'Pierre Maupuy.' A glance of interest from

Fouché, then the scratching of the pen. 'Found dead in a cat-house; the House Under The Clock.'

The quill continued to flap over the page, a scrawny bird. Fouché's eyes were up while his hand continued to write. 'Confirm the facts to me: first, this is Maupuy who was courier for the late La Porte?'

'He. I knew him by sight and I saw the body.'

'In this brothel?' Fouché winced inside at the word, the thought of public admission of lack of self-control.

'In the rubbish on the riverbank nearby. Stabbed in the throat. I asked around, spent some coin, traced it back to the Clock fast enough. Old Jeanette denied everything at first, but I shoved her around a bit and she opened up.' Fouché's eyes flickered wider a moment, his tongue cleaned his teeth. 'Found dead in one of her rooms. Says she doesn't know who or how, and I think she's telling the truth.'

'No trail?'

Guilbert shook his head. 'I'll have another go, but I doubt it anyway. The district's a sewer, and no one notices one more shit.'

A superior smile from Fouché. 'Someone seems desirous of eradicating La Porte's network – the King's network.'

Guilbert nodded.

'And one wonders why.' Guilbert nodded. Fouché would wonder why.

Fouché realized he was expected to give direction. 'I . . . I assume it would be hard to identify a murderer in such a situation.' Guilbert didn't disagree. 'Have we means to look for the people Maupuy contacted?' Nod.

Guilbert continued to recite: sins and violences, and Fouché took it all in with restless lips and always the pen scratching over the page.

The stranger was crossing the yard towards the steps, and from the shadows Lucie watched him.

'You learn anything?'

He stopped; he turned towards the shadow, and peered at her. Lucie didn't move, and he walked nearer.

'Your British. You learn anything?'

'Nothing to the purpose. Pardon me, Mademoiselle: an indelicate question.' She felt herself stiffen. The stranger's face was darkness against the sky. 'Does Henry have a . . . a woman – friend?'

'No one special.' She dared herself to look at him. 'There is a house in St-Denis. You understand . . .' The stranger nodded. 'And also . . . The foreigners. Madame Emma Lavalier and her circle. Perhaps there he has a woman.'

He was silent a moment, remembering the woman Lavalier and her salon, the sense of possibility, and transgression – and hostility. Then he was uncomfortable: she could see it in his mouth and his sudden shifting. 'Surprising – that . . . that a man should look elsewhere for . . . for beauty, when he could . . . ' – again the shifting – 'see it much nearer.'

She felt herself blushing faintly. 'No. No he is never. He is . . . he is correct.' He frowned, still uncomfortable. 'And Monsieur Greene is a gentleman and I am not good enough for him.' Still uncomfortable. It was almost funny; foolish, certainly. Lucie said, 'You and him . . . You're not like him.'

The stranger smiled – it looked weak, she thought. 'No. No we are not alike.'

'But you were friends.'

'Partners, time by time.' He smiled faintly at her thought. 'Sometimes perhaps opposite characters may be complementary.'

'You make friends with the other British?'

He shook his head slowly. 'I'm afraid I found them rather foolish. Charming company, I'm sure, but foolish.'

She considered this. Then she shrugged, and looked away into the yard.

He stepped closer. She felt him near. 'My French is limited, Mademoiselle. But I'm learning to read your face nicely. Your silences are worth a whole speech.'

She looked up into his face. *Read this*, she was thinking. 'I think they are dangerous, Monsieur.'

'Those dandies? Dangerous – dangerous to Henry?'

She watched the stable-boy carrying a saddle into the yard. 'France is . . . There is no peace. There is no safety. In Paris they kill each other in the streets. Soon the Prussian soldiers will be here and they will kill many people.' She shrugged. 'It's not that life is so wonderful anyway.'

He watched this silently.

'And in this dangerous time, your friend Henry Greene talks to many people. To French people. To English. To others. To anyone.'

He said, carefully, 'You mean that he is . . . spying, Mademoiselle.'

Lucie looked at him, felt her eyebrows lift as she considered him, suppressed her scorn. 'Come, Monsieur. You're simple maybe, but you're not so stupid.' She shrugged. 'Good money, I guess.'

He nodded, slowly. 'Tension. Rivalry. Competition.' He looked at her. 'Many good opportunities to do business.'

She considered him again. Perhaps he was stupid. 'Many good opportunities to die, Monsieur.'

———————◆———————

Throughout the meeting of the Committee of Supply, Fouché watched Danton. There are times when the whole Revolution seems to depend on Danton's drive, on his word. If one is concerned for the Revolution, one must watch Danton.

At that moment, Danton was silent. While other voices chirped and fluttered around him, the room seemed to be drawn in towards the glowering face. The eyebrows were pressed down in a frown, all the troubles of the Revolution weighing on that mighty forehead.

'Can France really be tha-'

'An appeal to citi-'

'A tax on – '

'The rich – '

'A sou – '

'A sou?' From Danton's overcast face, thunder. 'A sou!' And like creatures shrinking before the storm, the others withdrew into their collars. 'The Revolution was not built on your sous, sir; it was not bought like crusts! It's not bankers and clerks who will save us, but the simplest citizens of the street.' Now Fouché was frowning faintly. *What game is this? What happened to Danton's money worries?* 'We have no need of money. Were the Revolution poorer than the poorest beggar, it would endure, because it is believed – in the heart of that beggar and ten millions like him.'

The others began to relax. They couldn't quite see how the beggars would . . . But at least Danton was blowing over. 'Well, if the minister is confident – then I think we may all be more confid-'

'Yes, be confident.' It came as a growl from Danton. 'The Revolution is now too powerful to fail.' A great shrug. 'You must forgive me, Messieurs. You know I am not a man for these pocket-book essentials of administration. You tell me we should worry, and I'm sure you're right. But the Revolution will not fail.' The growl again. 'It cannot. The people will not let themselves be thwarted. With our enemies around us, we will only be stronger!' He was up now, resting heavy on his fists. 'The people will stop – at – nothing – to defend the Revolution and to carry its flag onwards! If it's gold you want, the people will find it; if it's blood, they will give it. The Revolution will not lack.' The final '*pas*' was spat, disdain for these trifles.

And Fouché almost laughed aloud; he restrained it in a cough. *It's brilliant, even for Danton. More worried than any of them about the Revolution's finances, behind-door he has with murmurs stirred these lesser men to anxiety, and when they cry back to him his murmurs he stands on the dignity of the Revolution and looks down his nose at such trivialities; then, at the instant when his fervour might calm their clerical fears, he instead lets them wind him up into a greater fervour of defiance about the crisis of finances.*

Fouché watched him, large in front of them and staring down from his defiance, with admiration. *This combination of little intrigues and grandstanding has given Danton enormous power in this moment. With his next word he could have the King in chains, or any of the men in this chamber, or a mob . . . doing what?* A little smile crept onto Fouché's lips, but the eyes stayed watchful. *What has he justified, with that little performance? What is he about to unleash?* Danton alone is dangerous enough; Danton when he whistles up one of his mobs can up-turn Europe.

Fouché wondered. *There have been tremors during the day, rumours swelling like yeast: men are gravitating towards the centre of the city; there is more bustle around the Hôtel de Ville; Santerre has been gathering* weapons. One of the intermittent spasms of the revolutionary fever? Or is something planned? What would Danton say next?

'We must let the Revolution take its course,' he said. 'It may not be stopped.' Fouché's eyebrows rose a fraction. Danton slumped down into his chair. 'I hope that we may prove its adequate servants.'

And discussion turned to the possibility of new measures for supporting the Army of the Vosges. Fouché gave Danton one final moment of consideration. Then his eyes dropped, and he leaned forwards, skimmed the line of figures and notes in front of him. *Danton has his games*, he thought; *I mine*.

Across the table from him, the two representatives of the Ministry of Finance sat upright, edgy, licked lips, waited for the examination to begin, rabbits before a snake. Fouché on the track of inaccuracy, of vulnerability, of error, is unstoppable and terrible.

Slowly, his eyes came up to them.

———— ◆ ————

Emma Lavalier let the men wait.

She moved her knee slowly, and a ripple rolled up the hip-bath to her face. She lowered her chin, and blew bubbles into the tide.

Marie had stuck her head in to announce Benjamin and Pinsent. *More hot water.* But her visitors! *More hot water.*

More hot water.

A day such as she was become used to. And a trial all the same.

Social calls. So they should seem. Visits that should be appropriate to a lady of her sort, visits to people that knew her and who were known to know her. She was known for a woman of independent but not unseemly social habits, and Paris was freer now, and it should be nothing for her to call on a female acquaintance and thereby exchange some words with the acquaintance's husband; to carry out certain pieces of business touching her financial affairs; to seek a meeting with a minister to intercede for a friend in prison; to exchange a civil word or two in the street.

But words carried greater weight now. To say the wrong thing – even to be present at the wrong moment – was prison. During Emma's visit

Thérèse du Morlay had murmured hardly a word and hurried from the room with no further pretence at propriety, leaving Emma alone with her husband. A wife should have been scandalized by the idea of doing such a thing, by the possibility of what husband and charming widow might do. But a betrayal of marital fidelity was the least of the possible betrayals now, and it was better to think of no possibility at all. Gossip about the worries of some of the principal revolutionaries, and the vulnerability of Brissot and Roland, should have been trivia; but to show interest in the gossip was to send a message, and to pass on the gossip was to declare an acquaintanceship. During her visit to the minister she had stated her ostensible mission – a triviality, the kind of triviality that before had oiled the springs of all social interaction in Paris – and when she looked into his face she couldn't tell if his next word was going to send her to La Force or call for some tea. A word could be expensive; but a life could be very cheap.

And underlying it all . . . the *atmosphere*. There seemed, indeed, something actually in the atmosphere, some vile humour of the air that poisoned the mood of the city and every human thought. Paris was sour milk, Paris was . . . a porcupine, a constant threat to over-sensitive nerves. People were scared, and people were angry, and people were watchful. Giving a merchant a coin for a ribbon was an exchange of suspicions. To say a word was to invite a dispute. Glances that would once have been indifferent or even admiring were now envious, bitter, and seething with the possibility of threat. In the rue de Cléry a man had spat near her feet, and no one had reacted; and she had hurried on.

You walked through Paris with the blade over your head at every moment.

One hand keeping her hair piled high, she bent forwards and lowered her face flat into the water. She was a creature of a different element now. She could drift away.

Children did it, she had heard: *If I cannot see, I cannot be seen.*

If I were invisible, then I would be truly free.

From some other element, some other world, there was a hollow thumping, and then a murmur. She came out of the water with a gasp and a dribbling of tepid water, and glared at Marie.

But I am not invisible: it was her glory and her curse to be the most noticeable of human creatures.

She stood, and the water exploded from her breasts and hips.

And so her triumph would be of bravado, and not of disappearance.

———————◆———————

After the committee: Fouché striding away along the corridor, driving the Revolution with each fast stride. 'Fouché!'

Fouché slows but does not stop; the Revolution will not be served by hesitation. 'A moment for an old man?' Danton, jovial and filling the corridor as he makes up the distance. For Danton, Fouché stops, and waits respectfully.

'Tidy work in there,' Danton says, and Fouché bows his head to acknowledge the point. He holds the pose a moment; *what new Danton is this?* Danton's shirt-front shows a trace of his breakfast. 'I own I sometimes lack the patience for your little surgeries of logic, but we need them right enough. Tidy work.' Fouché is looking into his face now, trying to work out what expression to adopt.

'I was asking Roland about you,' Danton says. 'Work out whether my irritation at you was justified.' Fouché smiles, instinctively; it's well judged – *he knows I wouldn't believe friendship*. Now Danton smiles down at him: 'Irritation might be, but respect too. Keeping us straight, Roland says.'

Fouché nods.

Danton's hand clutches hard at his shoulder. Fouché refuses to show the discomfort. 'Keep at it! The Revolution needs its Fouchés as well as its Dantons.' *For now*, Fouché thinks. 'Trust your instincts, and we will too.'

A nod, and he releases the shoulder and strides off. 'Don't get bogged down!' he calls back. 'We don't have Fouchés to waste.' The mighty smile, and Danton is gone.

Fouché stares after him. *Danton really is worried about something.*

———————◆———————

Sir Raphael Benjamin and Edward Pinsent had dismissed Emma's apology with thin-lipped courtesy, which Ned Pinsent had managed to build into an over-elaborate compliment. And Emma had thought: *Yes, damn you; for I am glorious and worth a little waiting.*

Benjamin had heard where there might be a party; Pinsent had heard there might be some discreet gaming there, arrangements for even a lady to amuse herself with a wager.

'I think those will prove the mildest games played tonight,' she said. Benjamin growled interest; he knew her eyes. 'There's a mob out tonight. Who knows? Another Tuileries, even. It's rumoured they'll head for that way again.'

And she knew Benjamin's eyes. He was calculating now, instinctively: risk and opportunity, red and black. This time it didn't take long. 'A mob is poor sport,' he said, and sniffed. 'Excitable sort of beast; unpredictable.'

'No sort of form,' Pinsent added.

'And with only a small stake you risk a hell of a loss.' The mischief rekindled in Benjamin's eyes. 'Unless larceny's our game this evening. Fancy a new pair of boots, Ned?'

Pinsent affected a groan of distaste. Everyone knew he was thinking about it.

'Don't,' Emma said. Between them the men were boys enough to follow the mob for amusement alone. 'There's something behind it tonight; policy of some kind.'

She'd meant it for a warning, but of course Benjamin was interested again, and the irritation hissed in her throat; and became a smile. 'You're a pair of great hearts, no mistake.'

'Madame Lavalier.' Benjamin was mock-gravity, but she could see his alertness. 'Amuse us with your rumours.'

DEPARTMENT 3

Paris/Centre, the 14. of September
The trading house of Kuyper & cie.

Holdings of gold: reckoned one half million livres; declared three hundred thousand livres.

Visited this day the agent of the Comte de Thomis, the nephew of Mme Le Sommer, Delannoy, and Becquey of the Assembly, all seeking to withdraw investment, even at fifteen sous in the franc, and Quinette of the Assembly interested to speculate, and a delegation of the lacemakers' guild.

Also for one full hour Soyer, of the house of that name. M. Kuyper in sour humour after the discussion.

A foreigner – probably British from clothes and voice – name unheard – called on M. Kuyper, and after agreeing to wait thirty minutes was seen in the outer salon. He was a business partner of the Englishman Henry Greene, and had come to Paris to join him. But M. Greene had been called away shortly before the stranger's arrival, stranger was not sure whither – had heard perhaps Geneva – and Greene had left no detailed instructions. Stranger knew that the house of Kuyper was on occasion in affairs with Greene, and was anxious that Kuyper suffer no inconvenience from Greene's absence: had he any obligations outstanding to Greene? M. Kuyper more cautious even than usual: M. Greene but an occasional acquaintance in affairs; a man interested in information more than cargoes, and of late but little; M. Kuyper would always be delighted to take a glass of wine with any man who shared his interest in the world and might usefully exchange information regarding matters of commerce and political economy, and was glad to know the gentleman; but no, there was no business outstanding; M. Greene had not been in for 3 or 4 weeks.

News of the arrival in Brest of the Gabriel and the Sainte-Marie. The Soleil now one week late to Toulon.

[SS K/1/X1/2 (AUTHOR TRANSLATION)]

In Fouché's never-resting brain, there came first a sense of familiarity – a musical resonance, as in the chants of the Oratorians back in Nantes: questions about the British in France. And within this a single chime, a point of memory: an Englishman named Greene.

Fouché stepped to the cupboard in the minister's offices that was becoming his cupboard, and retrieved another paper. *A stranger in St-Denis. Asking for Greene, known to this Department.*

Fouché put the two pages together, as if they might whisper to each other. *1. I must have some satisfactory system of referencing and across-referencing. 2. I must be admitted to the secrets of 'this Department'. 3. An Englishman called Greene, and another with a strange name, loose in Paris.*

Tonight we will march and burn, and don't it feel grand? The shoulders of men beside and jostling and it's a scrum and a surge, and we can feel our feet stamping into the ground and our arms strong. Behind in our ears are shouts and breaths and we gasp in the excitement of it all, and the shouts grow and merge around us and we throw our heads back . . . and – we – roar! Anger and hope are joyous and we roar, and the noise around us picks up our roar and lifts it into the gloom. We are stamping forwards shoulder-by-shoulder, and we have a purpose though we don't know what it is, and we are thousands. In front, the torches wave high and scorch the darkness. Tonight we will march and burn.

✣

Paris at night: for Lucie, all the cheap sins of man, and all the darkness beyond him. This habit of walking the streets alone had been hers for ten years and more, but she knew she would always be that first little girl – eight years old? – sent on an errand and losing her attention for a moment and realizing herself lost in the biggest, darkest, most deceptive, most mysterious place she could imagine. She had learned her way around now. But that meant knowing where she could not go – alleys that were too terrifying in her imagination, huddles of streets that turned their backs on the rest of the city and where she heard whispers of lost girls and unknown unpunished crimes, the places where the whores stood brazen and jeered and spat at another woman and showed her what the world could be. It also meant knowing *how* she must go: how she should walk not to be noticed; whom she should and shouldn't look at; how to look if she wanted a protective smile; how to look if she wanted something extra for her sou. She knew how to stand and how to look in a merchant's hall, and how in a pimp's pot-house.

Somehow she had found a familiarity in all this. She never relaxed, she never seemed to take a full breath, but she knew this place; it was a body she inhabited. She knew the pretences to adopt for the smarter squares, and in the streets that ran away from them and interwove like water down glass she felt invisible and thus, brilliantly, safer. In the chaos she could hide and survive.

Lately there was something new in the streets: everything was strained; sharpened. Once the faces had been complacent, or scornful, or the poor ones just deadened. Now everyone was edgy; feverish, with the wider excited eyes of the fever. Remarks became insults more quickly; fights started more easily. Everyone was *looking* for something, in each face and each word. Everyone was waiting.

It made the darkness even more welcome. She had a warm meal inside her, half of it given free for a smile and a familiarity. She knew that the shit collected on the left-hand side of this street. She knew the light ten yards ahead was a good light, a friendly sentry and where she would turn right. The sounds came distinct to her from the shadows: horses, carriages, arguments, feet on earth, words in corners, knives on plates, moans into ears. Somewhere in the distance, she could hear the familiar sound of a crowd.

✛

Still distant from the mob, the Hôtel de le Marine stared pale and cold onto the Place de la Révolution; waiting. In truth, the Department of the Marine only occupied one corner of the building: an administrative convenience in a time of confusion. Its grand upper level – the dozen columns of its portico, giant bars through which the building itself peered – soared above the archways of the ground storey. In the night, the archways became a sewer-grille, blackness and mystery.

Testimony: I only came out to meet a friend, no harm intended, messieurs, but then there were a few of us and we had a drink or so and then we couldn't pay for any more so we went outside – warm evening, you know, messieurs? – normally the drink makes you feel a bit cold when you get outside but it was warm enough – proper Paris summer evening – we were standing there in the street, no harm to anyone, fooling around a little I guess, and then we hear shouting at the end of the street, and what were we supposed to do? Decided we'd go and see what the ruckus was – well, didn't really decide – just naturally went that way – always a bit of excitement in the crowd these days, eh, messieurs? I wasn't leading, no; and I don't know who was. Dark, see?

Raph Benjamin and Ned Pinsent were in darkness. Warm evening, but Benjamin could feel the cool of the stone against his back. He adjusted his shoulders and enjoyed the thrill against his neck. *Sordid sort of habit for a fellow who was born to the lights and the wine.* He readjusted his hat. *Or have I become a fellow of the night who sometimes sticks his head out to play in the light?* He could see Ned Pinsent's outline a yard away, but the face was lost. *The dark has become the place where we thrive – and the place where we must hide.*

It's the Hôtel de la Marine now, but we've not started calling it that yet. For most it's still the Hôtel du Garde-Meuble: the Meuble; *the Furniture.* It's one magnificent side of the Place de la Révolution – we've only been calling it that for a month, but we're a bit more assiduous about forgetting the Place Louis XV. It was designed – in fact, the whole square was laid out – by the Royal Architect Gabriel, who also did the Opéra at Versailles, and the Petit Trianon for the older Louis's successive mistresses. The Meuble has more than five hundred rooms. Its two ornamental facades are allegories of Magnificence and the Public Happiness. At night it hangs over the square like a frown.

*Testimony: we were in a crowd – how many? I don't know, messieurs – you
don't, do you? You know – a crowd. And we're walking now – marching –
feel proud when you march in a crowd, don't you? – and these are our streets
now, we go where we like, no one to tell us not to, long live the revolution,
right? – But we were angry, yes. Shouting – there were shouts – not speeches,
just slogans – you know, whenever someone feels like it, yes? – Down with
the King! Death to the Prussians! – that's the stuff. But we're still angry,
because – begging your pardon, messieurs, but we're all still rather in the
shit, aren't we?*

I wasn't leading, no; and I don't know who was.

⁜

The Hôtel de la Marine – du Garde-Meuble – really was the repository
for royal furniture. And on the first Tuesday of every month, we used to
be able to go and admire it. The furniture itself was ludicrous, but the
fabrics . . . No single thing in our lives showed the richness – the luxury
of texture – of those damasks. As we wandered through those chambers
– each one as high as a house, dominated by the chandeliers that hovered
at their very heart with candles as tall as a child, endless falls of curtain,
every panel white framed with gold, purity and splendour – how were we
supposed to react? Were we supposed to *dream*? Of course not: only little
girls, perhaps, with their brittle desperations. Were we supposed to be
reminded of the futility of dreaming?

Our visits also gave us the opportunity to admire the Crown Jewels of
France, laid out in the Meuble in glass case after glass case, like so many
oysters on the slab.

⁜

*Testimony: did I know where we going? No, sir. No, not me. I mean, I guess
I knew which street it was and where it leads, but I can't say I noticed – it's
just the faces around you – that's all you can see – someone's shoulders right
in front of you and faces left and right and everything's orange and brown
in the torchlight and I remember the sound of our feet – we weren't exactly*

marching, but a lot of feet together makes a hell of a sound – and voices. Not particular voices – no one's exactly saying anything – lots of voices together. I wasn't leading, no; and I don't know who was. Guess you've never been in a crowd, have you, sir? No one leads a crowd.

✢

If one is concerned for the Revolution, one must watch Danton. And if one is concerned for Danton?

Fouché started south of the river, at the Club of the Cordeliers. Asking after Danton he got a couple of jokes and some third-hand ideas about where he might be, and realized that he'd only come to the Cordeliers because he assumed something extreme was happening. The pamphlet-seller Gaspard, handing out his last pages for free on the Theatines to get home for the night, thought he'd seen Danton. On the Pont Royal Fouché bumped into Bernadot, who asked after Nantes and his electioneering and thought he'd just seen Danton in the Tuileries gardens. Crossing fast onto the north bank of the Seine, Fouché saw one figure on the far side of the dozens of people drifting through the gardens and convinced himself it was Danton.

There are two Dantons. The Danton of the people, who can only exist when he has another man to act on; or preferably a thousand men. And the Danton of his own head, who must have solitude to think and to plan. Such, anyway, has been Fouché's preliminary attempt to understand the great figure of the age. If Danton is not in one of the Clubs, if Danton is indeed stalking through the Tuileries in the evening, then Danton's mind is occupied.

There was a moment when Fouché felt foolishness, chasing a shadow through the night. But Fouché is a fast learner, faster than anyone, and it is becoming clear that not only success but life can depend on anticipating the great moves of the Revolution just before they happen. And the greatest move will always be Danton's. And today Danton has been preoccupied. So Fouché followed him – followed the idea of him – through the Paris night.

✢

Testimony: I was on duty at the corner of Place de la Révolution and the Champs – my regular station, sir, across from the Garde-Meuble – the Hôtel de la Marine – and obviously I hear the crowd coming. Voices – shouting – and then I see the torchlight reflected on the windows in the rue Royale and so I can tell that's where it is. Honest with you, messieurs, I don't want to desert my post, do I? but you don't exactly know what to do. And the crowd's coming nearer because I see the light changing and growing on the windows in Royale and then I see the people – like a big animal coming out into the square. And of course I respect the voice of the people, messieurs, and we are free now, but still, crowd marching towards you . . .

⁜

'What the hell are we supposed to be doing here, Raph?' Ned's heavy murmur, and Benjamin winced. Then they both heard the crowd. Couldn't place it quite: somewhere behind them, except that the stone – the arches – does funny things to sound. Getting louder; getting nearer. *A crowd can be anonymity. But for two Englishmen in Paris, a crowd is a public and very dangerous place to be.* Two faceless shadows stared at each other, and tried to push themselves back into the stone.

⁜

In the rue St-Florentin, near the Garde-Meuble, Karl Arnim was waiting. He knew a small something of what had been promised tonight. *And this is my sickness: that I cannot avoid the temptation to be near it.* Dear Marinus would scold him for his arrogance. *Bravado*, he would say. And perhaps he would be surprised, that his so cold friend was drawn to put his hand in the flame. *But I will not cower from these penmen and peasants. If this mad Prussian is to be in Paris, let him be in the very heart of it all.*

Arnim glanced up at the facade adjacent, blank and cold. *I am alone here, and if they find me they will kill me. But I may be colder than that death, and greater than them all.* He felt his jaw clamp tight, and stared ahead.

⁜

Testimony: first the crowd was sticking together, but once they're in the square they sort of spread out a bit. Natural. Like they want to fill it. Like they own it. And then the crowd just sort of mills around in the Place. Shouting, and torches, and I think some fights break out. And that was when the damage was done. Windows, mostly, as you saw, messieurs. Show a man a stone and a pane of glass and nature takes over, messieurs. Then eventually the crowd moves on. Off along the Quai. So I followed. No, sir, I couldn't see who was leading.

❖

Even on the portico of the Hôtel de la Marine – its long public face – there are shadows: where the two wings of the building push forward slightly from the portico between them; beside, and behind, the columns; in and around the arches, of course.

Now, behind one of the columns on the Hôtel's mighty first storey, a figure steps out through a window, and looks around himself. Cautiously, he peers round the column into the Place de la Révolution. There's little light in the square at night, and in the area behind the columns he's well concealed. He moves a few paces to the end of the portico, and steps to the edge and takes an involuntary breath as he contemplates the drop to the ground. At his feet, tied to a piece of the ornamental ironwork on the nearest window sill, is a rope. He stoops, tugs hard at the knot, then stands, grabs the rope and licks his lips and leans backwards into space.

❖

Testimony: there was more trouble farther on, messieurs. Near the Pont Royal – sorry, messieurs, the l'Egalité – as you'll know. Somehow there was a lot more shouting. We found afterwards they'd got themselves a barrel of wine and started on that, which can't have helped. Shouting – more angry now – and a bit of scuffling on the edges and more windows gone. I heard someone got knifed, but you'll know more about that, messieurs. No, sir, I didn't see anyone stirring it up. How do these things ever start?

❖

In the darkness under the arches of the Hôtel de la Marine, Benjamin and Pinsent had relaxed a fraction as the sound of the crowd dwindled. Benjamin saw his companion's shadow lean forwards, and knew he was about to murmur again. But something distracted the shadow: the head flicked to the side, the shoulders stiffened, and the murmur was an urgent 'Raaphhh'. Benjamin, between two arches of the colonnade and looking towards the building, couldn't see what Pinsent – back to the main body of the building, between two doors – clearly could. Pinsent's shadow was still frozen. Then the head turned slowly, and even in the gloom Benjamin could see the insistent nod towards whatever it was.

He checked the two paces between them: the ground was dark – shadowed – but he was trying to work out what the light through the arches was doing at waist and head height. A breath, and he took two steps and pressed himself back into stone next to his companion – hands flat against the wall for reassurance, fingers curling around the edge of the doorway – and already his head was straining to see what Ned had seen.

It was rather obvious what Ned had seen. At the far end of the line of arches, standing half visible in the first of them, was a man. 'Came down a rope!' Pinsent hissed. And as Benjamin worried about the noise, and kept on looking, a sack appeared in the air above the man and came lower, lower on the end of a rope, until the man caught at it and guided it to the ground.

❖

The river stank less at night, and particularly in the summer nights Lucie Gérard enjoyed the cool of it. She enjoyed the emptiness that suddenly opened in the middle of the city. In the middle of all the accumulated details of the city's centuries of existence, layers of stone and shit and such an impossible concentration of tiny details of life crowded together into the biggest noisiest thing that anyone could imagine, suddenly there was a void. Nothing, like a strip of poisoned ground where nothing would grow. To her right there were the palace gardens, and she heard the noises of night from their shadows, the trees and hedges moaning and calling. Then the emptiness was behind her and the streets closed over her head.

Near her now, in an upper room in the Jacobins Club, Fouché watched Danton. He was learning a new Danton: more anxious than he'd ever imagined possible; somehow more human. But still the mystery.

Danton had been surprised at first, when Fouché had appeared in the doorway. But then civil, and for a moment almost genial. Neither, though, had wanted to talk and each was content to leave the other alone. Fouché sat on a sofa, pretending to read a pamphlet, his whole character in the narrow slits of eyes visible over the top of the pamphlet and flicking left and right to follow Danton.

Danton walked. Backwards and forwards the length of the salon. Chest out, arms folded behind him, eyes lost, sometimes stopping and sometimes glancing out of the nearest window into the courtyard.

Danton is thinking. *Danton is waiting*.

✤

'Looters!' Benjamin hissed.

'Enterprising fellows. Reckon they've left anything for us?'

Benjamin glanced to the outline beside him. 'After you up that damned rope, old lad.' He'd forgotten his nervousness about their murmuring. As they watched from twenty paces away, along the patchwork of darkness and lighter spaces between the arches, they saw another man let himself down the rope to the ground. He was followed by another sack.

'Is this what the rumours were about, d'you suppose?' Another man.

Benjamin hesitated. 'I'd assumed it was the riot.'

'Who'd predict a riot? How d'you control that sort of thing?'

'Whole country's a riot.'

Pinsent murmured sombre agreement. 'No chance we could pick off a straggler, I suppose?'

'Mmm. Rather depends how they – '

Immediately beside them in the darkness, something clicked and a door started to open.

✤

Testimony: wasn't a lot I could do at this point, messieurs. Found a mate and he said word'd been sent to the Hôtel de Ville and I thought: I know my duty, and so I trotted back to the Place de la Révolution. All quiet by now of course. But you know what they say, sir; Paris never sleeps, does she? Suppose the fact the Place was quiet made it easier to spot the goings-on.

✤

Sir Raphael Benjamin and Edward Pinsent, Englishmen of dubious character, in the middle of revolutionary Paris, on the edge of a riot, caught between a band of looters and the offices of the Ministry of the Navy. The door clicked and swung out towards them, the panes of glass turning the traces of light from the square under the arch and onto their faces, and a figure stepped silently into the night in front of them.

Pinsent moved first, some unlikely brilliance or a last instinct to shut the stable door, lunging forwards and pushing the door closed. A gasp from the figure and the reflected light flashed across him and Benjamin's pistol was following its own instinct and driving into the man's stomach.

The man was a gasping, gabbling shadow. His arms started forwards or upwards and he opened his mouth wider and was about – And Benjamin's pistol pushed harder into his belly and he moaned and stumbled backwards. 'Silent, damn you!' Benjamin hissed. '*Ta gueule ou ta vie!*' *Practical French for the English gentleman abroad.* The man shuddered, and very slowly reached into his jacket and Benjamin's trigger finger was tensing but the man's hand was out now clutching something. Benjamin could hear the roaring of the man's breaths. His own breaths, maybe. He reached out and grabbed whatever it was – cloth – but hard inside.

Now a voice and the suggestion of movement from the other end of the arcade, but Benjamin's instinct to look went uncompleted. A slam beside him and Pinsent staggered into his arm and then away, driving back against the door, and it rattled shut again against whoever was pushing on the other side. 'Damnit, man!' he called over his shoulder. 'The chase!' And Benjamin had the package in a pocket and with the pistol clutched in his other fist swung it in a single straight punch into the head in front of him, and as the shadow dropped the pistol arm kept turning and he fired at one of the panes.

The night exploded in glass and noise. 'Fly!' he roared, and they flew; shoulder by shoulder through the arch and into the square and immediately veering and making for the corner and wherever there was not light.

⁜

Testimony: like something out of a dream, messieurs, something from the playhouse. The Meuble was . . . like it was covered in people. Not covered, obviously, but there was one coming down the wall and someone moving below and voices. Guess it took me a moment to grasp it. But naturally I know my duty, messieurs, and so I run across the square and I give a yell and then there's another comrade beside me and we're both running in. Well, the lad on the wall has reached the ground and he sees us and he's away before we get there, but we keep going and as we get to the building another feller comes out. Like he doesn't know we're there – from the arches – and I knock him down almost before I've seen him. Then there's shouting and now someone else runs out further along and my mate's watching the man on the ground and I'm off along the arches and there's two or three figures running ahead of me.

Lucie was lost in the darkness, in the anonymity of the city. The gardens were behind her now, and grand buildings beside her and soaring high. She felt their scrutiny; felt her smallness. Then a side street off the Place de la Révolution and a carriage ahead, and she didn't want to turn around so she kept walking, head down; keep walking and there might be a comment or two but she could keep going.

But as she passed the carriage some animal curiosity made her glance up, at the window, and in the window was his face and she stumbled and gasped at the impossible coincidence of it. Then he'd seen her and pulled his head back and there was a shout – and more shouts now, and running – and the carriage was rattling away and she was staring after it and her teeth were clenched at the gut-turning tricks of her life.

Testimony: they had too much of a head start on me, sir, and by the time I got to the corner most of the men had gone. There was a carriage rattling away down the street and maybe they'd got in that. Hard to say. But not all of them, sir, and I kept on going and I'm glad I did because I caught up with one of them – the girl. Across the street and I grabbed at her arm and warned her good and clear and she just stared at me, all surprised, and here she is now, sir.

In a night of spectacular *coups*, the gendarme sounded like he'd got the prize.

2

The Fugitives in the Forest

In which M. Fouché's explorations bring him confusion
rather than clarity, and several persons experience the
discomfort of suspicion or pursuit

The Memoirs of Charles Maurice de Talleyrand

(extract from unpublished annex)

---

*In early September of 1792, I had left Paris for England. Formally my
mission was one of diplomacy, entrusted to use for the Revolution the
great skills I had used for the King, to avoid a war with the British. And
perhaps they hoped I would stir a little sedition. Already you may see
the contrast between the clear thinking of some of the men at the head of
the Revolution (ah, poor Danton . . . !), and the passions of the mob,
which those men thought they led but which had overrun them.*

*For, naturally, my own mission was rather different. You may call it
undignified, and yet is not the greatest skill of the diplomatist to preserve
for more valuable use tomorrow that which may be given cheaply today?
The record of the subsequent decades of my service to French — indeed
to European — diplomacy shows how valuable was my tomorrow. And
consequently it shows how absurd would have been the loss of my services*

in those wretched blood-soaked todays. I confess it freely: I fled, like
a cut-purse or a petty philanderer, and I am proud of it. How much
greater the vanity, to stay, as many of my acquaintance did, proclaiming
their importance and defending their dignity, and only realizing the loss
of both as the guillotine's blade dropped?

Persons of distinction were being dragged into the street and slaughtered.
Our dream of justice had been abducted and defiled, turned into the basest
instincts of the envious rabble: by their reasoning, a name or a scrap of
lace condemned a man or woman to immediate death; judicial process
meant a crude spasm in the mind of a beast. We had promised the world
the triumph of Reason: had not I contributed to the Declaration of the
Rights of Man? Did not I write the Report on Public Instruction? The
enfranchisement of disciplined brilliance might have created a new Utopie;
the unleashing of the public passions created an inferno.

And so I found a charming refuge, in an affectation of diplomatic
activity and the eternal stability of British society. (For is this not
your great gift to the world, Britain, that your people who consider
themselves the most free and flexible are at one and the same time the
most conservative and steady in the world?) I enjoyed your London, I
saw your Manchester, and I met the excellent men who were somehow
harnessing the terrifying social and economic power of the latter to
sustain unthreatened the genteel conventions of the former. I own that
I indulged in a little financial speculation; and what is that, but a purer
form of the political investments that we make to ensure a stable future
in all markets? I was introduced to Messrs Wormald and Bellamy and
Doctor Andreyev, and they tried politely to induce me to a formal switch
of loyalty. And I refused, naturally, for we all knew that there is no
such thing as loyalty in diplomacy, and that by crossing the Channel I
had crossed as many boundaries as I needed to, for the tide ebbs, and
the tide flows, and the tide endures. With Mr Bellamy in particular,
though, I began a most stimulating exchange of views, my clearer and
uncompromising insights something of a provocation and a stimulation
to his intellect which, though commendably ruthless, was, in the English
way, more dogged and conventional.

Meanwhile, in Paris, the mob increased its control of the streets, and thieves owned the night, and noble jewels were counted as cheap as noble throats. And the few deluded souls who continued to believe that their intellects could rule in such a France continued their little sophistries of administration, and watched uneasily as power in the National Convention continued to shift to the radicals. So might the citizens of Sodom have washed their linen on the last day.

[SS G/66/X3 (EXTRACT)]

———◆———

Fouché was at Minister Roland's office early. There before the minister, indeed, immediately off his seat as Roland approached along the corridor with birdlike steps.

'What happened last night? What happened, Minister?'

'You know something, Fouché?'

They danced and squeezed clumsily through the doorway, and Fouché felt the conversation start to do the same. 'I know nothing. Danton – Danton was ... something. What happened last night?'

'Danton ... ?' Roland saw the frustration in Fouché's face. 'The Garde-Meuble has been robbed: the royal jewels.' Fouché's guarded eyes opened wide. 'It seems the looters have been busy for days. The theft was discovered last night; most of the villains escaped.'

Fouché's face was confusion.

Roland said, with painful caution, 'You were mentioning ... Danton?'

Fouché gathered himself. 'I was sure that – that Danton was doing ... something. He was there.'

'There? Where?'

'In the streets, and then at the Jacobins.'

'You saw him ... ' – a whisper – 'involved somehow?' In the Interior Minister's face, the enormity showed: Danton the troublesome; Danton the essential.

And Fouché's voice changed. Calmer again; measured. With something of wonder. 'No, Minister. I saw nothing.' He shook his head slightly; frowned at himself. 'I suppose I was with him for two or three hours and I never saw him near the mob or near the Meuble.'

'Fouché, what was Danton doing? Anything... anything discreditable?'

'No, Minister; certainly not. No, I was with him throughout.' Roland did not look reassured.

And Fouché felt the confusion spreading on his face again.

I have made myself Danton's alibi.

———— ◆ ————

Less than a minute after they'd disappeared into the shadows beside the Hotel de la Marine, Benjamin and Pinsent had been on their horses and trotting into the Paris warrens. Trot not canter, not gallop, Benjamin with face tight and hawk's eyes, Pinsent glancing at him and holding himself back. Not straight for the nearest gate, because if a gate is going to be alerted and locked it's that one. So first to the east, trusting to gloom and the secret-swallowing anonymity of the back streets.

From the shadows beside them as they'd ridden, noises: dogs, and sins; and the voices of whores and drunks and beggars, calling out on instinct and expecting nothing. Once a hand reached for his horse, and Pinsent kicked it aside and rode on.

Then north again, and more light as they came to the gate. A greeting from Benjamin to the sentry, and Pinsent had noted that there'd been a bit of noise in Paris tonight, and the sentry had shrugged and they'd passed out of the city. Once they were clear, on some shared instinct they stopped and looked back towards the hulk of Paris.

'Bloody oath, Raph. Bloody oath.'

And Raphael Benjamin had breathed out for an age, and then grinned at him, and pulled at the reins and led the way into the night.

In the dawn, sour light and sour taste, Raphael Benjamin had remembered the package: the looter who'd thought him a bandit – *and am I not?* – and passed over something from his jacket, something presumably liberated from the Garde-Meuble.

Hopeful, but with his enthusiasm tempered by the lingering sense of chaos, of the narrowness of their escape, Benjamin had reached for his coat on the back of his chair. He'd pulled a little cloth bag out of the pocket. His mind had leapt instinctively for the possibility of coins – *a little something for the tables; ought to share it with Ned* – and then slumped a little at the smallness of the bag, the paltriness of the prize and the world.

Not coins. Wrong shape.

Everything in the morning seemed pale, but what fell from the bag into his palm and filled his hand was brilliant – flashing brilliant. A pair of little eggs, one shining white and one shining blue: jewels.

———— ◆ ————

Testimony of Joseph Douligny, thief: asked did he confess his crime, *yes, messieurs, I confess it – an episode of madness, messieurs, in a weak mind;* an episode that lasted three or four nights, of repeated violations of public property? *it was more of a business, messieurs – more of an employment;* asked what did that mean, *we'd never have thought of it, not even the guv'nor. It was put to us as a job. Anyhow, all Paris was burning these days, rioting and destruction; this was just another chance to knock the old regime, wasn't it?* Reminded that this was the property of France now. What were the arrangements for disposing of the treasure, *don't know, messieurs. I wasn't in charge of that;* asked how they gained access, *one of us knew there was a window did not close on the first floor. In the darkness we could not be seen climbing;* asked how many nights the gang had been busy, *three or four;* asked what did they take, *what we could – jewels – necklaces – rings – brooches – chains – pearls – gold and silver candlesticks;* including the four great diamonds of the Capet family, formerly self-proclaimed Kings of France? *I saw no diamonds;* pushed for honesty before the Tribunal, *honestly, messieurs, I saw no diamonds;* but your comrades took them, no doubt, *I saw no diamonds;* asked to name his comrades, *I am no snitch, monsieur; I say nothing;* you say nothing here, yet you have already said all you need to under interrogation. Asked who might it have been who set them on – assuming that that part of his story was true – what Frenchman could have contemplated such a crime? *funny thing, messieurs – when we were coming out we saw someone moving – under the arches of the Meuble – in the shadows – watching us maybe. My mate, he went to have a look, and he says he saw two or three men. He heard voices too – just a snatch.* Voices? *English, monsieur.*

———————◆———————

When Prosecutor Fouquier-Tinville attacks a prisoner, first his right hand swirls in the air as if summoning some heavenly power, and then it darts forwards in one endless finger to shoot lightning at the guilty person – anyone confronted by the power of Fouquier-Tinville is assuredly guilty. His left hand is forever at his hip, a source of balance, a pose of rectitude, while his right pulls the sparks from the sky. The head – unwigged, for Prosecutor Fouquier-Tinville is a man of the people, a force of nature – soars up and back as he summons all the dignity of justice, and then is dragged forwards by the finger into the assault, and seems to stare into the guilty soul before it. The words come at bewildering speed, relentless, irresistible, screeching up with hatred at the grotesque idea of crime against the Revolution, roaring down in condemnation. The truth of them is . . . Well, what is truth? If you say a thing with enough ferocity, with enough rhetorical brilliance, with enough passion, that is surely virtue enough.

The investigation into the *affaire* at the Garde-Meuble took almost a week to identify and capture several of the thieves. The prosecution takes as long. It is the spectacle that absorbs all France, and Prosecutor Fouquier-Tinville knows it is his moment.

When he turns to the judges, conclusion delivered, he bows like a servant. When he turns again finally to the crowd, he bows like a magician.

———————◆———————

Fouché and Guilbert outside the Tribunal, about to go their separate ways:

'I own I have not met many men like that Douligny, Guilbert.'

Guilbert smiled faintly, and then restrained it. 'Very properly not, Monsieur.'

'You have, I suspect.'

Guilbert nodded. Experience of the world; regrettable necessity.

'Well then. What did you make of him?'

Guilbert shrugged, then saw Fouché's unchanged attention, hawk eyes. *I shall not underestimate you, Monsieur*. 'No less trivial than he seemed, Monsieur. A rogue. The lowest kind of mercenary. Cut a purse or a throat for a sou.'

Fouché waited.

'Some men lie from habit; not him – he was less stupid than he seemed and talking most carefully – he's worked out what'll save his neck. But most men lie for a reason. I think he was telling the truth, Monsieur.' The hawk eyes opened wider. 'No reason not to.'

'A bandit, in his extreme, telling the truth? Now that, Guilbert, is surely interesting.'

———— ◆ ————

Lucie spent her life trying to blur into the background; to disappear. Slipping through the gaps in the crowd; speaking into the breaths between others' sentences. Now the whole world was watching her, and waiting to dispute her every word. She sat on a chair – a wooden chair, its plainness apparently designed to offer less to draw the eye away from her – at the centre of a storm of faces, all staring at her.

The appearance of Lucie Gérard before the Tribunal stuffed the chamber with its biggest crowd yet, squeezed tight, standing only, straining around and over heads in front to see the distant pale figure. She was on last, which meant they must reckon she had something worth saying. And a beautiful young woman – the rumours spread like stench through the streets; her beauty, her daring, her lasciviousness, her many allegiances – was a much better prospect than the series of undistinguished and unwashed looters who'd preceded her.

There was no doubt or variety about their staring: hundreds of faces swirling around her, with nothing else to look at, eyes fixed.

'Louder, Mademoiselle!'

She was naked. Her dress, white and simple, seemed strained and transparent at shoulders, breasts, thighs. Never been so exposed. Never been so terrified.

'Louder, Mademoiselle!'

'Lucie Gérard!' – hasty, desperate to appease.

She confirmed her family, her residence, her life on foot, St-Denis and Paris.

Around the banalities, her audience continued to weave their fantasies.

Two men were watching Lucie with particular attention, though each had placed himself with deliberate discretion; watching but unwatchable, Joseph Fouché and Keith Kinnaird gazed at the woman whose pale frail murmuring had become the centre of the world.

Lucie was prompted to relate her journey through Paris of the evening of the 16th. The temperature, the atmosphere of the city at night, whether she was tired – Fouquier-Tinville wanted his audience to be there, seeing Lucie and seeing what she did, following her like good servants of the Revolution, observers of the great crime.

Her voice small and steady, and the mob straining to hear. Occasional whistles of frustration when they couldn't.

Had she seen the mob? Heard it? No, she hadn't.

Did she see anything in the Place de la Révolution? No.

She wished she had.

And what then? Walking out of the square, along the rue St-Florentin.

And when then, Mademoiselle? What did you see?

'I saw a carriage, Monsieur.'

Describe it. She described it.

And, Mademoiselle?

She frowned; confused for a moment.

And did you see anyone inside this carriage, Mademoiselle?

A breath; a gasp. And Lucie nodded. His profile; his face.

Did you, by any chance, Mademoiselle, did you recognize this person?

Another attempt at a breath.

She nodded.

Then who was he, Mademoiselle? Tell us! Who was this mysterious figure waiting so close to the scene of this terrible crime, so close to this savage betrayal of the Revolution? Who was it?

Lucie stared into the fog of faces; a last breath.

'An Englishman, Monsieur; resident in St-Denis. His name is Henry Greene.'

Emma Lavalier sat so that the stone of the summer house seat was deliberately sharp against her shoulders, and stared out into the evening landscape and did not see it.

The shifting of the years, of fashion, and of finance had established the summer house as a minor curiosity in the grounds of the Chateau of Saint-Ouen, and then its last remnant. It was a mile from her own little house, reached discreetly; a place for solitude – or for privacy, at least. Trees dropped down a slope towards it on one side, and open country spread away on the other. A borderland: between landscapes; between past and future; between worlds that should not overlap. A place where two people might meet, and touch, and withdraw.

Emma had time to wait. The urgency of her summons to Benjamin had also impelled her to the rendezvous well before he could be expected.

It gave her time to think. About being a woman. About being French.

Hooves rumbled hard over the ground outside, and she came alert. Raph Benjamin was beside her within seconds, up over the steps with lithe strides and bending briefly over her hand and staring into her face. 'At your service, always.' He swooped down onto the bench beside her. He reached for her hand again.

She pulled it away. 'It has become less fashionable to be English, dear Raph.' His face showed his confusion.

Slowly, she reached for his hand, pulled it up to her face, and placed a kiss on the knuckles. She returned the hand to his leg.

'The theft of the royal jewels. They are connecting it to the English. Paris is boiling.'

Benjamin kept his face still. He had not told her that he would go to the Garde-Meuble, nor that he had done.

She leaned forwards, more earnest. 'Greene was seen there that night.'

'Greene?' Real surprise.

She examined his face. Real surprise.

She nodded. 'He was seen there; waiting near. Seen, and now named. And known as an Englishman.'

'But he wasn't – ' She waited. She could see Benjamin's mind working hard. 'We haven't seen him for . . . for weeks.'

Her words were firm. 'He was seen there. Word is going out, from Paris to the police and National Guard of all France; Henry Greene. It puts all the English here under suspicion.'

'But we didn't . . . ' Slow, deadened.

'Didn't you, Raph?' She smiled. 'What didn't you, exactly?'

He growled his frustration. 'Greene, damn him . . . ' And sat back against the stone. 'What in hell is he – '

A new voice from outside. 'My lady?' Quiet, feminine, urgent.

Emma was immediately alert. 'What is it, Colette?'

'There are officers at the house, my lady. They ask for you.'

The stone chilled her. Her eyes flashed to Benjamin's, then away, and she stood.

He was up beside her, hand reaching for blade. 'Take my horse, Emma. Get well clear. I'll – '

'Don't be ridiculous, Raph. What will that achieve?' And she stood and strode down the steps and into the trees.

———— ◆ ————

29TH SEPTEMBER, 1792

The Grand Tour made more lively

Sir,

Paris seethes with rumours and excitement after the affair at the Garde-Meuble – a coup of true bravura, by men of daring and strong bellies. In public minds a hazy notion of wounded national pride contests with ill-concealed admiration at the exploit, all mixed with the ever-present unease that in these strange times anything may be possible. The Legislative Assembly is the national authority in name only now, and all await the imminent formation of the new National Convention based on popular election, and await the innovations and arrogations that might spring from this new manifestation of the Revolution, with its unprecedentedly broad mandate.

There is still confusion at the deed of the Garde-Meuble itself, and the official investigation has only stirred the rumour-pot. There is speculation, indeed, that one or more of your own yahoos may be involved. If so, they're men of dash and you may tell them so, and they're damn' fools for risking everything in such a mad caper and shaking the temple for everyone, and you may tell them that too. More significant are the speculations about who within French society might be behind the coup.

Meanwhile Williams, the Welsh philosopher and radical preacher and peddler of good causes, is here at the invitation of Roland, of the Interior. For some unfathomable reason he comes accompanied by one Matthews, a sometime tea-dealer and all-the-time hot-head. An acquaintance of mine has heard Williams in the salons, and another reports his first meeting with Roland. Themselves they fancy they're come to make peace, or some such foolery; quite what our hosts have in mind I may not speculate.

Meantime I learn from divers sources of one Kinnaird, a Scot of uncertain provenance, recently arrived, somehow connected to the St-Denis gamblers of your acquaintance, and apparently with a notion of sticking his nose into the business of more discreet men than he. I don't know if he's of your stable; I rather hope not; but if so you'd oblige me by tightening his rein.

E. E.

[SS F/24/145 (DECYPHERED)]

---————◆————---

Fouché sharpened his quill with freakish speed, the blade flicking and clicking against the point back and forth in his vibrating wrist. A trick from school; a trick that reminded him of Guilbert's with the knife. He wondered what that meant.

Roland watched the performance uneasily. Fouché was useful. Fouché was odd. Fouché was not, somehow, controllable.

They were in Fouché's office. Fouché's office: a small room adjacent to the minister's, a mutual convenience – indeed, the size suggested that it might once have been a convenience – so that Roland didn't have Fouché lurking at his shoulder all day and Fouché didn't have to crouch like a schoolboy at another man's desk. The proximity – a connecting door, and he could be in any meeting he liked, be with the minister in a moment – was essential. Thrilling, for Fouché. He felt he had learned one of the great lessons of government: *titles are nothing; geography is everything.*

Roland was relieved. Fouché found himself pleased – dangerously comfortable, almost.

The minimum furniture, and the simplest: wooden table; upholstery on Fouché's chair because the clerks couldn't believe he'd accept less; two plain chairs for visitors. Already the room was dominated by paper: a cupboard covered most of the end wall, including half of the window in the corner; already every space on the shelves was the beginning of a pile of documents. Already Fouché was worrying that it wouldn't be enough.

'You are content to manage this affair yourself, dear Fouché?' It wasn't really a question; a courtesy only. To Fouché's hesitant suggestion Roland had immediately agreed.

'With your permission, Minister.'

'She is a . . . lady of renown.'

Fouché didn't know what that meant. He waited.

Roland licked his lips. 'Almost of . . . notoriety.' Fouché still didn't know what it meant, but he could make more of a guess. 'A lady of contacts. In different parts of society.'

Was Roland telling him to go carefully? 'And, it seems, in parts of foreign society too, Minister.'

'Indeed! Indeed. She gives . . . parties. And attends them. She has been once or twice to Madame Roland's salon.'

Fouché's eyes narrowed. It was almost a useful insight from the Minister, at last. Roland's young wife had made herself one of the pre-eminent hostesses of Paris. An invitation did not indicate any particular attitude of politics, but it did indicate significance. Social status, or money, or beauty, or brains, or influence.

'I confess, Minister, that I was unfamiliar with the diversity of English people in Paris.'

Roland was standing with his hands clasped in front of him. Now he opened them, as if demonstrating the size of the English community. 'Oh indeed! Diplomatists – certainly until they closed the embassy last month – and engineers, and travellers, and gamblers, and fugitives; a few writers and physicians, though it's more the other way, more French in England, if you follow.'

'And adventurers and thieves, it seems.'

'Mm. So it seems. It was smart paperwork of yours – drawing the links between them. This Greene, and so on.'

'Will they have smuggled the royal jewels out of France already?'

'Who can say? Perhaps it depends on whether they were . . . ah . . . official agents. Of the British Government. The British Admiralty has its spies. Their Home Office has its spies. And there were rumours . . . an older office – ancient – its name unknown.'

It sounded mediaeval. Fouché was caught between reverence and irritation. He was conscious of moving into new territory, again.

Roland said, with discomfort: 'It is not yet illegal to be a foreigner in France. We have always been . . . most cosmopolitan.'

Fouché nodded. 'But no more Prussians, anyway.'

'Ah . . . ' – for a shrewd navigator of the fastest political currents, Roland could on occasion seem extremely old – 'well now. Just one. Perhaps.'

Fouché waited patiently.

'When diplomatic relations with the Prussians were broken, their embassy was closed and all of their officers left – including the one with whom the government corresponded on matters of security, and the one we suspected of being responsible for Prussian espionage in this country. But it was always rumoured that there was another, greater man. Unattached to the embassy, and responsible for Berlin's most secret dealings. At that time . . . ' – the vagueness was left alone; everyone was too polite to mention that Roland had been the King's last Minister of the Interior before becoming the Revolution's first – 'he was our greatest mystery. Our greatest concern. A Prussian master of intrigue, at work in France.' Little smile. 'I fear that our ignorance made more of him than was warranted.'

'If he exists – now, of all times – he cannot be ignored.'

Roland's face opened in acknowledgement and impotence.

'How may he be traced? How may he be captured?'

'We tried to keep a few likely contacts watched. Not likely to achieve much.' Roland shrugged, elaborate and slow. Detecting frustration, even on Fouché's blank features, he added, 'A challenge for you, perhaps.'

Fouché said nothing, ignored the paternalism. *There is more reading to be done.*

Suddenly Roland was moving towards the precious connecting door, chirping as he went. 'Well, I'll leave you to your interview, dear Fouché.'

'Only if you're sure I do not impose, Minister.'

'Not at all! Not at all. Distinct advantage.' He was halfway through the door. 'Most helpful.'

Fouché watched the door click shut.

Why does Roland not want to be part of this?

Faintly, uncomfortably, the sense that there were more of the fundamental rules of government yet to learn.

———————— ◆ ————————

'He's cooked us, the bastard!'

'My dear fellow – '

'Don't fellow me, Benjamin: you tell me the devious bastard Greene hasn't cooked us somehow.'

Raphael Benjamin started to speak, to calm, and then hesitated; it did look as though Henry Greene had cooked them. 'Not deliberately, surely.'

'Really? Really?' Ned Pinsent was hot, halfway drunk and striding in a necessarily small circuit of his room. 'He disappears, drops off the world, not a word except to set us up in that lunatic mission to La Force – and now this!'

'It wasn't his doing we were on the spot.'

'You sure of that, Raph?'

'We heard rumour something was afoot at the – '

'Yes: rumour.' Pinsent's knee knocked the corner of the cupboard, and the words continued through the hiss of pain. 'That bastard breathes rumour, don't he?'

He stopped striding a moment, and looked at Benjamin. They remembered where the rumour had come from. Pinsent set off again, now with direction. 'I'll fight any man, but I ain't waiting to get hauled before the Tribunal.'

'They've no other names. There's no suggestion that we – '

Pinsent swung a box onto the table. 'You're brave, Raph, not stupid. Every ostler and bar wench for ten miles knows we're comrades with him. Only wonder is the gendarmes haven't kicked the door in already.' He was looking around the room for things to put in the box, and now made for the cupboard. 'I'm away.'

'Not to England, surely Ned.' Pinsent stopped. His shoulders slumped, and he turned. His face was hatred, and then it too slumped. 'No, they still won't have you, will they?'

Pinsent turned away and opened the cupboard. 'The provinces then. The coast. The Low Countries.' He put two cups into the box. 'Somewhere I'm not known.'

'They've taken Emma in.' Pinsent looked up, stunned. 'Questions only, I guess.'

Pinsent shook his head heavily. 'Damn this . . .' he said hoarse. The candlestick followed the two cups. 'She's well-known. And they've obviously found that Greene visited her.' Another shake of the head, another murmured curse. He stepped to the bed and tugged the counterpane off it.

'We can't leave her in their hands, Ned.'

Pinsent's head snapped round, the eyes more alarmed than before. 'No, Raph. No.' This time the head shook rapidly. 'Duty to a lady, and you know how I – how I – admire her' – Benjamin smiled very faintly – 'but we'd just as well book our places on the guillotine right off. It would only confirm we were involv- And I'm not damn well involved!' The counterpane went into the box. Pinsent made for the mantelpiece, reaching for the picture of the two girls.

A knock at the door.

They stared at the door, at each other, and back at the door as it knocked again.

Benjamin stood, was behind the door in two steps and had the pistol in his hand and cocked. He nodded at Pinsent.

Pinsent said, '*Oui*,' with difficulty.

The door opened. On Pinsent's face Benjamin saw the apprehension and then, most puzzling, an eye-widening surprise.

———— ♦ ————

Emma Lavalier's catalogue of revolutionaries:

peasants; bull-like bankrupt innkeepers; broken-toothed street girls; vicious jumped-up clerks; poets; bullies; demagogues.

Men of romantic grandeur; even greatness. Danton: the brilliant, the voracious, the dazzling. She knew some of them.

The mob, fired by frustration and poverty and all the things that have always sent men with ill-formed anger and ill-formed dreams into the street.

But never this. Immediately, in the eyes of the man in front of her, there is something different.

Pale hair; pale face. The eyes . . . somehow opaque; their colour, their glance, hard to catch. A young man, surely; with an old man's face.

His eyes had travelled down her body, as she stood in front of him, and she relaxed a little and let her body swell with his gaze. Even revolutionaries preferred their innocence comely.

Then his eyes came up again, and they were still so ghostly and so challenging and she began to fear.

Fouché's examination of her body had been instinctive. Like the glowing rolling contours of a classical statue, it invited the eyes. And like a classical statue, he knew it to be what men considered beautiful.

But he noted this, rather than responding to it. And so his eyes came back up to her face again.

Her face stopped him. It unsettled him.

For Fouché, women's faces have always been a blank: unreadable expressions from unimportant people – a mother, a maid. A mask, given to them by the adolescent expectations of men. But now, for the first time in his life, he wants something from a woman – he needs something – and he knows that a command won't get it.

What is this face thinking? What is this face thinking of me? For the first time, he must read a woman's face. He must decypher it.

The dark hair has started with poise, high on the head, but come awry a little. Strands of it hang loose around her exposed neck, the neck where the hollow of her throat is open and vulnerable. The features are ... The lips are closed firm, and this makes them seem thinner than they clearly are. The nose is small but strong, and the suggestions of brows sweep up like swan necks from it. The eyes at last?

She is not a young woman any more. But the face is still an exquisite thing – he remembers a lesson in the appreciation of the classical arts for boys too young to appreciate them – a fineness, a perfection of proportion in its elements. And colour: is it artifice or fear? Would applying a woman's pastes denote masquerade or confidence or merely habit?

Can one read quality in a face? Can one read guilt?

The eyes again: the eyes are dark, wide. They do not shift from him. When he makes contact with them, she breaks it first – he feels her insecurity, and he enjoys it – but whenever he looks away and looks back they are fixed on him.

She is watching me. She *is reading* me...

✣

Emma Lavalier has always been able to influence men, by physical presence alone. The subtle shifts of her body – a hem raised on a step, a thigh moving forwards, a full breath into her chest – distract and attract. The signs of vulnerability invite sympathy and desire: disarray of hair suggests a woman coming awake in her bed – it suggests the morning after and thus the night before; disarray of clothing suggests the violation that has happened or is about to. The hints of a loss of control – the wider eyes, the shorter breaths – imply weakness and invite an over-confident assumption of mastery.

Everything that one can know of Emma Lavalier are the exterior qualities: the messages of surface that distract a man from her self. Within this costume of lace and flesh, behind this mask of emotions, Emma Lavalier is hidden and unknown.

The exposed neck had been a careful calculation. Often a high collar suited her better – suited her height, and her face. Today, however, she needed to be vulnerable, not poised; and that meant the exposed neck.

And yet . . . in the France of the machine, to expose one's neck is the greatest vulnerability of all.

✛

Guilbert earlier, just an hour or so before, when Fouché had mentioned that he was going to be interrogating a woman: 'And what does Monsieur know of her?'

'Nothing, naturally.' Thin smile. 'Hence the interrogation.'

No smile from Guilbert. 'If Monsieur will give me more notice of these occasions, I will try to be of more service.' And Fouché had shrugged, covering the vague but irritating sense of his own naivety.

Within the hour, Fouché starting to fidget and watch the door more often as the interrogation came nearer, Guilbert had returned unbidden; Fouché wasn't sure that he'd seen the door open and close.

Guilbert brought a portrait of Madame Emma Lavalier, a tapestry made from fragments acquired in corners and shadows.

Her age and family were not exact. *Old Lavalier was a soldier who earned honour fighting the British in the Americas in the 'fifties, and a merchant who earned a bundle trading with them afterwards. So he could marry for lust rather than status, and did so. And then he'd hung around the court picking up duties here and there to maintain a bit of standing.* Emma Lavalier had been an adolescent nobody, but beautiful. *Twenty years younger than her husband, maybe thirty even, and she's a Cleopatra now so what she was like then, Monsieur, just imagine!* (Fouché could not imagine.) Old Lavalier had married this pearl, and then most conveniently died. *Stories of course, Monsieur: all kinds of gossip about lovers – she was a generation younger than him, and he was a bit of a fool despite his gold and she'd dropped from the womb with a trick, probably learned deceit at the moment of conception – and then rumours about how quick and unexpected he died.* But her beauty had made her desirable, and her married name had made her acceptable. *His death gave her freedom and adequate money to enjoy it, and she does so, Monsieur. Close enough to noble society to have enjoyed the right invitations, far enough from the court to have avoided trouble until now. Nothing flagrant, nothing controversial. Gossip about her liaisons of course, Monsieur* – and even Guilbert had felt it appropriate only to murmur the names of a certain count, and then, leaning in further, of Danton; Fouché's eyes widened, not at the idea of Danton's depravity but at the vast interconnectedness of the world's – *but she keeps them to herself. Parties at her house – near St-Denis – reputed lively – rumoured debauched, but isn't every party you can't get into? – but no trouble. Acquaintance with quite a few foreigners – including some English – regulars with her. Perhaps a lover.*

And Fouché's mind had whirled in this constellation of sins, and foreigners, and Danton, and he had tried to restrain it. Fouché had wondered about Lavalier and her world; and – as the man nodded courteously, and slipped away – about Guilbert and his world.

✥

Emma was trying to read the strange young man in front of her, and could read nothing. He had noticed her body; he had noticed her face. But they meant nothing to him. His complexion, his lips, and above all his eyes, showed nothing. It was like being watched by a statue. Or a snake. Her costume and her movements and her expressions were nothing. She was naked in front of him.

She felt bewilderment, and alarm, within the artfully arranged costume. The short breaths came unfeigned. And then a kind of astonishment: *Must I – for the first time since puberty – confront a man as I truly am, without a pretence?* And then scorn at herself. *Why do I fear this? If this precious identity has been worth protecting all these years, it must have a purpose now.*

She took in one deep breath.

Let us see who Emma Lavalier may be.

✥

To Fouché's utter surprise, the woman Lavalier smiled faintly. *What does this mean? Is this some new pretence, or some further mystery of woman?*

For a moment, the shameful flush of his naivety again, the provincial clumsiness he had smoothed away so carefully. *I have never encountered people such as –* Then the old familiar anger, immediately suppressed and supplanted as always by determination. *And they perhaps have never encountered one such as me.*

'Why have I been dragged here?'

'Madame, you will be so good as to name for me your acquaintances among the English community in Paris.'

The Revolution is France, stripped of its facades, confronting all of the aspects of its self.

———————◆———————

Keith Kinnaird stepped cautiously forwards into Pinsent's room. Pinsent's face was disturbing enough. Kinnaird was also glancing at the door, and wondering where the pistol was.

'Mr Pinsent? My apologies if I interrupt.' The door swung shut beside Kinnaird, and the pistol muzzle was an inch from his breast. He took a breath. 'Good day, Sir Raphael.'

The insignificance of the man, in the middle of the madness, had Benjamin smiling despite it all – the incongruity; the relief. 'Good day indeed. Come to sell us some spoons, my dear fellow?'

Kinnaird just watched him, apparently uncomprehending. 'Gentlemen, I heard that Madame Lavalier had been arrested – by the regime.' The Englishmen glanced at each other. 'You know, no doubt. I wondered if . . . if there was any word of her; if you knew what it meant?'

Pinsent waited for Benjamin.

Benjamin closed the door. 'Bit of a shock, to be honest, old fellow. They're brutes, these people, of course. But we hope this is some bit of chance or opportunism on their part.'

'You don't know why she's been taken?' Benjamin shook his head, and Pinsent followed him. 'I heard that Henry Greene had been seen near this extraordinary robbery in Paris.'

'Yes, indeed! Extraordinary, no?' Benjamin's voice dropped. 'You ain't seen him, I suppose?'

Kinnaird looked faintly surprised. 'No. No indeed.'

Once again, he was left uncomfortable in the silence in this room.

'Well, gentlemen, I ask your pardon for the intrusion. Good day.'

Benjamin opened the door for him, and then held up a finger, thoughtful. 'Good to see you, Mr Kinnaird. Um . . . if it's no inconvenience to you, I hope we might stay in communication. You'll be busy about your affairs, no doubt, and perhaps we may share any information we each learn.' A smile. 'Trying time to be English, and – Or, indeed, even to be Scottish.'

Kinnaird nodded cautiously. Slight bows, and he was gone. Benjamin closed the door again.

'What the hell was that, Raph?' Pinsent still had the picture in his hand, ready to place it in the box. 'The shiftiest fellow in France, and suddenly he's your dear comrade?'

Benjamin's smile as he turned, and his eyes, were shining hard. 'That, dear Ned, was opportunity at the door.' Pinsent didn't get it. 'Right now we need a distraction. And what better distraction, than the shiftiest fellow in France?'

• • •

Fouché watched Emma Lavalier walking away down the corridor, between two soldiers.

She was as tall as them, and seemed to be leading. He was staring at the back of her neck, at the muscles in her shoulders, still trying to read her.

As his glance fell away, he found Guilbert sitting immediately in front of him, looking up at him. Like some sort of faithful guardian. Or a watcher.

Guilbert stood, and bobbed his head in courtesy. He must have been there when the woman had left.

He seemed to have some trick of anonymity. Even against a bare wall, alone on his simple wooden chair, Guilbert could be unremarked.

Why is he here?

He had brought information about the woman Lavalier, and no doubt sought reward. Deserved enough, and Fouché was reaching for a coin when Guilbert's frown and dismissive tut stopped him. 'My regular payment is more than satisfactory, Monsieur.'

What then?

Fouché stood silent, waiting.

The currency of information.

'If you will spare me the time, Guilbert, I would be pleased to share such new information as I have.'

A little smile from Guilbert, and a fuller bow. 'Thank you, Monsieur. A most intelligent suggestion. It will make me more capable of serving you.'

I never know when he is sincere.

Guilbert sat. From his own chair, Fouché tried to look grand.

His methodical mind overtook his pose of casualness. 'The woman as you described her, Guilbert. A butterfly. A woman of diverse society. We had a prolonged performance of hauteur, of wounded dignity. She admitted acquaintance with some minor figures of the old regime, while trying to impress me with a few names of the new administration. She presents Madame Roland as a friend.'

'So does half of Paris.'

'She's been there several times. This was more than posture, more than pretence. She is a woman of connections.'

'Including foreigners?'

'She presented herself as a hostess for a most colourful society. She named Greene, the Englishman. Owned he had visited her home several times. Was happy to talk about him; describe him. A rogue. A disreputable charmer. She was wide-eyed at the idea of his involvement in the affair at the Garde-Meuble, but did not resist it at all. She spoke only of his style as a man, and let me make the political inferences. She made no effort to hide or diminish her association with him. But then, she must have known that we would know of it anyway.'

Guilbert nodded at the sense of this. Fouché took a deep breath, and his focus stretched beyond the office, before eventually returning to Guilbert. 'That is why she leaves me so . . . uncertain; unsatisfied, Guilbert.' Guilbert's eyebrows rose a fraction; it was a challenge to his own effectiveness. 'She generously confirms things that we already know or can easily check. She is associated with the most bewildering diversity of people. And all of her skill is used to present her own relation to those people in the most cautious way.'

'She named other names, Monsieur? Associates of this Greene?'

'She named other foreigners of her own association, but would not speculate about their relationship to Greene. I have a list here, which you must of course read.' His finger dropped onto a page in front of him, and Guilbert's eyes followed. 'Again, these are names we already knew, or could know. The Englishman Benjamin we have heard of more than once. Other names.' The finger tapped at the page. Guilbert watched it hungrily. 'Perhaps I shall interview some of them. Is it possible also . . . Guilbert, is it possible for you – someone – to monitor such people? Follow them? Their correspondence?'

'The Commune police keep any number of people watched, Monsieur; but they're not up to following.' Guilbert's head came forwards slightly. His voice was flat. 'You may command me anything, Monsieur. From this office' – a glance at the connecting door – 'you may command France.'

Fouché considered this, eyes more intent.

'It seems that the authorities cannot find this Greene, Monsieur.'

'They cannot. He is reported missing from his residence for some weeks. This is why we try his acquaintances. Madame Lavalier was the most prominent.'

'Perhaps I may try some of the less prominent, Monsieur.' It wasn't even a question. Fouché nodded, uncertain what exactly he was agreeing to. 'What was her manner, Monsieur? Regarding her acquaintances of the court; the foreigners?'

Fouché reflected. 'It was well-judged, I should say. No suggestion of guilt, but a hint of shame. She the innocent victim of the rotations of history.'

'Did she name La Porte?'

Guilbert the shrewd; Guilbert the incisive. *If only I might guarantee that Guilbert as my tool.* 'Alas, Guilbert, she somehow failed to own acquaintance with the King's chief of secret correspondence.'

Guilbert smiled politely at the sarcasm. 'You've seen her style, Monsieur. *Could* she have had such a connection?'

Again reflection. 'I judge – yes. She is not of that circle of the court, but she could have been useful enough and presentable enough to be of service to its officers.' He paused again, and again saw her in front of him, the eyes trying to read him. 'She has depths, Guilbert. I hope I do not seem fanciful. Depths beneath her society charms.'

'You think she could be dangerous, Monsieur?'

Smile. 'I think she could be . . . useful.'

Guilbert nodded approvingly, and Fouché had the uncomfortable sensation of feeling pleased with himself.

'Monsieur, if you find yourself on occasion . . . frustrated – thwarted – by such a person, there are . . . other ways.'

'Torture?' Fouché tried not to sound naive.

A shrug in Guilbert's lips. 'Sometimes an unfortunate requirement of the needs of justice, Monsieur. We will agree that justice must be pre-eminent. It is unacceptable that a criminal should be allowed to obstruct justice by mere silence. In such circumstances it becomes necessary to overcome this obstructiveness with pressure. Brisk and prompt pressure.' Fouché contrived a thoughtful nod. Another of Guilbert's shrugs. 'If Monsieur should ever think it . . . appropriate. For the needs of the Revolution.'

'Mm. Indeed.' Man of the world. 'Presumably there is some approval required.'

Again the shrug. 'For a case of lower profile, much may be achieved on your authority alone, Monsieur.'

Fouché considered this – faintly pleased and faintly awed.

Guilbert stood waiting.

'Well, Monsieur?'

What did he want? Fouché felt himself being hurried along through his own life. His face showed his uncertainty. Guilbert's murmur again: 'Monsieur, do you consider it appropriate for the woman Lavalier?'

There were two impressions in Fouché's mind: Emma Lavalier's untouchable scornful superiority; and the first hint of pleasure that he'd yet seen in Guilbert.

He felt his tongue tracing the circuit of his lips.

'I shall have it in mind, Guilbert.'

The suggestion of a smile from Guilbert.

'She lives in St-Denis, Monsieur.' Fouché looked up again. He'd thought the conversation over. 'Same as the British you were interested in. Same as where there was the unrest in the night, over those mathematicians causing trouble.' Fouché still didn't understand. 'The surveyors. Measuring the earth.'

The triangulation; the meridian. Half-consciously, as Guilbert spoke, Fouché reached for the shelf where he knew Bailly's letter to Lavoisier lay, describing the troubles of the astronomer trying to measure the meridian in St-Denis. He felt the texture of the paper as he picked it up, trying to weigh significance, read meaning. *The truth of France is ten million connections and attitudes and affections, and of these I know but a few dozen.*

Guilbert had stopped, seeing the letter in Fouché's hand. In this office, you deferred to paper.

Fouché saw Guilbert's expectancy, and passed him the letter. Guilbert obediently scanned it, flipping it over once to check that there was no second side of script, and then again in case the blank face told him anything more.

'Well?'

'I make nothing of it, Monsieur.'

'Nor I.'

'I mean that I actually do not understand the words.'

Fouché smiled. 'That is your future, dear Guilbert.' Guilbert seemed indifferent about his future. 'Two of the most advanced natural philosophers of the age, discussing the most exciting experiment. It is part of the Assembly's reform and standardization of all weights and measures.' Guilbert remained unimpressed by the prospect of change to his weights and measures. 'Bailly writes to Lavoisier to tell him of his student's activities. And no, Guilbert, I don't see there is anything to make of it.'

'Man's got a good story; wants to tell his friends about it.'

'Exac-' Fouché stopped, snatched the paper back, and looked at the all but blank reverse side again. '*Friends*, Guilbert! That's rather good. Friends indeed. What did you make of the "1/6"?' Guilbert shrugged. Fouché spun back to the shelves, and returned with the envelope. 'Now?' Guilbert swallowed his irritation. 'Envelope and letter written in a different hand!'

'A servant, Monsieur.'

'A copyist, Guilbert!' Still Guilbert refused to become excited. 'In which case the notation would refer to the first copy of six, no? I propose that the other copies would have the same hand as the envelope.'

'That's how they do it sometimes. But who makes copies of a personal letter?'

'Indeed. Indeed. And the copyist has the addresses.'

Very faintly, Guilbert sighed. 'Your pardon, Monsieur, but you seem a bit excited by this. From what you say, this . . . experiment isn't any secret. There's nothing in the letter that could be of particular interest to anyone.'

'Not the message, Guilbert; there's no secret there.' He sat, heavily, at his desk and placed the letter and envelope squarely in front of him. 'But the *means*.'

There had been a ghastly intimacy to it, her interview with the creature Fouché. Terrible; thrilling. It had felt like nakedness; like the greatest vulnerability. Like violation.

Emma had hurried home, cloak wrapped tight around her. Bathed, then walked two hours in the deepest part of the forest, bathed again. She wanted to be cleansed of her whole life. She wanted to hide, in some place where Emma Lavalier would never be found.

It wasn't the questions. She'd been deflecting and defying questions all her life. Not caring what people thought of her, she did not care when her answers caused disapproval, or her lack of answers caused frustration. It hadn't mattered whom she danced with; whom she'd slept with.

It wasn't the style of the questions. She'd expected confrontation. She'd feared pain – for a moment, in the street, before the gate, the officers either side of her, she'd found herself shuddering at the thought of actual pain; her flesh raw and screaming.

But the creature had been austere, even deferential, despite his remorseless persistence.

No. Her experience had been bearable – better, even, than she had feared. But still she sat and shivered as the bath water cooled around her.

Now she had dressed, and conservatively; austerely. Her ankles, her arms, and her vulnerable neck were all covered. She sat in the salon – she sat alone, upright on the sofa, holding her body tight and erect. And she reflected with a lurking sense of horror at what her world was become.

Anyone could be declared a criminal – not for what they did, but for who they were – and carried to the guillotine. Prisoners were being casually tried in the prisons and killed. Priests – *priests* – had been massacred in their hundreds. The Swiss Guards – formality, order, the power of a benign central authority – had been slaughtered at the Tuileries. The Princesse de Lamballe had been interrogated and harangued and thrown into the street and cut to pieces.

Death was no longer a contained, contingent thing – the consequence of crime or of disease. Death was everywhere, and utterly unpredictable.

From somewhere, there was a knock.

She had been escorted to her interview with the creature not knowing if she would return – or even if she would arrive. Each of the heavy wooden doors she passed in the passage towards him could have opened to drag her in and shut her up for ever. Whatever she said in the interview, her survival had depended on his whim. Every time the creature had opened his mouth – she remembered his mouth in particular, a thin bloodless reptile's slit – the word could have been death. He hadn't needed to threaten, because the whole of his regime, the whole of life now implied the threat. Violence was the breeze of the Revolution; violence was carried in the gutters; violence was in the blood.

Again the knocking. Whatever the truth, whatever lie she told, at any second she might be dragged away and massacred.

She heard the front door opening, the heavy click of the latch. Her erect body stiffened and strained instinctively, and she forced herself still.

She'd wanted the servants away from the house for the rest of the day. She wanted no humans. But now a human had come regardless; a human who did not care to be stopped by an unanswered door.

The world had changed. There were no laws any more. Least of all the old law that, faced with the grandest man of power, a beautiful woman could always find an advantage.

The front door closed heavily. Footsteps, and another click as the door to the salon came open.

---❖---

KINNAIRD, Keith — born 175? — given as the s. of Muir Kinnaird
of Corstorphine, shopkeeper, and wife Janet, but there is much to
suggest that these — the father, at least — were but foster-parents. The
timing, contemporary records, and certain tales from that time hint at
the chance that the boy Kinnaird was the issue of an unknown Jacobite,
either orphaned or abandoned by his father or by his father and mother,
during the last silly flickerings of treasonous plotting in the decade
following the defeat of the rising of 1745. The boy was schooled at
home and then in Edinburgh, and reputed sober, adept and persevering.
For a certain time he worked as assistant to his assumed father, then
struck out on his own in trade, developing a concern of unspectacular
but solid prosperity at first in Edinburgh, and then in correspondence
with Glasgow, the northern cities of England, and eventually via the
North Sea traffic. In the early 1780s he was in partnership, and later
intermittently in correspondence, with GREENE, Henry (SS D/93). In
London regularly 1780-1785; in Amsterdam at least once 1787.

[SS D/101/1]

---❖---

Emma Lavalier rose to meet Kinnaird like some goddess of dignity, and it stunned him as much as if she had been naked.

The lack of an answer to his knock, the absence of any servant to greet him, had been merely one more obstruction and discourtesy in many weeks of them. Expectations born of years in trade; of a lifetime as a Scot. A silent hardened scorn at the foolish painted men and women. He'd lifted the latch with the weary sense that, as usual, he must slip in uninvited, side doors and blank faces, must prosper if at all by the unorthodox path.

All so tiresome. All so inefficient.

And in that sensation, a moment's reassurance. His father: *no Scot was ever given anything for free, nor won what he did not first deserve. If you want it, you must take it. What you will become, you must make.*

The inner door. The echoing of the latch in the cool silence of the house. The door swinging away and the woman rising to meet him.

Now he saw her beauty. Not a thing of flesh, of lips and shoulders and breasts as other men saw; instead, he saw a creature for one moment in absolute control of herself.

For Emma, the appearance of the ridiculous English . . . Scottish man was a kind of reassurance of the perversity of her new world. The remorseless strangeness of it all. This salon had been her protected haven of life, of colour and amusements and passion. Today it was cool and empty and pale, and its only visitor was the man that none of them wanted or trusted.

She said nothing. She stood in silence, watching him; considering him. The leanness: nothing of relaxation or indulgence about this man. Lean as the animals must be, that prey or are preyed upon.

Kinnaird was accustomed to silence. But he was surprised by it now: he knew this as a place of bubbling revelry, of superfluous noise and superfluous life. Now it was frozen with stillness, paleness, and silence.

He was used to using his silence, but he had not expected it in her. He had glimpsed Emma Lavalier before, and judged her: a decorative object, a licentious spirit.

Now she stood cold in front of him. Her dress was some sculpted fashionable thing, in a blue so pale as to be grey, mingling with the dust that drifted in the light from the windows. The collar was high, and tight around her neck: he saw beauty not in the grace and elegance of that neck, but in the discipline that had closed and fastened it. She had been interrogated by the Revolutionary Tribunal, and her response was this greater composure. And her face . . . he saw it beautiful not because of its fine bones and cool complexion, but because in this time of chaos and danger it had become more austere and more serene. He had the impression he was seeing a truer Emma Lavalier than he had before.

'I apologize for the intrusion, Madame. I had heard of your seizure by the authorities, and your return, and came to enquire after you.'

'Here I am.'

'Well enough, I am relieved to see.'

'You show greater solicitude than any of my intimates.'

'Perhaps they are turned more cautious precisely because they are your intimates, Madame.'

'You are surely more cautious than any, Mr Kinnaird.'

'Your circle of acquaintance is hardly a secret, Madame, and the regime is all-seeing. If they want me they will find me easily enough.'

'Please pardon a discourtesy, Mr Kinnaird. But I do not believe that you came here solely out of concern for me.' The 'solely' said 'at all'. And still the extraordinary poise.

Kinnaird bowed his head in acknowledgement. 'I came to France to seek an acquaintance. Those who have been his closest intimates deny sight of him, and evade me. Now I learn that he has been seen in the fringes of the outrage that has all Paris talking. I wondered if your experience today had . . . helped you to find yourself more ready to talk to me; or if you had learned any more of Greene today.'

She watched him.

Her face was absolutely still. But he knew it was thinking hard.

'My experience today has certainly affected me. It has certainly not made me more likely to talk to you, Sir. And no, I learned no more of our dear friend Greene.' Kinnaird breathed. Waited. 'It was not what you might expect, Mr Kinnaird. No tortures. No abuses. The greatest terror in the world is, it transpires, an unsleeping bureaucracy backed by an unstoppable mob.' She pulled her chin up. 'They did not have to harm me to persuade me to name my friends.' The hint of a smile in the ice. 'My lovers.'

'Indeed, Madame, you were surely telling them nothing they did not already know.'

Now she smiled, brilliant and cold.

'Where is Henry Greene, Madame?'

The eyes, the voice, hardened. 'I do not know. And now I do not care.'

'Revolutionary Paris is not a place for solitary speculators, Madame, or highwaymen. Whatever his enterprise, however disreputable, if Henry is active he is active in league with others.'

At last she showed the faintest surprise. 'You are a child, Mr Kinnaird. Or a simpleton. In the most dangerous city on earth, you pursue a social inconvenience. Like a man in a fire or a battle, who worries that his pocket-watch has stopped. And as we scramble and scuffle you persist in asking us for the time of day.'

'Or like a woman who dances, as her friends disappear and her people are slaughtered.'

'They will not shake me from myself.'

'Nor me, Madame.'

'Our mutual friend Greene is a rogue, Mr Kinnaird. An opportunist, a gambler, a speculator. A dealer in anything he thinks will pay: a silk or a secret.' Kinnaird nodded equably. 'He has danced the line between England and France, between trade and fraud. The intimacies he whispers are of nations as often as women.' Kinnaird was unstirred. 'All this I told them today.' She considered him again, coolly. A shadow of a man. 'I wonder if I mentioned you.'

His eyes hardened through her affected levity. 'Did you mention me, Madame?'

Now she was interested. 'Would that worry you?'

He shrugged slightly. 'Not especially. It is merely useful to know, in order better to calculate my position.'

He was unshakeable. 'You are an insignificant man, Mr Kinnaird. An unremarkable thing, a shadow, a murmur.'

'Yes. It has served me well these years.'

'You'll pardon me, but it seems rather a miserable existence.' *He does not flinch. He does not waver.*

'No doubt, Madame. But it is mine. I was born without name, money or' – he nodded his head slightly – 'beauty. I can not command success, nor buy it, nor charm it. I make my way on my wits, and my character.'

'Admirable. Do they carry you far?'

'Far enough.'

'I dare say.' It sounded more sneering than she had intended, and she regretted it.

'Pardon me, Madame, but it is not I who is hunted by the Tribunals.'

She scowled slightly, and resettled herself on her sofa. Her dress spread evenly around her, the only colour in the room.

'You don't thrill one.'

'I don't seek to.'

'Do you dance, Mr Kinnaird?

For the first time, something flickered at the edges of his mouth. 'Satisfactorily, Madame.'

'Hah! Satisfactorily, is it?' The life was in her eyes, the movement of her face. 'I'll bet it damn well is. Do you have pleasures of any kind?'

Now he did smile. 'Certainly, Madame. But they do not depend on the regard of others.'

At this she stopped. It came like a slap, and it came like illumination. Once again, she felt the dream of solitude, of impregnability.

Slowly, she stood. Once again, he watched her poise with admiration: a mastery of muscles and of self, and yet again he wondered at her life.

She walked towards him, hand outstretched. It was gesture of courtesy and dismissal. He took her hand, bowed over it, and didn't lower his eyes from hers.

Emma kept her hand in his a moment longer. She recaptured the lightness in her voice. 'Two cold ruthless ghosts in one day is too much, Mr Kinnaird. Where are my bright glorious men?'

'Consigned to the past, perhaps, Madame.' She listened to him as to a death sentence. 'It is the age of the mob. Your men of glamour and colour will rise on the backs of the mob for an hour, or a month; but then they will fall, and fall hard.'

She considered it. And said, with wonder, 'And it will be the quiet, subtle men who endure.'

———— ◆ ————

On 2nd October, to mark the heroic resistance of Lille against foreign siege, Madame Roland held one of her legendary soirées.

It was a phenomenon with which Fouché was neither particularly familiar nor particularly comfortable. But the invitation, delivered earnestly via his chief, was now natural; and the opportunity, for a man of ambition, irresistible.

The Interior Minister was notionally the host, of course, but when Fouché reached the top of the gentle spiral of steps Roland could not be seen. Instead, Madame alone received him, taking his hand and matching his little bow.

'My husband tells me you are become, Monsieur Fouché, the very ideal of the servant of the Revolution.'

Fouché, with alarm, felt himself flushing – not in humility, but the certainty that he would not find the right thing to say to such a platitude.

'Madame, I . . . if I might emulate Monsieur Roland's intellect, and Madame's spirit, I might hope to become a better servant.' Thin smile, bow, and he stepped away.

When he glanced back, he saw that she was still watching him. *What has Roland told her of me?*

A little glow of pride, which he tried to quash. To be considered noteworthy by Madame Roland was a prize indeed.

He lurked uncertainly near the entrance, near his hostess. Courteous nods – brief exchanges of politesse – with those arrivals whom he knew. Villers. Fréron. Lefebvre de Chailly. More than one congratulated him on his election to the Convention. He was as struck by the number he didn't know, as by the number he did. There was a Paris – there were Parises – influential and important, of which he was yet ignorant. *I have more reading to do.* And then the realization that he had more socializing to do.

Which drew his attention back to his hostess. The heart, and some even said the brains, behind Interior Minister Roland's political skill. Amongst other things, she had written the speech a few months back in which Roland had pressed – arguably threatened – the King. It had cost the Interior Minister his position; and a very timely fall it had been, for now the King was a prisoner and the minister was returned to position – and his wife more influential than ever.

Not conventionally beautiful – so he had overheard; and so he could perceive if he thought about it – but the dark eyes, wide in the face, held him. Her open neck was wrapped in a foam of lace that swooped down her exposed chest to a single and large rose. Fouché caught himself; brought his gaze up again. *Am I becoming as other men?* Uneasy thought. 'Monsieur Fouché!'

He looked up, startled. Madame herself. 'The Minister' – her husband, but it was typical she should refer to his official title – 'is buried in business somewhere. Would you oblige me by escorting me in?'

And so it was on Fouché's hand that Madame made her ceremonial entrance to her salon. Her status as hostess, and her reputation as revolutionary, earned her a polite fluttering of applause from her guests. The applause was not for Fouché – except – and she would have been careful in this – as the man selected to escort her in, he was the one honoured after all.

A moment of alarm in Fouché: she and Roland had broken publicly with the Jacobins; Roland's position was precarious; *am I being adopted by a faction?*

Joseph Fouché, of whom much was murmured in the corridors of Paris: his least comfortable moment since arriving in the great city; and at the same time a stiff-necked cold-faced triumph.

Fabre d'Églantine. Robert. Philippe-Égalité himself. Joviality about the performance of the Convention in its first days. Ignorant speculation about the Austrians and the Prussians and what Dumouriez was doing. Then, inevitably, Danton.

There was some glamorous creature beside him, but it was to Danton that they all looked. His height, his bulk, his noise, drew the room.

Fouché looked at the faces gathered around the man, scorning their butterfly minds. What is happening? What do I think? I must ask Danton . . . *Yet I too am here in attendance.*

'We stubbornly maintain that our genius defines the Revolution, but Lille shows that our true genius is stubbornness!' *Witty enough to seem brilliant; loud enough to seem irresistible.* Fouché watched the performance; considered himself as attendant. *Is he what I must become? Is he what I must follow?* At last Danton happened to see him, and the eyes and face seemed to swell in recognition. *Is he what I must destroy?*

'I'm afraid I'm rather a hot-head, dear friends: throwing up the political battles, rushing out to face the Prussian monster; leaping for the stars!' He had clutched the arm of the woman beside him, a shrewd pose of comradeship, of drawing strength from lesser people. 'But damn me if I don't look down to find that the likes of young Fouché here have built a ladder up after me!'

Fouché flinched at the reference; assumed a slight. But then amid the murmurs of amusement he saw the approving nods in his own direction.

More confused: *Danton is complimenting me?*

More of his brain was rehearing Danton's words. Well-judged, of course: a vigorous polishing of his image, and his commitment, while offering seemly credit to those less glamorous than himself; respect for the necessary business of order and administration, behind his own claim to the heart of the Revolution. Very well-judged. *I respect this in him.*

But such a performance! All – And once again Fouché forced himself to look beyond his irritation.

This was all imposture. So where was the truth?

What is the opposite of the pose?

Danton is not hot-headed but rational? Danton never gives up politics? Danton does not think the Prussians are monsters? Danton is not amused and satisfied by my work in the shadows of the Revolution? No. Danton is . . . *Danton is uneasy about me.*

Faintly, unseen, Fouché smiled.

Danton at last released the arm of the woman beside him, and turned with elaborate show of patience to listen to a question, and Fouché glanced to the woman for the first time.

She was looking at him. She was, faintly, smiling. *She saw me smile.*

It was Emma Lavalier.

Fouché's face held cold. How could she possibly be here? Then he remembered Guilbert's reports of her connections, and Roland's, and her own claims.

He contrived a little nod. Restored the thin smile to his face. *She must be shocked to see me here! A reminder of her shame, surely; of her vulnerability.*

Emma Lavalier had slipped away from Danton's side, and was walking straight towards Fouché, hand outstretched to accept the greeting that he must surely offer her.

'Why, Monsieur Fouché! How nice to see you again. It was my great pleasure to have the chance to call on you. I trust I may continue to aid you in your vital work.'

Slowly, in spite of himself, Fouché lifted his hand to take hers; bent over it in courtesy. Then his face came up into hers and, oblivious to the features and expressions around them, the eyes locked on each other.

Fouché felt himself cold – and somehow thrilled.

Danton is an amateur compared to this woman.

Emma Lavalier was gleaming: bright eyes and dangerous energy; Benjamin knew the signs. She was exhilarated by how she had managed to make her place in the salon – she felt that she was catching up with Paris again. In the small hours of the morning – a house in Aubervilliers, a private room and a deaf-mute girl dealing and counting for them – she and Benjamin were playing piquet, she for higher and wilder stakes than he.

'Tonight, Raph, it behoves you to be losing to me a little more generously.'

'Always. In *élan* as well as cards.' He glanced at his hand. 'You breathe triumph. You are so relaxed?'

She considered it. 'No. No, Raph, I'm not. But I find that a game I thought closed to me has re-opened.' She smiled. 'More intricate than ever; more exciting.'

He smiled back, then said through it: 'More dangerous.'

She sniffed. 'Perhaps.' Nodded slightly. 'They haven't knocked on your door yet.'

'Perhaps they can't find it.' He revived the smile. 'Perhaps I should knock on theirs.' His glance dropped to his cards again, and his voice with it. 'I have wondered at that.'

'With the army fighting the Prussians, they haven't enough men to face you?'

He bowed. 'No doubt. More likely they are still cautious about bringing in foreigners. And they don't know what exactly to accuse us of. They won't provoke a scandal with the English yet, not if they can help it.'

'You think so?'

He shrugged. 'For now . . . ' Eyes up again. 'In truth, they could come for me when they chose. They may not know all of the games that I play, but they must have my name, from any of half a dozen channels.'

Emma Lavalier's glance dropped to her own hand. 'Raph,' she said quietly; 'you haven't asked if I – '

'A gentleman, Emma, does not ask a lady about her interrogation.' To the cards again. 'Point of three.'

Guilbert always appeared with the air of the gutter somehow clinging to him; the dungeon. His habitual silence echoed with the pains of others. When Fouché looked at his strangely white hands, he immediately wondered what Guilbert had washed off them.

Here, in a corridor of the Tuileries outside the Committee room, he was a reminder of a grubbier France, or its envoy.

'You were not satisfied with the interrogations of the thieves of the Garde-Meuble, Monsieur.' Fouché glanced to left and right; Guilbert's eyes were steady on him. 'Your instincts were sound, of course.' The voice flat as ever. 'Monsieur the Prosecutor is an amusing actor, but a poor interrogator.'

Fouché waited.

'The thieves are insistent' – for once a faint emphasis; it resounded with what the thieves had had to undergo to maintain this insistence – 'that they stole many treasures, but did not steal the great jewels. They did not enter that part of the Meuble where the great jewels were kept. They did not properly know of it.' A pause. 'They have little reason to lie about this point.'

Fouché, mind still half in the Committee's discussion of the role of the police in dealing with deserters from the army, took a moment to follow the implications. 'But that would mean . . . a second robbery, Guilbert? Some great coincidence, or some double deception?'

'I mistrust coincidence, Monsieur.' There was a distant hint of distaste. 'Likewise the over-elaborate.'

Fouché nodded, trying not to seem naive. 'So . . . ?'

'They insist they were put on to the business by a man unknown to them. A man always shadowed or masked. A Frenchman.'

'He incited their grand outrage as cover for his own quieter affair with the jewels?'

'A clever arrangement, Monsieur.'

'But what manner of Frenchman, Guilbert?' Guilbert had nothing to add; he stayed silent. 'One working in the royal interest, perhaps? Recover their treasures – for bribery?' Fouché's eyes widened at his own thoughts. 'For *escape*?'

Still silence. *Guilbert does not speculate; is it a wise habit?* 'But the English,

Guilbert! An English voice heard in the shadows. The Englishman seen in the carriage outside.' He felt himself fluttering around Guilbert's stolidity. 'Three robb-?' He stopped before Guilbert could re-express his mistrust of the over-elaborate. 'An Englishman in concert with a Frenchman?'

And always, striding away in front of him, the shadow of Danton in the night. *Why was he so distracted? Is that merely his habit? Is that the extent of his distraction at the Prussian threat to France?*

Why does Danton haunt me?

———————◆———————

From the suite of His Serene Highness the Duke of Brunswick, as at Verdun, the 3. October

Sir,

the indecisive engagement near the place called Valmy has made appropriate a reconsideration of the military and political position of His Serene Highness's forces. There is, naturally, no change in the strength or spirit of our Prussian troops, but His Grace's prudence and greater vision make him averse to rashness or mere adventurism at this delicate time, and the excitable situation in France, the unpredictability of their irregular troops, and the proper military concern – so different from our opponents – at the possibility of so substantial a force as our own trying to live off unknown terrain so recently scoured by the French horde, do counsel against any hasty incursion.

Arnim has had a whole plum in his mouth for the duration of this paragraph, working and sucking at its flesh until the juice and the fibre are all swallowed. Now he leans forwards slightly, and spits the stone in an arc towards the fireplace. It drops silent into the ash. He wipes his mouth.

Your position and our hopes in you are accordingly unchanged. Prussia will soon lead the advance of stable government back into France, but will naturally do nothing injudicious for her own interests or fighting men while the position and attitude of Louis of France is unresolved. This proper patience while we await the moment most propitious for victory, and the undesirability of any diplomatic complication intervening, makes it more essential than ever that no embarrassments be allowed to emerge from the historical relations of the Court of France and the Court of Prussia.

[BUNDESARCHIV BERLIN-LICHTERFELDE, RESERVE COLLECTION; AUTHOR TRANSLATION]

It is, in its way, so magnificently full of half-truth and deception that they might stand as a second layer of encypherment. Arnim's tongue explores his teeth, seeking the fugitive plum flesh. From all he's heard – from all he's read between the lines of the revolutionary bulletins, with their uneasy bravado and their clumsy deployment of military terminology – the Duke of Brunswick has no need to retreat. But he's obviously not advancing at any imminent moment. The lines of strategic nonsense can be ignored. *Brunswick has some larger game.* The matter of the position and attitude of Louis . . . Arnim smiles. Berlin and Brunswick don't want revolution triumphant; but they're happy to wait for a while as the King, and the Revolution, and royalist rebels eat away at each other, swallowing French money and lives.

And at last he considers those potential embarrassments. He reaches for another plum, stroking the bruised velvet skin. Never far from Karl Arnim's mind these last months: the secret correspondence of the King of France; and the dangers and the opportunities it contains.

———————— • ————————

Why does Danton haunt me?

Danton: all of the loud bullies of Fouché's life.

Sitting behind Roland, Fouché watched over the minister's shoulder as he spoke to the Committee. He was aware of the blur of faces beyond. If he were in the minister's position, this would be his view.

An odd uncomfortable exposure, this presentation before the Committee. A schoolboy with his catechism.

Fouché the schoolboy had liked it to be known that he knew things. He liked better the knowing of something that no one knew.

He knew what the minister was saying. They had discussed it. Roland's voice warbled indistinctly ahead of him.

Question: what could Danton be worried about? What could he have done that would make that vast character shameful – fearful? There have long been rumours of Danton's improprieties, his financial peccadilloes, his lavish life. *'Who is that well-dressed fellow?' 'A friend of Danton.'* The catch-phrase that eats at the purity of the Revolution.

Refined question: as Danton is not a melancholic, a catcher at fancies, what practical thing is it that he fears? What discovery does he fear?

More refined question: what proof might there be of some misdeed? Either a witness, or a . . . a document.

Fouché dreamed of documents. He lived in them. He devoured them, digested them, and built the matter and pathways of his mind from their smallest details.

Now, as the minister's carefully modulated voice sounded somewhere nearby, against the background of blurred faces, Fouché wondered about the power of documents. And he wondered at Danton and documents.

Witnesses have died: Laporte, the King's confidential secretary, on the guillotine; the go-between Maupuy in a brothel, his corpse slung on a dunghill. The Princesse de Lamballe, closest confidante of the Queen, savaged in the street.

It was getting harder to investigate the royal correspondence. A challenge, to a man who lived on documents.

------◆------

The stranger, the man who called himself Kinnaird with such apparent discomfort in his strangled accent, proposed a walk. Lucie had not found a reason to refuse.

That alarmed her. Normally the lie – a commission, a malady – would have come instinctively, natural reaction to the prospect of uncomfortable company. But the stranger seemed to hold her. Polite concern after her appearance before the Tribunal. Dull blank face. Cold sharp eyes.

There was still some summer in the warmth of the air. But the sky was autumn: white; dead.

It was an ugly time for a walk.

The stranger led them out of St-Denis town, past the dyeing factory and towards the river. He didn't speak.

It took a while for Lucie to notice it.

She knew where they were going.

She walked a pace behind him, and to the side. She could see his profile, and she wondered what he was thinking.

The river appeared through the trees; a pale wall. Lucie felt her heart thumping in her.

'Where now?'

He stopped, and turned to face her. Dumbly, she gestured to the left, towards the glade. 'Very well,' he said, and started to move again.

They came to the glade. The stranger hesitated, then walked to its centre, and turned. Lucie had stopped.

'Well, this is charming.'

He didn't say it as if it was charming. So quiet; so steady. The glade spread around him. The light coming off the river made him look colder. Lucie looked past him to the trees fringing the glade, to the rough undergrowth; not to him.

'What are those buildings? Downstream there?'

She glanced. 'Mills. For spinning.'

'Must be a pleasant place to come of an evening.'

The banality was unnerving. He cannot be so mild. He cannot be so tame. He was watching her still. What is in the undergrowth of this man?

She shrugged.

'And the Paris road . . . must be just up there, beyond the wood?' He gestured.

She nodded.

'Convenient place to meet someone coming from the city, I guess.'

She shrugged.

'Henry use this place sometimes, do you think?' He anticipated the shrug. 'I'm trying to understand his habits, Mademoiselle.'

'Yes he met people here sometimes. Different people. Yes I could name some of them, but it won't do you any good because he met lots of different people in different places.' Now he looked a little startled. 'And yes, he was supposed to meet someone else here, that same day he was supposed to meet me, but I don't know who.'

He didn't know where to go with it. 'Had he been anywhere – met anyone before that?' It was a stupid question, and her scowl told him so. 'I suppose you don't – '

'He'd been away the night before. No, I don't know where.'

'You weren't sure about the day. But you seemed sure there was a party at Madame Lavalier's in the evening. What do you think of her?'

Not the kind of question she was used to. He was waiting for an answer. 'Does what she wants. Doesn't care what people think.'

It was said dead. 'That doesn't sound good to you?'

Now there was life in her voice. 'You have to be rich to be free.'

He nodded, soberly. 'Is there a reason why you would remember there was a party that evening?'

Lucie looked down, and continued to look down.

'Mademoiselle?'

She looked up. 'Guests. Foreigners. At her house.' She glanced down, and up again. The stranger was still waiting. 'I hear these things. Invitation messages. Interesting for the local fingers. And – '

'Fingers?'

She held his eyes. 'Pickpockets, Monsieur. All those horses needing holding, all those carriage doors needing opening. Beg a sou, lift a franc.'

'And you tell the . . . fingers, about such occasions.' Cold smile. 'You've never gone in for pickpocketing, I'm sure.'

'Never, Monsieur. The boys used to like me to do the talking for them – *allow my brother to carry your bag, Madame* – they trust it more with a girl – but that's completely different. And years ago.'

The stranger was looking lost again. And again it made her feel more comfortable.

Still he was unknown. And still she wanted to know what he knew.

———————◆———————

There is something odd in Guilbert's face. Normally a man silently at ease in his environment, Guilbert is . . . uncomfortable. It's so unusual as to be startling. Paris is supposed to be celebrating confirmation of the news that Brunswick is retreating beyond the Rhine; Guilbert seems unimpressed.

'A problem, Guilbert?'

The face settles at Fouché's challenge; the discomfort disappears. *Admirable self-control.* 'An inconvenience, Monsieur. An irritation.' Fouché's expression invites more. 'You asked after the Tourzel women – Madame the royal governess, and her daughter.'

'Indeed.' Fouché's mind is ahead of his words, beginning to feel the strangeness. 'Imprisoned in La Force.'

'No longer, Monsieur.' The words are flat.

Guilbert watches their effect on Fouché. The face hardens. More like a skull than ever. The hawk eyes widen and darken. The eyebrows rise. It's not surprise: it's distaste; it's a reconsideration of a servant's usefulness.

'Have I misunderstood the purpose of a prison, Guilbert? Have I underestimated the power of revolutionary *liberté*?'

'The prison is not well-administered, Monsieur, I regret. Habits are bad. The morale and morals of the custodians are poor. In this time of . . . change, Monsieur, the routines and responsibilities of interrogation and imprisonment are chaotic. Different authorities have different influence, and the custodians are trying to keep everyone happy.'

'All true. And?'

'Sometime in early September – the killings had started in the streets – the two women disappeared.'

'I don't pay you for fancy, Guilbert.'

'Monsieur. There are no records. No authorizations. But no escape was noticed. So – '

'Nothing was noticed? This happened in early September – two of the closest intimates of the royal family yet living, enemies of the Revolution – and no one notices when they disappear from La Force?' Fouché's anger is at the situation he cannot control. At something he does not yet understand.

'Naturally I have investigated, Monsieur. A custodian who remembers an unknown visitor. Arrangements that allow the authorities to commit and remove prisoners without bureaucra-'

'We are the authorities!'

'We are some of them, Monsieur. If I may, Monsieur, the structures of authority are complicated.' Fouché's face is stone. 'I judge that over the course of two nights, the two women were removed from the prison, by someone who knew the place enough and had enough authority to get in and get them out.'

Somewhere in Fouché, glowing within his frustration and bafflement, an admiration is growing for the daring and skill of men who can make Paris work in this way.

Guilbert sees the face soften, sees the reflectiveness. 'If Monsieur will tell me more of this context, I can try to serve him better.'

Fouché pulls himself straighter in his chair – a scarecrow; a skeleton. He folds his hands in front of him.

Guilbert loathes the performance; mistrusts the inhuman nature.

'I interest myself, Guilbert, in the documentation of royal espionage. The correspondence, in and out, of those in concert with the King. His familiars, his collaborators, his co-conspirators. Those in France who participated in his corrupt government; those involved in the financial games and frauds that sustained his regime and enriched its creatures. Those abroad with whom they dealt. I am interested in uncovering something of this correspondence, Guilbert, because someone else seems interested in covering it up. There are no facts, no traces, no grounds for suspicion that might be levelled at any man. But I am interested in why so many men and women connected with royal communications seem to have disappeared.'

Fouché smiles a death's smile, over-stretched lips and sharp teeth. 'I am interested, Guilbert, in Danton.'

And now there's the faint discomfort in Guilbert's face again. *Hallo . . .* Very cautiously, flexing his toes in his boots, he finds himself reconsidering his position. *Here's trouble.*

———— ◆ ————

FROM THE MINISTER PLENIPOTENTIARY
TO FRANCE

To the Secretary to the Congressional Committee on
Trade and Diplomacy, Congress of the United States,
meeting in Philadelphia

October 4th, 1792

Sir,

the National Convention of France has produced its
latest novelty. Declaring the Republic 'one and indivisible',
it has reaffirmed its rejection of monarchy and offered a new
provocation to its opponents. A skeptic might say that these
defiant bravadoes do generally accompany some new sensation
of external threat or vulnerability, but this Republic continues, if
yet sure neither of its oneness nor its indivisibility, hale enough.
As if in emulation of the robust spirit of the declaration, the
town of Lille, in the north of the country, is declared in the
latest reports from that district to have resisted the Austrian
siege. If that be true, and if, as is anticipated, the Austrians
withdraw to regather their strength and find a new district to
supply their commissary needs, it is like to be succeeded by some
new French expansion in that direction. For the Revolution,
though it go sometimes forwards and sometimes backwards,
seems never inclined to stand still.

I had the honour to attend last night the latest soirée of
Madame Roland, wife of the Interior Minister and the somewhat
brittle heroine of the moderate revolutionaries. Danton was
there, which suggests that Roland and Madame are still close
enough to the main thrust of the movement – or, indeed, that
Danton still covets the impression of moderation, or more
likely the impression of ubiquity. Roland and Brissot and the
old moderate Jacobins hope for an easing of the tensions and
a reconsolidation around steady government – by themselves.
More radical voices represent the hunger of the populace for

stronger measures – or, I would suggest, they follow it. For the massacres of September, inside and outside the prisons, have given the people a taste for blood and not satisfied it. Thousands of persons of quality have been slaughtered, the example of Paris carried to the provinces and eagerly emulated; I learn of one datum recording that in August and September 1,395 persons died in Paris of whom 420 could not be identified because their bodies were so mutilated or burned. Generations of jealousy at the privileges of the rulers, combined with fear at the threat from Prussia, have been unleashed and the men who presently claim that they lead the Revolution are more in the position of the man who keeps a wild beast and must either find food for it or himself become its supper.

You will recall from my earlier reports that the King had entrusted to me, near the end of July, a small portfolio of his correspondence – some two dozen documents pertaining mostly to our relations, which I elected to destroy, and a few papers of personal sentiment for his family but no political significance, which I continue to preserve. My informal researches have shown that on the night of his flight from the Tuileries Palace last month, he entrusted to Madame Campan, of his entourage, another portfolio, which she has in like wise burned. Clearly, the bulk of the royal correspondence was elsewhere – and presumably is so still. I learn that more than one party, French and other, is eagerly after it.

I continue to hold in trust for the King the residue of the funds which he also entrusted to me on that occasion in July, and to account diligently for the expenditures which I have drawn from those funds either to secure the advantage of fugitive adherents of the former regime or to pay the expenses of those members of his retinue to whom I am pleased to continue to offer the hospitality of the Legation.

Morris.

(DECYPHERED; US NATIONAL ARCHIVES, DEPARTMENT OF STATE RECORDS RG 59)

A private supper for Fouché, at Roland's home. The food was indifferent, which meant nothing to Fouché; the intimacy, in this fortress of political respectability, was everything.

And as quickly the thought followed: have I been seen? Will it become known that I was here? Does that remain desirable?

'Monsieur Mi-' The door opened behind Monsieur Minister and a pair of satin-wrapped breasts appeared in the centre of Fouché's vision. By the time he'd looked up further, Madame Roland was standing beside her husband. Fouché rose – thigh catching under table top and knife rattling off plate and onto floor – to greet her.

'Monsieur Fouché: we make you too busy a servant of the Revolution, I fear.'

'Your hospitality – Madame – your hospitality is reward too much. Madame, I cannot sleep while the minister is awake.'

She smiled gravely – handsomely.

'We would welcome your conversation, my dear.' Roland's sincere partnership with his wife. *Yes!* Fouché thought instantly. Then worried at whether he really could have the conversation he wanted, with her present.

'I would not dream of interfering,' she said. 'And I have a guest of my own. Good evening, Monsieur Fouché.'

Fouché had started to sit, stood again, caught his fork as it teetered, and took her offered hand.

As he watched her pulling the door closed behind her, Fouché's unconscious mind took up his sentence. 'Monsieur Minister, I concern myself with the royal correspondence.'

Roland's eyes came up from his plate. He waited, silent.

'Monsieur Minister, what was found in the Tuileries after the departure of the King? Have we everything?'

The Minister of the Interior's eyes widened, and they gazed bleak: alarm; disapproval. He placed his knife and fork down on his plate. Then he frowned at Fouché, stood, frowned again, retreated to the wall watching Fouché over his shoulder all the time, seemed to reflect, walked to the table again and sat. And again frowned.

The Minister's tongue explored his lips. 'Ah . . . If, Fouché, I knew your interest . . .'

Fouché's mind was grappling with the Minister's performance. *How much can I not know? Is there still so much secret, even from me?*

How, then, to present my interest? 'A concern at . . . at the threat, Minister. Louis was known to have correspondence with the courts of Europe. After the Revolution first began to bring him under proper control, he no doubt corresponded in a treasonous manner, to invite foreign action against the Revolution. No doubt he received replies; perhaps he kept copies of his own letters. Such correspondence would show not only his treasons but also his . . . were there any . . . his intermediaries in France.'

Interior Minister Roland had survived a long political life, and a tumultuous change of regime. He chose not to answer.

Is it me? Of what can I be suspected?

'Hence my question, Minister.'

The Minister's tongue made another patrol of his lips.

Or, if I am not suspect . . . ?

'Nothing was found, Fouché.'

'That's – that must have been disappointing, Minister.'

The Minister's eyes, normally so benign, were cold.

'Indeed. Naturally there was great interest. As you say – the question of Louis's corruptions and betrayals.'

It was all too bewildering. 'So . . . So it is thought destroyed, Minister? Burned?'

'We must assume so. A most natural proceeding.'

'I ask, Minister, because several persons connected to the royal correspondence have recently died or disappeared. It seems to indicate some . . . unfinished affair.'

Silence.

Why would the Revolution's Interior Minister be so wary about the King's correspondence?

'But there was nothing . . .' Carefully, Roland shook his head.

Because the Revolution's Interior Minister was previously the King's Interior Minister.

The door opened behind the Minister again, and Madame Roland was at the table before either of the men was halfway stood. She waved them down again. 'I shall see my friend out, Roland, and then I shall retire for the night.' The Minister murmured acknowledgement. 'Goodnight to you, Monsieur Fouché.' Out came the hand and he grabbed at the fingers, thrilling at the touch of their tips. 'We are grateful for your company.'

He had half-stood again; 'Madame.'

She smiled soberly at him, and bent to kiss the side of her husband's head, and Fouché gazed down the shadowed tunnel between her breasts. *I am not a child! I have a wife; this is not unknown ground. So why does this female trouble me?*

As the door started to close again, Fouché caught a glimpse of Madame Roland's guest making for the front door. Just a glimpse of the back of her head, hair up and an exposed upper back.

Somehow, the hair and the back seemed fami- *Control yourself!*

————————◆————————

Emma Lavalier closed her bedroom door behind her, and pressed her body back against it.

The world shut out. She would even do without Colette's gentle fingers for her toilette.

Colette had prepared the room: the bed ready, the curtains drawn. The hem of the curtain shutting off the bay window was rippling faintly; Colette had opened the window. The idea of cool – the prospect of the sheets against her body – felt like relief.

There was something wrong with the bay curtain: it didn't hang true; it ... bulged slightly, halfway down.

She pressed harder against the door, fingers stiff and strained. She tried to see through the curtain.

She should get out. She should summon the servants.

She took a great breath, and it trembled like a sob.

Increasingly I must face my sins alone.

She started walking towards the curtain, her steps measured and counted and bringing her closer to another unavoidable confrontation.

Another breath, and then she wrenched the curtain aside.

Raph Benjamin was sitting on the window-sill, back against the frame and one leg propped up. Lavalier swallowed her gasp, her thumping heart.

"'S the trouble with the Revolution,' he said, 'plays havoc with morality.'

'I've all the control I want over my morality, thank you.' She cupped his jaw between her thumb and forefinger. 'If I want you I shall summon you.' She scratched softly at his cheek.

Affected amusement at this. The voice came harder: 'Our encounters are become rather furtive, dear Emma.'

'You never used to complain at privacy, Raphael.'

The old grin. 'Private I like. Private I encourage. But furtive is different. Furtive is merely undignified.'

He was right. She was becoming more . . . cautious, was it?

'If I may, Emma, one of your charms – one of your very many charms – has always been your readiness to enjoy life. To . . . to embrace it.' Rogue's smile.

'And you life personified.' She said it flat. 'Benjamin, if you propose to review my lost charms like a fat grocer in a brothel, we may end this encounter now – furtive or otherwise.'

Colder smile. 'Even so.'

She shrugged. 'Life seems . . . more serious.'

Should she just satisfy him? To shut him up, to prove him wrong, to restore his hope in life. To restore her own.

No, not even for that.

'I was at Roland's house this evening. The Minister of the Interior.'

'I have heard of him.'

'Calling on his wife, at least. He was having supper with a colleague. A young man named Fouché. He is Jean-Marie Roland's latest cultivation: a tiger of the Revolution.'

'And what creature of revolution are you, dear Emma?' There was admiration in his voice nonetheless.

'I overheard this Fouché asking about the royal correspondence. Apparently they didn't find any.'

'What of it?'

'You don't think that's interesting?'

'Burned it all, presumably.'

'And if they didn't?' Benjamin shrugged. 'There's nothing that would . . . would worry you, Raph?'

'Ah, my *billets-doux* to dear Queen Marie, you mean? Messages of support to His Majesty from me and all my Prussian friends? No, there's nothing of that – ' He hesitated open-mouthed, and then brought his lips together and whistled a few notes of a tune. 'But good old Greene, now . . . Surely not. Surely that's out of his league.' He picked up the tune again. Lavalier watched the face, watched the mind working. Watched fondly. 'But if the revs are interested in ripe letters, now . . . ' The tune again for a few notes, slower, and flatter. 'What's the name of that Dutchman of yours? Rumours about him and the Prussians. Pleasant fellow. Dull.'

'Oh – Marinus.' She smiled. 'I like to see you scheming.'

The rogue's smile again, and his eyes searched her body. 'And that little compliment is all the warmth I may expect tonight?'

A brief sigh, and she bent down, and kissed him full on the lips; his hands came up to her body. Then she began slowly to push him off the window-sill into the night.

———— ◆ ————

The paper system of the revolutionary Ministry of the Interior was that inherited from the royal Ministry of the Interior, except that some – though not all – of the men who guarded it had gone. Fouché had approached it ready with justifications and ploys, and found that no one objected to him simply looking at whatever he fancied. Or indeed taking it.

Looking at it was easy. It was everywhere: piles and dossiers and crates of papers, in different rooms of three different buildings. The successive political upheavals and the constant changes in staff, in priorities, and indeed in the whole structure of the state had meant a series of abortive attempts at reorganization. Fouché spent a dispiriting morning wandering angry between ministry buildings and former ministry buildings, and even to the Assembly archives in the Convent of the Feuillants, looking in each for the more established porters who could tell him where the documents were. Occasionally he would find some. The royal paperwork had become as fugitive as the royal family, huddling for shelter in diverse grand buildings; and trying, as it seemed to Fouché, not to be noticed.

Roland saw his frustration. 'Your documents, Fouché?'

'Minister. It's absurd. The most elaborate administration in Europe, and the most luxuriant, and all traces of it have disappeared.'

Roland shrugged sympathetically, and turned to go.

Then he said, 'It may have been destroyed, you know?' Fouché looked doubtful. 'I recall that we had record of one – no, two – incidents. The King gave some documents to the American ambassador and the ambassador destroyed them; we had a man who saw it. And our investigations of the chaos at the Tuileries showed that some documents were given to Madame Campan, and she also destroyed them.'

Fouché considered it. *Another lesson, perhaps.* Should he rely on men, not papers?

But he didn't trust the men.

'Americans, Minister?'

'Another factor in your calculations, dear Fouché. But our revolutionary allies.'

Fouché scowled. 'Unless the ambassador and the woman Campan left with a suite of wagons, what they later destroyed must surely be incidental. The royal correspondence must have been vast.'

'Indeed,' Roland said, trying to care. 'And yet . . .'

———————◆———————

'You are the British, who lodges at the Tambour?'

It was muttered, flat, and like an accusation. Kinnaird found himself checking a second time that the man wore no uniform, looking beyond him.

He nodded, some ancestral prudence making him think he could more easily pretend a misunderstanding if he hadn't actually said anything.

'I have a message for you; a rendez-vous.' Kinnaird's eyes widened. He managed to turn the expression into disinterested enquiry. 'Tomorrow. Ten of the morning. The shop of Petiot in the Galerie Marillac.'

Kinnaird nodded again. And now he had to speak. 'Who? Who am I to meet?'

Now the young man looked quickly either side of himself. 'Another British: Henry' – the H was uncomfortable for the French mouth – 'Greene.'

A garbled French pronunciation of the so-mysterious words. For a third time Keith Kinnaird nodded; slowly now, fate and his heart thumping hard.

———————⋄———————

Pieter Marinus's house was anonymous: narrow, its three floors apparently failing to shoulder their way between the two more substantial buildings either side, and just off the rue Martin. The anonymity had perhaps been an unconscious choice; the proximity to the Porte St Martin and a fast way out of the city had been deliberate.

He had the key in the lock when he sensed someone near him, shifted his eyes to catch movement, heard 'You are Monsieur Marinus?' He looked at the speaker. *Time to get into the house? Time to run? Drop the key, or throw it?* A lad. Poor. Dull-faced. He looked beyond the lad – saw no one – scanned the street around him, trying to catch movement in windows, figures in doorways.

The key stayed in the lock, unturned. Marinus held his hand up near it, ready to strike or push out or to get inside.

'I am Pieter Marinus.'

The lad didn't seem impressed. 'Message for you, Monsieur. You're asked to a meeting tomorrow, ten of the morning. The shop of Petiot in the Galerie Marillac. The message is from a British named Henry Greene.'

Marinus felt his stomach lurch. He fought to control his expression, fought to stand still, urged his mind to think.

He nodded.

The lad stood there. Sniffed.

Marinus placed a coin in the lad's hand, and the lad considered it, and shrugged, and turned away.

———————⋄———————

Fouché was at his desk. The desk was covered with papers. Not covered completely – for the papers were organized in precise piles, precise in the congruity of each pile and in its relation to the adjacent piles. Occasionally he would, by way of experiment, move a paper from one pile to another. Sometimes, when he felt that his mind needed refreshing, he would transpose the positions of two piles, adjusting their relation to the others.

Guilbert was through the door before Fouché had properly registered his knock, and Fouché looked up startled, as if caught in a secret.

Guilbert's haste was unusual, though his voice of course was flat.

'Your pardon, Monsieur.' Fouché nodded, as if this pardon were actually a transaction. 'A detail from the Commune.' Fouché nodded again. 'As you know, the Commune police have their informants and their spies. They mostly inherited them from the Prefect of Police, which means they were informants and spies under the King too.'

'Trade must continue, Guilbert.'

'Right you are, Monsieur. I know your concern for the affairs of foreigners, Monsieur. You spoke of rumour of Prussian business in the city. So I keep in touch. The Commune police have an eye on the house of a Dutchman – once suspected of intrigue with the Prussian embassy, before it closed – and yesterday they saw a messenger stop there. The messenger is one of their occasionals. Why get paid for a message once when you can get paid for it twice?' Fouché nodded. 'He'd delivered the same message to an Englishman. Invitation to a meeting.' Fouché felt his impatience beating in him. 'The invitation came from Henry Greene, the man seen outside the Meuble when it was being burgled.'

————— ◆ —————

The street was a chaos of noise and movement and dust, and Kinnaird stepped through it uneasily. All shops in this district, and stalls filled the street between them, and his vision was bright with fruit, and the fat rich smell of fruit swirled round him, ripening too fast in the summer heat; from every stall and shop-front someone was yelling his variety and his quality and his price, like so many rival church bells, and Kinnaird's ears rang with this competition of excellence and the bubbling of voices around him in their unfamiliar language. As an exercise in commerce he wondered at it; made some comparisons, some calculations.

He stepped and slipped through apple cores and half-tasted peaches and discarded leaves and orange peel and spat-out plum stones and an ooze of slops that glistened on the cobbles and were sticky under his boots. Ahead the dust was worse, and he saw workmen with aprons and a scaffold of timbers against one side of the street, other men on ladders, a bustling of buckets and pulleys. There was a splash beside him and a curse, as one of the fruit-sellers tried to damp down the dust around his stall and glared hopelessly at the building works. Kinnaird stepped forward quickly as the slick of water reached his boot.

A workman came staggering past with a bucket of water, and another following lazily, and Kinnaird stopped him to ask for the Galerie Marillac; he had to ask twice, shouting, and the man pointed beyond the works. Kinnaird skirted the bedlam of activity, watching the workers, appraising them as he'd appraised the stores. The dust was sticking to the liquids on his boots now. There was a tavern to his right. He could smell cheap wine and hot grease.

The Galerie was an elegant entrance of fake columns, and through it a flagstoned hall and a wooden staircase. Beside the staircase a man was slumped against the wall, but straightened as Kinnaird hesitated beside him. Kinnaird said, 'Petiot?' and the man gestured up the stairs with his thumb.

'You are Monsieur Marinus?'

Kinnaird stopped, foot on the first step. 'No.' Suddenly the sense of his isolation, the need to be innocent of whatever Henry Greene was doing. 'No, my name is Kinnaird.' The man frowned at the unusual word, and relapsed against the wall.

Halfway up the staircase turned back on itself, and the noise of the street dropped. Kinnaird heard his boots on the boards; heard their creak.

At the top of the stairs, silence. A passage stretching to left and right of him, a line of perhaps a dozen frontages, each a single-room premises that would also look out onto the street. Above some of the frontages there were signboards: Chapeaux; Dusollier & Fils; Société Bretagne. Among the *fils* and *frères* he looked for Petiot.

The arcade seemed deserted. Not completed? So why the signboards already there? He took a step to the right. Through the window of Dusollier & Fils he saw shelves, all dusty, and a low cupboard adrift in the centre of the shop. He walked on.

An eruption of noise behind him, and he turned fast. A man had stepped out of one of the frontages, with a saw and a short length of wood and a fat laugh directed back into the shop. The man started down the stairs.

Kinnaird watched him go, and turned forwards again. Again the silence, though now he could distinguish through it the sounds of the work from outside, and from behind him, through the unclosed door, the carpenter's mate hammering at something.

Ahead, at last, was Henry Greene.

Now he saw the name 'Petiot' painted elaborately over the next doorway but one.

Through the smeared window next to him, he could see the workmen on their scaffold, repairing the wall around the window space and installing a window frame. Through the glass, and the silence, they seemed far away. Their world was distant, and boisterous. His was not.

He came level with the premises of Petiot, took a breath, and looked through the window panes.

It was empty.

Another abandoned shop space, dusty boards and racks of shelves. The street window in the place had shutters, closed except where one panel hung loose on a solitary hinge and let the day in. Among the ghostly residue of Petiot's business, the beam of daylight caught a chair left in the middle of the floor and scorched it silver.

Kinnaird hesitated, and found himself about to knock.

He frowned, and tried the handle. Stepped inside. Frowned again, and closed the door behind him.

He walked the perimeter of the room, considering it as a commercial premises. Its capacity; the quality of the woodwork; the location; the light.

At the door again, again he hesitated.

He walked to the chair, brushed a hand over the seat, and sat. He thought about the man downstairs; about the name he'd said.

He thought about Henry Greene.

———— ◆ ————

Raph Benjamin entered the tavern through its back door, a lithe figure swaying deftly between the swinging pots and the servants who bustled to and fro, a salute to the cook who glanced at him indifferent, a finger placed on the lips of a maid about to complain, bending to kiss the hand of his hostess and so into the main room at the front of the building.

Mid-morning, trade was slow. There was one man hunched over the counter, gazing at a beaker of wine as at his cheating lover. An ancient sat stiff against one wall, breathing in long gasps and intermittently lifting a cup of water two-handed to his lips. Benjamin nodded as he passed. Silhouetted against the front window was Ned Pinsent, a big stiff shadow.

A tuft of his hair was standing up unruly, and Benjamin felt a moment's fondness for the shadow. He clamped his hand down on its shoulder, and Pinsent jumped.

And subsided. 'Oh. What ho, Raph.'

Benjamin slipped down into the chair adjacent. 'Any sign of our bird?' His eyes were adjusting to the contrast between the interior and the daylit street outside.

'Punctual to the minute.' Across the street, builders were swarming up and down a timber scaffold. 'Give me a Scotch grocer for punctuality. Few minutes ago now.'

The woman placed a beaker down in front of Benjamin, held his eyes a moment too long, and he grinned at her.

Then back to the blaze of daylight. 'Excellent. Any activity since?'

'Not a flicker. No sign of t'other fellow.' Benjamin grunted, indifferent, and took a mouthful of wine, and grimaced. 'What are you anticipating to happen, Raph?'

'Almost certainly nothing. I don't trust any messenger, but I don't much trust the efficiency of the *crapaud* police spies either. Nine chances in ten nothing happens and he gets bored and he's gone inside the hour. But him blundering around Paris prattling about old Henry takes the attention away from us. That's all I'm after.'

Pinsent watched him for a long moment. 'You ain't in touch with old Henry, are you, Raph?'

Benjamin glanced at him, then back to the street, and Pinsent started to scowl. 'Raph, you – hallo!' His head came forward and he pointed upwards out of the window.

The workmen were bricking and plastering a new window frame into place in the facade opposite. Now a leg appeared on its sill, and a body swung out onto the scaffold, and stood for a moment blinking in the shock of sunlight.

In the tavern opposite, cheerful laughter from two Englishmen sitting at the window. As they watched, Kinnaird exchanged stares with the workmen on the scaffold, then pushed past them and clambered uncomfortably down the ladder and looked about himself and hurried away up the street.

Benjamin's hand was on Pinsent's shoulder again, and he was still chuckling.

Pinsent said, 'You got things arranged in St-Denis?'

'Most tidily, my dear fellow. A couple of gifts for our friend.' And he glanced out of the window again, and along the street to where a figure could still be seen hurrying for the corner, dust billowing from his boots as he went.

———————— ◆ ————————

Over the course of his weeks in France, Keith Kinnaird had come to feel comfortable in the rooms at the Tambour. He had no interest in luxury, and in this the Tambour could match his needs more than adequately. It was kept tidy, the air was fresh, and it was his.

But now, for the first time since his early cautious exploration of the rooms, they felt alien. They felt like Henry Greene's rooms again.

For the first time in those weeks, Greene's face came clear to his mind, and he wondered at the man.

He watched the Tambour for an hour or more before he brought himself to go near. It wasn't fear, or a calculation of risk. It was Greene. Greene was present again, Greene was around him somewhere, and Greene's rooms seemed to belong again to their former inhabitant.

Kinnaird felt more temporary, less certain in this place.

The door to the rooms stuck for a moment. It felt different even just to stand on the threshold. He was back where he had started: a stranger; an unfamiliar place; a friend who was everywhere and could not be found.

He stepped forwards into the living room, seeing it as for the first time again, looking to see Greene sitting in a chair, or slouched against the doorway to the bedroom.

He did one circuit of the room, touching the things that he knew to be his: the few books huddling at one end of the shelf; a shirt drying on the back of a chair. He'd left the front door open, and through the gap the day outside shone bright and free onto the walkway. The doorway seemed narrower; constricting.

The threshold didn't only feel different: it was different. The doormat – a failed attempt at a rectangle, cut from a sack – was askew and riding up onto the door sill. That's why the door had stuck; that's why it had felt faintly unfamiliar to stand there. He took two steps and pulled the mat straight, and saw the corner of paper underneath.

A single page folded in half, and then a sliver of it folded again to close it.

Kinnaird stuck his head out the door, looked left and right along the Tambour walkway, and down into the yard. He straightened the mat, closed the door, and looked down at the paper again.

His surname was written on the outside, in rough capitals. Inside, in the same lettering:

DEAR KINNAIRD – COME TO PETIOT, GALERIE MARILLAC. OUR PLAN PROGRESSES. H. G.

[SS K/1/X1/6]

He placed the letter on the table, stared at it a moment, and then made another circuit of the room. Not touching anything this time, just looking at each object. He looked down at the mat again.

Then he looked towards the bedroom, and walked to the connecting door. He stared around the room, and made a similar patrol. He sat down on the bed, and looked warily around again. The door to the living room; the open window and the trees beyond.

He stood, and there was a thumping at the front door.

He stood rigid, no breath, and then craned his head round to see the door. Again it thumped, and its panel vibrated and the light caught dust coughing from the cracks. '*Police du Commune*! *Ouvrez*!'

Thumping, and thumping, and Kinnaird crept dreamlike into the sitting room. On the table was the note from H.G.. '*Ouvrez*!'

'Hey!' A new noise, a new voice, a new direction, and Kinnaird twisted round in confusion. 'Hey British!' It sounded like – like *Lucie*, and it came from the bedroom.

'*Ouvrez*!'

He recoiled from the door, edged backwards into the bedroom, clutching for sense anywhere. The bedroom was empty. Lucie's voice was desperate, a restrained shout: 'Quick, British!' It was coming from the window. In two steps he was there, saw her below him on a horse, heard the front door to his rooms slamming open with a crunch somewhere behind him and first one leg was out of the window and then the other and he was flailing for a hold, and swung in the void a moment, *am I to spend my life panicking out of windows?* and then dropped to the ground. He staggered, stood, found himself next to the horse's flank and swung himself up behind the girl and immediately the beast was moving and he was swaying and fighting for balance and they were away.

Fouché was wolfish. As he appeared in Roland's doorway, eyes shining and jaw set fervent and smile full of appetite, the Interior Minister felt himself pulling back slightly. 'It seems we have an English conspiracy not a Prussian, Minister!' He had a set of papers rolled in his hand.

Warily, Roland beckoned him into the office.

'You will recall, Minister, that a few weeks ago we had reports of a Britisher of name Kinnaird in St-Denis, asking for another Britisher named Greene.' Roland did not recall, but Fouché was invariably right on these points. 'He moved into Greene's rooms in St-Denis. Then we had the affair of the Garde-Meuble, and the report by one witness that an Englishman named Greene was close by and observing. So we set to hunt him down. Investigation of Greene shows a man of diverse contacts in Parisian society and the foreigners in the city.' Roland nodded. It sounded credible, though he hardly –

'Now, Minister! This morning we learn that this Greene has invited two men to a rendezvous. One is a Dutchman. Questioned, he acknowledges receiving the message but says he ignored it. Only a vague memory of the name Greene, no intention of accepting such a brusque and informal summons from someone with whom he has no relations. The other, though . . .' Again the smile. It really was rather alarming. 'Kinnaird did go to the rendezvous. We rushed men to the place. Our postern reported his arrival. But for some reason, before the man Greene could arrive, Kinnaird decided to escape by a window. Our people were too late to surround him there. But they went immediately to his rooms. On a table, a note from Greene repeating details of the rendezvous. Folded in a book, a letter from Greene to Kinnaird. Under the mattress . . .' He placed one of his papers on the desk. Roughly square, it was not text but a hand-drawn map. 'A sketch of the streets around the Garde-Meuble, and the entrances.'

Roland nodded. He looked up into the hungry eyes. Nodded again. *What does he expect me to say?*

Fouché gestured to a chair, and the minister beckoned him to sit, with some relief.

'Minister. Would you oblige me by telling me what we know of British Government secret activities in Paris?'

───────── ◆ ─────────

They rode for two miles at a canter, until St-Denis was lost behind them and they had been swallowed by open country and then trees. Kinnaird had started with his hands clamped on Lucie Gérard's upper arms, until she'd shaken them off, and then clutching uneasily at her hips. After the first mile his body, if not his mind, had relaxed a little and he became aware of her body: the bones of her pelvis in his hands, how slender her back was.

By a river she pulled the horse up, and guided it off the track into the trees.

Kinnaird slipped off the back of the horse as soon as he could. Lucie followed, and led the horse by the reins to the water's edge, and it dropped its neck and began to drink. Lucie patted the mare's shoulder, her hands small against the sheeny muscle. At last she turned to Kinnaird. He was standing stiff among the oaks, staring at her, hands very slowly clenching and unclenching.

'Deep breath, Monsieur.'

He stared hard, and then did as he was told. She nodded approval.

He took another.

'Why – ' He shook his head; tried again. 'What – '

She frowned in pity.

Kinnaird took another breath.

'Thank you,' he said; 'I think.' Lucie nodded indifferent. 'Though I might have been better talking to the police than running from them.'

'Trust me,' she said. 'You wouldn't.'

She'd never seen a man look more lost. Still so cold, still so buttoned-up. But, in this glade of sunlight and green life, so out of place in his dull clothes. And that cold face so powerless and so confused.

'This is the Paris of the Commune. Easy to get arrested. Very hard to get freed again.'

'But I – '

'No one likes to admit a mistake, do they? Better just agree you're guilty of something and keep you locked up.' Her voice was flat, humourless. Her weary world.

She began to recite to him, more insistent. 'Henry Greene has always been danger; always suspicion.' She saw him reflecting on this. 'Now he has been seen right where the crime of the year was happening.'

'Seen by you!'

She shrugged. 'I was supposed to be silent? You want me to join his conspiracy too?'

'What con- Is there a conspiracy?'

'Isn't there?' She turned away, feeling his stare against the back of her neck, and pulled the horse up and around.

'Where are we going?'

She mounted. He hadn't moved. 'I know a place.'

———— ◆ ————

Pieter Marinus prowls his house a full hour, a fretful fidgeting hour, an hour of quick breaths and forgotten resolutions and familiar objects touched and rejected, an hour in which his shoulders, his knuckles, never seem to relax.

On the shelf in his salon, the violin waits. He knows he cannot touch it yet. He's utterly out of tune with its perfection; he knows that any sound he produces from it would squeal or stutter. Great God, the clumsy alarm in his hands might break its fragile neck.

He wants to see Arnim. He needs the Prussian's eternal solidity in front of him, needs Karl's hand on his shoulder, needs the breath of his kiss on his forehead. Karl is certainty. Karl is rightness. Great cold stubborn Karl is something warm in this mad world.

Of course, the one thing he must not do is go anywhere near Karl Arnim. The act of a fool. The act of a Judas.

As Marinus tells himself this for perhaps the tenth time, he starts to feel some flicker of professionalism and sense inside himself.

I am panicking. I must not panic. If I do not panic, then I am no longer a man who panics. If I am not a man who panics, then there is no need for panic.

It was not the first time he had been interrogated by the police of the Commune. The lot of a foreigner, and a man of affairs. It is the frequency of his contacts with official Paris, the trivial encounters with its bureaucracy, that makes him such an unlikely intermediary of spies, and therefore such a good one.

But there had been something about this interrogation: the unexpectedness of the original incident, perhaps; or the horrible expectedness of the summons after he had been given, in the public street, a message from the most sought-after criminal in France. Once again he hears the name Henry Greene in his ears, and it echoes and stabs and nauseates him like some unwashable shame. He has done so much to justify La Force or *la guillotine*, but he has never done anything as crass and brutish as what the man Greene did at the Garde-Meuble, and he has never in his life done anything so clumsy as to merit hearing his name linked with a known conspirator in that shocking manner. If he had sought the favours of the most ancient, wrinkled raddled whore down by the Celestins, the pox would not have been more certain than the sickening hammering at his door the following day after that ghastly encounter with the messenger boy.

The delay had been the only surprise. The delay had made it worse.

He reflects, again, on his performance before the policemen. Earnest. Bewildered. *Honest.*

Yes, I believe I have met the man named Henry Greene on certain occasions.

Unconsciously, he had started to fiddle with his little finger, mimicking Arnim. Once he'd spotted and suppressed that instinct, his next had been to wish that he too had a ring of poison, so that he too might be able to look down on the world.

At the house of Mme Lavalier and . . . once at Christiansen's.

We exchanged courtesies, but never spoke any subject, nor yet a full sentence one to another.

Yes, certainly I heard of the terrible incident at the Garde-Meuble. Yes, I had understood that a man of this name was connected.

Sincerely – that had been a mistake, he keeps telling himself – *I was shocked to receive an invitation to a meeting from Greene. Such were not our relations. And, of course, after his connection to the affair at the Meuble he was a most suspicious person.*

I cannot imagine what his purpose was. Perhaps as I am known as a man of affairs, of trade and intermediation, particularly in the Netherlands, which is of service to many gentlemen who find themselves restricted by the current condition of relations between France and her neighbours. Perhaps his interest was purely commercial – he'd been talking too much at this point. He winces at the memory – *perhaps he had some transaction related to his crime. All I may say is that I never for an instant considered acting on the invitation.*

Of course I shall report any further contact. I am delighted to serve the cause of good order, and I trust that a time more conducive to normal business relations may supervene soon.

He badly needs to see Arnim. To get reassurance: from his hand; from his mere presence, mighty and enduring.

To *give* reassurance. *I said nothing imprudent. My tale was simple and –* hilariously – *honest*.

He knows he must not.

His fingers flicker near the violin, and withdraw. He feels feverish.

He knows that he must assume he is watched. He knows that this makes him a contagion to Arnim. His stomach lurches at the thought. Arnim must not see him. Arnim must – will – shun him now.

It is a little death.

In his resolution – *it is a martyrdom* – once again he finds professionalism. Even a little pride. Karl would honour this steadfastness, this wisdom. *We are men greater than our emotions. We are men greater than our world*.

Slowly, steadily, his hand reaches for the neck of the violin, frail and exposed. He grasps it, feels and knows the weight of the instrument as it swings down to the vertical in his fingers, hangs in its beautiful symmetry, and then swings up under his chin. Immediately there is Bach, measured and mathematical and reassuring, the notes flowing flawlessly.

Almost flawlessly. He stops, lets the bow drop a moment, then lifts it again. *Damn Henry Greene.*

———— ◆ ————

A stone pavilion on the edge of the woods of the Chateau de Malmaison. The stone was cool to sit on, and the cool and the thickening darkness heightened the silence.

It was a nightingale dusk, a dusk for whispers and hints and faint melodies, a dusk for shadows of love.

'What is this place?'

'One of the adornments of one of the properties that the former King will not be using any more. He hunted from the house a few times, and no doubt came to this place for other sport. If you didn't know the place, how and why is it one of your rendezvous?'

Karl Arnim was a large shadow against the stones, darkness against their moonlit chill. He was an absence. 'I identified the place for its qualities – distance, isolation, views; it is easy to observe who comes, and not be observed oneself. I cared not whether it was a royal arbour or a poacher's privy.'

'Rather fancy for the latter.'

'Your King was wont to play at shepherds, was he not? So why should not poachers have their palaces? Oh, I forgot: they have.'

The newcomer laughed, low and boisterous. 'It ain't so much of a holiday as all that.' And he bent and slapped Arnim's leg, jovial. 'Eh, my shadow?' Arnim restrained his flinch. The other looked around the pavilion, stepped to one of the window spaces, and took in a great breath of the night. He ran his hand up the smooth stone. 'Neat enough: if our shadows are seen here, we will be thought two lovers and no more.'

Arnim grunted. 'A grand seduction indeed.' He watched the figure in front of him, big and black against the moonlight. 'Will you take a little wine, my dear sir? A pastry?'

The figure turned. 'I'll take it all!'

Arnim gave him time; watched him as he sat back against the stone, bottle in one hand and pie in the other, heaving them up into his mouth alternately. When the food was finished, the figure let out a great sigh.

Arnim said, 'You're on a tightrope.'

The man grunted. 'And all Europe waiting for me to fall. Hah! And half of France too.' The head turned. 'You too. You're waiting.'

Arnim shook his head. 'I'm a diplomatist, my dear sir. I dislike falls. Too much violence. Too much unpredictability.' He leaned forward a fraction. 'Think of me as the net, for when you fall.'

A chuckle came out of the gloom. 'I'll remember that.' His shadow broke suddenly, irregular and moving and now thrusting forwards. He had produced something from the recesses of his darkness, and Arnim took it. A box, the span of his hand in width, highly polished under his fingers. 'A token for your master. An offering. That his restraint may endure. That the tightrope performance may continue.'

Arnim enjoyed the texture of the wood in his hands a moment longer, then placed the box on the bench beside him. 'The net will be here,' he said.

A grunt. 'And that.'

Silence. Arnim said, 'It's always an honour to meet, my dear sir; but there is a risk to it.'

Another moment of silence. 'And for you, old friend. And for you, eh?'

'Know that I shall always match you, stake for stake.' A pause. 'Something worries you?'

Now the shadow distorted again, and loomed forwards, and tapped Arnim's knee. 'And it should worry you too, you hear?'

'Enlighten me, do.'

'The royal correspondence.'

'What of it?'

'We never found it. Well, parts of it, of course. But not the real stuff. Not the diplomatic exchanges. Not the secret business.'

Arnim's voice was quieter, cold. 'Not destroyed, then.'

'You'd like that, wouldn't you? Mm, we'd all like that. But no, it's out there somewhere.'

'One means no disrespect to his divine Majesty, but is there no end to the idiocies?'

'Someone's got the dossiers – one of the entourage who hasn't been picked up yet, perhaps; or perhaps they're hidden somewhere.'

'Mm. And you are looking, I presume?'

'Yes. And if you've sense you'll help.' The shadow leaned forwards. 'I assume there's a few things in there to keep you awake. Your people ain't as cold and clever as all that. Bound to – '

'You think it could be found? By someone other than you?'

'Since I don't know where it is, I have to assume that someone could fall over it at any time. And there's a least one man looking for it. Fouché, Roland's creature.'

'I don't – '

'Mark him. He's a jackal, with energy and with brains.'

'I have read the name, perhaps.'

'He's in everything. Busy-busy. Interests himself in the affair at the Garde-Meuble too.'

'I take it you would not lament, should some accident befall him.'

Just a chuckle in the gloom, and Arnim couldn't be sure what it meant.

'Meantime, we must hope he can be kept on less treacherous paths.'

The other man grunted, and took a great swig of wine.

Their handshake, when they left, was wary but then solemn. The other man said, 'You wander Paris, alone, for Prussia. You truly do not fear, my friend?'

Arnim gazed at him. 'I consider outcomes. I calculate likelihoods. Thereby I recognize and tolerate the possibility of less desirable situations; nothing more melodramatic than that.'

'Death would be rather undesirable.'

'Death is not so hard, my dear sir. But regrettable when there is still so much life.'

A chuckle, stretching into a kind of growl, and the man was gone into the darkness.

Arnim stepped out of the pavilion, and as his foot touched earth he felt himself in a different place. The absorption of the interview, the world of the mind and the heart, vanished. He was back in revolutionary France, and its night was full of dangers.

He touched the ring on his little finger; his control over his own destiny.

Staring into the darkness, he began to see the patterns. In the same way, as he immersed himself in the silence he began to hear its infinite constituent noises, and to classify them. Leaves: leaves still clinging to branches swaying in the breeze; leaves on the ground swirling; and the shorter rasp of leaves moved by a boot. Creatures: birds – he'd had an uncle who could identify them by their call – and mammals. Mammals small and large; mammals careless of their own noise, and mammals trying to restrain it; mammals innocuous and mammals dangerous. He must distinguish the individual details of the French silence as he might the instruments in an orchestra. He must sense every element of the world, from a tempest to a breath.

Particularly a breath.

Fully five minutes after he had begun to watch and hear the night, Arnim was ready to move. A natural walk out of the pavilion – in case by chance he was observed – and around it. From the back of the pavilion, thirty paces through darkness, which must separate him completely from the place he had been. Then some three hundred paces on foot, first on a track known by particular trees and stones he had noted in the moonlight as he came, and then on a kept path which showed clear in the moonlight. Now he must abandon concealment, for nothing is more obvious than a man trying not to be seen.

Something burbled in the darkness.

Something of nature? Water – or animal?

The burble again, from low to his left, and now it was more clearly a chuckle.

Animal.

A deeper growl joined it.

The basest of the animals, indulging in the basest of its habits. He walked on.

Immediately a man loomed at him from the path, a shadow to mirror his own and nearing him. They passed close. Hand tight on the blade in his pocket, Arnim murmured a courtesy.

The courtesy was returned, and the shadows passed on through their element. Within two minutes he was on his horse, and within five the horse had carried him to where he'd left the carriage. As he came near the road he slowed the beast to a creep. Ahead, the outline of the carriage in the moonlight. And then a hand: the palm of a hand, projecting out of the trees just a yard or two ahead, an uncanny message that floated to him out of the night. He pulled the horse to a stop. He stroked its head slowly, willing it still, willing it easy.

He stayed like that, bent over the neck as his eyes scanned what little he could see of the road through the trees, and still the hand floated in front of him.

Suddenly from the road there was more noise in a moment than he'd heard in a quarter hour: running feet, a shout, a thumping and more shouting, and as Arnim fought to control his muscles, fought not to startle the horse with his tension, he heard a cry and something land heavy on the road. Running feet again, and then silence.

Still the hand floated, a minute more, and then slowly it fell away into darkness. Arnim let the horse amble forwards again, and immediately Theodor was beside him and taking the reins and leading the animal towards the carriage. 'I guessed it for some road-robbery, Meister,' he murmured; and Arnim nodded and dropped down from the horse. By the time he was settled into the carriage the horse had joined its companion between the shafts, and then they were rattling through the gloom towards Paris.

———— ◆ ————

Somewhere in the heart of France, Lucie and Kinnaird were swallowed by the forest. An hour after the trees had risen up around them, Kinnaird had forgotten that there had ever been a horizon. Life had become a narrower, darker thing. He was smaller, crowded and jostled by the trees he was trying to make his way through. He was hunted now, of course; a rodent hurrying through a burrow. In this world of undergrowth and darkness, a world of greens and shadows that flickered and shifted and shrank away and then loomed forwards, the idea of a Paris – a created place of people and buildings and noise – was not distant but impossible, to his shrunken fugitive mammal mind.

After two hours, he no longer believed in daylight. The trees had become the columns and buttresses and arches of some ancient cathedral, gnarled and warped and ceaselessly moving around them, a place of pagan mystery and sacrifice where they had been entombed. Among its black eaves, lights flickered and then died, emblems of a lost ancestral sun.

Or the muscles and fibres of some vast stomach, that seemed to roll and churn around them as they meandered.

He had grown fanciful too, then. But his senses gave no sign that, when they had been taken into the tunnel of trees, they had not also been taken into the ground – not only into the darkness but downwards, drifting and spiralling. And slipping backwards, too, into an earlier age of the earth. Here the Lord had not finished His seven-day work. It was a world of half-formed things, with much yet uncreated.

From the darkness, noises: there was running water somewhere nearby for half an hour or so, some river of eternity from the heart of the earth; there were hints of creatures – from above and around them cries and calls and chattering of birds and explosions of wings, from the undergrowth a restive rustling of something foraging; the mournful creaking of the trees as they moved and followed the two intruders; the constant watching and whispering of the leaves. And smells. It would never be dry in this place, and the air was thick with must and mould and damp soil, and sudden savoury bursts of herbs that had him turning his head to catch them before they drifted away.

They were on two horses now, after a hasty purchase at an inn. In the madness, his one piece of good fortune had been that the police had come before he'd taken his purse from his coat, so they'd money enough for now. The shared horse had been uncomfortable and conspicuous, and he needed it not to tire. And as, gradually, Kinnaird had started to lose some of his alarm, he had become more aware of his ambiguous position on the animal, with a beautiful and vulnerable young woman against his chest and thighs.

Lucie was riding slightly ahead of him. She was a wraith within the forest light, appearing and disappearing between the intermittent rays of the sun, some spirit of the trees, suggestive and deceptive.

'You don't talk,' she said, head half-turning back towards him. 'You don't complain or anything.'

'You're disappointed? Surprised?'

'Men talk.' She was looking ahead again now. 'Men complain.'

'It seems that no Frenchwoman is ready to think me a true man.'

'You're not a normal man.'

They rode on in silence.

Three hours after their disappearance from the world, the landscape changed for a time. The dark sky of foliage thinned and, to Kinnaird's awe, opened to reveal daylight. He gazed at it like a primitive seeing the eclipse. The ground was broken, erupting in massive rocks each the size of a house that loomed over the track and made the vegetation around them thinner.

Kinnaird was gazing up at one of these, wondering at its age and feeling his smallness, and when his eyes dropped to the track again he was stunned almost to falling. A man had appeared around the next bend, walking towards them on the track, and it was as startling as the recreation of the sky had been.

His surprise made him uncertain: was he supposed to react? Were they supposed to hide? Obviously not. But . . . he realized how comfortable he had become in their disappearance from humanity.

As they came level, the walker dropped his head so that his face was hidden under the fringe of a hood; and his hand, Kinnaird saw, was held oddly poised at his hip as he walked – on the haft of a knife.

On some instinct of propriety, Kinnaird turned his head slightly so that he did not seem to stare.

The trees closed over them again.

A mile later Kinnaird saw something moving in the trees. The coverage above was still heavy, daylight only intermittent, but the trees around them were more widely spaced and in a patch of dappled shadow, of greens and greys, he was sure he saw a figure. And then the phantom had disappeared into the patchwork of colours again.

Moments later it happened again. This time it was distinctly a man, standing on a rise in the ground thirty paces off and watching them. His face was covered or shadowed, and a second later it had disappeared into the undergrowth.

Then a face appeared among the shrubs at the side of the road, and Lucie's horse shied and skittered, and after staring at them wide-eyed the face vanished.

Kinnaird was looking for faces and figures now, so much that it took him longer to see a shelter hidden in the trees off to his right. A crude thing of branches and fronds and cloths, its colours and shapes blending with its surroundings. Then it was gone, but he was alert now and he started to see more of them. The same improvised lean-tos, and then one built of branches and cloths around the ruined walls of some ancient cottage. In several places there were cooking fires lit, smoke drifting up to merge with the shadows. There were more figures now. Those nearer the road would see the two riders, and some would stare and some would turn quickly away.

Kinnaird edged his horse up level with Lucie's. 'What is this place?'

'I think this is our destination.'

'It – This?' It was another world, populated by another species. Kinnaird had never felt so alien.

'It is a place I have only heard of. A rumour.'

He glanced at her face a moment longer, pale and set on the track ahead, restraining the urge to look at the faces that stared; he glanced and wondered again at her uncanny mix of fear and wisdom, at her strange relationship with the world.

'Hold!' A man on the track in front of them, and again Lucie's horse skittered. The man had a sword in one hand and a pistol levelled at them.

Lucie's voice came low and flat. As usual, she found she was trying to make herself more passive, in the presence of a threat. 'Who are – '

'You walk from here.'

'What if – '

'You walk from here, or you turn and go back the way you came.'

He looked lean, and capable.

Kinnaird said, 'You ask us to trust you, sir?'

'I don't give a damn. Walk, turn back, or die where you are. Your choice is no concern of mine.'

—————— ✦ ——————

Fouché hesitated in front of the royal palace of the Tuileries – felt his uncertainty, and pulled himself straighter.

He reviewed the palace, as one more document placed in front of him.

The Tuileries as symbol of monarchy; *I as subject*.

The Tuileries as architecture: a hundred years in the building and rebuilding, from Catherine of the Medicis to Louis who called himself the Sun King, a grand statement of power in the grandest city in Europe by the grandest family. An endless wall of windows – hundreds? *thousands*? – running along the Seine and then filling his horizon now, gazing down on France. The monstrous central dome; dominance only. *I as awe-struck peasant*.

The Tuileries as history, more than two centuries of it. Left behind by its kings when they preferred to create a court of fantasy at Versailles – far from the Parisians, hungry and angry. Until the Parisians forced the last of those kings back to the heart of his capital, to a place with so many windows that the hunger and the anger could not be ignored. And when the National Assembly – that precociously, dangerously large gathering – needed a place for its deliberations the only hall big enough was in the

King's palace, so here they had come, to dictate terms to their captive landlord. From here the royal family had escaped; to here they had been dragged back. Now the royals had been imprisoned, and France was ruled from this place by the National Convention. *I as insignificance.* So much had happened here: the great drama of France.

The Tuileries as *stage . . . I as spectator.*

Or I as actor?

Fouché looked around him: at the satisfying formality of the gardens, the ornamental trees sharp against the evening sky; at the palace of privilege abandoned by a discredited monarchy.

I am entitled to be here now. I exercise influence here now.

The Tuileries as disputed ground; *I as rightful servant of the rightful regime.* The Tuileries as battlefield; *I as victor.*

No uncertainty now.

But if this is a stage, what tragedy was played here and what comedy? What masquerade, what trickery might have been managed while eyes and ears were distracted with grander spectacle?

Only two months ago, now.

The 10th of August:

Paris boils. Counter-revolutionary forces are getting close to the frontiers of France. The Prussian Duke of Brunswick has publicly threatened the destruction of Paris and her people if King Louis is harmed. The Assembly has summoned the National Guard from the provinces to defend the capital. They hang around the streets like the summer heat, pestering the women and pilfering under cover of revolutionary slogans. You can smell the fish on the troops from Normandy; the lads from Marseilles are singing their new song, upheaving Paris one tavern at a time. There are rumours of a Secret Committee of radical mayors and borough chiefs; the Secret Committee is hearing rumours of its own. For the first time someone has dared to say that the King is the threat to France. On the streets they're demanding action. Paris has two governments – two *Communes* – each in emergency session, in adjoining rooms in the Town Hall and squabbling over the writing paper and trying not to look at each other on the stairs. The illegal Revolutionary Commune rules the dissolution of the legal one, but keeps three of its officials on; one of them is Danton. Impatient and mistrustful and angry, a feverish organism with artisans and armed shopkeepers running in its veins, the city of Paris is *becoming* the Revolution. But Louis has 4,000 men to defend him in the Tuileries; there's surely no suggestion of a physical threat.

Testimony of Roederer, Prosecutor-General of Paris: the King's complacency was his undoing. In any case, gentlemen, he could not have overcome the will of the Revolution, could he? I'd been in the Tuileries all night – you'll say it was reckless of me, that I was in danger, but this was my duty, and a man does what he must, eh? Well, it was chaos right enough. The women were flapping and refusing to go to their rooms, what with the rumours that were slipping into the palace, but most of the King's party seemed more sleepy than anything else. I fancy they'd supped better than usual. Monsieur le Maire, dear Petion, turned up promising to defend the King – one doesn't want to impute counter-revolutionary sentiments to the fellow – probably felt it was the sort of thing he ought to say. But he obviously didn't feel too comfortable because in the small hours he managed to escape the palace – lucky fellow! – and find safety in the Town Hall. I'll be honest with you, gentlemen: I didn't want too many Frenchmen to shed their blood on a point of constitutional order, not if the thing could be managed peaceably. The problem was the National Guard who were still in the Tuileries: if they held for the King, I could see there'd be a hell of a fight. But I managed to persuade their commander that he himself should come to the Commune to negotiate, which I'm happy to say he did, and revolutionary justice caught up with him pretty fast there, didn't it? That left the King himself. Not that he was looking so regal any longer, gentlemen, but Frenchmen are good soldiers and he might have rallied them. I confess I'd not expected an actual attack on the palace – you'll pardon me, gentlemen, but surely none of us had anticipated the bravery of men and women impassioned by the revolutionary ideal, had we? Right through to dawn the palace was restless, but no one believed there'd be a physical threat against the King; they'd had a couple of years of this sort of thing, Varennes and so on, turned the poor man grey, but no one had ever been touched, had they? Then with dawn we saw the crowds gathering: endless lines of people coming out of the side streets and gathering around the palace – wonderful sight, gentlemen! A new dawn indeed! No longer individuals: this was Paris – this was France!

– as one mass, determined and unstoppable. *This was when I advised Louis to abandon the palace and seek the mercy of the Assembly. This he did in an instant: no debate, no hesitation – he could see right enough the danger outside the walls – just gathered his immediate family and away they went across the palace garden. Well, gentlemen, you may say it was deception of a sort, but can you blame me for it? Condemn me if you will, gentlemen, but I stand proud that I saved the lives of many Frenchmen, who might have died at French hands and may now instead offer themselves against the foreign foe.*

And so it begins. The National Guardsmen begin to drift away, twos and threes from the backs of detachments, from the farthest cannon: officers are still rallying them, but everyone knows the King's gone and all that's left to defend is an empty palace *so what's the point, and bugger it, why would you?* The crowd's gathering, alive with shouts and bayonets and coming on straight; they're divided by units, and you can tell them by their uniforms – *tell 'em by their stink* – spot the difference between a unit of salty Bretons and a unit of Picardy peasants a mile off – and among them, rougher and madder, are the Parisians. Fewer bayonets among the Parisians: they brandish the tools of their hundred trades, and they mean to do violence with them, and suddenly a bayonet don't look too bad a way to go compared to a cleaver or a hammer or a dose of the pox so rancid the smell alone'd kill you, and *blimey, ain't that your old woman over there?* In the front ranks of the Guard, men look at the endless relentless swarming of the mob and reckon *this ain't for me; you worry about your own carpets, Louis.* When the mob reaches the National Guardsmen, it does so with cheerful insults and slaps on the back.

Not so the men of the Swiss Guard. Perhaps it's a mercenary's commercial probity: it don't do for word to get around that a Switzer'll take a gold piece but then drop his musket at the first sign of a riot. More it's desperation: the Swiss Guard don't have comrades and relatives on the other side of the lines; even their employer has hooked it, and with tens of thousands of angry peasants all that blood-boiled energy's got to go somewhere, and the Swiss know where. They stand and fight, from the windows and alcoves and doorways of the Tuileries palace. And as the crowd pauses, roars, and comes on euphoric the Swiss are annihilated, shot and bayoneted and clubbed and hacked to pieces.

Fouché replayed it all, indifferent. His interest had stopped on one point only. *There was no time to prepare their escape; no time to tidy their indiscretions.*

Testimony from June of the previous year showed no great destruction of documents before the flight to Varennes: the King too hesitant about the proposed escape, and then someone sensible in the royal entourage warning against any unusual action that might give them away before they'd even left. So whatever correspondence had collected since 1789 and the family's installation in the Tuileries was still there when they were dragged back from Varennes last year, the summer of '91. Throughout which time Louis's treacherous correspondence with the enemies of the Revolution and the enemies of France would have been most active. And since which time he'd had another year to fester and plot. *And when the Tuileries had been attacked on the 10th of August, and the family had fled, they'd had no time to tidy their indiscretions.*

Since the Convention had set up shop in the Tuileries, Fouché had become confident about walking in regardless of its history. Now he walked towards the great dome with nerves alight. He needed to walk back into a moment of its past. As he came nearer, the dome soared and fell over him and he was swallowed by the old palace.

The palace was silent. He was used to it all chatter, he and his colleagues in the Convention hurrying to and fro, the rustle of business between them. The silence emphasized how cool it was: tall white walls, long windows, pale air. The air was so clear he knew he could hear for miles; could hear for years. Invariably he turned right as soon as he entered. Today he turned left. The floor seemed cleaner. Where the Convention now gathered, the palace parquet had felt more boots in a month than in the previous century. Not in this part.

He was on new ground now. Curiosity was the untidy habit of the undisciplined and under-employed, and it had never led him away off the direct path to the Convention chamber. Indeed, he'd felt an unspoken sense among the nation's new legislators that to stray into unnecessary parts of the building would reflect an unhealthy interest in the luxuries of monarchy. As if even the most ardent revolutionary, finding himself suddenly alone among the gilt and the grandeur, might begin to dream forbidden dreams of power. An unnatural inclination to solitude was, after all, the first step to a crown.

For a man alone in the Tuileries, strange perils lurked.

Fouché reached the foot of a vast staircase; stopped; kicked at the first step with his toe. The stone echoed. There'd been carpet on these stairs, but it had been taken somewhere. A flinch in his mind: there'd been rumours of pilfering, of corruption in the administration of seized state assets, and he must remember to pursue the matter.

The plasterwork was spotted with musket fire here, angry white blotches and a plume of dust on the floor below. The Swiss Guard had tried to mount a defence from the landing; they'd held for two exchanges of fire, and been overwhelmed.

The stairwell was bigger than any house he'd ever lived in. It seemed lighter, airier, than the sky. A mirror, a full storey high and miraculously undamaged, dominated the space and doubled it. No one had known what to do with it, presumably.

He took the first step onto the stairs, and again heard the echo of his trespass all around him. He tapped onwards and upwards, tiny in the vast space and wondering who was looking down on him. He was straying into the histories of kings now, into their lives. The staircase split, and he had to decide whether to circle left or right to reach the same point. A trivial choice, yet one that few men would ever have had to make.

He turned left. At the top a gallery, stretching away left and right, polished parquet floor glowing in the sunlight. Occasional stains on the floor, where someone had died and vanished. Like the mirror, the larger items of decoration remained: curtains gathered in golden columns beside the windows for which they'd been specially made; tapestries showing men and beasts two or three times life size. He walked on, feet louder on the parquet than on the stone, sole inhabitant of this monstrous space. He was treading the steps of kings now. They had strolled, and played, and looked down on Paris from these footprints. The gallery had heard their daily movements, over centuries. It had heard their latest descendant's panicked flight, a month back. Its scale had surely shaped their twisted belief in their own greatness.

Fouché hesitated; looked up and around himself at the luxury. Felt a treasonous twinge of enjoyment at possessing it all for a moment.

And heard footsteps.

The echoes of the kings of France, no doubt. Their ghosts, searching in vain for their inheritors.

Fouché felt a stab of panic; realized that the panic wasn't fear, but shock at how the cursed place had made him fanciful. Cold Fouché, *Joseph le mort*, two minutes in a palace and walking with ghosts already.

The footsteps were coming louder. No good would walk alone in this place. He walked on, trying to keep his own steps quieter, but the answering steps grew louder as he neared a corner. The tap and tap snapped at each other like duelling foils. A few steps from the corner, footsteps clattering and heart matching them, ready to confront whatever the worst of this corrupted place might be, and then he was at the corner and turning.

Danton.

———— ◆ ————

Kinnaird and Lucie were escorted to a cabin a minute's walk off the forest track. Gestured to enter. Told to sit.

They sat. Lucie had relapsed into silent passivity. A wooden cabin, one lantern on a tree-stump in the corner.

A whole community was here, in the dark heart of the forest. Among the trees were stone buildings repaired with branches and cloths, wooden huts, and shelters that were becoming part of the trees they leaned and twined into. In a few minutes' walking they'd seen at least two dozen people, men and a few women, dressed in every variety and mixture of clothing – rags and ragged finery. Most watched from a distance; turned away. A bold solitary child had stood in the open, watching them pass. A big blank face; a big blank stare. It increased Kinnaird's feeling of loss. The world wasn't even suspicious of him any more; the world was become indifferent to Keith Kinnaird. Or perhaps it was just pale Lucie that so absorbed the child.

The door to their cabin opened, and a shadow filled the space. Filled it: a man, tall, and broad in the shoulder. The lantern-light flickering on his face found its crags: a handsome face, pale – but the eye sockets were black.

He sat and faced them. He said nothing.

Deep in the sockets, Kinnaird began to perceive the glimmering of his eyes.

'Do you know where you are?'

The voice was a shock after the silence. The mouth was another black hole.

He'd spoken to Kinnaird, but it was Lucie who replied. Neither her face nor her voice were focused on the man.

She said: 'There is a place inside France that is outside France.' Kinnaird stared at her. Her voice seemed far away.

Now her eyes flicked up from her lowered head. 'That is the place I was told of once. That is the place we're looking for.'

The man nodded. No emotion showed in the shadows on his face.

Lucie said, 'Me a night or two. Him . . . ' – she shrugged. Another nod.

At last Kinnaird's bewilderment found its voice: 'What is this place?' The other two looked at him as if surprised that he could speak at all.

'Part of the estate of the Château de Pierrefonds,' the man said quietly. 'Until the owner joined the *mécontents* and Richelieu had the château destroyed. Left a ruin for a century and a half. Otherwise just a few outhouses left. The forest is reclaiming them. Now . . . Now it is a place that does not exist, for people who do not exist. Who are you?'

Kinnaird shifted on the bench. Lucie was sullen.

'If you are to enjoy this place with us, we must know the worst of you. Who are you?'

He knew to turn to Lucie first. 'Lucie. Father an apothecary. I carry messages. Today I help him.' She nodded towards Kinnaird.

The eye sockets turned back to Kinnaird.

'I'm . . . I'm Keith Kinnaird.'

'My greeting to you, Keith Kinnaird.' The unfamiliar names were remade with difficulty. 'Now who are you?'

Kinnaird's face screwed up in discomfort. 'I am . . . I am falsely accused of – '

'Everything is false now. And here we all think ourselves virtuous.'

'I am accused of conspiracy against the Revolution.' Best not to mention Greene and the link to the Garde-Meuble, and the suggestion that he knew where the royal jewels of France were hidden.

'Congratulations.' There was no life in the sarcasm. This was a man who'd lost those sparks; he was becoming part of his forest.

They sat in silence. The man gazed at them.

Kinnaird heard voices outside. Everything in the forest was murmur.

'You can stay. I think there's a shelter a hundred paces or so to the west; two men moved on yesterday. No one owns property in here, not any more. You find a place to sleep, you sleep.'

Kinnaird nodded.

'Here we are fallen aristos, evicted priests, thieves, frauds, bankrupts, murderers, beggars and whores.' He grunted. 'All beggars now. Perhaps all whores.'

'Dangerous men, then?'

'Naturally. But on the whole not to each other.' The eye fixed on Kinnaird. 'And not to you, presuming that's your concern. Each of us has his enemies outside of the forest. None has any call to make new ones inside.'

'We're safe here, then?'

The man shrugged, and turned away.

'What name do you go by, sir?'

The man stopped in the doorway, turned, and considered Kinnaird. 'I am Aucun,' he said after a moment.

'You are . . . No one?'

The man nodded slowly. 'I am now.'

---------- ♦ ----------

'Your pardon, Minister.' Roland's face came up, ever-mild, ever-cautious. 'I seek your advice: your . . . experience.' Fouché's flattery had no obvious effect; Roland's face stayed mild and cautious. 'I have continued to contemplate the lost papers of Louis: his secret royal correspondence.' Roland licked his lips. It might have been a gesture of uncertainty; it certainly hadn't been pleasure. *Why would this worry him?* 'I conceived the idea that some documents might still be in the Tuileries – there having been no opportunity for the royal family to remove them or destroy them.

Perhaps I am wrong; perhaps it is unlikely.' Roland made a noise; an attempt at encouragement. 'Or even were they not there, the fate of the papers might be known by those familiar with the routines of the palace.'

Roland waited.

'I wondered Minister – as you yourself were once – ' Roland's eyes went wide and his lips thinned: the fear that lurked in all men who had had any association with the old regime had leapt up and caught him by the throat. Fouché saw it and hesitated and waited for Roland to control his face again. 'In your constant effort to work for the interests of France and her people against the tyranny of the King, Minister, perhaps you saw something of the routines.'

Roland considered Fouché. And then considered his words. 'Only a very few in the palace – the King himself, and one or perhaps two men – would have known what was actually done with secret correspondence. The only likely men are fled or dead.' Then, just in case: 'We, ah – We can't interrogate the King; not like that.'

'Mm. I was thinking though, Minister, not of the King's confederates. I was thinking of servants. Simple men. Not privy to the correspondence, but seeing the habits and procedures of the King.'

Roland pursed his lips, a brief pose of contemplation. Then a little shake of the head. 'No. I doubt they'd know anything.'

Fouché nodded. 'Ah well.'

He watched the top of Roland's head, bent over his papers once more. Contemplated the head, the man, as a factor in his investigation.

And again he saw Danton. Saw his face, in the Tuileries.

Of all the revolutionaries, the one who best suited a palace was Danton. He might not profess to like monarchy, but his mighty size and his mightier vanity demanded a palace.

There'd been a moment, as they first stared at each other, when Fouché had wondered if Danton hadn't after all taken up residence in the palace. Why not, since he ruled the Paris mob more than Louis had ever done?

But Danton's face had been wrong. No satisfaction, no ease, as the two men had stood at bay across the parquet, the sunlight through the window panes setting out the chess board between them.

Surprise first. Danton hadn't expected to be found in the palace – and then, second, he wasn't comfortable about it. And as Fouché had registered the surprise, he'd seen something else: a trace of what the surprise had replaced, perhaps, or an echo of Danton's strange situation, wandering the Tuileries alone. Danton reflective; Danton perplexed.

And then, as ever, Danton's self-control had reasserted itself. Eyes never leaving Fouché, his face had spread into a monstrous smile. And then he had turned aside and beckoned Fouché onwards with an elaborate bow.

'What you want, dear Fouché' – Roland's voice was distant, distracted – 'is old Xavier.'

------------- ◆ -------------

Lucie Gérard and Keith Kinnaird's residence was framed by a pair of beech trees, three paces apart, with a rope strung between them at waist height; over this there were blankets and what looked to Kinnaird's inexperienced eye like deer-skins, with loose branches and rocks holding them into a tent shape. There was a gap in one quarter of one side, presumably a blanket of satisfactory enough quality for the previous guests to have taken it with them.

By unspoken assumption of competence, Lucie went off with some of Kinnaird's purse to find supper. The price, for a loaf of bread and a sliver of cheese, was ludicrous. The economy of the France outside the law favoured those at the bottom of society: those who could bake, or hunt – or steal. And stolen food came expensive.

They ate in silence, heads thick with weariness and the gloom. And then they dropped with the sun, wrapped in their clothes. Lucie watched Kinnaird as he settled, waiting for something. Then, uneasily, she lay down near him.

Kinnaird's eyes blinked in the darkness. He'd only slept out a few times in his life, and lingering uncertainty about the creatures of the French forests as well as his murderous neighbours kept his consciousness glimmering a little longer, amid his vast exhaustion.

'Lucie,' he murmured. 'Why did you save me?'

But she was asleep. In the small hours, the forest utter black and alive with tiny noises that seemed monstrous, he woke to find her against him, her back and rump against his chest and stomach, as if they were riding again. He lay there uneasily, reflecting on this, until he drifted into sleep again.

When he woke with the dawn, she was gone.

⸺⬥⸺

ALERT:

to all **MAGISTRATES** loyal to the **REVOLUTION**, to all detachments of the **NATIONAL GUARD**, to all agents of policing and justice in **FRANCE**
the **NATIONAL CONVENTION** seeks the testimony of
M. XAVIER BONFILS

sometime steward in the Royal Household of the former Kings of **FRANCE**. The said **BONFILS** may be reassured that he is not suspected nor accused of any crime against the **REVOLUTION**, but he has information vital to an investigation pertaining to the security and good order of **FRANCE**. Any loyal **FRENCH CITIZEN** who assists in the location of **BONFILS** and his rendering alive to any agent of authority of the **REVOLUTION**, is to be **REWARDED**. Once to hand, **BONFILS** is to be sent immediately with armed guard and all reasonable comfort to the **OFFICE OF THE MINISTRY OF THE INTERIOR, PARIS**.

ROLAND

Danton was a vast shadow looming over the Interior Minister. Danton was always a vast shadow looming over him. Roland sighed.

'Dear Roland, if you want a new valet there must be an easier way to advertise.' Danton flourished the paper and dropped it on the Interior Minister's desk.

Vaguely, uncomfortably, Roland had the sense that he needed to guard his words.

'A formality.'

Danton still loomed. 'Really?'

Roland shrugged. 'There are . . . certain aspects, of . . . recent events that would benefit from a . . . fuller explication. The manoeuvres of Louis. His negotiations with his supporters – his foreign supporters.'

Danton lowered his head, like a burden that strained him, until he could catch Roland's eye. 'The roads to every border are packed with the King's retinue making for safety. The Maison du Roi was – what? A thousand officials? Two? The grandest aristos in France; the King's closest advisors. And you're hunting his butler?'

'Fouché has the idea that – ' Something like a growl came from Danton's throat, his head down and dangerous like a bull's; he reared, turned, and strode out of the room.

<hr />

Oh, the adolescent infamy of it: Sir Raphael Benjamin, breeches still awry, perched on the window sill and contemplating the drop into the darkness below. *Don't a man ever grow out of this?*

A gentleman's experience of the world kept a part of his mind alert to sounds of alarum even when his conscious attentions were properly absorbed by a lady. In this case, they'd been properly and blissfully absorbed by certain intimate garments of the lady under consideration, and by the treasures therein. And still some part of his brain had heard a door slam and a shout, and somewhere in him a voice had said *hallo* . . . and he'd felt the lady stiffen, and he'd been up in an instant and considering the windows. A plunging kiss into her breasts, a rich kiss on her lips, something more genteel on her hand to mark the restoration of propriety and he was at the door and remembering where the stairs were beyond and trying to remember what happened at the bottom of them. As he opened the door the maid was right in front of him, a gasp of shock and the biggest bluest eyes and he pressed a finger to her lips and grabbed her shoulders and moved her aside. There was another shout downstairs, the sound of servants hurrying, and the stairs were no good now. Along the landing to where an open sash window beckoned to him, and he threw it fully up and tried clumsily to sling one leg over the sill. It wouldn't go, and he wrenched his breeches into some kind of order and tried again. Athwart the sill and head in the night, he looked down into the darkness of . . . some yard? How far down? Something glimmered below him. Tiles on a roof or water in a puddle? He stuck his head back in.

The maid was still watching him. Something flickered around her lips. Footsteps on the stairs behind her, and her expression became polite interest, and she suppressed a smile. Benjamin took a deep breath, blew her a kiss, ducked his head out and swung his other leg over and twisted and scrambled, got his hands gripping the sill for an instant then let himself drop. His feet hit roof, it held, he staggered and kept moving. Off the roof and keep moving, feet splashing and slithering through God knew what. He heard the sash shutting behind him, as he found a gate and slipped through into the world. A fifty-yard jog, a coin to an ostler, and he was up on his horse and away.

Because one never knew, he took a similarly roundabout way back into his own rooms. For entry or exit, there are times when a gentleman needs a back door. In the case of the current premises, a back wall, a back privy roof, and a back window. Free from foolishness with maids and uncertainties, he was in through the window and laughing softly at the mad sport of it all before he saw the figure slumped in his good chair.

Darker kick of guilt. The chair was turned away from the window; he couldn't see a face.

A mighty snore. Benjamin kicked at the nearest leg. 'Get up, you oaf.'

Ned Pinsent came awake with a grunt and a stare, glared at his host and settled back into a doze. A bottle of wine was on the table beside him, two thirds empty. 'Breaking into mine was easier than buying your own, eh?' Pinsent only grunted. 'Blast your nerve.'

Pinsent raised a heavy arm and extended a finger towards the far side of the table. 'Lad brought that.' A folded paper showed grey against the wood. 'Didn't say if it was from a lady or her husband.'

It was a sealed packet, Benjamin's name and his address here written on the outside.

Inside was a separate paper, sealed, unaddressed. He broke into this one, and Pinsent watched his face as he read. Very deliberately, he released the paper and let it drop to the table.

'All right, Raph?'

Benjamin's face was grim, and then it murmured a curse, unusual and vicious.

Sir, I give you greeting from home.

We have, I think, a mutual friend in St-Denis. He has, I fancy, on occasion involved you on our mutual behalf. We find that he is unlikely to be able to do so at the present moment, and so I take the liberty of communicating with you directly.

It may suit us both were I not to detail any personal acquaintance between us, and to avoid the idle use of names in correspondence passed over uncertain ground in uncertain times. Suffice to say that, whether or not we have met, you and your particular — not to say distinguished — character are well known to me, as are your circumstances. I may mention how much I was struck by the boldness of your action in the matter of Lady L. S. and the Trinity Plate, and by your spirit of enterprise in Worcester in the spring of the year '88.

A gentleman of sporting instinct and unpinched boldness is worthy indeed in these uproarious days, and might do good service were he to apply himself in a deserving cause. If I may particularize: as all thinking men continue to observe most closely the daily more remarkable developments in France, it has not gone unremarked that the authorities in Paris have set themselves to locate a man named Bonfils, formerly a servant in the entourage of the King. Now, it happens that there is an element here, all men of sober and patriotic sentiment, who would not be sorry should the French be thwarted in their aim.

I recognize, dear Sir, that this proposal finds you in a moment of discomfort, not to say vulnerability, and I regret any suggestion of discourtesy in seeming to exacerbate your predicament or indeed to work upon it. Clearly, should your family's efforts to preserve the general, and especially judicial, ignorance regarding certain past indiscretions prove unsustainable, it would place them in a more distasteful position at home, further disadvantage your own prospects here, and indeed serve sensibly to increase the fragility of your situation in France.

I confide that you and our mutual friend would find yourselves natural allies in this affair, should you find him at all.

I close by expressing my sincere regard for you, Sir, and for your continued good health.

[SS 2/96/1]

'What's the Worcester and indiscretion stuff, Raph?'

Pinsent had snatched at the letter before Benjamin could stop him.

'None of your damned business, is what it is.' Benjamin's voice was distant.

'I ain't the only one who can't get home so easy, is that it?'

'Not at all, Ned, I adore this cesspit and I'm here for my health.' No humour.

'No names in the letter. These sound like the same outfit who had their hooks in Hal Greene.'

Benjamin considered him a moment. Never wise to underestimate old Ned. 'Yes, Ned, they do.'

'Hal Greene who got us sent to La Force, and to that shambles in the square, and has now disappeared into the shadows to continue his chaos with greater freedom?'

'He, Ned.'

Pinsent was affecting indifference, but he was sitting up now, eyes open and earnest. 'Which all goes to say: this'll be a particularly damn-fool notion, then.'

'It will, Ned.'

Pinsent settled back into his chair, and avoided eye contact. 'But, ah . . . You ain't in a position to refuse, eh?'

Fouché had schooled himself to pay attention to other men. However tiresome and fatuous they might seem – and most indeed were – he had come to realize that it served him to know their characters better: their pretended strengths and their weaknesses, their impostures, their desires. In schoolrooms, in small-town politics, and now in the National Convention of France, he marked the bullies and the milksops, the wooden virtues and the brittle dislikes, the ambitions and the fears. So now in the Convention chamber he ignored the sweating press of bodies to his left and right on the bench and leaned forwards, a pose of interest in the opinion of the representative from Ardèche, and a close attention to the man's expensive coat and his assumption that the property of the individual was a truth that need not be debated or proven. Merely conventional, of course, but – a sudden acrid smell from somewhere near him; *God, but I loathe the dumb herd habits of my fellow man* – merely conventional, but the gentleman from Ardèche seemed oddly fragile in his insistence on the point.

Knowledge is power; a paper or a man.

Farther along the bench someone was shifting – stretching, or bending to murmur, or preparing to rise – and the movement rippled along to Fouché. He resettled himself between the shoulders either side of him, saw once again with distaste the ears of the man immediately in front of him, raised his gaze and scanned the hundreds of faces ranged around him in the chamber: sleeping – however that was possible in the crush and the bustle – staring, sweating, shouting. France is recreating herself in this place, and Joseph Fouché watches for the weak points.

As his gaze reached the doorway, down and to his left, among the men standing in the gangway he saw Guilbert, staring deliberately in his direction.

Eventually, the man from Ardèche ran out of steam, with a last celebration of the fact that in the new France the rights and estates of a man of virtue were no longer subject to the exactions of the clergy or the whims of corrupted ministers, and Fouché stood – *I fancy, Monsieur, that the prospect of a parcel of land or a lawsuit would quite overmaster you* – and shuffled his way through the press of legs to the aisle.

He found Guilbert in the corridor. 'I hope you will judge the intrusion worthy, Monsieur.' Fouché said nothing. 'This: a letter has just arrived at the rooms in St-Denis previously occupied by the fugitive Greene and then by the fugitive Kinnaird. In English, addressed to Greene although the letter itself uses no names. It encourages him to obstruct our hunt for the royal servant Bonfils.'

A little thrill: 'He is significant after all, Guilbert, that little steward!'

'Of course, Monsieur.' It was a nice flattery, and Fouché enjoyed it.

'So significant that the English want to stop us getting to him. What might he know, that the English are so desperate?'

Guilbert stayed silent. Guilbert did not deal in what men might know, but in the facts he persuaded them to tell him.

Then something else. Once again, the shadow of something shapeless and unsettling. 'But these English, Guilbert . . . They know what concerns us, and – How do they know, indeed? And – '

'From our alert for the man Bonfils, as I guess.'

'So they have agents – within France – who notice such things, and who judge immediately their interest in the matter, and who act. Act, Guilbert! Judgement, decision, instruction.' His eyes were bright. 'It is admirable that, Guilbert.'

'They don't know we're reading their letters, Monsieur. That's not so admirable.'

Theodor did not enjoy his trips to the market for Meister Karl. He was a man of the Pomeranian plains, and the endless over-soaring maze of the Paris streets felt like constant suffocation. He'd roamed Europe with the army, until the explosion of a cannon had ruined him, and took the view that cities were to be looted and burned and nothing more. He prowled the lines of stalls, careful of his feet on the pulp-slicked cobbles, careful of the hands that might reach for his purse. Even the women were less fun in the cities; paint and cheap tricks and nothing to get a hold of.

He knew the items he wanted in the market; he would find the best quality available for those items; and he would leave. No extravagance, no loitering. He walked the square once, to know the options. *Reconnaissance.*

Good fruit, the French had. And they were good traders. He'd never campaigned in France; the foraging and the requisitioning would have been good sport. But he didn't like them, for men. He wondered how they fought.

Two pheasant there; they would satisfy. Immediately he was in front of the stall, pointing. A fat woman next to him began to protest; he ignored her. The merchant sized him up, liked the look of something unfamiliar about his face or dress, and said a price. Theodor shrugged, pointed to his ear, shook his head. The man flashed a handful of fingers three times. Without gesture or hesitation Theodor found ten sous and handed them over. He didn't demean himself by bargaining with these people. Delighted to have got more than five, the trader had the birds tied and over Theodor's basket arm in half a minute, and Theodor was turning away.

He felt the unnatural movement against his coat; sensed the body behind him.

The cannon had ruined Theodor's hearing, but thirty years of soldiering had forged muscles and sinews that would never slacken. Rather than turning, he first reached his right hand under his left shoulder until he found the ferreting palm and gripped it fierce, pinching until even he heard the scream, and now he was turning, to his left, swinging basket and arm against whoever was behind him.

The whoever was a boy, now sprawling among the cabbage leaves and chicken shit. The boy gaped up at him, and then nodded wide-eyed towards the basket.

Theodor looked down, and saw the slip of paper now stuffed against his cabbage. He looked back, and nodded once, and the boy scrabbled away over the cobbles and up.

Theodor brushed the paper, but did not open it, before handing it to Meister Karl. '*Im Markt.*' He left the Meister to it.

Arnim nodded, and opened the paper. It was a printed proclamation from the Interior Minister, seeking a former royal servant named Xavier Bonfils. Scrawled in ink across the bottom corner was a single word: *non.*

Fouché's pleasures, such as they were, had always been of the mind; never of the flesh, or the chase. Seeing at last the pattern in a Latin conjugation, that was exciting. Assembling the chain of argument to overmaster his opponent in the seminary, that was thrilling. The other things smacked of loss of control; he left them to the beasts.

Then he'd seen something in Guilbert's face, as he'd set off on the trail of the royal servant Bonfils. Guilbert, who had always been congenial because of his reserve, his phlegmatism. Suddenly there'd been a bustle about this steady man, and something shining in the dead eyes. Impassive implacable Guilbert had been excited, because he was hunting something. Even though he had no conception of the importance of what he was hunting: of the answers that might be given by the man he hunted; of the enormous significance if his prey did have information about the royal correspondence.

Fouché felt his own intellectual stimulations blending with the hunt. Roland had told him of a great Prussian diplomatist and spy, thought to be active in Paris. He himself was beginning – by the exercise of his logical intellect – to explore the network of British emigrés and their activities. And now he found himself . . . in a competition with these men. In a race.

Roland's summary: the Prussian; and that office of the British crown, anonymous and ancient.

He rarely thought of what Guilbert actually did, to produce his results. He found it hard to imagine these other men, the foreigners. But he knew them for obstacles to his own success – for rivals, and he would not be beaten.

Roland, on the royal servant: *old Bonfils, that's the man. The steward's steward. Behind the titles and the rituals, the man who made the royal household function. Rather a curious little fellow, if one noticed him at all. But one didn't, really. Invisible, yet saw everything.*

Fouché liked the idea of Xavier Bonfils.

Isolation had left Pieter Marinus feeling futile. He could rouse little enthusiasm for what little business was to be had. France seemed a greyer, duller place now. The prices were rising in the markets, and faces were meaner, and more vicious. People of quality and of life were shutting themselves up indoors. If they ventured out, the men of culture and discretion with whom he might once have enjoyed a little conversation, they did so cloaked and hasty.

Only the angry boisterous men walk comfortably.

The rue Allent was a little oasis in the brutal world: a street of quietness and proportion, as he walked in it this pleasant evening; the houses elegant and even; not a street of the rich, but a street of quality. And Nº 17 was the house of Docteur de la Musique Noyons, as well it might be, with its curtains all tied regularly, with the paintwork of its windows fresh, with the step well scrubbed; and Monsieur le Docteur Noyons had a manuscript attributed to the hand of Lully himself, with which he was loth to part, but if he could find a gentleman of discernment to whom to sell it, he would be reassured that necessity had not forced him into irresponsibility.

A last blossom of delicacy in this new harsh season.

Marinus knocked.

And waited. He knocked again, a little firmer. The door, unlocked, gave a fraction.

He hesitated, called a timid 'Hallo?', and pushed. The door swung open. He stepped in, with another polite hallo.

The hall was as elegant as the exterior and his imagination had promised. Chequerboard tiles and subdued quality.

'Bolt the door, and kindly come into the kitchen.' The voice was muffled. He did as bid, and followed the passage towards the back of the house. Just before the final door he glimpsed movement beside him, realized it was his own in a mirror, and in that second also saw a figure through the half-closed door who would have been able to see him in the mirror. He had already pushed at the door, and it was swinging open and his unease was growing with the opening and he took a breath and forced himself to stand his ground, and at last he could see the figure full, and he gasped.

It was Karl Arnim.

Their greeting was courteous, warm.

'But – how? and how can – ?' Marinus stopped himself. 'Forgive me. Obvious and trivial questions.'

'Not at all. Most understandable. You must please excuse the deception. Rather childish, but it seemed imprudent to use either of our houses. Now, as you are not the authorities I need no longer skulk by the back door. There is a bottle of wine and some fruit in the parlour, and I do not propose to pass a moment longer than necessary in this servant's squalor.'

The peaches were fresh, and the wine excellent. 'And Doctor Noyons? He is a friend – an ally?'

'Doctor who? I never heard of him.'

'The owner of this house.'

'I have no notion who he is. The name was contrived to fit the story. The address was convenient. I knocked this afternoon and used the power of revolutionary authority, the threat of unearthly terrors, and a couple of coins to induce the owner to vacate his establishment for an hour.'

'But why?'

Arnim looked up from his glass, amusement. 'May not a man enjoy a bottle of wine with an acquaintance, even in these hard times?'

'Triviality does not become you, Arnim.'

'Very well. I confess I am obliged to ask for your assistance in a little affair. Somewhat distasteful, but regrettably essential. You know that I am concerned to prevent the revolutionary authorities finding the secret royal correspondence that might be embarrassing or dangerous to my patrons. I learn that they are somehow closer in their hunt. I must take more active measures to obstruct them.' He took a mouthful of wine, savoured it. His eyes came onto his companion again. 'You are somehow uncomfortable, my dear fellow.' Marinus looked even more uncomfortable. 'I have it: you grieve that you will not, after all, get your hands on a Lully tonight.'

'You could have sent me so much instruction in a two-line paper, and stayed safe.'

Arnim reflected on this. 'Hardly civil, my dear sir. And besides, where should be the pleasure in that?'

Marinus gazed at him. 'Karl Arnim: a mighty soul, a poison capsule on his finger, and immortal. Is that it?'

'Let us not be sentimental, dear Marinus. I practise prudence in the face of the threats of these revolutionaries; but they shall not unman me. Karl Arnim goes where he pleases.'

———————◆———————

Guilbert's relationship with the sergeant of police of Meaux had started badly. He knew the man and knew his character from his face alone. Competent. Steady. Rather stupid. Not disposed to work. Guilbert had asked if there'd been any sign of the man Bonfils, wanted by the Ministry of the Interior, and the man had stood slowly and looked at him as if he was trying to throw his weight around unnecessarily, and suggested that they nip over to the Rose to check, *nowhere else he'd have stopped, the Grenadier and the Sphinx are too far off, might get ourselves a little something while we're there*, and Guilbert had felt the slow irritation in himself, *you should have* – But he swallowed it. 'Right on every point, brother.' *Dullard.*

In the Rose, the innkeeper's book showed that Bonfils had stayed the previous night.

Guilbert had turned slowly to look at the sergeant, again fighting down his anger. If the man had been doing his job, Bonfils would have been held already. The sergeant was looking at him, but there was no sign of embarrassment. *Too bloody stupid even to see it.* 'Right-ho,' the sergeant said. 'We'll pick him up tomorrow then,' and he turned back to the innkeeper.

The innkeeper had looked at them both, uneasily. Guilbert's face, if not the sergeant's, had showed him that somehow he was implicated in something regrettable.

'Well now, old comrade,' the sergeant started. 'Inconvenience for us both, if my friend here from Paris can't catch up with his important witness because we didn't see him.' He'd nodded slowly at his own thought, and Guilbert had watched him with interest. 'Satisfaction for us both, and we'll split a drink, if you happened to be checking his luggage to see that all was in order, and found a hint of where he was going.' The voice rumbled on quietly. 'Or, say, you were helping him on with his coat and making sure no coins fell out, and you overheard him talk to the ostler or the coachman and say where he was headed.'

Guilbert watched it with appreciation. The man knew the rhythms of his own little world.

And the innkeeper had said 'Montmirail', and smiled in relief.

Now Guilbert and the sergeant of police of Meaux sat side-by-side on a bench, toasting their unbooted feet against the sergeant's fire. Companionable. The unspoken shared pleasures of men of shared experience.

Guilbert was telling him about how he'd frightened old Xavier Bonfils's sister, and the sergeant was nodding slow approval.

———————— ◆ ————————

On the other side of Meaux, Sir Raphael Benjamin was reviewing his situation with the help of a bottle of wine.

'Montmirail,' the innkeeper at the Rose had said to the two men at the counter, and standing just three paces away Raph Benjamin had heard it clear.

The destination was handy confirmation. The fact that there were other men after the royal servant was not a surprise. But damned risky nonetheless.

It had been easy enough to find out who Bonfils was, with a police and National Guard hunt out for him. The gossips knew Bonfils had lived in Paris, but had not been found there yet. Benjamin had long cultivated the acquaintance of a sergeant of the National Guard quartered at the St-Denis gate of Paris, and his sergeant had confirmed the search – *way I have it, I'm to let the whole Prussian army past me here long as I get this valet* – and the lack of success to date.

The conversation with Emma Lavalier had been short, and sour. He'd claimed a note from Greene asking him to learn what he could of the search for Bonfils. Emma obviously doubted the story. As she was so in with the revolutionaries these days, she might hear something.

'If you must make me a whore, Benjamin, you might have the character to make me your whore, and not just pass me down the line.'

'I'm obliged to play the pimp and not the prince, Emma. When my life is as easy as your new friends', you will no doubt find me as charming.'

He took a mouthful of wine, glanced once around the shabby inn, fit setting for his mood. His anger at his predicament had made him graceless. Another mouthful. And Emma had been uncomfortable because he was right.

Her face when she'd told him, a day later, that Interior Minister Roland had information that Bonfils had a sister in the rue Rameau, where the police had called and found nothing. Her voice: cold; blunt; and somehow very sad.

Another mouthful, in the Sphinx inn.

He recalled the boldness; it flushed him like the wine. He'd watched the street outside Bonfils's sister's house a full hour; watching for watchers. Then the knock, and the paper pushed under the door, a calculation of the wariness of Bonfils's beleaguered family. *A servant of the master of the servant.* It had worked: the hint of loyalty to Bonfils's King, guarded enough for the sister to feel she wasn't committing a crime by owning the relationship. She'd opened the door, a scared pale thing. Benjamin had got no farther than the hall. He repeated his loyalty in the same discreet terms. He said he knew Bonfils had been here – and it worked; she didn't deny it. He said he knew Bonfils had gone. He wondered if she knew whither. The sister had shaken her head. *He gave no hint?* Shake of the head, the eyes big and pinked in the pale lined face. *Madame, I can help him . . .* And then she'd snapped, hissed. 'He's gone, the old idiot. An old idiot with his old dreams, wandering out into the mud; didn't know where he was going himself, probably. Hardly any clothes even. Just a little case. Silly little man, with a silly little case under one arm and his silly book clutched under the other.' Then she was shaking her head again and hurrying him out and choking on her own breaths. A last inspiration on the doorstep: *your brother, Madame; where was he born? Where was his boyhood?* And she'd looked at him with something like relief, and he'd known he'd won. 'Montmirail.'

Another mouthful. And then his attention shifted.

A man had walked in and gone straight to the counter. He'd murmured something to the innkeeper behind it – big brute; hangdog face – and then he'd *shown* something – something cupped in his hand – and the innkeeper had nodded to a door beside him.

Benjamin forced his eyes down to the table. Mustn't show attention. It was curious, because another man had gone the same way a little while earlier. Benjamin hadn't seen any of the hand business, but now he realized there had been something furtive, something that had jarred.

He glanced up from his goblet. The new arrival had gone, through the door by the counter.

One had gone in and not returned. Now another had followed. Not the privy.

Wine-warmed and curious, he felt the appeal of the forbidden and the chancy. And if it was a card game, perhaps they'd welcome another for the pot. He was up and at the door in three strides. 'Privy through here, is it? Tha-'

'No, Monsieur!' The man's arm was out and blocking his way before the words were finished.

Pretending irritation rather than his actual satisfaction, Benjamin considered the arm, and then the face. *I'll take that as confirmation.* The man recovered himself. 'Your pardon, Monsieur. The privy is through the door over here.' Benjamin let himself be led.

The layout was ideal. The privy was on one side of a back yard, and the windows looking onto the yard surely included that of the forbidden room. Benjamin tolerated the minimum time appropriate for the pit, then slipped back out into the yard. He considered all of the windows of the inn; none showed a face, and the yard was deserted. He crossed to the window that he judged to be the one he was after.

Eventually his sight adjusted enough to realize that he was staring not at a curtain but at a storeroom in total darkness. He moved along one.

This window did have a curtain – a bit of sack, anyway – and there was light behind it. He pressed his ear hard against the glass.

' – priests hiding at the farm already, and they can't stay. It's folly to think things'll be back as they were, not anytime soon.'

'The Prussians are – '

'The Prussians are gone, and they'll not be back awhile.'

'His Majesty lives. His Majesty –'

'His Majesty is prisoner of the Revolution, and whatever happens he'll not be able – '

The door opened and someone splashed across the yard to the privy. Benjamin turned slowly, checking that he was all in darkness. Then he slipped back across the yard to the door.

Not a private card game. Not an obliging daughter or maid. Instead, a bit of local royalist conspiracy.

He returned to his bottle.

Greene, who used to be such a blade, had got more interested in the secrecy and the sport, and dragged him in willy-nilly. The occasional spree around Paris – the memory of the two jewels, still safely hidden – was one thing. Cheap wine and rural hovels and running errands for unknown grinders in London was something else. Anger – hot and twisting in his gut – at that letter, with its haughty certainty that they had him by the balls and he'd do what they wanted. Another mouthful of wine. Sickness at his fugitive existence, the pitiful reality of his family, the nasty aftertaste of glorious sins. Another mouthful.

Raph Benjamin the sportsman was fading. And so was Emma Lavalier.

He'd presence enough to stop drinking. Yes, the innkeeper had a room free, and yes of course Monsieur would be their most honoured guest, only a king's ransom of a tariff – one sou per louse – and would Monsieur be kind enough to give his name for the register?

His name? Yes – the authorities were become most insistent on these bureaucratic points. The innkeeper looked more hangdog than ever.

And Benjamin hesitated: his fool's errand, and here he was putting up at the meeting-place of the local royalists, and the insistent bureaucrats struck him as a much more efficient force than the local gentry whingeing about the priests hiding in their attics.

'My name's Kinnaird. Keith Kinnaird. May I spell it for you?'

————— ◆ —————

Lavalier had come to realize that, more and more, she was surviving in oases – private oases, somehow hidden from the desert outside. Her salon, alone. The stone summer house with the woods behind and the open landscape before. The garden of the Carmelites. A bath. And her dressmaker's temple of fabrics. She could have fittings at home, or leave the business to Colette, but she liked to walk and she loved to hide in the little parlour at the front of the shop, nestling among the bolts of cloth and imagining herself drifting among the swags of lighter material that seemed to drop from the skies.

It was quiet and cosy; it was elegant, sitting on the best chair and sipping at coffee. She was treated with regal distance, by the dressmaker occasionally popping in to check she was still comfortable, by the faint curtseys offered by the maids who came to chase their mistresses' commissions, and indeed by the young scruffy messenger boy who came in on an errand with his younger scruffier friend and, seeing Lavalier sitting in state, made a theatrical bow. She could feel safe and she could think.

Connections with others had ceased to be merely amusements, and become affiliations, and they risked becoming accusations. To be associated with the right person might be useful. To be associated with the wrong person would be dangerous. The strange Scotsman, Kinnaird, had been at her house twice, and now he was a fugitive, hunted by the revolutionary authorities. Dangerous for her. Raph Benjamin wasn't a hunted fugitive, but that was probably because the authorities didn't know half of what he got up to. She wondered where he was now. To meet any foreigner was become an act of diplomacy, or of treason.

And her French acquaintances? The divisions were becoming more stark. The Rolands seemed so moderate – so safe; but Roland was weak, and vulnerable now, and whispers were becoming discussions. Danton? Danton was untouchable, surely. But prominence brought its own risks.

It was becoming impossible to be loyal to everyone.

Someone else was passing in front of her; it startled her a moment, because she hadn't heard the door. A young woman walked through the parlour towards the back, saw Lavalier, made a curtsey without catching her eyes, and continued on her errand. Half a minute later she was back, message delivered, and making for the front door.

'It's . . . Gérard, isn't it? I think . . . Lucie?'

The young woman stopped, and turned to face her.

'Lucie Gérard, Madame, yes.'

'How does your father, Lucie?'

Lucie had broken eye contact, and was talking to Lavalier's feet. 'He's ... he's well, I supp-'

'I was being polite, child. I know your father's state, and I know the state of prices and trade.' Lucie looked her in the face now, unsure.

'How ... how do you do, Madame?'

She was a pale uncertain thing in the quiet of the parlour, like another swoop of lace drifting with the air currents from the front door. Lavalier smiled. 'Thank you for the courtesy. I suppose you know my reputation, Lucie.' Lucie said nothing. 'Well, the market's as bad for women like me as it is for apothecaries.'

Lucie glanced at the cocoon of fabrics, of which Emma Lavalier in her lovely frock was the natural inhabitant. 'You seem settled enough.'

'I hope so, Lucie. That seeming is everything. Dupont silently allows me to increase my debt here, partly because he thinks that other women will follow me, less notorious and more solvent, and more because none of us – none of us, Lucie – wants to admit that it has all become impossible.' Lucie was trying to understand it. 'Will you take a little coffee?'

Lucie glanced towards the back, and the hidden majesty of Dupont. 'Thank you Madame, but I shouldn't.'

'I decided a long time ago to give up on "shouldn't".'

'And you've found a way to live on it, Madame. Me, I've had to take the other way. No one sees me, Madame, and that suits me fine.'

It was a lovely, wild, lost face. Lavalier wanted to stroke it. 'Yes. Yes, I see. And you lost your mother ... some time back, I think.' Lucie nodded. 'I confess I understand nothing of the mother's instinct, and little of the daughter's, but it's a strange path you've had to walk, isn't it?' Still silence. 'And yet you endure. You survive. I see you everywhere, always walking, always in the background, always ... just always. You took messages for some of my British friends, I think. For that extraordinary Scotsman.'

Lucie nodded.

'And now they are all running and hiding, and my salons are more boring. I thought the police would easily catch the man Kinnaird.'

Lucie considered her a moment. 'Not him. I thought so too, but not him. Something ... strange about him.' Emma was attentive. 'Like he's so stupid he doesn't know to give up.'

Emma smiled at this, nodded. 'I've never met anyone like him. So insignificant. And so unnerving. I . . . it's almost that I fear him – not because he's dangerous, but because he might be right, and he might be stronger than any of them.'

'He's sweet on you too.'

'Sweet? I'm not – '

'He can't work you out. He thought he could, now he knows he can't.'

Emma relaxed again. 'From him, that's flattery. Still, with the National Guard of every town in – '

'He's away safe. Where they won't find him. If you're worried.'

'How do you kn-'

'He's away safe.'

'And there you are again, Lucie. In the background, and enduring. Remarkable. Lucie, how do you find the new . . . the changes?'

Lucie shrugged, but it was calculated. 'What's changed?'

Lavalier wondered at it a moment. 'You just . . . continue to drift? Oblivious?'

'Men are the same. World's the same. The shit continues to flow, Madame, whoever's sitting on top.'

A door slammed at the back of the premises, and they both started; then caught each other's eyes again.

Lucie Gérard curtseyed, and Emma Lavalier nodded deeply; conventions restored.

At the front door, Lucie turned back. 'Thank you for . . . Thank you for talking, Madame.'

'It was my pleasure.'

'Madame, has your purse been over there, on that table, all this time?' Lavalier nodded. ''Fraid you might find it's lighter now. The Ribot brothers. I saw them come in. Little Matti distracts, littler Marc has a rummage.' She hesitated. 'I know these people.'

Lavalier didn't look at the purse. 'Thank you for your concern.'

'I could tell you where they live. If you've missed anything.'

'Thank you for the thought, Lucie. The indignity of chasing them would be worse than the indignity of being tricked. Besides, the purse contains only a few sous. What's valuable' – she pointed between her breasts – 'is tucked safe in here. And little Matti isn't ready for that yet. What a woman shows and what she values are different.' She smiled, but it was hard. 'You see Lucie, I know these people too.'

------- ◆ -------

His Majesty had always impressed on Maitre Bonfils the importance of flexibility. Impressed it – a word of jocularity, for such was his humour; had he ever had cause to complain at some actual failing of flexibility in Bonfils it would have been once only and Bonfils would have been out of the royal service for ever – and valued it.

Alone in the dirty lane, trudging through the evening to the dead house, his life shattered and himself thrown out like last night's pitcher of piss, left to rediscover himself after four decades, surely his flexibility was being over-taxed. Could His Majesty really have intended this? Imagined this?

He trudged on towards his . . . his *home?*

His Majesty was imprisoned now, by murderers and rebels and the world had gone mad.

His Majesty had always impressed on Maitre Bonfils the importance of correctness. Impressed it by manner alone, by divinely given assumption of utter deference and of the most perfect attention to his needs. And valued it in so far as Bonfils remained the only commoner permitted – after decades of faultless service – conversation with His Majesty, and that only by invitation and when the affairs of the royal household required it.

His present condition was surely not correct.

He had been travelling for many days, from the madness of Paris towards some dull animal feeling of sanctuary in the village of his forefathers, and he smelt like it. Days of summer heat, cooking his sweat under the formal coat it would be sacrilege to remove in public. Intermittently some fluctuation in the breeze would raise his own stink to his face, and his nose would shy and strain. Ghastly indignity; the most unimaginable lapse of standards.

He'd only arrived late last night, and the house was musty and unknown, and immediately this morning he'd trudged back to the village to arrange food and the possibility of a servant.

There was a stain on his left sleeve, down near the cuff, and he could not remove it with brushing or water. There was grease in it, he knew. He thought he knew whence it came, too: the tavern two nights back, the walls clammy with years of damp and the endless condensation of kitchen steam, a brute of a man serving him – *What is service, Bonfils? Service is utter devotion to the needs of the master, Maitre* – an unguarded movement of recoil when the man spilled soup on the table – oh to be able to whip such a man, to be able to banish him from such employment for ever, to break him – and his sleeve brushing the wall. He shuddered at the thought. Even in the greying of evening, the patch on the sleeve glowered darker.

He felt self-pity rising in his gut. Felt his face crumpling, and tried to collect himself. This landscape – these fields, these mourning royalist willows – was supposed to be home; the land of his people, the place where he had been born, a mother's warmth and familiar rooms and spring smells and running barefoot to a river and knowing friendship for the first time. But he had left it as a young boy and remembered little. He felt nothing for it, and this might be the saddest loss of all.

The house was his pension, bought ten years previously on advice tendered in a moment of excess informality by the Comte de Fleury, and visited only once – a curiosity, when the royal household had visited the Champagne in the spring of '87. Now it was to become, he supposed, the rest of his abandoned masterless life.

His left foot felt damp. He shifted it slightly inside the boot. *The good footman shall train his body to be able to stand in perfect stillness one full hour, and then train his mind to endure longer.* The tricks of a life spent in the most obsessively formal chambers in Europe.

There was a hole in the boot, surely. And no one to fix it.

You are permitted no feelings, Bonfils, until your duty is done! Old Pierrepont, his predecessor; his master. *When is your duty done, Bonfils?* Dead these twenty years now, surely. *My duty is never done, Maitre.*

He walked on.

The Revolution was seeking him. He had read the proclamation. There had been little else on his mind for the last forty-eight hours. After the indignities the wretches had forced on His Majesty, did they now want to punish his servants too?

The road was a corridor. The stones that showed paler in the last of the sun were the gleam of light on a polished floor. The avenue of trees passed regular and stiff beside him as he walked, like the sentries at Versailles, unseen eyes that watched him as he approached the Royal presence. He trudged on, dead to his aches, mind numbed as a junior foot-sore footman.

Still, perhaps it was better to present himself. He had seen the violence of the Revolution, and he had seen its unstoppable power. He could never outrun those mobs; he could never hide. Better to present himself and answer their questions honestly.

Obedience. Correctness. Virtue.

Old Xavier knew himself not so old. But his fifty years – forty of them in the royal service, dust boy to steward, never a day of sickness, never a moment of inattention – felt like a century. The darkness had closed around him, alone and abandoned in this lane, and the world had changed and he was ancient.

At last the house, dead in front of him and in his heart. He opened the back door – it was still wrong to use the front – and felt his exhaustion swelling as he stepped into the parlour. And then his heart burst in his chest.

There was an appalling tattered figure slumped in the chair and leering at him.

He spun away, mewing in fright and scrabbling at the door again. It opened, and the evening was blocked by an enormous shadow rising over him.

Guilbert had woken early and ridden steadily to Montmirail without a break. He'd gone straight to the Hôtel de Ville and, blood up from the ride and chase, required assistance in the search for the man Xavier Bonfils. The clerk seemed to know the name, seemed to remember the family had had property in the area. With the vague but ominous power of the Ministry of the Interior hanging over him, he'd hurried off to make enquiries about where in the district Bonfils might have gone.

Guilbert had taken his boots off, and found a lump of bread and a half-empty flask of wine.

Feet up, he had considered royal documents, and foreign agents. And he had considered Fouché, and then Danton, as if testing the uncertain rungs of a ladder.

The clerk had been back inside two hours. Xavier Bonfils had bought a house in the area a few years back. A courteous nod, and Guilbert had pulled on his boots and been up and out and mounting his horse.

———— ◆ ————

After his little imposture as the Scotsman Kinnaird at the Sphinx, Benjamin had left by the back door and taken the opportunity to reinforce the imposture at the inn of the Rose. He contrived to find the innkeeper there alone – earnest hand on arm – sombre whispered words – 'Pray do not say one word, dear Monsieur. You must not incriminate yourself, I beg you' – natural alarm on the man's face – 'But if you serve the noble cause that I believe you serve – the cause of legitimate and godly rule in this country – know that you have a friend in me'.

The innkeeper looked even more alarmed; glanced over Benjamin's shoulders. Benjamin had nodded reassuring sympathy. 'You had my dear acquaintance Bonfils here, I know. No, no: not a word. On his way homewards, of course. It has been a hard time for good men.'

And the innkeeper had nodded, and Benjamin had savoured it.

'How long ago did he leave? I had wondered if I might catch him on the road.'

Late morning, the innkeeper had said. No coach had been due for a couple of days, and Bonfils had taken a horse instead.

'Just a horse? He had nothing to carry?'

'He carried nothing. Left his little bag here with me to send on when the coach comes through.'

And Benjamin had nodded, again the sympathy, and again he'd laid his earnest hand on the man's arm. 'Your commitment earns my deepest respect, sir, in these times.' Then his other hand came discreetly over the counter. 'I have written my name on this paper, in case you should wish to pass it to friends who need a friend.' Last heavy nod of sympathy, enormous tip and away into the night.

Or not quite away. First he'd loitered in the darkness, waiting until something – in the end it was a most opportune brawl – brought the innkeeper outside. Then he'd slipped back into the inn and into the storeroom. There were three bits of luggage there, but only one was a bag small enough to match the innkeeper's and the sister's description of what Bonfils had carried. The catches opened to Benjamin's knife.

He wasn't sure what he was looking for. Some new hint about the man, about why he might be useful to the revolutionaries or to London. Some extra information about where he was going. Something that would enable him to seem to know the man better, or to influence him. Whatever useful thing he might have found in the little case, it wasn't there.

The man had been some sort of servant to the King, and for a prolonged period. If so, this case was a pitiful residue of a life. Some clean shirts and stockings. Two candlesticks. A pair of tiny matching volumes: a bible and a prayer book. A block of soap. A brush for shoes or coat. A spare set of false teeth.

It made his quarry seem smaller, his errand less grand. He'd closed the bag, and slipped out into the night again, this time for good.

He'd slept rough. Well out of the way of whoever else was on Bonfils's trail, straw under him and a warm darkness above. Then a day's ride, and he'd gone straight to the inn in Montmirail and started asking and a chain of three people in the locality had led him to confirmation that Bonfils had bought a house there, and told him where it was.

Now he was back in the inn, a good day's work behind him and a bowl of soup and a bottle of wine in front.

———————— ◆ ————————

Silence once more in the house of Xavier Bonfils. Silence from the figure in the parlour chair.

An eternal silence in the house of Bonfils: Bonfils was gone, and would not step through the door again. He had never spoken aloud, in this house he did not recognize, and now he never would. So there was not even a whisper of an echo of his voice, somewhere in the woodwork or vibrating the spiders' webs.

Soon the creatures that had been disturbed by his arrival, the creatures who had come to live in the gaps in the house, would return. They would make more noise in this place than Bonfils ever had, and they would possess it more.

Still the figure in the chair waited.

Around the building, jostling close to it, the trees whispered to each other in the breeze, perhaps contemplating how soon it might be seemly for them to reclaim the wood that had been borrowed for the construction of the house.

Xavier Bonfils was slumped against one of the trees, staring empty-eyed at the home he would never now achieve. The wound in his chest seemed small – a last gesture of restraint; something that might be lost in a crease; just another stain – but it was sufficient. The knife was clutched in his hands.

The figure in the parlour chair waited, and continued to grin. A wild, strained grin, locked in a distorted face, placed on top of a figure that did not slump and bend as it naturally should, a figure ragged and clammy and most unnatural.

A figure that had been dead for some time.

A figure who, more than most, might well grin at the strangeness of it all.

The figure of Henry Greene.

3

The Unquiet Dead

IN WHICH THE NEW METHOD OF PHILOSOPHICAL ENQUIRY
INVIGORATES M. FOUCHÉ'S INVESTIGATION OF THE ROYAL HERITAGE,
A SCOTTISH MERCHANT MAKES A TOUR OF REVOLUTIONARY FRANCE,
AND SIR RAPHAEL BENJAMIN FINDS A CAUSE

The Memoirs of Charles Maurice de Talleyrand

(extract from unpublished annex)

---

*At around this time my hosts in London invited me to produce what they
termed 'an appreciation' of poor Louis's correspondence. Ill-judged and
damned ill-spelled, was my first reply, but they would insist. In part I
think they hoped to entice me into sharing, by the back stairs as it were, a
summary of the European secrets that were known in Paris. In part I think
there was some game of politics being played among the London government
bureaux, and my hosts wanted material to justify a call on the secret fund
in order to support intensified operations in France. (Their fathers ran
espionage work from their private fortunes and raided the secret fund to go
gaming, of course; but England is become of late a more officious place.)*

*I offered them a kind of menu de dégustation of French secrets.
Nothing genuinely secret — for what is? — but a sumptuous selection*

drawn from the trivia of European deceit, and hinting at the main dishes. The great men in Paris, royal and revolutionary; Mirabeau, and the Prussians; Franklin the American, and the curious overlaps between American and British espionage — an intense and brilliant rivalry, except for the men at its heart who in my experience were commonly working for both sides. I gave them, you see, enough to be properly alarmed.

And I tried to make them understand the true threat of the royal archive: not what it revealed about anyone in particular — though that was bad enough, for me, and for many other great men, in Paris and London and a half a dozen cities besides — but what it revealed about everyone. The nature of European secret diplomacy, and of Louis's mad hoarding, was that everyone of note across the continent could somehow be implicated. With the mob ready to decapitate you for a scrap of lace, the mere appearance of your name in the royal correspondence could easily be fatal. More than that, a whole way of life would be exposed, the entire system of civilized European discourse. No one of sense was fighting to save aristocrats — generally the least useful and the least charming and the least cultured of people — but there was an essential fight to save aristocracy.

In this battle of the good order of all society, the lives of the individual agents and officials — innocent or otherwise, whatever that meant — were as chaff in the wind.

[SS G/66/X3 (EXTRACT)]

* * *

Benjamin contrived to lurk on the edge of the gaggle of idlers watching Bonfils's house and the activities of the authorities. There wasn't much to see now, but there wasn't much else to do either. So the half-dozen of them swapped rumours or smoked a pipe or just stared at the empty house.

'Two dead,' someone was saying, with a kind macabre satisfaction. 'Owner and – '

'Bonfils. Just bought the place.'

'Bought it years ago. Bonfils and a stranger.'

'Robber. Bonfils caught him and there was a fight.'

'Bonfils killed him, but took a fatal wound.'

'Killed himself, he did. Remorse.'

'Royalist conspiracy. They fell out. Bonfils couldn't live with the fact that he'd ruined the whole – '

'I heard – '

That would do, Benjamin thought. Surely the evil string-pullers in London would be happy enough. *Thwart the French in their aim*, the message had said. Dead was surely thwarted enough.

He wondered who the other man had been.

———————— ◆ ————————

'This does not help us, Guilbert.'

'I regret that, Monsieur. My approach could have been dif-'

Fouché was talking over him. 'We learn, Guilbert.' *Jumped up*, Guilbert was thinking, *but the ideal man to work for*. A hard-working man could go a long way working for a man like this. 'There is frustration in this outcome, but also we draw something from it: with such interest in the man Bonfils, we know that he was significant. We know that there is more to learn. Somehow, we must learn the secret that he fled to protect. Now!' – he straightened the paper in front of him – 'what of the other man?'

'Your pardon, Monsieur. I think this the more interesting point.' Fouché waited. 'Markings in his clothes, and a letter in his pocket, suggest it was the Englishman Greene. Henry Greene.'

'Greene?' Fouché's eyes widened. 'The agent? Now that's too tidy, Guilbert!' He hesitated. 'Bonfils killed him?'

'Difficult to know, Monsieur. The body was not lately dead.'

'How long?'

'Difficult to know. I have seen bodies, Monsieur' – the understatement came flat as ever – 'but it is impossible to know. A physician could say more.'

'Wait, Guilbert . . .' Guilbert waited. Fouché's eyes had narrowed again, the hawk circling. 'How are we sure that it is this Greene? A set of clothes, a letter . . . ' Guilbert nodded. 'Could someone who knew him identify him for us?'

'If you can find someone you trust, Monsieur. And the face had . . . suffered.' Fouché looked uncomfortable. 'From his lodgings it is known that the man Greene had visited a surgeon within the last month, who pulled a tooth. We will find the surgeon and he will examine the teeth. It is a good method.'

Fouché nodded. It was a good method, and he marked it as something else he had drawn from the day. Still his hands flexed and unflexed under the table, frustrated at the many things he still did not grasp.

ORDINARY REPORT

Department of Haut-Marne
18. October 1792

Meaux; routine check on inn Rose, known to be visited by Royalist sympathisers. Recent residents as follows:

night of the 13th – Juppet B., Bezieres P. (priest?);

night of the 14th – none registered;

night of the 15th – Bezieres, M. & Mme Dunay Th. (questionable – liaison);

night of the 16th – Jacques (surname not known), Bonfils X., Valery H.;

night of the 17th – Valery H., Lepin H.

Boy reported a foreigner active in the inn, night of the 17th, asking questions. Under questioning, landlord admitted this was Kinnaird, K. (name circulated in Ministry Bulletin nr 78), travelling Paris-Montmirail.

[SS K/1/X1/12] (AUTHOR TRANSLATION)

Danton was in with Minister Roland – Roland referred to such visits as Danton's orbit, his measured tour of the sphere of the Revolution to show his light – when Fouché pushed unbidden through the connecting door.

Fouché chose to come, and chose to push through unbidden, precisely because he knew Danton was there. 'Minister!' He said, urgency and determination, and then affected to notice Danton and offered him a generous bow and kept going towards Roland's desk and kept speaking. 'An immediate order for your consideration.'

Though he did not shift his focus from Roland, Fouché thought he could physically feel Danton's unease. He pressed on. 'I am uncomfortable, to be honest, Minister. I know you prefer to go slowly; I know you do not like these determined measures.' It was an understatement. The words 'immediate order' had soured and paled Roland's face, and he'd pulled back from their manifestation on his desk. 'Naturally I prefer that hope and patience alone may protect us. But for duty I am obliged at least to offer you the possibility of this measure to protect the Revolution.'

'Come now, Fouché! Surely poor Roland doesn't need – ' But Roland's hand had come up and Danton had stopped, and Fouché was fighting to suppress his delight. And now Danton saw his mis-step.

'Dear Fouché,' Roland said, stiff with dignity, 'I have nothing against determination and speed when wisely guided.' Fouché's words had been a calculated chance at prodding Roland to action. Danton sticking his head in was a guarantee of it. 'You are concerned for the Revolution?'

And now Danton couldn't risk interfering again.

'The Revolution does not panic, Minister. But I don't like this recent development. Foreign agents have murdered a French citizen simply because he was the object of an enquiry by your office, with the aim of thwarting our investigation. The English are clearly implicated somehow in these affairs: the outrage at the Garde-Meuble; the murder. Perhaps I sounded melodramatic earlier: perhaps it is only prudence that we give ourselves the possibility, within the law, of investigating the most dubious of the foreign residents.'

Roland kept his eyes on Danton, said 'Prudence indeed!' and signed.

Ned Pinsent was half-asleep in his chair, eyes somewhere between the picture on the mantelpiece and another world, when his door started thundering. Three knocks – fists – against it and the catch was shuddering. He jolted forwards in the chair, gaped at the door, half stood, and again the thundering. He took a deep breath, and a step forwards, and was reaching for the pistol when the door crashed in and there were muskets in the gap and uniforms pushing through behind.

By the time Raphael Benjamin had made it back to St-Denis his satisfaction had shrunk. The death of Bonfils would presumably keep Greene's London shadow-men happy, but it didn't feel like much of an achievement. And after several groin-numbing days in the saddle he was tired and bad-tempered, and cursing London and Paris and the various places where he'd been forced to spend the last few days.

He stomped through the open front door, aware of the effect of his dirty boots on the tiles, and sure enough there was a loud 'Oh!' squeaked out nearby. He hesitated, weighing sarcasm and knowing he was too tired to be polite. He glanced to the side towards the noise, down at his boots and the smear behind them, and back up at the noise. The landlady was standing in the little parlour from where she always spied on the world, and staring at him. 'You're here!' she added.

'I'm here,' Benjamin said, unable to think of anything to add.

'You're . . . you're welcome.' She said. 'As always.' And she smiled.

It was the most bewildering aspect of the journey. He spent a moment trying to absorb the phenomenon of a pleasant landlady, shook his head and made for the stairs.

And stopped.

Something different is something wrong. He took two paces backwards, and ducked round into the passageway towards the back of the house. 'You're not going to your room, Monsieur?' came from behind him.

'I'll take a piss in the yard, Madame,' he called over his shoulder. 'Better than doing it out of your window as usual, eh?' Into the yard, he glanced around the squalid space and made for the gate in the back wall – head down, suppressing the urge to look up at his window. He pulled at the gate; it wouldn't move. A shout somewhere behind him, muffled, and his hands were on top of the gate and he vaulted up onto it and down the other side and heard the sash rattling up and as he touched the ground and crouched with the momentum there was an explosion behind him and something thumped into the gate. He scrambled away along the alley, head tucked low and feeling his shoulders broad and exposed.

<hr>

More alone than he had ever been, lost in an outlaw forest somewhere in the middle of a land in chaos, Keith Kinnaird – merchant, sometime Secretary of the Warriston Philosophical Society – stared into the darkness and considered his life.

He'd always considered himself a solitary man: courteous, but not sociable. Independent. Taking nothing; expecting nothing. More than twenty years he had made his own way in the world.

He'd always considered himself an outsider. A changeling to the couple who'd raised him, and who grieved for the history of rebellion and shame that he represented. A restless soul, fighting the shopkeeper's eternal urge to conform. A man who had to trade to eat, in a world built on money but affecting to despise it. A Scot, in an English universe.

And France had seemed to offer so much. Henry's letter had seemed so enticing. The chance to use his talents, in a society recreating itself with unprecedented freedoms. He'd never had much use for fraternity, and equality had always seemed an illusion; but what might not be possible for a Keith Kinnaird, given liberty?

And now he looked around the forest, this place of perfect liberty.

For centuries, Scots had looked to the wildernesses for their freedom. And here in this wilderness he saw what that freedom meant. Desolation; desperation; barbarism. Humans become animals, in the heart of the most civilized country on earth. It was the corrupted betrayed embloodied freedom of the Wallace, of the great Montrose, of MacDonald of Glencoe, of the abandoned victims of the '45. The same promise of a dream: your own land; your own life to live; true freedom. And the same nightmare in the end: families pale and starving and hunted, hiding in the bracken, trying to live off nuts and berries, so eternally cold and wet, hoping feverishly to hide away for ever from human society.

Then he wondered at the dependencies of men on other men. He felt first his vulnerability, his weakness: how very frail he seemed, how foolish, compared to the man Aucun – compared even to Lucie. He'd always found himself composed, whatever the challenge. Now that felt a silly little pride; vanity only. He was alienated, adrift and afraid.

Something began to whisper in the wind above him, and the few leaves still on the trees whispered it back. The whispering became drops of rain, spattering the undergrowth.

He was nothing.

Kinnaird felt the first drops on his face, saw a picture of himself with a muddy trickle rolling down one cheek.

Here. Now. This, after all, is who I am.

And something else:

I live yet. The Scottish nation, all its mercantile strength, was born of slum-bairns and mud-washed fugitives. *And if I can live in this, what might not be possible?*

Edward Pinsent was not an obliging prisoner of the Revolution, and somewhere this glowed in him as a point of pride. Somewhere deep inside – somewhere instinctive, for he had made no conscious decision to resist.

He'd had a few years of schooling, two decades or more back, until father and schoolmaster had decided that no one was benefiting from the transaction. Now, discomfort and tiredness and loneliness and hopelessness had stripped away those decades of life and experience, and revealed the stubborn bewildered schoolboy Pinsent at their core. Solidity his only characteristic, and endurance his only resistance, against the endless protests and punishments at his failure to be more courteous, more obedient, more prompt with his answers.

Questions always startled him; made him clam up. He retreated inside, until the thrashing was over.

The cell was damp, and no light came in through the grille high in one corner; but he had it to himself mostly, and he'd kept a bundle of straw dry enough to sit on.

He wasn't counting hours, or days. They would pass, somewhere outside him. They always would.

Fuck the pluperfect tense.

The door rattled loud, and swung in, and lamplight caught one and a half eyes gleaming in the gloom.

'Up and out, old ox!'

Pinsent levered himself upright against the wall, suppressing the groan and the strain it cost him, and turned his back and undid his breeches and began to piss into the bucket.

'Get a bloody move on! Nice day out. Someone to talk to.' A hand pulling at his shoulder. He shook it off, half-turned, and contrived to piss on the nearest boot. 'Oh, f-' and the back of a hand caught him across the mouth and his head smacked against the wall.

He stumbled up the two steps into the corridor, doing up his breeches and chuckling. At the top, the usual ritual. The manacles appeared in front of him; he lunged forward to knock them away; the guards pulled him back; musket barrel into his back and then he let his hands be chained. The guards laid hands on his shoulders to push him along, and he shook them off and walked anyway, and they were used to it now and let him. Faces lunged forwards into door-grilles and bars as he passed, fingers clutching and straining, and he nodded to them all. 'I give you good day, Madame.' 'Dear Sir, I trust you are feeling a little better.' 'My respects to you, dear Doctor.' 'Ah, Mademoiselle, you tempt me as always.'

When there was no one to talk to, his face closed again, dirt and stubble and two bruises and a half-closed eye. Up more stairs, and another corridor, and then out into the courtyard and he winced and shied at the light. The guards had to steer him towards the archway. The relief of shadow again, and jovial comment from one of the sentries at the gate, and he told him to bugger off, and there was rattling, and the gate swung open and they pushed him through and the gate clanged shut again. Ahead he could see a coach, fringed with daylight at the end of the archway. Somewhere inside he registered that a coach rather than a cart meant no execution today. Somewhere inside he registered that the coach meant another interrogation.

A shove and he stumbled forwards, and pulled himself up straight and walked towards the coach. Simple black business, four-wheeled and cheap. Closed coach. *No one wants to see Pinsent on Founder's Day*. A guard pulled the door open in front of him, another shove from behind, and he growled and reached his chained hands up for the frame and pulled himself up and in.

And then a shot, and a shriek of alarm from the horse, and the beast must have reared for the coach went swaying and twisting and Pinsent stumbled to his knees in it; behind him shouting, the guards were starting to – and then another shout, 'Escape! Stop him!' – and slumped against the seat he saw a figure race past the open doorway behind him and now the guards were turning and moving uncertainly after it.

Then the roadside door of the coach opened in front of him, and in the blinding daylight there were horses and a figure and 'Up you get, Ned! Jump to it, you idle sod!' And he was scrambling up and through the door and falling into place on the horse and immediately the beast lunged forwards and away and he was clinging on.

Half a mile later Pinsent came fully conscious again, properly registered the man on the horse beside him, well-sat and gazing into the street ahead and still steering both horses. Hawk's eyes and somewhere in the mouth the suggestion of a smile: Sir Raphael Benjamin on a spree.

Pinsent said: 'You came back for me.'

————— ◆ —————

Hunger forced Kinnaird to learn faster. Without Lucie's charm, credibility, and fluency in the language he'd been paying ludicrous sums for the simplest food. At this rate he'd spend his whole purse in a week and still be living in a tree.

A faint memory, from as far back as memory went; the reality of a childhood in rebellion-wracked Scotland. *Get smart before you get hungry.*

He felt his empty gut; felt his frailty, and knew the danger. Promising it would be the last time, he allowed himself to spend another fortune on a loaf and some cheese, bought from P'tit Pierre, one of the two unofficial kings of the forest republic. Pierre – who with the dubious irony of his class was anything but *petit* – lived in one of the few stone buildings with something like a complete roof. He'd created what passed for luxury: a chair, blankets, a metal bucket he could light a fire in as a stove. On a shelf, the debris of the brutal economy of their community: two cracked beakers; a pair of women's boots, which Pierre had arranged as a kind of ornament; a prayer book; a pair of spectacles. When Kinnaird had arrived, he'd been whittling a stick with a large ivory-handled knife.

He handed Kinnaird the cheese, wrapped in a foul cloth. 'You want sausage?'

'Thank you, no.' Pierre shrugged, with a glance of complacent pity at the desperation of a man who would not pay a week's wage for a sausage; and as he turned away his fat swaying shoulder knocked against another knife, which had been embedded in one of the timbers framing the building. He stared down at it – a cheap, simple blade – stooped and picked it up and tossed it onto the shelf. Kinnaird had been considering the swaying movements; he fancied Pierre had one leg shorter, or wasted.

Pierre sat, and picked up the ivory-handled knife and his stick from his table again. His absorption and a few gouges in the stick showed he was trying to make something decorative. It still looked like a stick. Kinnaird nodded at the knife. 'I saw that in the hands of a newcomer yesterday; lawyer from Versailles.'

Pierre's eyes came up under his brows. 'You see it in my hands today.' He gazed at Kinnaird, defiant but then uncertain. 'That's progress!' And he pushed out a big laugh.

Kinnaird smiled like an idiot. 'I'll tell you what, P'tit Pierre; I make you a proposal.' Pierre watched him, holding his bravado. 'The fortune I've paid you, you could get to America maybe, or make yourself king in Paris. No need to bother with the little stuff now.' He could see Pierre swelling. 'You could throw the sausage in for free.'

Pierre grinned at the hilarious idea of generosity. He sucked his teeth.

'Sausage now – very expensive, sausage.' He shook his head. 'I like you, English. You're a funny man.'

'You're too much of a trader for me, Pierre. Very well then. Something useless, for a funny man.' For a moment he'd worried that Pierre might actually give him the foul sausage. He affected to look around. 'That old knife, now. The little one. To celebrate progress, and lawyers who don't ask questions.'

Pierre watched him, not sure what he thought and what was funny any more. 'My old knife?'

Kinnaird shrugged, and nodded at the ivory handle. 'What's the value of the mouse, against the lion?'

Pierre considered this, then looked up again. 'I'm the lion in this forest!' He grinned at Kinnaird the mouse.

Kinnaird nodded in admiration, as if he'd just realized the comparison. Actually he was remembering a rich boy from Greenock who'd fancied himself a tobacco importer, fat and rather stupid.

With half a loaf and some cheese in his belly, and the little knife in his pocket, Kinnaird sat for an hour in the fringe of the forest watching the lads who came from a village referred to only as 'The Windmill' to trade eggs or bread or beech oil or things they'd stolen from their neighbours. He watched Pierre and the few like him, furtive and hasty nearer the daylight, make their trades and hurry back into the trees. He saw the quietest, most cautious of the lads. And then he followed him.

Halfway to the village the boy turned to confront him. Kinnaird held the knife blade forwards, as a weapon. The boy stayed silent, the eyes on Kinnaird and watchful, and Kinnaird knew he'd chosen well. He switched the knife around in his fingers, so the handle was forwards, and now the boy looked at it. Finally Kinnaird held it upright between them, and explained that when the boy returned with three chickens, two of which needed to be in lay, the knife would be his. After that he would get a fixed sum, once at dawn and once at dusk, for any mixture of items he cared to bring according to an agreed tariff.

Inside twenty-four hours Kinnaird had brought the forest economy forwards by three centuries, replacing the mediaeval era with the mercantile from his branch-and-blanket headquarters. Inside a week he had doubled his original purse, and a lawyer, a former tax farmer and a couple of murderers were in his debt. Soon afterwards he bought a horse and emerged from the forest.

———— ◆ ————

'You came back for me.'

Pinsent heard his own words as if distant. His vision came slowly. Raphael Benjamin bubbled into focus.

The words seemed to surprise him; he was even uncomfortable. 'My dear fellow . . . A bit of theatre, and a coin for a lad to divert them.' Then he was busying again. 'Ned, you look atrocious.'

One and a half eyes flickered. 'Accommodation distinctly average.' He realized he'd been asleep before. 'Raph, I must know – '

'We need to get you washed and shaved, and if we can't do something about those bruises we're better laying up here rather than having you frightening the children. And I'd rather not lay up.'

'Won't the bandages do?' Once clear of La Force, Benjamin had lost them in the heart of the slums, put a bandage around Pinsent's face and a sling over one arm and a blanket around his shoulders, turning a manacled fugitive into a wounded soldier. This had got them out the city, and for ten miles, to the cheapest tavern that still offered a private room. There Benjamin had fed Pinsent broth until he'd passed out.

Pinsent's hand came up to feel his head, and he remembered the manacles. 'And ain't these the bigger problem?'

'Manacles I can change, Ned. Your face, alas, I cannot. And the bandages do draw the attention rather. For now, sleep; we won't move until dusk.'

Pinsent slept. In the evening, as the blacksmith of the village of Cergy was letting his fire die with the sun, he was startled by two shadows who appeared behind him. Their faces were masked. One of them stepped forwards, and the blacksmith took a tighter grip on the tongs he'd been holding, and waited. The shadow thrust his hands forwards, revealing manacles. The blacksmith's eyebrows came up.

The other shadow placed two objects on the workbench in front of him: a pistol, and a gold coin.

The blacksmith shrugged, and pulled the manacles onto the anvil.

In the dawn, Pinsent woke again. Benjamin saw, and pointed to a loaf of bread and a flask of milk on the floor. 'Get your strength up, old lad. Can't have you snoring all the way to Switzerland.'

Pinsent absorbed the room: its cheapness, the smell, Raph's bed placed to block the door. He flexed his wrists, feeling the absence of the manacles. Then he took a mouthful of milk and buried his face in the bread. He was talking before he'd finished swallowing. ''Fore God, Raph, what's been happening?' Benjamin, sitting tidily on his bed with his back against the door, frowned mildly at the question. 'Hal Greene! What about him?'

'What indeed?'

'That – that he's dead!'

Now Benjamin came upright. 'You said what?'

'You don't know?'

'Ned, I'll guillotine you myself if you don't talk straight.'

Pinsent finished another mouthful, watching the other carefully. 'It's all they would talk about. All they wanted to know about. Hal Greene mixed up with some royalist plot, and found dead.'

'But where? How?'

'There was some servant – used to be the King's valet or something – '

'Wait – You mean Bonfils? Was the name Bonfils?'

Pinsent frowned, and saw the irritation. 'You'll pardon me, I'm sure,' he murmured, grim, 'if I ain't crystal on the details.' Benjamin nodded, impatient. 'May have been the name. He was murdered, some little town somewhere, and Greene was found beside him, dead and stinking the place out.'

Benjamin slumped back against the door.

'You know anything about it, Raph?'

Benjamin gazed at him, and said nothing.

Pinsent returned to his breakfast. After a while, he said: 'I didn't tell them anything. Nothing to the purpose, you know?' Benjamin got what he was talking about, and smiled. 'Not Emma's name. Not yours.'

'Course you didn't, old fellow. Civil of you.'

A silence, and then the stolid wonder again. 'You came back for me.'

The eyes of the genius Lavoisier would not meet Fouché's. They stared up, into the infinite, and would never deign to drop to the representative of a terrestrial power.

A servant had checked, and then invited Fouché in. And it was in the entrance hall that he first saw the legend: saw the wide clear eyes gazing up and away from the earth; saw the mind working, saw the dreams.

What kind of man puts up a portrait of himself in the front hall? Didn't have time to tidy his papers when he'd been forced out of his offices at the Arsenal, but managed to bring out the prize portrait. The existence of the painting told him something. And if Lavoisier owned it, then it was Lavoisier as he wanted to be seen.

Fouché considered the image again. It depicted a man of prosperity. It depicted a man of *purity*. The Lavoisier in the picture was doing something noble; and Lavoisier was humble in his contemplation of . . . of whatever was to be seen in the notoriously brilliant mind. Chemical speculations as the mysteries of Olympus.

The servant was whispering to him again, and Fouché followed through into another room. The servant left him and closed the door, and Fouché took the opportunity of solitude for further exploration. There was a table across the room with papers on it.

He was halfway towards the table when he glimpsed movement, somewhere on the edge of his vision.

At the far end of the room, in front of a window, a man was sitting at a desk and bent over some work in front of him.

The rounded back, the wigged head, were absolutely still. Only an arm moved, slowly, to touch something obscured by the body; then the other arm shivered as he wrote.

Fouché stood still, caught in the middle of the rug, and waiting.

The man at the desk did not turn. Adjustment of something with left arm; shiver of writing with right.

Fouché waited. Eventually he said, 'Good day to you, Monsieur le Professeur.'

Nothing.

Is he deaf? Surely Lavoisier was not so old. Louder: 'It was most kind of you to agree to see me.'

Adjustment of something with left arm; shiver of writing with right. Shifting cautiously round, Fouché could see more clearly what the man was working at: a glass vessel of some kind, on a metal stand, with metal pipes protruding from the top of it.

Surely he had seen the movement now, even if he hadn't heard. Fouché was irritated, but a kind of awe restrained him. He was not accustomed to being other than the cleverest man in the room; but the cleverest man in this room was the cleverest man in the world.

Fouché contrived a mighty cough. It produced no effect. He thought about continuing to the papers on the table, but discomfort wouldn't let him. After another minute he sat in the nearest chair.

Coal burned dull in the grate. *He feels the cold, even in a mild autumn.*

He considered the room – the furnishings showed affluence, and absolutely no distinction or unnecessary elaboration. The room was no more than comfortable: a rich man's book and paper store.

He considered the rich man's back, across the room.

Antoine-Laurent Lavoisier: trained as a lawyer; trained as a geologist; presented his first paper to the Academy of Sciences at the age of twenty-one; gold medal from the King at the age of twenty-three; by the age of thirty he was changing the way men saw the world. Where most men saw the air, Lavoisier saw strange invisible fumes and powers; things you could not touch or see but which burned. Lavoisier saw not air, but spirits he named oxygen and hydrogen. Lavoisier saw the world in closer detail than any man had ever seen it.

Fouché waited.

Also: a tax farmer, a gunpowder broker, and the husband of a charming and much younger wife.

Fouché shifted uncomfortably on his chair.

And as if inspired by the same unseen power, the back across the room shifted for the first time, and stood. The man turned, and came to Fouché. 'Young man, you're most welcome. Please don't stand.' A bell touched, the servant immediately in the room, drinks ordered. The hospitality was entirely normal, and there was no acknowledgement of Fouché's wait. Lavoisier pulled a chair round to face him.

Fouché met Lavoisier for the second time. This was an older Lavoisier: the nose, the eyelids, the jaw, had gained a little flesh and lost their sharpness. Gone with them was the sense of freshness, and purity. *The face of a tax farmer, not a dreamer.*

The eyes, though, still had an innocence as they considered Fouché. And innocence was what he was supposed to be doubting.

'You must forgive me, young man, but I don't – '

'Joseph Fouché, Professeur. Of the cabinet of the Minister of the Interior.'

Lavoisier stiffened in the chair. Fouché read alarm, distaste, discomfort in the souring face. 'Of course. I am at the service of the Revolution, Monsieur Fouché.' He tried to cross his legs, but the pose of relaxation did not last more than a moment. 'I realize that it was necessary for me to leave my post at the Arsenal, but I trust my work here will continue to be of use to the authorities.' He'd stopped pretending now, and the voice got faster. 'There is still much to be done to improve the quality of our powder. Kellermann and Dumouriez are still advancing against our enemies, yes? How many cannon?'

Pause. He was actually, Fouché realized, waiting for an answer. Fouché shrugged, back in the schoolroom.

'A small improvement in the quality of the powder – it's a matter of its properties during the combustion reaction – will create a significant improvement in the strength and reliability of the detonation. We may also, I think, safely expect to see a more efficient expenditure of powder – a lesser charge for the same effect. You will rapidly understand the benefits, young man, to the treasury and to our straitened resources.'

Silence. Fouché wondered if he was supposed to clap.

Instead he said, gesturing towards the apparatus on the desk: 'You continue your . . . your investigations, Monsieur le Professeur?'

'Investigations? I am not a magistrate.' Fouché the errant pupil again. 'To investigate is to follow a trail of footprints, not knowing whither they go. To *experiment* is to devise, based on great knowledge, an hypothesis, and then to design tests that must, by unavoidable logical implication, prove or disprove the hypothesis.' He began to tick off the steps on his hands, stiff-fingered. 'Hypothesis – test – observation – inference – synthesis.'

'I under-'

'And repeat!'

'I –'

'France is mediaeval, young man. A land of spirits, of superstitions, of credulousness. Do the peasants expect the touch of Danton to cure them of the pox?' *Quite the opposite, probably.* 'My great hope of the Revolution is that it drags this primitive land of ours into the age of reason. We must trust to nothing but facts: these are presented to us by nature and cannot deceive.' Lavoisier's lips were dotted with spit in his excitement. 'Reason – experiment – observe! This is the only law we must follow.'

'The National Convention –'

'The Convention is a gathering of mammals. A herd. Each of them is so much chemistry: a chemical process, a burning of fuel to maintain heat and the working of the organism.' Fouché was feeling uncomfortable. 'Chemically speaking, we are little more than the fire in my grate there. If I had been allowed to continue my experiments on respi-'

'But you weren't, Professeur, were you?' *Enough of these dreams.* 'You made your fortune as a tax farmer, not a natural philosopher, and the people felt the pain of your taxes before they felt the benefit of your philosophizing.'

Lavoisier deflated in a long sigh.

'In the end you were little better than the bishops, selling pardons and positions to clothe their mistresses.' Lavoisier's body and face started to contort. 'Professeur, I respect you for your mind – you . . . you have a purity of mind that I admire. But the Revolution . . . it demands conformity, not genius.'

Fouché stopped. It was not an idea he'd had before.

Lavoisier was nodding. Slowly, unhappily. Eventually he said: 'As chemistry, young man, we are all alike. You may reassure your comrades of that. But the same chemical substance may be manifest in utterly different forms.' As he regained familiar ground he regained confidence. 'You see the coal burning over there? In chemical terms, a lump of that coal is the same as a diamond.' He smiled at the wonder of it, smiled at his own certainty.

Fouché's face showed his uncertainty, and he fought it down. 'We may have to give up our diamonds, Professeur, to keep the coal burning.' *The King's diamonds*, he was thinking.

Again, the unhappy nod. This time Lavoisier stayed silent.

Fouché gathered himself. 'Professeur, I had the responsibility to monitor your premises in the Arsenal, after your departure. I found a ledger, and a sheaf of notes. They were sent on to you here.' Lavoisier nodded vaguely. 'I recently found that one other item had been misplaced in my office. A letter to you, from Monsieur Bailly, that had arrived after your departure from your former premises. I take the opportunity to return it to you.' A very precise copy was in the appropriate dossier.

Lavoisier showed no inclination to casual gratitude.

'Monsieur Bailly describes to you certain experiences of his acquaintance, the mathematician Delambre, during the present expedition to measure the meridian.'

A half-nod. 'I shall look forward to reading it.'

Fouché stood to leave. 'One more point, Monsieur. A minor curiosity merely.' Lavoisier waited warily. 'We noted the marking "1/6" on the letter, and wondered at it.'

Lavoisier shrugged. It was not a natural gesture, indifference, to this mind.

Fouché watched his face. Saw the wariness.

'Curiosity, Monsieur, as I say. In the ministry we are naturally attentive to these trivial details. Even in the correspondence of a man of absolute public reputation.' They both knew that Lavoisier was short of this, and falling fast. 'Even unwittingly, a man could obstruct or assist the ministry most significantly.' He smiled. 'Such a volatile time.'

The chemist was not a natural dissembler. The face was stone; the eyes were hatred.

It was a child's hatred. The passion of an infant mind caught out in a deceit, or deprived of a toy.

'I wondered if it might be a copyist's mark. If the same message – this very innocent message, between men of reputation – was being sent to others.'

Lavoisier forced a smile. 'You're quite right, Monsieur Fouché. I'm delighted to satisfy you on the point. Always happy to assist the ministry, naturally.'

'I am sure of it.'

'We are a small circle of . . . of acquaintances. Men of a philosophic inclination. Theorizers and experimenters. We were once brought together for a particular scientific enquiry and, finding each other's intellectual society congenial, resolved to maintain a correspondence wherever our activities should take us.'

It sounded credible; and innocent. Fouché felt disappointed. 'It sounds a most natural proceeding.' He forced a smile of his own. 'And you very naturally adopted the services of a copyist who would both copy any message to all members of the group, but also manage the sending onwards.'

'Quite. Years ago now, and we rarely make use of it. But I informed the copyist of my move here, nevertheless. The note you have, from Bailly, must have been sent before I did so.' His voice went flat. 'Rather an upset time.'

'I would be fascinated, Monsieur, to know the enquiry that brought you together.' *I would be fascinated to know the names.*

Lavoisier grunted. 'It was a foolishness – a charlatanry, indeed – in the time of . . . of the old order. Several years ago: the . . . mid-eighties. Eighty-four. His Maj- That is, Louis called a Commission of Enquiry. It was the Secretary to the Commission – insignificant old functionary; he's dead now, I think – who found the copyist and established this arrangement.' He smiled, and there was discomfort again. 'Monsieur Fouché, you have discovered the secret of the Friends of Magnetism.'

---

1. MAY 1784

In Paris, an unnatural theorem is to be scrutinized

Sir,

Louis the KING has conferred upon MESMER, the physician of Vienna and darling of the salons, the uncomfortable honour of a Commission to examine his outlandish speculations.

Mesmer – and the outline of his speculations – has been mentioned in earlier reports. (I sent you myself his notorious Mémoire with its Propositions.) Such is his renown that he has moved from only private practice to conducting séances involving small groups, and I have now had the opportunity to attend one of his matinées and to see the phenomenon for myself.

It is a most peculiar performance. Participants, some ten or twenty devotees or persons afflicted with all degrees of sickness – my companions included among divers others a lady much troubled with headaches, a lad who has not walked since birth, two lunatics, and a quack I know to be in the pay of one of Mesmer's rivals – sit in a circle in Mesmer's parlour, around a curious wood and brass and glass vessel some three hands high. This Mesmer calls the 'baquet' – we would say the pot, or the tub – and from it protrude a number of metal rods which the participants are obliged to hold against their persons, specifically against the most afflicted portion. Thereafter a rope is run from the device to one of the party, and thence to the next person, and so on round, until the circle is completed and the rope returns to its source.

I append a sketch of the device, and am endeavouring to obtain closer technical specifications.

This experience itself is felt by some to have perceptible effects upon the fluxions within their organism, and the impact is greater when Mesmer himself approaches, and, without actually touching, moves his hand nearer to the subject. Witnesses have reported the most remarkable shocks and even convulsions at the mere proximity of the man.

Such, he proposes, is his animal magnetism, which he elaborates as being the power exerted by one human body of more potent motion upon a weaker, transferring by magnetic force its electric currents into and then through the fluids that pervade all organisms.

I confess, Sir, that I departed his salon with more of a headache than when I arrived, but happily there is a more robust review of its effects. His Majesty, concerned by the popular enthusiasm for the phenomenon as much as by its questionable implications for natural philosophy and for religion, has now decreed that a Royal Commission of Enquiry be established to consider the existence and true operation of the hypothesized magnetic fluid. His Majesty is also, I understand, acutely concerned at the implications of such a phenomenon as a means of perverting the normal function of authority and deference in society.

The Commission will comprise several medical men, natural philosophers including BAILLY the astronomer and LAVOISIER the chemist, and the American representative, FRANKLIN. Sensible of the various complications and potentialities that that name involves, I shall endeavour to remain au courant with their deliberations and determinations. E. E.

[SS F/24/38 (DECYPHERED)]

———————◆———————

These are the days of Keith Kinnaird, a fugitive free in France.

In Chateau-Thierry, a conversation with two farmers and, later, a grain merchant about what the eastward campaign of the volunteer army has meant to them.

In Coulommiers, supper with a schoolmaster. Too much of the local cheese, and discussion of mathematics, and the power of reason, and its relation to government and loyalty.

In Montereau, half a day watching the movements of the barges on the Seine.

In Montargis, with the saffron sweet in the air, a coffee with a retired merchant and the sale of a copy of Montesquieu's *Lettres Persanes*.

In the outskirts of Orleans, icon of resistance to the English invader, a discussion in an inn on the Dutch republic and the importance of Britain's Asian territories, following the loss of some of her American colonies.

If anyone asks, he is a merchant. He makes no pretence to be French. If asked, he is Irish – in these strange days the least controversial of the British islands. He says that he is trading in the wake of Custine's Army of the Vosges. This doesn't always endear him to the farmers or his potential competitors, but it explains him satisfactorily to those he meets – especially those in uniform. In his bundle, across the back of his horse, he brings a few books which he can offer for sale, by way of introduction to certain sorts of men.

But I *am* a merchant.

I used to be a merchant.

Keith Kinnaird is no longer resisting. He is moving in France, with France. He is learning her currents: of trade; of people; of information.

He is making a tour of northern France, keeping his distance from Paris. He is not yet ready to risk returning to the capital; but he knows that time must come.

He is not ready to leave. Kinnaird has unfinished business in France.

———— ◆ ————

Guilbert had got used to waiting while Fouché finished reading something. Reading had never been Guilbert's way into the world – writing was a dead, deceptive kind of communication. But some men were needed to read. The Monsieur made good use of it, and to be fair to him he was prodigious fast and on occasion would read while listening, and hold each clear in his head.

Guilbert wondered at that head.

When the head came up it was smiling faintly, lost in something.

Eventually it focused. 'What do you have today, Guilbert?' Fouché hadn't noticed that he was adopting something of Lavoisier's treatment of guests.

Guilbert shrugged. 'As usual, Monsieur, military success means folk are more impatient at home: more fights; more robberies. The police are stretched; the Paris Sections are grumpy. The investigation into the royal diamonds is blocked completely. No one's talking about who was really behind it, and no one's interested to push. No word on the British fugitives. We've turned over the lodgings of Benjamin, who hasn't showed up yet, and Pinsent, who was sprung from La Force. Nothing. They met other foreigners frequently, but no one knows anything. They were close with Greene, but we knew that anyway. We've questioned a few other British – keep 'em worried, yes, Monsieur? – and they're frightened enough to talk but they've nothing to tell. There's a watch on all the city gates, of course; on every city gate in France; but ten sous'll buy new papers, and ten francs'd buy the guard himself.'

'And . . . the other man?'

'The mystery. The Kinnaird. He galloped out of St-Denis and disappeared from the earth. We don't know who rode with him, and we don't know who's helping him. Every district in France is watching for him; no one's seen anything.'

Fouché was gazing into the distance. Guilbert had expected more irritation.

'You were reading something . . . pleasant, Monsieur?'

The faint smile came back to Fouché's face. 'Fascinating, Guilbert. Not the subject, but the process. Several years ago Louis commissioned a circle of great philosophers to review the claims of Mesmer. Have you heard of him, Guilbert? – the physician – remarkable cures by the use of magnetic power.'

Guilbert nodded. 'Him and a few like him. Holds his hands on young women's bellies, or thereabouts, does it a powerful long time and claims he's a wizard when they start to feel funny. Might set up as a physician myself, Monsieur. He makes money at it too. They made a good thing of him in the music halls.'

It was a distraction to Fouché. 'The Royal Commission was quite a group, Guilbert: Lavoisier, whose letter we had, and Mayor Bailly who's fled, and – '

'Nantes.'

'Yes, and Lagrange the mathematician, and the American ambassador, and others like them. I have been reading some of their reports. They showed that Mesmer's theories were nonsense, of course. Magnetized trees, Guilbert. Magnetic water. But they way they did it!' He was pacing, and turned back, and his hand was gripping the idea in the air. 'Their method:

experiments – comparisons – brilliantly devised to show the truth. They conducted sixteen different tests, and in each they had some subjects apparently supporting the hypothesis and some not. Multiple subjects, to remove the possibility of error. Testing the hypothesis positively and negatively, so there could be no doubt about their conclusions. They didn't destroy Mesmer with philosophy, but logic.' Fouché's predator eyes were bright. 'Logic, Guilbert!'

Guilbert nodded. Most of what he heard in these buildings was magnetized trees.

<hr />

From the front window of the Ship Hotel in Chartres, Kinnaird was watching the traffic outside. He'd never been able to see a wagon without wondering what it contained and where it was going. Now that habit had become a purpose: the currents of France – her blood – were her trade. Chartres was on the main road between Paris and Nantes, on the Atlantic coast, and Nantes was rich with the trade in sugar and coffee from the Americas. Kinnaird measured the character and strength of France by the wagons that flowed along these arteries.

The Ship was prosperous, but quiet this morning. His only company was a man of about his own age, dressed as prosperous and quiet as the establishment and sitting discreetly in the gloom away from the window. And a young man, flamboyantly dressed and with a sword at his side, had been in the room when Kinnaird arrived, had left shortly afterwards, and come and gone twice since then.

Kinnaird was making himself consider the people that passed as well. Their currents were also significant: the movement of uniforms told of military campaigns, and of police bureaucracy. Everyone else was moving – just as people always moved – out of hope or out of fear. He was becoming interested in the hopes – whether a deal, or a job, or a dream of liberty in radical Paris – and the fears.

Just outside the hotel's window was the barrier at the city's western entrance, where the National Guard could monitor goods coming in and out, and monitor people. A bare pole between trestles, four or five uniforms guarding it and checking everyone who wanted to pass. If someone wanted to go westwards, to the sea, or turn northwards into Normandy and towards the English Channel, they had to pass this barrier.

The young man rattled into the room again, his sword catching against a chair-back. He strode to the window, near Kinnaird, and looked out. Dark hair, dark eyes, good bones. And hellish impatient. He glared into the street, the dark eyes cursing whatever was not yet there, glanced at Kinnaird and then sat down uncomfortably, wrestling the sword into place between chair and table.

Kinnaird took a sip of wine, and resumed his consideration of the wagons and people outside.

He had been a week on the road himself. He was making himself more comfortable in his strange, shadowed life. He had found a way to travel, to exist, to find company and stimulation, without fully being himself, and without apparently drawing unnecessary attention to himself. He had to assume that the name of Kinnaird was still dangerous, but the Kinnaird who had jumped out of a window and galloped in panic away from the National Guard now seemed a figure of history.

The young man stood up again, with a clatter, and pressed his forehead against the window as if the glass against his skin might cool his fervour. He turned, glanced at Kinnaird, and sat down again.

Kinnaird considered himself a sensible man, but knew himself stubborn with it. He had never expected anything in life, he had worked for everything he had gained, and he had tolerated the unfortunate losses and the unripe deals; but whenever he found resistance, he set himself to overcome it. France had resisted Kinnaird, and Kinnaird would not turn and run.

And still he did not know why he was hunted.

Another clatter broke his thoughts. The young man was looking about himself with the usual disregard for his sword.

'You're not a trading man,' Kinnaird said politely, quietly. 'I guess you wait for someone, and they must be someone special.'

The young man glared at him; the dark eyes – sad eyes – considered him from boots to brows. Then the glance softened. 'You are not French, I think.'

'I am not.'

'English, from your accent?'

'Irish.'

Now the face brightened in a smile. 'Ah, my Celtic cousins! We are fellow romantic souls, my dear sir.'

'If you say so.'

The young man had switched into fluent and elaborate English. 'Myself, I am Espanish. That is to say, a citizen of the Basque lands of the north, hence my consanguinity with you and your people. You would honour me by allowing me to present myself. I am Don Francisco de Borja de Lasheras, caballero, and diplomat of the Embassy of the Kingdom of Espain.' He stood, clattered, bowed elaborately, and sat again.

Kinnaird contrived a bow from where he sat. 'You honour me by your introduction, sir.'

'And may I presume to seek your name, sir?'

Kinnaird said quietly, 'I'd rather give an honest man silence than a lie.'

The face darkened, and then glowed in the smile again. 'Ah! I knew it – a mystery! A romance!'

'Like your own, perhaps.'

The young man swooped down into the chair next to him. Over his shoulder, Kinnaird saw the clatter re-attract the attention of the man in the corner.

'There is a lady,' the young man whispered.

'I thought there might be.'

'Mademoiselle de Charette. A lady loyal to her faith and to her crown. She escapes by this road. I have esworn to protect her, and have ridden as her invisible escort these two days.'

'She's a lucky girl.'

'Mine is the good fortune to be able to serve her. I have killed two men already in her cause.'

'Oh.' For the first time in weeks, Kinnaird was starting to feel that he wasn't the most disreputable man in the room. 'Er . . . congratulations.'

'But now, this barrier will be a test. I fear this may be the crisis.'

'The young lady is . . . disguised?'

'With her father, yes. But those soldiers, they check everyone most assiduously, you observe? She is not . . . But no matter! Now that I am here, if she is suspected I may deal with those ruffians myself and allow her to escape to esafety.'

The two of them were silent for a moment, contemplating the barrier outside, the blurred figures of the men guarding it, and the rather ominous prospect of the young man's proposal. Kinnaird was wondering if it mightn't be wise to leave sooner rather than later.

'I'm wondering,' Kinnaird said mildly, 'whether you might be of more service to the lady making your distraction just before she gets to the barrier. Distract attention away from her, rather than drawing it.' He smiled apologetically. 'More subtle, perhaps.'

Again the smile. 'You are right, dear sir! Esubtlety . . . That is the thing, is it not? It shall be so.' He stood violently. 'I bid you adieu! If I ever have the chance to thank you . . . '

'If you survive the next hour, young man, and return safe to your embassy, and if a man with no name should ever write to you seeking your co-operation in some matter of advantage to our two countries, then you would have the chance to show gratitude in a way that would benefit all of us, including the young lady.'

A grand bow from the young man – nod from Kinnaird – and he clattered out.

Kinnaird breathed out slowly, and returned to his consideration of the street outside. His mind began to fill again with the men and women tramping backwards and forwards in front of him, the intermittent flow of carriages and carts through the barrier, the habits of the guards as they checked those who passed.

Somehow, in the midst of it all, the lunatic was the most congenial and humane company he'd met.

He sensed someone moving near him.

He didn't turn.

It was the other man in the room, sitting down silently and beginning his own scrutiny of the road.

Neither looked at the other.

Fifteen minutes later, a cart appeared to the left of Kinnaird's vision, coming from the direction of Paris towards the barrier. A driver sitting up front, and what looked like a lad in rough clothes among a dozen barrels at the back.

Still the ebb and flow of traffic through the barrier.

Kinnaird had seen his silent companion's hands clench into fists.

Then a wild shout and the thunder of hooves and for a moment the window was filled with darkness as a horse charged past, making for the barrier at mad speed, the rider swirling a sword around his head and clutching a pistol along with the reins in his other hand. As they reached the barrier the sword swung down near one horrified guard, the pistol fired at another, and the horse took the barrier in one mighty leap, the rider soaring above and held on by ankles and momentum only, and the hooves sent another guard sprawling and in an explosion of shouts and dust the horseman was through and racing for the trees in the distance, and the guards were grabbing each other and pointing and some were running after the rider and at least one was running back into the town, and in the Ship two men watched wide-eyed.

'Merciful Christ . . .' Kinnaird's companion had his hand over his eyes.

The dust began to disperse.

There was only one guard at the barrier. A horseman coming in from the countryside had been waiting when the Spaniard had executed his rampage. Now he yelled something to the guard, and the guard hesitated, and then let him into Chartres.

The horseman passed the cart of barrels coming in the other direction; the noise of the wheels grew more distinct, and the cart pulled to a halt at the barrier.

Kinnaird's companion was staring through the window.

The guard hesitated. The driver – an old man, he seemed – said something. The guard said something back, and the driver pointed to the barrels and said something else. The guard looked around himself, hurried to the back of the cart, and thumped the nearest barrel with his fist.

The fists of the watcher were white.

Apparently satisfied, the guard hurried back to the barrier and raised it. The cart began to move forwards into open country.

Now Kinnaird's companion turned to him.

'Should I be grateful to you for that spectacle?'

Kinnaird shrugged slightly. 'Not as spectacular as it might have been.'

The man nodded. The cart was clear now.

Kinnaird considered the man again – his clothes, his face – and said: 'You're a trading man, I think, sir. And of some success, I fancy.' The man did not answer. 'Unusual for a man such as you to pay such attention to a single load of barrels. Whatever it was.'

'Empties only. It came in full from the coast; unfortunately we can't always make the return run pay.'

'My point is doubled. Care for details made me most of my success in trade, but I still think I'd have trusted the driver with a cart of empty barrels.'

The man nodded. He looked at Kinnaird, and smiled. 'The people. One likes to keep an eye on one's people. Check they get home safely. Usually without the aid of romantic enthusiasts.'

Now Kinnaird nodded. 'I assumed it was something like that. A Christian act. But I still think that the Spanish lad helped his lady friend a little.'

'Perhaps he did at that.' The man offered his hand. 'Jarreau.'

Kinnaird shook the hand, and considered the face.

'Kinnaird,' he said.

A frown opposite. 'I think I have heard the na- . . . You are he . . . !' Jarreau sat back in his chair. 'My goodness, Monsieur Kinnaird. You are quite the most notorious merchant in France. You must find the trade here stimulating indeed.'

'On my word, sir, I do not know why. I find myself notorious, for feats that I do not know or acknowledge.' He saw the disbelief. 'Sincerely.'

Disbelief became a kind of wonder. 'In which case, Monsieur Kinnaird, your misfortune exceeds your notoriety.'

'France has been a strange place.'

'Come come, Monsieur. As a man of affairs, you know that the first principle of doing business in a new town is to familiarize yourself with the customs and habits of the people. In revolutionary France, the customs and habits are passion, fantasy, envy, revenge, suspicion, fear and blood.'

'Sounds like my first day in Glasgow. You're on the right side of it, at least.'

'Side?' Jarreau seemed genuinely surprised. 'You have the most curious approach to business, Monsieur Kinnaird. I support no "side". I pursue my own principles, and I hope I do so discreetly and prudently.' He sat straighter; he saw Kinnaird's approval. 'And if you'll pardon a discourtesy, I'd be obliged if – given your present profile – you stayed as far away as possible from my operations.'

It hurt. But Kinnaird nodded. 'I understand. But I hope to . . . to stabilize my affairs, and resume more discreet and satisfactory dealings. Perhaps we might then find mutual advantage, Monsieur Jarreau.'

Smile. 'We might indeed, Monsieur Kinnaird.'

The town of Évreux looked like it might be rather lively, and Raphael Benjamin resented having to keep himself confined to an inn on the outskirts. On the second night he left Ned sleeping and slipped out to size up the pleasures of the place. But he knew of no safe doors to knock on, no warm welcomes he could trust; and when he saw light through a shutter, or heard laughter from some hidden conviviality, they felt like taunts.

When Pinsent asked where they were going, he cursed him because he didn't know himself. Eventually he said something about Évreux being on the way to the Channel. Pinsent said, 'England, Raph? You mean we could go back?' And they both knew it was an empty hope.

After his tour of the unwelcoming town in the small hours, he'd lain awake, reviewing the rather insubstantial record of his accumulated years. Sport enough, but was it really supposed to have led him no farther than a French tap-house, too scared to get a woman or a good meal?

With the dawn he'd cursed himself for self-pity, and gone down to command an early breakfast. Soon after he'd sat, a couple entered the room. They didn't see him at first, not until they'd asked for food. When they did see him, the effect was peculiar. Immediate concern, a glance at each other, then down, and a furtive glance sideways in the unlikely hope that the kitchen had produced their breakfast before the order had even reached it.

Benjamin considered his dirty coat, and his fugitive state. He felt his unshaven chin, and irritation at yet more people who would not know him.

An old man and his – no, surely not wife, not unless the old man was the richest luckiest devil in France; daughter, more likely.

Either way.

He kept his eyes on the old man, until when the old man happened to look up Benjamin gave him a respectful nod. The old man reciprocated instinctively, then looked down. The exchange naturally got the woman's attention, and she couldn't resist glancing up herself, to find Benjamin's eyes entirely on her. *Very charming curls.* He let the smile spread over his face, and gave her a little nod too. She looked away.

He didn't see them again. He heard they'd started taking their meals in their rooms. Which was damned unsporting.

————————— • •—————————

'News, Guilbert? You have that look about you: somehow well-fed, somehow still hungry.'

Guilbert didn't really register the point. 'Monsieur is most . . . pleasant. And I have news. The surgeon has examined the corpse we found in Montmirail, in the house of Bonfils. He confirms from the condition and arrangement of the teeth that it is the man he treated a few weeks back. The Englishman Henry Greene.'

Fouché nodded, slowly. 'That's tidy, Guilbert. It confirms the English as somehow complicit in royalist plotting.' Guilbert was impassive. 'Which, as you are presumably thinking behind that mask, we would in any case have assumed.' He winced. 'But how, Guilbert? We may speculate well enough what they aim at, but how do they work?'

'Monsieur?'

Fouché smiled. 'You are the good agent, Guilbert. You want to know the intentions of our enemies. Me, I take it for granted that they intend to defeat the Revolution and restore the discredited King and his corruptions. I need no surgeons or tortures to tell me that. But how do they intend this, Guilbert? If I knew their methods – if I knew their *connections* – I would have a chance of confounding them.'

He watched Guilbert; eternal, unyielding, indifferent.

'What do we know of the death of the man Greene?'

Guilbert shook his head once. 'Knocked on the head, Monsieur. Something rough: club or stone, maybe.'

'A murder, or – or a fight? Bonfils could have killed Greene?'

Guilbert's faint insubordinate shrug. 'Perhaps, Monsieur. But they didn't think he'd been in the district long. Perhaps that's wrong. Perhaps it's possible the Englishman came to put some pressure on him, and Bonfils refused, and they fought. But –'

'Or Bonfils wanted help, and the Englishman refused, and so – ' He stopped, and glared at Guilbert. 'But this is mere speculation! This has no value.'

'No, Monsieur. Anyway, we still cannot know when this Greene died. Certainly well before the servant Bonfils. Weeks.'

'We must do better, Guilbert. We must shake the English harder!'

'Yes, Monsieur.'

'We have the body of Greene still?'

'In the cellars, Monsieur. We've put him in a box – he's not fit to be lying around, Monsieur. And it means he's ready for burying.'

'For now we keep him. There may be something . . . In the clothes, say.' He smiled uncertain. 'This Greene, Guilbert, alive or dead, has been a mystery and a confusion. I want that mystery and confusion working to our benefit for once.'

'Old Arnold, now.'

'Mm.'

'Drowned when the packet went down off Boulogne. Thomas.'

'Mm.'

'Fever. Dunkirk.'

'Brussels.'

'Course it was. Course it was. Reading his bloody Gibbon to the end. Three.'

Ned's day of the dead, Benjamin called it. Pinsent's habit, when trying to cheer himself up, of reciting a catechism of past acquaintances who hadn't survived quite as long as he had thus far. 'Seven.'

'Marten.' They were in Benjamin's room, playing cards through a day that would never end.

'Fight with a gypsy. Folkestone.'

'That was Marston, ass. Twelve. Marten's in Rome, living with a whore.'

'So says he. That's fifteen, Ned.'

'Got you that time, eh? Twenty, and a pair.'

'Mm.' Rome sounded warm, and easy, and lasting. 'Twenty-eight.'

Benjamin wasn't admitting that he didn't know where they were going. Pinsent was too uncomfortable about it to ask any more. 'Go.'

'We're set well enough here, aren't we, Raph?' Benjamin watched him. Pinsent wasn't looking up as he spoke. 'Fairish food and wine; pack of cards.'

'Well enough, Ned.'

'What were those papers you were writing? Never saw you use a pen so much.'

'Some more distractions for our hosts. They'll find from this correspondence that the Scotsman has been amazingly active against them.'

'Hah. Always the scheme. Always keeping your options open.'

Benjamin knew his options. They didn't feel all that open. He'd been repeating them to himself for much of the last forty-eight hours, and throughout Pinsent's litany of dead men. Switzerland. Italy.

'Vanstone.'

The Low Countries didn't look too clever, not with the French revolutionary army driving for the sea.

'Never really knew what that was, did we? Bloody awful he looked, at the end.'

East, into the German lands? Were they so desperate?

'That fellow who got stabbed by the pimp in Calais. Never knew his name.'

What worried him was that he didn't seem able to make a decision.

'And old Hal Greene now, of course.'

Sometime in the evening Benjamin had gone down to command some more wine, and see what food he could scrounge. In the main room of the inn a man was talking loudly to the innkeeper, while the innkeeper used a rag to smear a slick of wine and crumbs along the counter and back again: a coachman, it seemed, still cloaked and muffled against the wind and complaining about his troubles trying to find adequate rooms in town for his passengers, an old lawyer and his sick wife.

Both men seemed to take it for granted that the Old Willow Tree would not be adequate. Benjamin had taken advantage of the innkeeper's absorption to check the register.

A breath of air out in the twilit street, trying to find freedom in it, and a piss. Back in the inn, the young woman had appeared. He watched her from the doorway as she gave her instructions, enjoying just the hints of her profile under a scarf, enjoying the sound of her voice. There might be freedom in there.

Others in the inn had been watching her too, he'd noticed. The dream of freedom was proving elusive in France.

'We don't know how he died, do we, Ned?' He looked up from his cards as he spoke. Pinsent shrugged, and he nodded. It was no longer necessary for death to have a means, or a reason. 'Go.'

Wrapped tight in a pouch and tied close to him, he could feel the two royal jewels. Surely he'd sell them. Surely he'd be able to live forever on the proceeds.

'Six.'

But not yet. For some reason, not yet.

He didn't like the fact that he'd not told Ned. Kept meaning to. Knew he never would. But he didn't like the idea of being a secret thief. It was cheap. Sordid.

And somehow these jewels were more than money. They had significance. They were political. Had he indeed taken them to look after them – the act of a gentleman; a courtesy to a king?

'Raph, you ever wonder how you'll go? When it's your time?' Benjamin looked up, scowling at it. Pinsent was watching him earnestly. 'You know: fever, or fight, or whatnot?'

'Noisily, Ned. I shall go noisily.'

Pinsent chuckled, grateful.

At some point within the preceding twenty years, the salon of the Swan in Vernon had had pretensions: its drinkers and diners sat in booths framed by classical columns; candelabra on each table were supplemented by a chandelier in the centre of the room; behind the serving counter a long mirror doubled their light. And during the preceding twenty years, life had called the bluff of those pretensions. The plaster work on the columns was crumbling and pock-marked; it looked as if the mice had got into the salon, or a skirmish of muskets – and the general condition made both scenarios seem credible. Two of the bolts holding the chandelier to the main beam had given up the struggle a while back, and the cobwebbed constellation hung askew and would swing and creak when the door let in the wind. Damp had got down behind the mirror, distorting the wall and cracking the glass, so that according to the reflection one section in the middle of the salon did not exist; another molten triangle of mirror next to the soup tub was missing, and the rest was tarnished and blotched, showing the Swan's few patrons as blurred ghostly things.

To Keith Kinnaird's eyes too, one of them seemed to have passed on. A back, the back of a head, slumped over the counter. Fingers had failed and abandoned the effort to reach a goblet just inches away, a resignation mirrored in the seam gaping down the back of the coat. The man behind the counter was ignoring the body.

The door opened, and the chandelier creaked into the silence and the wind ruffled the hair on top of the slumped head.

Then laughter, sharp and ugly, and the door closed and the wind dropped and the hair subsided. Kinnaird glanced at the mirror and watched two blurs glide behind him to a table, heard voices, the only sound in the salon. As the waiter passed on his way towards them, Kinnaird gestured to his own glass, and continued to watch the body at the counter. The voices rose and fell nearby. The waiter returned with beakers of wine and water and poured from each into Kinnaird's glass.

'Revolution's been good to you, Trichet,' one of the voices said; Kinnaird was always interested to find people the Revolution had been good to, and heard flattery and bitterness in the voice. Trichet observed that he had been good to the Revolution. Chance for men of ability to get their just rewards. Escape the parasites, he explained more judiciously. Wipe them out. His companion noted that Trichet had done more than his share in that direction, and they both seemed to think this a good thing.

'Fucking aristocrats,' Trichet spoke with pity rather than venom. 'All those silks and titles and generations; and none of it'll save them.'

Kinnaird's interest faded, recaptured by the scene at the counter. The slumped head had creaked upwards on the neck, and seemed to be trying to find itself in the mirror. Whether because of the mirror's fog or its own ghastly pallor, it failed. Then, with the solemnity and surprise of a Lazarus, the body lifted into an upright position on the stool.

One forearm slipped and the body slumped with it and swayed backwards and forwards on the teetering stool; clutching desperately for the counter, at last it settled into the vertical again. A man little more than twenty, surely; very drunk, or beginning to feel the after-effects of it. He now held himself very erect, determined to defy the stool, and the eyes stared into the mirror's clouded distance.

Kinnaird watched the performance for a moment longer, sympathy and amusement, and then returned to his wine and the contemplation of provincial French politics.

A quarter-hour later he left, a coin on the table and a nod to the serving-man. It was fully night outside, and colder, and he stepped to the side and back into the shelter of the building to button up his coat. Some kind of wooden terrace arrangement a step above the street; perhaps they sat out here on summer days. As he strained at the button at his collar, Trichet's companion emerged from the salon, and then Trichet behind him. Polite goodnights, and the companion stepped down into the street and walked quickly across it and away.

Trichet hesitated a moment on the step, doing up his coat, and he was still standing there when a shadow launched itself out of the salon and wrapped itself around him and drove him off the step and down into the darkness. The body – two bodies – writhed and rolled, one behind the other and arms entwined, and something flashed and there was a scream – terrified, short – and Kinnaird stared and could not move. Still the bodies rolled, and the upper – Trichet; it must have been Trichet – levered itself up off of the other and staggered upright and Kinnaird glimpsed a streak of red across his neck. Now the other was half-upright and lunging again and as Trichet stumbled sidewards a hand swung round and the knife stuck in his arm. He squealed, gasped, flapped round to reach the handle, and floundered back into his attacker; the attacker went sprawling backwards and down, and Trichet dropped to his knees. The attacker came up into a crouch and was lurching forwards again at the unprotected back when Kinnaird caught him by the collar and dragged him back. Anticipating the attack and not feeling it, Trichet twisted round and gaped for an instant and realized his chance and struggled up and ran into the night, the blade still sticking out of his arm between the fingers of his clutching other hand and glinting in the last of the light from the salon.

Kinnaird let go of the collar, and stepped back. The shadow wriggled away from him and slumped against the step, gasping deeply. 'I – I didn't . . .'

'Well, no,' Kinnaird said when it didn't go any further. 'Not very successfully, anyway.'

It was the young man who'd been at the counter. He stared up at Kinnaird, and then his shoulders shook and the gasps became sobs.

———— ◆ ————

Eventually Ned Pinsent had stumbled away to bed. The innkeeper had divided most of his original bedrooms into two, to maximize the money he could screw out of the solitary travellers who were his usual trade. The possibility of solitude was keeping Benjamin sane. He had also noticed that his neighbour was the young woman. The old man was the other side of her, in a room of his own.

Benjamin put another hour or more into the correspondence he was creating for his own, more exciting Kinnaird. It was past midnight when he heard movement from the room next door.

Door open a crack, he watched the young woman – her head covered and face obscured under a shawl – making for the back stairs. She was moving carefully over the boards. Then from the window he saw a shadow appear in the yard; saw another shadow meeting it.

When the young woman returned ten minutes later, she opened her door and slipped back into her room with the same caution she'd taken to leave it, face in shadow and eyes looking everywhere. She started to close the door, looked round, and gasped. Raphael Benjamin was sitting in her chair.

He stood, gave a small bow. 'Your pardon for the intrusion, Mademoiselle. May I suggest that you close and lock the door?'

She stared at him, fear and then – the chin coming up and the eyes hardening – something like defiance. *Very charming curls, and very lovely dark eyes under the dark hair.* She closed the door, and locked it. 'Who are you?' It was a murmur, but hard; fear and defiance to match the expression.

'I am your guest, Mademoiselle, but may I invite you to sit? The conversation might be more congenial.'

She ignored it. 'Who are you?'

'A gentleman traveller abroad, Mademoiselle, with leisure to wonder why a charming and apparently innocent woman, with every advantage, should be so scared.'

'You make many assumptions in a short sentence.'

'Your manner throughout your stay has been more than furtive. You are registered as Monsieur Bertin of Versailles, and his niece Mademoiselle Terray. Unfortunately for you, I think I came across the family once; I'm fairly sure that the uncle's dead, while yours still looks pretty spry, and I know that the niece curdles milk at a goodly distance, while you're distinctly lovely.' She felt the colour coming into her cheeks, and it only stiffened her dignity. 'One of your few public appearances in the last twenty-four hours was – in a sudden show of boldness given the number of people in earshot at that moment – to announce with elaborate clarity your desire that your trunk be stowed in the storeroom because you would be here for a few days at least. I've had an odd life, Mademoiselle, not without disreputable moments, and I know the preparations for a backstairs bunk when I see them.' Her eyes were hard and wide and she gazed at him. 'Above all, your reaction now. You're scared of who I might be – you're scared of who anyone might be – and you don't risk drawing any attention to yourself. That's why you haven't screamed the inn awake, and nor alas have you shown any temptation to take the proper advantage of an Englishman and a closed door.'

Still the chin was high. 'I maintain my options, Monsieur. Depending on who I find you to be.'

'*Charmante* . . . I compliment you, Mademoiselle, for your spirit as well as your curls.'

'You have a name?'

'Not tonight, Mademoiselle. And I do not ask yours.'

'What then?'

'Merely to assure you, Mademoiselle, that there are two Englishmen in this hotel whom you may trust, and to urge you and your father to call on me if I may be of service.'

It seemed to warm her. He saw it in her face, and the way she breathed in and out more deeply. 'I thank you for it, Monsieur. There is no – That is to say, at the moment our plans are not clear. But I will . . . ' – her eyes dropped, and came up again – 'it would give me pleasure to be able to call on you.'

She let him kiss her hand with genteel courtesy, and her fingers stayed there long enough to suggest that warmth was starting to overcome fear.

———— ✦ ————

The young would-be assassin's name was de Boeldieu, and though he stopped sobbing soon enough he continued to shiver, so much that Kinnaird wondered if he might actually have a fever as well as the beginnings of a monstrous headache. He straightened the man's coat, led him to a different inn and bought him a cognac.

He sat in silence, watching the young man, and waited.

The young man stared at the cognac, took a mighty gulp of it, and slowly lifted his head to look at Kinnaird. Then he closed his eyes in some pain – his head, or his memory.

He pulled his shoulders, and then the troubled head, to a poised vertical. 'I should thank you, sir,' he said.

It was a good face, Kinnaird thought. Good bones; something left of the leanness of youth. The coat, and the shirt beneath, had once been good too.

'I hope you'll forgive an impertinence, sir,' Kinnaird replied, 'but you don't sound grateful.'

A slow, uncomfortable, heavy smile. 'You have saved a life, and no doubt you deserve credit for it.'

'Two lives, perhaps,' Kinnaird said.

'I'd rather both were extinct than neither.'

Kinnaird considered this. The young man took another mouthful of cognac, and once again pulled himself up.

'I apologize, sir. You have done a deed of the worthiest intention, and bravely.' He thought for a moment, then said with greater weight, 'That swine murdered my father.'

Kinnaird frowned. 'You don't seem a family for street brawls.'

'By the bastard process of their bastard regime he murdered my father. I . . . ' – again the closed eyes, again the pain – 'I was not a good son. I swore I would be a better after his death. I am training – there's a man in the district – I was trained with the sword when younger, but I paid no attention; now I will train like a prodigy.' He glanced down, clenched and unclenched his hand; another wince, the memory of the clumsy attack with the knife.

He took one long breath, and at the end it threatened to break into a sob again. 'I have waited for such a chance. Mourned. Waited.' Kinnaird saw again the figure slumped at the counter. A sharp breath; pain. 'I failed.'

Kinnaird began to ask him about his family. They talked for hours.

Benjamin slipped back along the corridor alive to every creak of the inn's wood, to every whisper of air. He was straining to notice movement around him so much that he only half-noticed that his door opened without the key, and by the time he'd fully noticed it he was in and the door was closed behind him and he was looking at the stranger sitting in a chair by his bed.

For a moment the stranger was alert, body poised, watching for his reaction. But Benjamin stayed silent and still, and the stranger picked up a glass of wine from the floor beside him, and took another sip. His eyes stayed on Benjamin.

Benjamin said, 'Comfortable?'

'Tolerably, thank'ee.'

Benjamin nodded, and looked carefully around the room from where he stood.

'You'll pardon me if I seem over-curious or inhospitable, but who are you, and what the devil are you doing in my bedroom?'

The stranger hesitated before replying. Benjamin took half a step forwards.

'I'm a man like you: with a knife and the knack to open a lock with it.'

'You're English, I think.' No comment, no denial. 'And for some reason it amused you to sneak in here while I was sneaking in there.'

'I wasn't about to intrude, and I ain't about to ask any questions. Did she survive the experience?'

'I've a pistol as well as a knife, if you're planning on getting discourteous.'

'A pistol, indeed? Among the footpads and philanderers of Évreux you must be a very king.' Benjamin scowled; considered him. A young man: late twenties? Simply but well dressed. Dark dressed. The cloak was hardly necessary for the weather.

'It seems I've something you want, anyway.'

The stranger sat up. 'Quite right, Sir Raphael!' And he smiled and sat back. 'I want you.'

'You'll get more of me than you want, boy, and you'll be lucky to make it back to Boulogne on a stretcher.'

'A typically reckless wager on your part, that. If there's a chance you could restrain your tap-room bravado for five minutes, at least, I'll – '

'Who are you?'

'The man who's been pulling your strings the last nine months.'

'You said what?'

'Can I please encourage you to sit, Sir Raphael?' Benjamin did not sit. 'I have been steering Henry Greene, and he has been steering you.'

'Hah.' But Benjamin was listening.

'In May he appeared to become rather drunk with you – perhaps not an unusual proceeding – and coaxed you into a most amusing bit of sport, didn't he? You set up as highwaymen for a night, and stopped a coach coming in from Rouen, apparently at random. You and he and your friend Pinsent shared a purse – enough to keep you in port and whist a month at least. Greene didn't share with you the leather portfolio he'd taken, did he? Said it was nothing, said he'd got rid of it as soon as he could.' The stranger shook his head at his own words. 'The contents came back to me, and via me to London. In July you were in the Low Countries. Change of air, bit of sport. Greene subsequently sent me some most interesting observations regarding the state of the fortresses between Dinant and the Channel. On the fourth of September, at Greene's direction you stirred up a riot around some surveyors in St-Denis. On the night of the sixth you broke into La Force – stout work that was, by the way – to liberate the charming Mademoiselle de Tourzel, and you were back the next night to bring out her mother. I could name another half a dozen such incidents. Some of them you knew were Greene's idea. Some you probably thought were your own. All were actually mine.'

Benjamin stared at him, refusing to show a reaction. He took a breath, walked to the chest of drawers and poured a glass of wine. Then he kicked a chair into place, and sat.

'Now, Sir Raphael, you're too much of a gentleman to believe that you've ever accepted payment from Greene for this work. But you've accepted his generosity blithe enough, haven't you? Fruits of his business speculations, and so forth, shared among friends.'

Benjamin took a fat mouthful of wine. 'So, I repeat: who – or what – are you?'

The stranger smiled mildly. 'I'm the British Government, Sir Raphael. Or, at least, the only bit of it that'll ever talk to you.'

Benjamin's eyes scanned him. 'You ain't diplomatic, and you ain't military.'

'No. Nor am I the parish clerk, a London waterman, or ever like to get into the House of Lords. I'm a department of the Crown you wouldn't recognize if you heard the name; and you probably never will at that.'

A slow nod. 'And you're here to . . . what? Snoop on the Revolution?'

'This and that. His Majesty's Government is naturally concerned to understand what's happening in France. The threat.' He smiled. 'The 'opportunity.'

'And that's got harder since Gower closed the embassy.'

'Indeed. And sometimes we like to avoid embassies, anyway.'

'Quite right; the wine was always damned average. And you broke into my room because you got a touch lonely and wanted to hear a familiar acce-' He caught himself. 'No . . . ' Benjamin smiled. 'No, you're here for them, aren't you? My poor hunted neighbours: the old man and that glorious girl. I'll bet His Majesty's Government is falling over itself to welcome escaping royos. Think of all the loot they'll stump up for you.'

'We will show that in one country, at least, property and the proper order may be respected.'

'Don't preach to me about the proper order, boy.'

'Your speculations about my motives are irrelevant here, and best kept to yourse-'

'I reckoned they were planning a midnight flit. But it's smarter than that, ain't it? You . . . You would be the coachman I saw, shouting about the old man and his sick wife.' The stranger watched Benjamin's brain working, faint amusement. 'And the old man and the sick wife, they've . . . what? Disappeared somewhere in town now, I presume.' He considered the stranger's face. 'No . . . No, they don't even exist, do they? But they will soon, won't they, when you sneak my neighbours down into the coach and make for the Channel?'

Now the smile was wider. 'You sound almost impressed, Sir Raphael.'

Benjamin swallowed the scowl. 'Credit where it's due. I took you for a messenger; a clerk, an errand-boy. But this is man's work.' His mouth twisted. 'May I offer any assistance?'

The stranger considered him, as if the suggestion were impolite, then shook his head. 'I thank you no.' Benjamin waited. *Gods, the arrogance of this puppy.* 'My plans will pass well enough, without assistance.'

'So what do you want, then? Before I kick you down the stairs.'

A sneer on the stranger's face; and then a moment of doubt as he considered the possibility of this. 'I want your loyalty,' he said.

'You want what?'

'You understand the meaning of the word?'

'By all means describe to me, privy-sweep, what your government has ever done for me to expect my loyalty.'

'It ain't a contractual arrangement, Benjamin.'

'Fine by me. Good luck on your trip to the Channel. Hope you don't get buggered to death by any syphilitic revolutionaries.'

'You've been busy, Benjamin. Every scheme, every outrage – even the ones we don't arrange – we suspect you. Greene was reported to have been at the Garde-Meuble when the royal jewels disappeared. And when we heard it, we assumed that he had shrewdly recognized their value – ceremonially, politically – and got himself involved. But now there are doubts. Greene turns up dead and rotting. And I ask myself: what if he wasn't at the Garde-Meuble? What other Englishman might have been involved?'

'What do you take me for?'

'Precisely what I know you for. You wish me to list your previous escapades? Chronologically, categorically or geographically?'

Benjamin smiled, grim. 'Well, ain't you the smart boy? But if you're expecting co-operation, you've a damned ill manner for it.'

'There was a time, Sir Raphael, when France must have seemed a jolly place for a gentleman on the lam. All that Continental tit and no questions asked about where your gold sovereigns came from.' He crossed his legs and folded his hands in his lap. 'But now the sovereigns are running down, and the prices are going up, and after the last couple of weeks even the whores'll think twice before letting an Englishman lift their petticoats. You got your friend Pinsent out of La Force, and a hell of thing it was too.' He leaned forwards. 'Who'll get you out when it's your turn? Who'll save you from the guillotine?'

'Make your point, damn you.'

'A man might be starting to think that home ain't so bad after all. A man might be starting to think of what he might do, to regain enough credit with the authorities that they might overlook certain past . . . indiscretions, and let him slip ashore at Folkestone one dark night.'

Benjamin's face was bleak. He knew himself hooked; hated it. 'You have that power?'

The stranger didn't reply, didn't even smile. The face glowed, hardened with the arrogant certainty.

Benjamin took a deep breath.

'I'll bear it in mind.'

The stranger nodded, considering his face. 'Do,' he said, and stood. 'Royal jewels and royal secrets, Benjamin. A couple of months ago, the stuff of an evening's sport. Now they're the stuff of empire.'

'So?'

'A man could gain his reputation over them. Or lose his head.' He lifted the sash window. 'Think on't, would you, old fellow?'

———— ◆ ————

By now, every inn in France has one or two of the poorest lads in the district who lurk in the rankest corner of the yard at the most unsociable hours of the clock, desperate to beg a sou for an errand, or just to steal it. You have to have spent a fair bit of time in the inns of France to have recognized the invariability of the arrangement.

Sir Raphael Benjamin had done so. Curiosity kept him awake that night, had him watching from an unlit window in the small hours when the coach appeared at the opened gate to the inn yard. From this vantage point, he saw movement in the darkness of the yard.

Soon, the man calling himself Monsieur Bertin was handing the woman calling herself Mademoiselle Terray up into the coach. Then he stepped in behind her, the coachman lurking and urging speed with murmurs. The door clicked shut, and the coachman began to climb up into the driving position.

From the other side, 'Mademoiselle!' A face thrust up into the window and Mademoiselle's heart thundered in her chest. She felt her father beside her, heard unformed protest starting in his mouth. 'A coin for a poor man, I beg of you!' The coach was swaying on its springs as the coachman made it up on top. She heard herself starting to refuse, to refuse everything, to refuse the idea that they might have been caught at the moment when safety seemed possible at last. Her father's arm coming past her to push at the head in the window. Then a hand around the back of her neck and she was yanked forwards into the window opening. 'Or a purse for your pretty neck!' And something flashed in the gloom and pressed sharp against her throat.

'What's happening down there?' Hoarse whisper. She could only choke. Something like a moan from her father, called out of the nightmare.

'Throw your money out, or I cut her throat!' The coachman was straining to look and the coach was swaying again. The robber glanced up, but his knife stayed at her throat. He pulled her head down farther, knife at throat, and ducked closer to the coach so he was shielded from above. 'Now! Money or her neck!' She could smell his breath, feel its heat against her face. The old man was reaching for his purse and the coach was swaying wilder.

The knife dropped away, and the robber groaned as his arm was wrenched around. She saw him twisting, the shadow distorting in front of her. She felt the night air fresh against her face. The shadow continued to turn and there was another shadow behind it, and they seemed to be dancing and she knew from their taut corners that they were straining for the knife. Then an arm came high and swooped and the robber went stumbling back, and the second shadow slid forwards and punched again and the man went down and still.

Another face loomed at her out of the night, out of the second shadow. 'Benjamin, Mademoiselle; at your service always.' It was said loud enough for the coachman to hear. She recognized him, sighed long in relief, and Benjamin stepped in closer.

His voice was lower, faster; his face was close to hers, so they became a single shadow. 'When they welcome you to London, insist on meeting the most senior man responsible for your escape. And give him this.' She gasped: something cold had pressed against her chest, and now he was pushing it down between her breasts. 'A gift for His Majesty, from the King of France and from Sir Raphael Benjamin. Yes?'

She nodded.

'Good; thank you. But don't,' he added, 'give him this.' He pressed forwards and kissed her hard.

'Step away, Benjamin, or I'll put a ball through your skull.'

'Quite right, my dear fellow. Good journey now. Well done on your successful mission.' The coach jolted forwards and then began to roll smooth and with growing speed into the night.

Benjamin watched it until it vanished, then turned towards the inn again. The girl's hair had been dark like Emma's.

There was a groan from the shadows near his feet.

Benjamin helped the young robber up. 'Next time, lad.' The lad was still unsteady. 'For now, it's back to the shit-heap for us.'

<hr>

There wasn't much fun to be had as the sergeant of police of Évreux. Such, at least, was the opinion of the sergeant of police of Évreux himself. There was a fat-headed idea that his job was all about power, and that his power had only got greater with the Revolution. But it never felt powerful. He spent most of his time compiling *Reports Ordinaires* for the Hôtel de Ville and for Paris. Never written so many bloody words in his life.

He'd be compiling a *Report Ordinaire* following his visit to the Old Willow Tree, that was becoming wearyingly clear. The landlord of the Willow was roaring angry, and he was demanding to know why the hell the police weren't doing anything to stop these kind of outrages, otherwise what the hell was the point of them, and the Revolution was supposed to have been about stopping this kind of abuse, except it bloody wasn't, it was just more outrages, and certain fat policemen who thought they could cadge a free bottle whenever they fancied it; and the sergeant – who considered himself no more than imposingly built – was thinking *one more crack from you, Pierre, and you'll be getting a very sharp reference in my* Report Ordinaire, *and see how you like those onions.*

Law and order, he was hearing, had broken down completely in Évreux. First there'd been the old man and his young niece, all terribly grand and highest-standards-expected, and now they'd only gone and done the pedlar's flit and not even a sou paid for the meals, let alone for two rooms. And just after he'd discovered that, he found that two others – two foreigners, he fancied, and he shouldn't have suspected any better, and what the hell was the point of the Revolution if it let people like these tool around France robbing honest trading men? – had gone out the back-window too; not a sou from them either, and they'd had one of his blankets and all.

The sergeant of police tutted loudly, told the landlord to shut his trap about the Revolution if he didn't want the Revolution giving him a permanent shave, and plodded around the premises reviewing the various scenes of outrage.

The old man and the woman, their rooms were more or less clean; no trace of who they were or where they'd gone. Their trunk, in the box-room, contained a couple of bricks and some old clothes.

The rooms of the two foreign men were also empty. They'd travelled lighter, the landlord was saying as they stood in the second of the rooms; come and gone with what they stood up in. The room was a sad shell: a mattress and two chairs and a candle-stub. The sergeant was enquiring whether the foreigners had stolen the chandelier, and the landlord was suggesting that they'd probably used it for a bribe at the police office, and in a show of restoring order the policeman kicked the mattress more squarely into the corner. The movement exposed a few new inches at the base of the wall, and as it did so a sheaf of papers fell forwards.

They'd been slipped down between the head of the mattress and the wall. And obviously forgotten by the foreigners in their outrageous escape. The policeman and the landlord both reached for them. Not money; the landlord pulled back.

Perhaps a dozen handwritten papers, folded in half. The policeman couldn't make much of them – didn't look like any French he'd ever seen. He wondered how you were supposed to add things like this to the *Report Ordinaire*.

———◆———

Fouché was trying to discipline himself to work by logic.

It didn't always seem to produce the results desired.

Sometimes he would think of Lavoisier: the proud brittle old man, who had changed the world with his rational deductions; but who could not escape the world, and had in the end proved an incompetent navigator of its currents.

What is the lesson of Lavoisier?

He had kept some of the records of the Royal Commission on his desk.

He found it soothing sometimes to read their measured style, and to follow their steady solid steps. They were a kind of music. And he kept them on his desk as a totem: a sign to himself of the man he was.

The desk was not as tidy today as it should have been. Papers were not straight; they overlapped; piles were not distinct. Of late he had been working longer in this room, and the effort to maintain his control of all of the information that floated and dripped through the ministry had left him sometimes feverish; energy became haste became distraction.

A knock, on the edge of his consciousness, and Guilbert was in the room.

Fouché was still looking at his desk. He'd become proud of his facility with the information. The faster the papers came in, the faster the information was assimilated to its proper place in his mind.

'They're waiting for you, Monsieur.'

Fouché did not feel like going to the Convention to discuss the government's obligations for costs incurred by the administration of Saint-Domingue. That was not his Revolution.

He was patrolling behind his desk now. It stood between him and Guilbert. His fingers brushed at papers.

His eye stuck on the bottom of a piece of paper, protruding ugly from under another dossier and at an angle. Within the text, his eye caught a name: Lavalier.

Emma Lavalier, who knew foreigners. Emma Lavalier who knew Roland, and Danton, and so many people. Emma Lavalier the suspect. Emma Lavalier the potential asset.

He lifted the top dossier, and his spread hand made to straighten the paper that mentioned Emma Lavalier, momentarily eased by the even order of the printing.

Which was strange. Because he could not imagine or recall why the woman Lavalier should have appeared in a printed document. He had written reports of her, and fascinating reading some of them were. But nothing printed, surely.

Instead of straightening the document, he pulled it towards him. It wasn't a document about her, or about St-Denis. It was one of the papers of the Royal Commission.

– in this experiment as throughout, the Commissioners were most careful to ensure that no prior or innate susceptibility, instinct, preference or prejudice should be able to tarnish the purity of the result. Thus a diversity of subjects was tested, some with vessels that had been magnetized and some with vessels that had not, and on this occasion in order to have one subject who was known to be of open mind yet also free from any possibility of favouritism towards an external interest, our Secretary Lavalier was prevailed upon to take –

Lavoisier's words to him: an insignificant old functionary had been their secretary; the man was dead now; the secretary had arranged the copying, and thereby established the arrangement of communication that was still working years later.

And this man had been named Lavalier.

'We have had occasion, Guilbert, to discuss the value of coincidence.' The age would be right. Emma Lavalier could easily be the widow.

Guilbert waited.

'We must learn from Monsieur le Professeur Lavoisier the address of the copyist, who was the hub of communication for the Friends of Magnetism.'

Another anonymous little town in northern France. Another cheap inn. Another bare room. Another shared bed.

'Don't think me ungrateful, Raph. But if I wanted to spend the rest of my life bunking with rogues in provincial taverns I'd have joined the theatre or the army.' Pinsent dropped down onto the bed, and it sagged and swayed alarmingly.

He struggled up to a sitting position. Benjamin was looking out of the window, and checking the fastening. 'Interesting thing about you, Ned. When you start complaining properly I know you're feeling in better spirits. What about me, anyway? You're hardly an asset if I want to entice a petticoat home.' He sat on the side of the bed and groaned as he pulled at his boots. 'Thank God you've lost a bit of weight this last week, or I'd barely get a corner of the mattress.'

'I ain't facing the wall for any man. If you want your cock easing you can go down to the parish pump like the rest of us.'

'Heartless, Ned. Heartless.' Back towards his companion, his fingers felt instinctively for his purse, and then for the lump strung against his chest.

'Still there, is it Raph?'

'Eh?' He didn't turn.

'Whatever you've had stowed in there since we left Paris. I know it ain't a heart.'

Benjamin turned, and pulled his shirt open enough to show the pouch. 'It ain't money, alas.' He closed and straightened his shirt. 'But it might buy us a ticket to London nonetheless.'

Pinsent was grave; watchful. 'My geography may be sketchy, but we ain't heading for the Channel any more. Nor Switzerland.'

Benjamin shook his head. Then he folded his coat, propped it against the foot of the bed, and stretched out in the opposite direction to his companion. 'I had a visitor back in Évreux,' he said, looking at the ceiling. 'Not that royalist peri, sadly.'

Pinsent waited.

'We'd always wondered, hadn't we, about the men behind Greene? Bit of business or a bit of politics. Keeping him afloat, giving us a bit of sport.' He glanced down, at Pinsent's face, still watching. 'Don't think we had any illusions, did we? Had a rough idea what was going on, and doing well enough out of it.' Pinsent grunted. 'Well, I met one of them at last.'

Pinsent's head came forwards. He still didn't say anything.

'Just the sort of turd you'd expect to be slipping down the gutters of government. The sort of malicious Christian beast they used to set up at school to lord it over the other boys.' Another grunt. 'Anyway, with poor Hal off the books, they're short of a hand or two to do their dirty work.'

'And in return?'

'Loyal service to His Majesty, get the slate wiped clean.' Silence. Edward Pinsent was contemplating the condition of his own slate.

'So you're staying? Hide in the bushes and wait for instructions?'

'I ain't just hiding, Ned, and I ain't just waiting.' He sat upright. 'First thing is to get the Revolution off my back. Off our backs. Damned if I'm spending my days skulking in some provincial pot-house. These last weeks I've been building that creeping Scotsman up as the main act; British spy and royalist agent. Well, it's time to put their attention there once and for all.' He eased himself back down onto the makeshift pillow.

Pinsent considered it for a time; watched his friend; watched the grey profile, the eyes lost in the air. Then: 'You believe 'em, Raph?'

'Mm?'

'Do your duty and hie for home, fatted calf and the thanks of Parliament?'

'You don't believe them, I take it.'

'Men have been setting themselves up over me all my life, and not one of 'em's ever said a straight word. You're being – '

Benjamin's fist thumped down on Pinsent's leg. 'Damn you, Ned! I don't have a choice, do I? What else is there?'

<hr />

Fouché sits surrounded by papers. Individual sentences from them murmur back and forth over him, an unruly conversation he strains to understand.

n.b. – Meaux, Sphinx tavern, a safe haven and men of good character in the district, where + may shelter.

. . . It is essential, dear K, that the man in question not survive to tell his tales to the revolutionary authorities . . .

Another route: St-Denis gate (first watch after sunset) – Pointoise cross – (fresh horses Magny, the Sun) – Dr J. Belyue – fresh horses Fleury – or boat with G. from Pont l'Arche – Honfleur either inn or school.

. . . I have quite deceived the British fops of St-Denis. With my old acquaintance Greene now out of the way, dear Monsieur, now I am freer to collaborate with Pr-

. . . maps you seek may be provided by the usual source in the rue de Verneuil. Vespucci will serve as your key.

[SS K/1/X1 VARIOUS] (AUTHOR TRANSLATION)

Fouché is known now as the master of documents. The sergeant of police of Évreux knew he'd found something significant, and the dozen handwritten papers galloped to Paris, and in Paris to the ministry, and in the ministry they were naturally carried straight to Fouché.

It's the *Pr-* that catches the attention, of course; the last breath of an unfinished letter. On an instinct of discipline, Fouché has forced himself to consider alternative interpretations – *Pr*ofesseur Lavoisier? *Pr*o-royalist elements? *Pr*ominent somethings? – but it was discipline become affectation. The interpretation is obvious and striking. This solitary British spy, working with the Prussian, the man reputed the greatest of the spies and the greatest threat to France.

And this Kinnaird, Fouché's respect for him is increasing dramatically. Kinnaird features in every outrage. The story of his escape has told of his daring. His continued survival has told of his skill. And despite being hunted, he is everywhere and active.

He had been reported in Meaux, at around the same time as Bonfils was passing through the place, immediately before Bonfils's death. And another report has reached Fouché from Évreux. A pair of royalists, the Comte de Charette and his daughter, had been tracked thus far, but in Évreux the trail was lost. Subsequent enquiries have shown that from Évreux they were somehow spirited away, no doubt to the Channel and to safety in England. In Évreux is the mysterious Kinnaird, and in Évreux hunted royalists are miraculously saved.

Fouché spends two full hours noting and cross-referencing, commissioning copies of other reports that must be associated with these, adding his own marginalia based on other related documents. Then he regathers together the sheaf of papers, trying to hush the voices.

The dossier on Kinnaird is growing fat.

***

'Crossroads, Ned.'

'I am aware of the concept, Raph.' The road in front of them went left towards Rouen, and right towards Paris.

'In more meanings than one.'

'You ain't about to get prosy, are you? Not on my empty stomach.'

'Listen, old fellow.' Benjamin was gazing out into the fields. 'I've been playing the solitary fox a bit recently. Not very comradely.'

'Recently?'

'Well, I – ' Benjamin had missed the sarcasm, until he glanced at his companion's face. Pinsent was watching him with something like pity.

'Raphael Benjamin, you've been playing solitary fox since the cradle. And because you're the luckiest devil who ever lived, the rest of the world has cheerfully opened its purse or its legs and followed along, to see where the fox might lead.'

Benjamin was uncomfortable. 'What I'm trying to say is – '

'What you're trying to say is damned impertinent. Some men lead their pack, Raph, and most men are in the pack. But it don't mean that those of us in the pack are all Hackney clogs. When I find better sport, or some fading madam who needs a congenial mate to guard the door and keep an eye on the books, I'll take my leave of you and good riddance. Til then I'll tag along, thank'ee.'

'I'm playing for myself, Ned. I own it.' Benjamin was gazing at the junction again. 'We've favours enough owed to us. You could scrape enough to get home, and you've a good enough tale to tell of what we've done here. Get out while the going's good, will you?'

'But I won't, Raph, will I? Now get along before I become discourteous.'

'Yes, Ned.'

The horses began to trot towards Paris.

'It's a jolly enough life, Raph, and there's always sport out there. But the road never ends, does it?'

'No, Ned.'

———— ◆ ————

On 4th November, according to the register, a party of Americans visited the ministry. A courtesy visit, Roland called it, when arranging that he should only be obliged to spend five minutes with them before leaving them to Fouché. One at least was new off the boat at Le Havre. Coming to review arrangements at the embassy. Fouché was thinking: *You don't send someone across the Atlantic to review arrangements.*

Fouché didn't know what he thought of Americans. English, Prussians, Italians: such men he could place. Americans . . . Americans were something new. France had helped them in their rising against the English, of course. But . . . new. Unknowable.

He thought of Franklin, the former American ambassador, and his strange contacts in Paris. He thought of the current American ambassador, and his involvement with royal documents.

He knew immediately which the new arrival was as soon as the three men entered his office, and knew him for the senior. The man in the middle was not much taller than the two either side of him, but he was substantially bigger. Not fat, just . . . big; solid. He didn't appear to possess a neck. And above all, Fouché thought, he was controlled. His movements, even just stepping into an office, were simple and certain.

His eyes too moved little, and moved sure.

He sat carefully, as if the chair might not hold him. Given the size of his shoulders, it was a distinct possibility.

'Mr Fowch is the minister's principal aide,' one of the companions said.

'He's the coming man, aren't you, Mr Foosh?' the other said.

Fouché smiled thin humility. It wasn't easy to follow that.

'I've been hearing about you, Monsieur Fouché,' the man in the middle said. His voice was as solid and sure as everything else about him. He pronounced the name correctly, except that he over-emphasized the second syllable, so that it seemed to drift away. 'My name is Murad.'

'You're most welcome to Paris, Mr Murad.' Fouché gave a little bow, and finally found a reply to the earlier comments. 'Such energies and abilities as I have are devoted to our citizens, and our allies. I am honoured to have you here.' He found his fluency both nauseating and somehow satisfying. *Necessary arts.* 'You are . . . visiting your embassy, Mr Murad?'

'That's right.'

'Some . . . concerns? Some problems?'

'No.'

'A long way to come.'

'Yes.'

Fouché smiled. Murad didn't smile.

'We shall be happy to offer you any assistance you may need.'

'Thank you.'

There was silence. Fouché was irritated, uncomfortable, with this impassive man who even as a guest would make no effort at politesse. In this office, the guests were supposed to be uncomfortable, and their tongues were supposed to be looser.

One of the companions, looking uneasily between Fouché and Murad, started to say something about the Convention's recent declaration but Fouché spoke over him. 'Your embassy has been much caught up in recent events.' He spoke deliberately sharply.

The American said nothing. He nodded, very faintly, but it wasn't clear if it was acknowledgement or appraisal of Fouché.

'The American minister was given a dossier of documents by the former King, before he was overthrown.' Silence. 'Did you know that?'

'I did.'

'Indeed. Perhaps it would be more convenient if we took those documents now. They are the property of the state.'

Silence. Then one of the companions said, uneasily, 'Monsoor, are you asking for the documents?'

Murad's eyes flicked to him. Then back to Fouché, as he said: 'I think if Monsieur Fouché knows the documents were given to our minister, then he knows the documents were destroyed.'

Fouché turned his anger into a smile. 'Indeed. But – if I may ask explicitly – would you be so kind as to check whether there are any other documents, undestroyed, temporarily in the hands of the American embassy, which we may take back?'

'We will check. We will give back to you any documents that are the property of the revolutionary government of France. We shall keep any documents that are the personal property of Louis, or that have become the property of the American minister.'

Fouché nodded slowly, forcing the smile into place. 'Naturally. Much caught up, I said. Unofficially too. Even your Mr Franklin is still a figure.' For once, he thought he got a reaction. The American's eyes seemed to narrow. 'He was a member of a circle of notable correspondents some years ago, and still some of this circle write to each other, and still copies are sent to Mr Franklin. Presumably via your embassy, now that Mr Franklin is no longer minister and has returned to America.'

Silence.

Fouché kept the smile; took a deep breath through it. 'I speculate that you have come to Paris, Monsieur Murad, to make investigations based on those documents from the Tuileries. I speculate that you are on a mission of espionage.' Murad stayed silent. 'You don't answer?'

'You didn't ask a question.' Even the sharpest retort came steadily from the big American. His voice never changed. His body never moved.

'You don't object to my making such an assertion?'

'It's a free country now. So we are told.'

———— ◆ ————

Emma Lavalier and Raphael Benjamin considered each other from discreet opposite sides of the stone summer house.

'You're grown thin, Raph.'

'I've been running fast.'

'And discreet. Thank you for finding me here.'

Benjamin scowled. 'I'll be out of the woods soon enough, I fancy. But until then I shouldn't dream of inconveniencing you.'

'My most charming fugitive.' They exchanged an old glance. 'But what's the point of it all, then? We are merely defending life, when life is grown tedious and empty.'

He smiled. 'It will return, that old life. I've just been playing the game a little more quietly for a spell. Hal Greene covered us all in shit, somehow. But I've now created a much more enticing bait for the authorities. It seems that our strange Scottish acquaintance has been most active in his misdeeds around France, and I've made sure there are documents to prove it.'

She considered this.

'For all of our sakes, Emma.'

She nodded.

They stood.

'Was it truly care for my reputation, Raph?' He frowned. 'And not your own? You are a private doubt; I am a public question. Who is more dangerous to be seen with?'

He stepped forwards. He took her hand.

'My poor Emma,' he said. He kissed the hand, and turned away into the afternoon.

Later, that evening, Emma Lavalier and Manon Roland found each other in a corner of the salon of Madame Henaut.

'Dear Emma, my vanity sometimes tells me that I am in touch with the real France. And then I see you, and I remember that you know more than anyone.'

'Dear Manon, only the trivial details known by the maid or the foot-soldier; we are all in your shadow.'

'I fear that Paris is gossip only – noise and nothing real. Today all they discussed in the Convention was the squabble between Custine and Kellermann. What of their armies? What of the foreign threat?' Bewitching smile. 'But for news of dangerous foreigners I must ask my Emma.'

Careful. It brought back the conversation with Raph. Her ambiguous position. Her over-prominent reputation.

She contrived a pose of dignity.

'In truth, dear Manon, I am grown rather distant from my foreign friends. The British, in particular. It no longer seems appropriate for a Frenchwoman to be seen with such people, when one knows a little of their games. One in particular – I know that your dear husband, and Monsieur Fouché, have been most anxious about him – the man Kinnaird . . . He was at my house once, you know. But now I learn him to be most dangerous.' She shook her head. 'It is a matter of duty, I think.'

Manon Roland nodded.

It will have to serve.

In a carriage, swaying and jolting over the cobbles, Murad the American was once again the centre of gravity.

'You didn't feel like confiding in our friend, sir?' one of his two companions said, head bobbing against the square of daylight.

'I did not, Mr Shields.'

'If the British are reading our correspondence, the French might have useful information about it,' the other said. 'British names. Contact men. Channels.'

'I presume they do. That reptilian gentleman didn't look like anyone's fool.'

'The French are the closest thing we have to allies. I reckon they rather feel we owe them for supporting us in the war. Now they're fighting the same fight as us. Same ideals.'

Murad's head swung slowly to face the man.

'You ever see one of those machines – those death blades – in Philadelphia?'

The companion shook his head uncertainly. 'No, sir.'

Murad still hadn't blinked. 'Uh-huh. You plan on ever seeing one?'

Surer now. 'No, sir.'

'Reckon I've fought for liberty as much as any man.' The other two nodded. 'And I believe powerful strong in equality. And in the right company I'll take a little fraternity. But I won't tell these people how to run their Revolution; and I'd choose that we be left alone to run our republic likewise.' He sat back against the upholstery. 'Now: tell me about the lady.'

Raphael Benjamin.

Sir Raphael Benjamin, Baronet.

Baronetcy tenuous, obliged to fly the roost, temporarily resident in the anus of Europe, where baronetcies and all such are being outlawed.

Estate: one dashed fine coat, the clothes I stand up in, a change of shirt, a blade, a pistol, a purse of small coins, and promissory notes from a collection of whores, gamblers and dead men; and one of the French royal jewels.

The tavern ain't going to accept a diamond for the room. Deference's gone right out the window.

Society: none.

One broken Englishman, farting and snoring on the adjacent palliasse. Good old Ned.

None too glorious, is it, Raph?

Emma.

But Emma finds me . . . what, now? Uncouth? No, she ain't that snooty. Dangerous? Perhaps, but not in any exciting way.

Emma finds me unnecessary.

Society: none.

Memories of companionship, of glittering roaring evenings, of aces bold in the candlelight, of ivory bodies under the moon.

A Paris slum, an ageing man on a palliasse, dreaming of flesh that has sagged and died now. None too glorious. One of nature's aristocrats, now too damned close to nature.

Ned's catechism. Smith, and Yeo, and Swan. Good men old and rancid before their time, derelict and embarrassing in tavern bunkrooms.

Sure I have no more reason to live than they.

The London shadow-men. Bullies, blackmailers and pimps.

But a cause. A chance.

A spree. A sport. A prize.

Documents. A royal servant fleeing Paris, with the last scraps of his identity and loyalty.

Well, we've all tried that.

The servant Bonfils, who had died so strangely, in the company of Hal Greene. Also dead; also strangely.

I shall not cough and slouch my life out. They shall not find me on a lousy blanket in the puddle of my last piss; they shall not throw my corpse out with the night's pot.

In the chaos of this new France, there shall be distinction, and brilliance, and glory.

———————◆———————

Fouché rode out of Paris with his habitual unease. The daylight that glared at him as he emerged from the shadow of the St-Denis gate, and the mean smudges of rustic houses in the landscape, seemed as the German forests must have seemed to the legions of Caesar. Simply being on horseback was discomfort enough.

The beast began to lope and lurch towards St-Denis. Lavoisier had named his copyist – a man in St-Denis, a man who doubled as the apothecary.

Fouché lived in ideas. In information. The physical was no more real than what it represented: support; treason; possibility. Even faces were only as real as what they showed or hid.

But he had realized, uneasily, that he needed to see St-Denis.

He saw the apothecary's house, and wondered at it. Like many such places, it served as a post office, a point of reference where messages might be held for local people.

This was the place where the copyist worked for the Friends of Magnetism, copying and circulating their letters to each other. Chosen by their secretary, the late Monsieur Lavalier, who as a local man no doubt knew the place and would have come to a reliable arrangement with the copyist. Near enough to Paris for convenience.

What is the significance of this?

Fouché couldn't find it in the two-storey building, the fading plaster and the slumping window frames, nor in the few men sitting inside.

Men of prominence, doing work known to the state, contrive an arrangement for their correspondence. There was nothing illegal in it; nothing strange.

And Lavalier? It was probable that Emma Lavalier knew of the arrangement her late husband had made. Was she in communication with men like Lavoisier, and Bailly, and Guillotin, and the American Franklin? What if she was?

What could she be to them? Fouché couldn't see Lavoisier attending one of her dubious parties.

I am over-thinking this.

The significance is not in the connection between Lavalier, and Lavoisier, and anyone else. The significance is information. He thought fondly of his desk, back in bustling vital Paris. *This is a world where information is power, and where information flows in infinite and unimagined channels.* He conceived of the world as a vast net, individuals of greater and lesser significance connected by strings of correspondence, copied and couriered through otherwise useless places like this. Power was not about strength: which person you threatened, or which road you put your army on. Power was how you understood and sensed the movement of information in the net.

I must read it.

Guilbert should be instructed: he should use his police agents to control this place. Not the people: but the information that came and went.

I must read it all.

He saw the inn at the sign of the Tambour, where the man Greene had lived, and the man Kinnaird.

The British provocateurs had inhabited these streets. Somewhere here, the woman Lavalier held her notorious salons.

It seemed a vile place, to Fouché. He gained no new insights from his visit; but what should he have expected of physical things? Reassuringly, the meanness diminished the significance of the people he was trying to understand. They could not be much, in a place like this. The sight of Paris, massive on the horizon as he awkwardly turned the horse around at last, was a great comfort.

Lucie Gérard saw him, from the shadow of a clump of trees. He reminded her of Kinnaird, so pale and out of place. He made her feel cold.

Emma Lavalier saw him from her window, and wondered if every day he visited every street in France.

Once again, Raphael Benjamin went to call on the sister of the late Xavier Bonfils. This time he wrote first – *a visit of courtesy, of condolence; the hope that the community of servants of the master of the servant might demonstrate their continued concern for one of their number in her sorrow.*

She'd taken the bait. Even in these times, the possibility of charity outweighed caution. Again, Benjamin found her face behind the door, pale in the gloom of her mean home. She let him in to the parlour this time, and she was silent until he was seated.

She'd prepared a little speech, he could tell. As soon as he'd sat down she was off, fists clutched together in front of her and eyes blinking hard as she recited. It was very kind of the gentleman to call. It was very heartening that she was not alone in the saddest moment of her life. She knew nothing of politics, she would not say anything about the King or about the government, but she hoped that in these difficult times there might still be rewards for loyalty, for men of good heart and honest faith.

Benjamin had a speech of his own, and it followed accordingly. What it must mean to lose a brother. Bonfils as a symbol of loyalty in the most uncertain times. The importance of those who were left preserving – in a most discreet way, naturally, Madame – their values and fellowship. Regrettably in these hard times there was so little to spare, but if she would overcome herself enough to accept a tiny gift of sympathy from one who admired her brother . . . No, he insisted – and he really had to, and it bloody hurt, and he wondered again how much he was going have to spend to buy back his name. *Damn sure that Louis and London could afford this better than I can.* If he, Keith Kinnaird, could ever assist her, she had only to write to him in St-Denis or mention his name to other sympathizers.

She accepted: a little curtsey, and he saw her desperation in the tight clutch at the purse. Monsieur must accept some wine; she was sorry that it was not of the best.

It was of the worst, but Benjamin suffered a polite couple of sips.

Then he asked – *perhaps a strange request, Madame, but we pay our respects as best we can to the spirits of those who have gone before* – to see where dear old Xavier had stayed while he'd been here. She hesitated, then nodded, and ushered him out. He didn't take the wine with him.

The bedroom was on the second floor, tiny and barren. Benjamin walked to the centre of it, trying to seem solemn.

He didn't know what he was looking for.

Something about the man, Xavier Bonfils. Something about his character, or his habits. Something about the book he'd been carrying when his sister had last seen him, a book obviously special to him. What might have happened to it, between the moment when he walked out of this house with it tight under his arm and when he arrived in the inn in

Meaux without it. What it might have been, to be so precious.

The walls were whitewashed; the timbers were bare. The bedstead was crude, and the bedding had been removed. There was a chair beside the bed, splay-footed and rickety, with a crucifix lying on it. There were two spindly iron candlesticks on a bare mantelpiece. It was a skeleton of a room.

He turned a full circle, slowly: trying to show gravity, trying to take in the room. The woman was watching him from the doorway.

Between the two candlesticks, a nail had been driven into the wall. Something no bigger than a hand's breadth or two had hung here. The whitewash had covered the nail.

He had no idea what the book might be. But – particularly if he decided to keep a hold of the second jewel for rather longer – this strangely important souvenir of the royal palace would be something to sweeten London.

The crucifix had a hook at its head; so that the son of Mary could take one more nail. The crucifix usually hung on the wall.

Bonfils's sister was still in the doorway, watching.

Your brother was a man of faith, Madame, I think.

Yes, he most certainly was. Nothing excessive, of course. Nothing showy. A good Catholic. The little he had he gave to the Church for charity. He always sought the company of men of the Church. Thoughtful, dignified men. Like poor Xavier.

Benjamin could hear the emotion rising in her voice, could feel himself getting irritated. *There might be something in it.* 'And, dear Madame – contain yourself, I beg you, for his sake – did our poor Xavier receive any letters before he left?'

Through red-nose sniffs, she nodded, and Benjamin felt his excitement grow. 'I remember, because it seemed such a relief to him. As he read it he kept saying "a good man, a good man", over and over.' Benjamin waited, heart thumping his impatience. 'The librarian of Meaux, he called him. A good man.'

Her voice was breaking again, at the thought of the good men. Benjamin was remembering his games as Kinnaird in the inns of Meaux, tracking the last journey of Bonfils to his death in Montmirail. And he remembered now the cathedral looming over Meaux. He made his courtesies as fast as he could.

'My trail grows cold, Guilbert.' Fouché's hands moved like a magician's over the papers in front of him. 'The ink begins to fade on these. No pattern. And nothing new.'

Guilbert nodded. Guilbert stayed silent.

'The secrets of the royal correspondence of France are as far from me as ever.' His voice was soft; a pale voice, to match skin and hair. 'There must be so much. And it's somewhere in Paris. Or am I wrong, and everything was destroyed?'

Guilbert said, 'There are other people we could bring in.' His fingers flickered, so fast that Fouché wasn't sure he'd seen aright. 'Other questions.'

Fouché contemplated him. 'Guilbert, I think you could rack every royalist in Paris and they wouldn't know the truth. Or we wouldn't recognize the truth.'

Guilbert gazed back. It seemed to him worth trying. He said: 'If you don't find these documents – if they stay hidden – are they dangerous?'

Fouché shrugged. 'I can't know, dear Guilbert, can I?' His eyes changed. 'But the possibility! Think of the possibilities in that correspondence. To have every traitor in France, every two-faced trimmer, in one's hand. To know of Louis's intrigues with the other kings.' The enthusiasm cooled. 'And I fear we're losing a race. I fear there are other men out there, who seek these documents, and they are more active than we and they may know more than we.' His hand wavered over one page. 'This Kinnaird . . . this prodigious agent of intrigue. He is everywhere – and we are nowhere!'

'If they know more than we do, and we could find them or follow them somehow . . . '

Fouché's smile was dead. 'It's a charming notion, Guilbert. But it's meaningless, isn't it? Unless . . . ' Guilbert waited. 'I wonder about St-Denis, and that damned apothecary's shop. If we have nothing else to try, we might try something there.'

To the librarian, Cathedral of Meaux

Sir,

I write as a friend and servant of a cause much troubled in these days.

I write as one of a community who knew dear Xavier Bonfils, and knew him for a loyal and pious man. Those who knew him and those who believe in what he believed in do all surely regret his death, victim of one of ten thousand anonymous violent hands that do torment this land.

[Approximate translation; original French very confused at this point.]

I believe that in his flight from Paris our friend entrusted to you some token of his past, which he believed too precious to be risked on his solitary journey. And in truth he was wise, for had he not done so it would already been in the hands of his murderers. Nor could he have found dearer surer hands than yours to receive it, for he was ever a man of faith.

And yet I speculate that you might find this token a burden. I speculate that you might, particularly after our friend's death, fear that the continued possession of it should bring you and your establishment into danger.

Know, then, that I have it in my power to take this token into safer keeping — to take it, indeed, quite out of the power of those who would use it for ill. Know that if you should find it to your benefit to be relieved of this burden, it may be arranged with the greatest speed and secrecy, and in the full assurance that the objects of our dear Bonfils in entrusting it to you will be upheld.

If I may assist you in this way, send me word at the house of Gérard in St-Denis.

Your dignity and security is precious to those of us who respect the old values. Please believe that I would do nothing that brings you risk or shame. Believe that we look to your endurance as a sign of what we prize. Believe my hope that we might share happier times.

In true faith, I remain yours,

Keith Kinnaird

He reappeared out of the infinite early one morning, a grey thing in the pallor of the dawn, standing in the chicken shit with the round-shouldered slouch of all the beggars until Lucie opened the back door and his shoulders came up and then his head and the eyes, those cold eyes, were staring into her again and it was as if the last weeks hadn't happened.

Every instinct told her she should ignore him, close her eyes and hope he vanished, slam the back door and escape through the front.

He gazed at her, and she thought: *it is all mad*.

Lucie shrugged. She turned, and walked back into the house, leaving the door open.

From the battered chair, just as in his first visit to the house, Kinnaird watched her.

'How do you, Lucie?' His voice was low, warm.

She scowled through this and his other courtesies about her father, about trade. 'You're still hunted,' she said.

'Yes.'

'You should have stayed in the forest.'

'For ever? There's no point in hiding, Lucie, if it's not to be ready to return.' Her weary scowl at this wisdom seemed familiar to him, and he felt it like reassurance. 'How is St-Denis? The people I know?'

'Same police as ever, same games. But . . . everything matters more now. Everyone goes more careful.' He nodded. 'The other British – the two you knew – they're still fugitives like you. But I saw one of them.' She smiled, cold. 'Easier for them. They're not as famous as you.'

He didn't return the smile. 'Madame Lavalier?'

'Goes to Paris a lot. She has to be careful now. She stands out. Enough to be known; not enough to save her.'

He nodded again, sombre.

'What do you want, Kinnaird?' He didn't answer. 'Why are you here? What now?'

'Now I'm back, Lucie. I'm back and I've unfinished business here. I want to know how my name has been upturned; and I want to right it. And I still want to find out what happened to Hal.'

'Why? Why not let it all lie? What does it matter now?'

He just looked at her. His expression hadn't changed at all. Fixed on his face: a faint wild smile.

It was infuriating. 'You can't stay here!' She added, more measured: 'I mean, St-Denis isn't safe. The police know all about the foreigners here. They're watching the Tambour. They're watching my father, Kinnaird: the work he does; the letters that come and go.'

He considered this. 'Interesting. I only came to say hallo, but that's interesting.' He stood. He came forwards a step. 'I need you, Lucie; I need you as my go-between. I've a place to stay – not far from here; they're people I trust, for they're outcasts like me. But I need you to be my contact with the world.'

She watched him.

'I'll pay, obviously.'

'Ten francs the day. And I continue my normal work. People'd notice otherwise.'

'Mm. I was thinking twenty. Let's call it fifteen. But you'll be mine. Pont de Neuilly at dusk each day, and whenever else I get you word.' Another step forwards. 'You'll be my ears and my eyes, Lucie. You'll help me feel my way into St-Denis and even into Paris. You'll be my guardian angel.'

Again she shrugged. *It is all mad.*

In the doorway, behind him, she saw him stop, saw his head turning slowly as he quartered the ground.

'What happened to you, Kinnaird?'

She had become adept at pronouncing the name – or a more elaborate version of it, giving a weight to the vowels and the long-buried 'r' that no tight-mouthed Scot or ignorant Englishman ever did.

Kinnaird liked it. He turned back to her. 'You were . . . you were a rabbit,' she said, matter of fact. 'And I left you in the wildest forest in France.' She glanced down at her lap, then up into his eyes. 'And I knew it would kill you.' At this Kinnaird smiled, and nodded slow. 'But you survived, and you came back.'

'Lucie, for a Scot – the forgotten son of a race of forgotten sons – the whole world is a forest. We learn fast.'

'Anything for Kinnaird?' The parlour of the apothecary in St-Denis was quiet – one other man there, slumped on a chair and staring into space. Benjamin had moved carefully through St-Denis, and in the shop he came close to the counter to ask the question. He didn't think his face was known, but there had to be a chance that someone somewhere might know the real Kinnaird.

The Scotsman hadn't been seen for weeks. *Followed old Greene, perhaps?* Little chance of him getting the letter first.

The man behind the counter was fidgety. 'Ah, but yes, Monsieur Kinnaird!' One risk dismissed immediately: the Scotsman either didn't use the place for his letters, or was too unmemorable. Benjamin had had an explanation ready, but it was much better to be thought Kinnaird. 'For you we have two letters.'

One was all Benjamin needed.

Dear friend,

your message came to me like cool water in the fever. The confirmation of the death of our friend is sad indeed, and yet we have surely become used to sadness in these terrible times, and must begin to fear that we shall never find any ease for our torments before we have enjoyed the great easing which comes to all true men of true faith.

Sincerely, your proposal would be most convenient. I do not wish to retain that which is not properly mine. In the turbulence, I cannot properly guarantee the good-keeping of the book. If it could be returned to those more fitted to possess it and better able to care for it and all that it represents, I should be doubly relieved.

You may visit me at any time of day or indeed night: we are used to visitors to our library, and travellers in search of a bed. Your name will alone secure you what you seek.

[SS K/1/X1/30] (AUTHOR TRANSLATION)

Benjamin's heart thumped once, a burst of satisfaction as soon as he skimmed the message. His letter, in the congenial guise of Kinnaird, had hit home. Bonfils had wanted to protect his book, whatever it was and whatever its secrets. Or perhaps he had wanted to escape it: an uncomfortable and incriminating link to his royal master. Either way, he had left it with his acquaintance, the librarian to the Bishop of Meaux, in whose care it might be safer and more anonymous.

Still lounging against the counter, he read the message a second time. The man was scared. He read it in the generalizations, in the absence of salutation or signature. The hint that a night visit might be preferred; the eagerness to be rid of the royal family's mysterious book. The willingness to overlook the faint possibility that it was a deception; which it was, of course, but not as the man might have thought.

Most men were focused on individual preservation, and with their heads down and their bags packed for an emergency might hope to come through the instability unscathed. But this man . . . their whole world was destroyed. Whatever happened in the wars – whether or not the Prussians found the gumption for another try against the citizen armies of France – it didn't seem likely that world would be restored. He tucked the letter into his coat.

Benjamin no more than glanced at the opening of the other letter to Kinnaird. A triviality – *have the package that you hoped for* – some damned bit of merchantry – *obliged if you would collect it from* – He refolded it, pushed it back across the counter. 'I'll leave this second one here for now. Reminder.' *That's right, old fellow; carry on trading turnips while some of us scheme and shine for Britain.*

<hr />

An attic in Aubervilliers; cheap lodging conveniently – or uncertainly – between Paris and St-Denis.

'I've sport tonight.'

Pinsent began to rise from his bed. He was looking paler now, Benjamin thought; flabbier. 'Hold up; I'll – '

'No. No, that's all right, old lad.' Hand on shoulder. 'Solitary fox tonight.

Foil rather than sabre, eh?'

'Foil rather than – ? Oh, go to hell then.'

Benjamin smiled. 'For that jaunt I'll have you with me, old lad.'

———— ◆ ————

Later, in the squalor of St-Denis, dirt streets and greying plaster walls and mean low eaves, there suddenly flashed a dart of beauty: something clean and proud and alive. As soon as he saw Emma Lavalier walking down the street towards him, Benjamin hesitated.

She was walking along the other side of the street. Her head was erect, her gaze direct forwards. She did not engage with the scene around her, with the lesser people. He knew that she was being careful where she trod, but the gaze never broke and she seemed to glide.

It was romantic fancy, of course. He felt a curse growling in his throat at his own foolishness. *Emma gets shit on her shoes like everyone else.* She was a dozen paces away, serene.

Half a dozen paces away she slowed and stopped, and first her eyes and then her head turned to him.

They watched each other's faces for a while; enjoying it.

Then some question in her face, some . . . apprehension.

Very slightly, Benjamin shook his head. Then he nodded, formally, and kept his head down until she had walked on.

But with Emma, the shit's grateful.

He watched her go: her rump, her back, her shoulders, the high neck and the hair under her cap, the hair shining black, a crystal of coal left in the ashes.

———— ◆ ————

From inside her chemise, Lucie produced a folded paper. It took a further moment for Kinnaird's mind to move from the chemise to the paper.

'For you.'

His name was on the outside, but not as a salutation inside.

Monsieur, we have the package that you hoped for. We should be obliged if you would collect it from the premises of our agent Lessart in the rue Sainte-Anne at your earliest opportunity. The door will be opened to you at any time. We trust that we may continue our co-operation, for we apprehend that we may be of further profit to you.

There was no signature. But beneath the message a symbol had been drawn with half a dozen strokes of the pen: a crude crown.

Kinnaird frowned at it for a time. Then his eyes came up, to find Lucie's. He watched her. She stared back.

She broke first. 'It's a trap.' His eyebrows rose. 'Isn't it?'

He stayed silent.

'Well, do you know what it's talking about?'

He shook his head. 'No, Lucie, I don't.'

'Well then.'

Kinnaird smiled. He looked, to Lucie, somehow hungry.

'But if someone is trying to trap me, I cannot ignore it.'

She stared again.

⸻ ◆ ⸻

Manon Roland and Emma Lavalier circled and nuzzled each other like cats. Discreetly across the tea-table, world-wise and toying with small talk, they sniffed at each other's charm, felt each other's influence, licked at each other's style. Lavalier wondered at Roland's salon, her power, her contacts; considered the modish revolutionary look she had started among women of her society, the hair worn shorter and loose cap and chemise, considered the seductiveness of a woman in the ill-fitting clothes of a man, of a clean woman with just a bit of dirt. Roland as ever wondered at Lavalier: the stories of her parties; the people she must know, the knowledge she must have. She considered the poise of the creature opposite her, the fresh lace and the faded satin, an artful preservation of an older style; considered the lure, for men, of new ideals and lost dreams.

They spoke of Prussians; and parvenu lawyers and untrained soldiers; and Manon Roland's fears about Roland in the Paris climate and the unpredictable winds of the Convention; and Camille Desmoulins and what men saw in him and what women saw in him; and what to believe in, without church or religion or king. Circled and nuzzled each other like cats.

'I don't believe I saw Robespierre at your last salon.' *Is he the future, and are you with him?*

'Have you seen Danton lately?' *Where is the Revolution, and do you know any more?*

'The faces of the women in the Tuileries mob!' *What role is our sex to play in this generation?*

'It is such a pleasure to be out of the crowd.'

'Such a pleasure to spend time with you.'

Together, intertwined, we might be more resilient than any of them.

The door clicked open and they both looked up, interrupted, watchful.

'My dear . . . ' It was Roland. 'Fouché takes his leave of us.'

Fouché followed his host into the doorway – 'My respects as ever Madame, to you.' – made his little bow, kept his eyes on Madame Roland's face and bust, a simple cap and a rough chemise – somehow sturdy, somehow vulnerable . . .

. . . and saw that Emma Lavalier was across the table from her, watching him. Somehow startled? Somehow superior?

Always you.

Always you.

'You know Madame Lavalier of course, dear Monsieur Fouché.'

'No man would ever know as much as he would hope to, Madame.'

'Monsieur Fouché knows more about me than I know myself.'

'Always Madame Lavalier suggests some new question.'

'Always Monsieur Fouché has the answer.'

'Tonight perhaps, Madame!' Adrenalin had got Fouché through the exchange, but now defiance replaced inspiration. 'Tonight perhaps we may know more answers than for a long time.'

Roland, floundering on the fringes of the exchange: 'Fouché is tireless, dear ladies. Even as he is here, he is managing his operations. Tonight he will capture a dangerous enemy.'

The ladies watched him, and Fouché enjoyed their regard.

'The British known as Kinnaird. Tonight he enters my trap.'

Emma Lavalier watched his satisfaction, while concentrating on the rigid muscles of her face.

She had a vision of France as a desert, of Fouché and Kinnaird as lithe feral rodents hunting each other among the rocks.

Was there a chance they might destroy each other, these lean uncomfortable men, and leave the world to Manon Roland and Emma Lavalier?

A day's riding from Paris, Sir Raphael Benjamin found the cathedral tower of Meaux rising out of the wheat fields. Towers, really: one monstrous square beast soaring up into the darkening sky, and a shorter thing with a pointed roof, and a gable end crowding between them for air, and buttresses and finials and whatnots; the whole thing more like a city itself, with different centuries of development jumbled together. Beside it, the roofs of Meaux were no more than foothills in the landscape.

The evening turned purple, and black, and the colour of the cathedral turned with it, the yellow stone getting paler and colder until finally finally the great edifice rising out of the landscape was a ghostly thing under the moon.

Benjamin had two men riding with him. Men for hire. Their task was simple enough, and probably unnecessary, but there was no need to be reckless. Their task probably wasn't even risky. Nevertheless, for some reason he hadn't wanted to put Ned to it; perhaps tonight he didn't want Ned's stolid chatter, or perhaps the old devil deserved a night off.

But now, strangely, he found that he did want Ned's stolid chatter, not the silence of his two paid servants.

Religion had been attacked by law, and priests massacred in the streets, and the cathedral of Meaux was more strange than ever, bulky and exposed and lonely on the landscape. The bishop was keeping his head down somewhere. But the building was still there. Even the Revolution would take a while to erode it. And within its precincts, there was a library. There was no longer a bustle of voices in the cathedral, no longer the hurry of monks and worshippers, the whispers of surplices and sins. But there were still books. And guarding the books was a librarian.

The librarian would have been a natural companion to Bonfils, the fugitive servant to a king who was no longer a king. Bonfils would have taken this road to Reims often enough in the royal entourage, and as the entourage passed through Meaux the bishop would have received the King, and in their shadows two quiet servants had found an affinity. And when Bonfils was wanted by the Revolution, and fleeing Paris for his old home in Montmirail, and when he found that his precious book was actually a burden, what more natural refuge for it than his acquaintance, the librarian of Meaux? What better place to hide a book than in a library?

And now Bonfils was dead; but the librarian was still there, in his library, a solitary scared man trying to preserve his little temple of papers while the world burned.

———— ◆ ————

Fouché walks away from Roland's house still inspired by his own image in front of the two ladies.

Then he starts to walk faster, as he thinks more about Lavalier.

A policeman must follow her home from Roland's. To check she doesn't attempt to pass a warning. The mysterious Kinnaird has been to her house at least once; this much is known.

It's a precaution only, and the policeman need not wait once she gets home; in truth, the trap is closing and cannot be avoided now. It's more a curiosity, then: to see if she could try to pass a message, and if she would.

Or might the Rolands . . . ?

The mystery of the jewels, the mystery of the royal documents, these have remained obscure. But the British agent Kinnaird is connected to everything.

At the ministry, he sends a policeman hurrying back to Roland's to pick up the trail of the woman Lavalier.

Then, stiff in his chair, he lets his mind fill with a British agent, and a Prussian agent, and the network of the Friends of Magnetism, and how they all might be interlinked.

Somehow, he doubts that Emma Lavalier will risk herself tonight. She had seemed comfortable at the Rolands. Almost comfortable with him. She knows where the power is now, and it's not with a fugitive British spy.

———— ◆ ————

Kinnaird considers the walls of Paris. As they appear to him now, behind the chaos of smaller buildings that have started to spread out beyond the city, glimpsed but never seen whole, they seem unworldly: a presence that does not fit with the normal society around them; something vaster, something indifferent to humans. Cities were the places where he had thrived. Wherever men concentrated together, a man of thoughtful and enterprising disposition might find honest benefit.

Now he must look at them anew. With their gates and their guards they are a trap. And yet, with their density of humanity, he must think of them as an escape as well. The letter brought by Lucie could certainly be a trap, too. But he cannot go back, not now.

He's on the fringes of the city, near St-Denis. He can see it across the fields, an insignificant and benign thing compared to the mass of Paris behind him.

He hasn't forgotten his escape from the Tambour. The madness of that moment, skittering around the rooms like a wet hen and finally throwing himself out of the window, still makes his heart hammer; still comes to him like fear. And the foolishness of his predicament, so confused and so panicked and so utterly the tool of other men, still comes to him like shame.

It had been the turning point. The moment when his dreamy bewildered meandering in this place of chaos became instantly more real, and more dangerous. The hammering at the door, and suddenly the madness of France wasn't happening around him any more; it was happening *to* him.

Or had it been earlier? A letter, opened in an Edinburgh coffee house.

Henry Greene, reaching out of the past and of unknown so-interesting France. And he had let himself be plucked out of Edinburgh – the most steady, the most promising, and today probably the safest city in Europe, where his biggest danger had been that a Glasgow wholesaler might try to horn in on a contract to ship a crate of tea. Now he's in the chaos, and the agents of the Revolution are hunting him.

He starts to walk. The turning point was when he became conscious, and when he started to react. And he's not in the chaos; he is become part of the chaos. And in the chaos, a man with open eyes and quick mind and steady heart may do something. Revolutionary France is one vast marketplace, of ideas and loyalties and lives. Nothing restricted; anything at a price; everything for sale. And Keith Kinnaird is out to trade.

———— ◆ ————

As a boy, Saint-Jean Guilbert had tortured mice.

Not physically. When he bored of them they died quickly, crushed or cut. They were so small, there was no suffering in them.

What he liked to do was confuse them. Make an enclosure of logs and stones and watch them scurry in circles. Squash the enclosure a bit, watch them scurry. Maybe set a stub of candle in there, see how they reacted. Squash the enclosure more. Wonder what they were thinking.

He'd catch the ones who came into the house, sitting in the dust and crumbs at dawn until they emerged. Or he'd walk out beyond the fringes of the town and lie down on the edge of a field, hand waiting in one of the furrows that they travelled.

Guilbert knows that his satisfaction in his current employment is directly linked to his pleasures as a boy.

He sits well-wrapped. Always important when waiting. He watches the door. His eyes never move from the door.

Sometimes the mice knew they were trapped, and sometimes they didn't know they were trapped. They were always trapped.

———— ◆ ————

In Meaux, Sir Raphael Benjamin is thinking about nuns.

Traditional dream of a spree, of course: locked in a nunnery. Just you and the old feller, no one else can get in, you and the old feller and all that fresh milky flesh under those rough skirts, behind those high walls, giggles and gasps and bless you all my dears.

The walls of the Convent des Ursulines are cool around him.

No nuns, alas. Place deserted, hence its great appeal to a man looking for a spot in the centre of Meaux, stone's throw from the cathedral, where he might do a bit of business away from anyone who might be watching.

Somehow rather a waste, though.

Benjamin can feel the pouch against his heart. Its subtle weight; how it moves against his chest as he breathes.

The Convent des Ursulines, deserted, night-stifled, is all things considered a grim barracks of a place. Endless whitewashed corridors. Doorways dark wood, evenly spaced all the way into the distance. His mind wanders along long white corridors that open out in front of him to reveal dark doorways, and he shifts on the chair and scowls at his night. From the outside the place is a blank-faced thing, the few windows high and tight, the whole forbidding. Inside it's all cold, and echoes. All pale, all stone, and all you can think about is the life that's no longer here.

Must have been grim even then. It echoes because there's nothing soft here any more, nothing plush or upholstered or comfortable. But perhaps there had never been anything soft here.

Damned strange sort of a life. Bunch of cold shrivelled women locked up with the echoes.

Surely somewhere, though, there had been a flicker of warmth: in some private moment, a rough cloth lifted briefly, a glimpse of flesh, something truly alive.

But none else there to enjoy it. In the entrance hall of the Convent des Ursulines, Raphael Benjamin sits alone on a simple wooden chair, and dreams of something young and amazed on his lap, and waits for the moment of his transaction.

———————— ◆ ————————

Emma Lavalier stares out of her window, at the moon, at the night.

The watcher has gone. He'd followed her home – she'd been aware of him by the end of the journey – and she'd seen him from her window still watching, but after only a few minutes she'd seen the shadow of the tree trunk stretch and split and then the man walking away.

She has the vague idea that the police had been better at it under the old regime; harder to spot. But you never knew.

Somewhere out there in the night, Fouché is hunting Kinnaird. She has a clear vision of their faces: always anxious, always hungry, always unsatisfied, scurrying in the moonlight.

Raph Benjamin is somewhere out there too. His face seems more comfortable to her; and so, probably, is whatever he's doing.

And now, forehead against the window pane but never as cool as she hoped, she sees all of them: boys, muttering in the shadows, playing their strange games.

They are hidden games, far from the moonlit lane outside. The lane is utterly still; nothing has moved since the departure of the watcher. Perhaps it was enthusiasm that made the revolutionary police more obvious.

Or perhaps they have a different intention. Perhaps the object is not to catch malfeasance, but to make it impossible; to show everyone that they are watched all the time.

And if everyone knew they were being watched all the time, how much of life would die?

----------◆----------

To anyone watching, at this middle hour of the autumn night in the Year One of the Republic, the front wall of the precincts of the cathedral of Meaux is imposing and blank and deserted. Beyond the wall, hints of the cathedral itself and the other buildings around it rise towards the moon, strands of pale stone suggesting the mighty facades and elaborate carvings hiding in the shadows. But at the entrance gate, the cathedral and the other buildings that make up its community turn their backs on the world. And given what the world's been up to recently, who shall blame them?

A horse clops hollow over the cobbles to the gate, and stops, and a figure with an elegant coat and a well-wrapped face gets down from the horse. He knocks at the gate.

He waits patiently, his figure largely hidden by the horse.

Another horse follows, and stops a short distance away. Another figure gets down, this one dressed simple.

Within half a minute, a small door within the gate opens, and the first figure is murmuring to the porter, and being hurried inside. The second figure ambles forwards, so he's holding both horses, in front of the gate.

Another minute, and the door opens again. The elegant coat steps out, there's a brief exchange with the man at the horses, and the coat goes back in again. The second figure trudges away, pulling both horses behind him.

———— ◆ ————

Keith Kinnaird can hear his own footsteps on the ground, such is the silence.

Making an impression. Kinnaird resonates at last.

He tries to walk more softly.

He remembers Lucie, her hand in her chemise, her anxiety. *It's a trap.*

Lucie. There was a worldliness to the young woman. He'd stuck too long with his first impression of her: the discomfort in the world, the clumsiness. But she had lived in the world; survived in the gutters and the shadows; and it made her, even half a generation younger than him, wiser and stronger.

Lucie has no loyalty.

It came like the betrayal of a friendship, or an *amour*. Lucie might be curious, and she might even be fond, but she is not loyal – to anything.

All of France around him in the darkness, waiting, and he unseen.

Somehow it has become impossible to avoid the world.

He thinks of the woman Lavalier. The most exotic creature he has ever met: she belongs in a Medici palazzo poisoning, or the Turk's seraglio. Yet also the most worldly. There is a kind of honesty to the woman Lavalier.

It is because she does not care, about anything.

If someone is trying to trap him, he cannot ignore it. If there's a weevil in the biscuit, you don't keep on eating.

Is it a trap? He stops philosophizing and reviews the facts and possibilities. Where he has been and who has seen him. The odd letter. His interest to the revolutionary regime. *What do they know of me?*

He stops walking. *Of course it is a trap.*

He considers the darkness around him. He tries to make it familiar. Tries to feel that it is his. *It is all a trap.*

He starts to walk towards his destination again, through darkness that wraps its arm around his shoulders and starts to rifle his pockets.

Is this who I am become?

———— ◆ ————

Guilbert waits. He feels the wall against his back; adjusts his shoulders; checks that he is still totally hidden in the shadow.

He's hungry.

Not for food.

This is what waiting is: appetite.

He doesn't have – he doesn't even wonder at – Monsieur's little obsessions. This document or that man; the puzzle; the politics. For Guilbert it is only the hunt, the daily search for food; for prey.

Monsieur thinks there is a goal – he believes in conclusions, in victories. Guilbert knows there's just life, just eating to survive, for as long as you can, because the only alternative is death. Monsieur believes you can observe the world like the natural philosophers and make your deductions. Guilbert knows there's no pattern, and no answer; just a lot of animals, bumping into each other like cattle in a barn at night.

His eyes never move from the door.

He's an animal too, no less than any. But he knows it; and he has a knife.

———— ◆ ————

To anyone watching, the stillness of night has returned quickly to the front wall of the precincts of the cathedral of Meaux.

Anyone watching is presumably wondering about the man in the fine coat still inside. He is still inside, which is presumably reassuring to the watcher.

Such is Raph Benjamin's satisfied calculation.

He himself is still secure like chastity in the Convent des Ursulines, around the corner from the cathedral gate. His first paid man is still in the cathedral, enjoying a glass of wine perhaps, or looting the plate for all Raph cares. The man's work is done: he had entered, collected the book, emerged briefly and used the cover of his horse's body to slip the book into the saddle bag, and disappeared into the cathedral again to fill the mind of the hypothetical watcher, while the second man led the two horses and Xavier Bonfils's precious book away into the night.

Now the book is Benjamin's, delivered to the convent by his second paid man, hefted in his hands and then slipped into a bag and slung over his shoulder.

Raph Benjamin is playing his own game this night. *And that's how you win: at a game that no one else even knows is being played.*

Raph Benjamin: his own game, and his own rules. He's resisted the urge to look at the book.

———— ◆ ————

If it's all a trap then there's no escape and no use fretting.

Kinnaird feels his footsteps pounding into France. He can see the door ahead now.

He curses the fatuous French philosophizing that's rotting his brain.

What would a practical man do? One of the adventuring men, like Sir Raphael lace-edged Benjamin, immortal and charming?

Kinnaird considers his surroundings. Looks for opportunities to left and right, tries to remember what he's passed already.

When do I run? What triggers it? What is the clue? What if there is no Lucie Gérard with a horse?

Should I run now?

He sees himself, ludicrous, running through France chased by shadows. He knows that he can't run.

Not because I'm proud and not because I'm slow, but because I'll look so damn' ridiculous.

The door is clear in front of him.

------------◆------------

Guilbert whispers into the darkness beside him: 'In the porch. Nice and tidy.'

He knows that the darkness is listening.

'Soon as he's through the door.'

The darkness grunts its understanding.

Guilbert commands the night.

------------◆------------

The details of the night roar at Kinnaird. His feet pound and the resonance shudders through his legs. The air scrapes across his face. He hears trees and house timbers moving. The door looms vast in front of him and he sees the iron studs that decorate it, sees the cracks in the woodwork, seems to see through the cracks and strains to see the other side.

He reaches forwards and his hand balloons before him and stretches for the door.

------------◆------------

The latch cracks like a musket shot and Guilbert is moving. He knows that as he moves the men with him start to move. 'Soon as he's through the door,' he whispers, to himself now. Then words and human senses are lost and he's moving faster. His prey must have no time to turn, no time to run; Guilbert will be in front of him as soon as he's through the door.

------------◆------------

The door swings open in front of Kinnaird, the crack widening and lightening and his whole existence opening out, and: 'You!'

Emma Lavalier herself has opened the door to him. Kinnaird starts to speak, starts to bow.

'You! But you are hunted: you're to be arrested this night!'

'But why, Madame?' There must be a candle somewhere beside her; perhaps she's holding it. Its colour flickers on her forehead, her nose, her chin, her shoulders, her breasts. Somewhere in the gloom, there are two tiny points of light in her eyes. Kinnaird feels himself breathing hard. 'I must know, Madame. What is told of me in Paris, among the men of influence whom I know you know? Why do they try to trap me? Of what am I accused? You are my only way to understanding, and my only way to cleansing my name.' She is more powerful to him than ever, more mysterious. 'I am innocent, Madame, and harmless!'

'You are the most dangerous man in France! If you have sense you will fly from here, to save your neck; and if you have courtesy you will do it to save mine.'

He watches her a long moment. Then he turns and disappears into the darkness.

———————— ✦ ————————

Benjamin slipped out through the convent door into the porch.

'Hold!'

His heart burst in his chest, and he felt the jewel thumping back against it.

Unspent, damn it.

A man close in front of him, men; and a voice. 'We sent the empty message to the apothecary's, and we waited for you to call for it. And now we can pick up your contacts too, and whatever they brought you.' Benjamin felt his whole body, a screaming tempest of senses. *Sir Raphael Benjamin has lived, and damn you all.* 'So: you are the one called Kinnaird.'

'Y- No!'

The final flickering of a candle in the darkness; a last gasp of individual passion and pride. His blood was up and his blade was out; but Sir Raphael Benjamin died quietly.

4

The Saltpetre Factory

In which two trading gentlemen find an unlikely sympathy,
Mme Lavalier reflects on the new age, a Prussian master-
plan reaches its climax, and the Comptrollerate-General
for Scrutiny and Survey takes a hand

The Memoirs of Charles Maurice de Talleyrand

(extract from unpublished annex)

*As the chaos grew within the borders of France, so it spread without.
On the 6. of November the volunteers of Dumouriez beat the Austrians
at Jemappes. Ironic that, had I been the healthy braggart so desired by
my illustrious father and my illustrious uncle and all of their illustrious
forebears, I would have been commanding such a battle — or perhaps
slaughtered in some pointless skirmish early in the Revolution. Militarily
it was a nonsense in every way — even the stupidest of the Talleyrands
could have seen that — a victory of irrational incredible charges, by idiots
against regular soldiers, causing vastly greater casualties among the
French than were suffered by the Austrians, who prudently withdrew,
and followed by an equally imprudent French advance into the Low
Countries, after which ensued within months both a more dramatic and*

lasting military reverse and the complete alienation of the population.

But at the time, such an empty-headed euphoria for the Revolution! Brussels fell within a week. The bizarre confidence of the Revolution grew, in both its leaders and in the wild instinctual mind of the mob. The territory of France was definitively cleared of foreign foe, and became thus susceptible to domestic division. And the army learned the power of its over-passionate volunteers, which was a doubtful lesson, and the power of artillery, which was wiser and more enduring.

In Paris, this ensured the apparently irreversible advance of the bloodthirstiest elements, the Marats and the Robespierres and the St-Justs, and consequently the impossibility that a prominent man of reason and discretion should quit the tranquil avenues of Kensington for the ensanguined gutters of Les Halles. Having unchained the mob, the leaders of the Revolution grew increasingly desperate to find red meat to feed it; corpse after corpse was flung into the insatiable jaws, and the administrators continued their investigations to discredit the very men who had done most to ensure the stability of the realm for so long. When I learned, from my hosts in London, of the ministry's pursuit of the royal correspondence of Louis, I knew that I could not in safety re-cross the Channel.

[SS G/66/X3 (EXTRACT)]

———————◆———————

'Intriguing business this morning.'

'Indeed?'

'Our latest guest from Paris: Mademoiselle de Charette.'

'Ah, she's supposed to be quite the peach. Breeches already straining all along Pall Mall.'

'As you say. Anyway, she asked to call on me.'

'My dear fellow; is there nothing you will not endure for your country?'

'She insisted. Discretion of the service be damned. Swans in, demure curtsey if you please, and polite thanks for what we'd done to get her and the old man out.'

'Charming.'

'Think nothing of it, says I, and hope to see you both in the park sometime. Then – this the more interesting part – she reaches down into her top hamper, and – '

'She what?'

'Well, one's met a few more French girls in the last year or two, but this was new on me too. Reaches down, and then pulls something out. A damned great jewel, if you please; a blue diamond.'

'You had to refuse, alas.'

'Here's the point. It wasn't a touch, and this ain't just any bauble: it's *the* bauble. One of the French crown jewels. One of Louis's royal diamonds. I think it's the one they call the Bleu de France.'

'Smuggled out of Paris in Mademoiselle's tits! But we thought – '

'Disappeared one dark night, terribly unfortunate and suddenly the revolutionary government's flush with cash. Seems it wasn't quite like that. Not with this piece, anyway. It transpires that an English hand found its way into the machine. Got hold of this diamond, and saved it from the mob.'

'Whose hand?'

'You'll blink at this: Benjamin.'

'What? Not Raph Benjamin?'

'He.'

'I assumed him dead of the pox in Naples. That or hanged.'

'He's been knocking around France a while now, between the guillotine and glory. We've had our eye on him. The way La Charette tells it, he had a hand in her escape. And he gave her the jewel to bring out.'

'What a blood.'

'Ain't he? Jewel to be passed on to me, for our safe-keeping. Thing is, I rather think the girl ought to get the chance to tell her tale discreetly at court; otherwise she'll have it all over Kensington in a week.'

'We can't have that.'

'She's quite emotional about it all; especially about him.'

'All rather a romance for an impressionable French chit, no doubt. But that's worthy service by Benjamin.'

'Indeed.'

'Might be time that name was welcome in the drawing rooms again.'
'Indeed.'

———————— ✦ ————————

At this time, the workshop of François Gamain, locksmith, is easily found. Gamain is known for his skill, and by diligence and courtesy of manner he has built up, over fifteen years, a reputation among the finest houses in Paris. Gamain is only a craftsman, of course. But he's a discreet craftsman and, if a locksmith should embody one quality, surely it's discretion.

Gamain's workshop is on the rue de Rennes. The street is definitely not of gentlemen, but the northern end of the street – and in the rue de Rennes this is what matters – is close enough to St Germain to have caught a little of its affluence. Gamain's workshop is on the ground floor, behind an elegantly painted sign and a sturdy door.

Gamain's home is harder to find. It hides underneath the workshop, reached through a small door in one corner of it.

At precisely noon, on any day when he is not summoned by a commission to work on site somewhere, he passes through the small door and down into his lodgings, and as he settles onto the stool Madame Gamain's arm swings in with a bowl of soup and he lifts the spoon and begins with even sips and the steady rhythm of the spoon, down and up, to take his lunch.

Madame Gamain makes good soup.

Two decades of craft – fitting locks, fixing locks, designing locks, making locks, and occasionally picking locks – have trained Gamain's mind to see the world as a lock. The mechanism behind the plate. Behind any problem, behind any situation, he sees the axles, the pins, the wheels, the cogs, the springs. A blockage he feels as a tightness in the muscles of his chest and stomach. The unblocking he feels as a great breath of air. He, he knows, is the key. For whatever challenge his customers present, he is precision and delicacy and easy in and *hup!* open.

Madame Gamain makes good soup. There's fullness to it, but not a heaviness, and that's important, especially for the noontime meal: sustenance that does not dull the faculties. Keep the fingers strong, keep the brain turning.

Madame Gamain is talking. About how she cut her finger in the cramped kitchen space, doing work that the maid should have been doing but wasn't, and it's all because their lodging is so small and dingy and isn't it inappropriate that a man of his success should still be huddling under the stairs like this? Gamain is aware of the noise of her, like the chatter of a customer behind his shoulder as he kneels on his old felt mat and works at a lock.

The Revolution has been winding itself up like some gigantic mechanism. Gamain attends meetings and discussions. Meetings of like-minded men, men of craft and men of discretion, who interest themselves in the proper functioning of their world. Gamain feels the springs tightening and straining; he senses the distortion in the fibres of the metal. Himself, he slips through the mechanism smoothly. Even in the Revolution, there are still doors of difference and distinction; there are still secrets. Trade is steady, for a locksmith of repute.

At a quarter after twelve, Madame Gamain swings around her husband's shoulder, still talking, and the bowl swings away and Gamain rises and turns and climbs back to his workshop, with measured steps.

———————— ✦ ————————

Roland found himself calling into Fouché's office more often than Fouché called into his. He acknowledged it wearily. He had never been a man on whom other men tended to call.

'Another coup, Fouché?' Fouché saw him, stiffened – *Ah, but how long will my little authority last amid these jackals?* – and stood. 'Another success?'

They stayed standing. Uncomfortably, Roland realized that there was another man in the room, off to his side, a dirty smudge on the edge of his vision. Fouché's creature; Fouché's brute. The man Guilbert. Roland nodded vaguely at Guilbert. Guilbert seemed not to see him.

'I claim no great glory, Monsieur le Ministre. We make progress. The Revolution – '

'Of course!' *I begin to loathe these* bon mots. *When did the Revolution become a person, anyway?* 'You thwarted a counter-revolutionary plot. You destroyed a foreign agent. A fine night's work, surely.'

Fouché shrugged. *His modesty becomes false; I must watch that.* 'I would have preferred him alive, to answer to justice and to reveal more to us of royalist schemes. But satisfactory, Minister. Satisfactory.' He stood and, two-handed, presented a small leather bag. 'I have the honour, Minister, to return to an officer of France one of her prize jewels, recovered from the British thief.'

Roland, all fingers: checking it, startled, and then looking up again in wonder. Fouché felt warmth in his chest. He'd contemplated some grander performance in the Convention, and then doubted he could carry it off. He trusted Roland to advertise the credit fairly, and he knew this approach would strengthen his own reputation for discretion; for *humility*.

Roland was grabbing his hand, shaking it flappily. 'Wonderful, dear Fouché! My compliments. My compliments. I shall . . . And – and what of the book?'

Now Fouché felt discomfort. He looked down. The book was perfectly centred on the table, and open.

'Some prize, is it? Codes, or treasons?'

Fouché shook his head, uneasy. Still the book started up at him. 'It is . . . It seems trivial, Minister. It is the steward's register; his log book – his account of what comes in and out of the palace, which tradesmen visit, what is purchased and delivered – '

'Any record of those documents – the secret correspondence?'

Of course not, Fouché thinks. 'No, Minister. I have studied it most carefully. I fear there is no mystery in here. The steward Bonfils kept the book out of some . . . some foolish instinct of duty. A souvenir of his service, no more; his last attention to his vanished life.'

'Visitors significant, perhaps.'

'And the visitors are not people of significance, Minister. The steward was not exposed to the visits of the King's courtiers. These are nobodies: the men who come to fix new carpets; the men who gild the banisters; a visit from a locksmith; an architect's assistant making plans for an extension; a doctor for the royal pets. It is a record of the obscenity of the court – you could feed the army on what Louis's palace devoured in a week. But no treacheries.'

Roland was nodding. He'd lost interest. He turned to go. 'The King was always mad about locks. That locksmith would be his tame one.'

Fouché's eyes came up: 'His – ?'

'He was fascinated by locks, Fouché!' Roland had turned back. 'The mechanism, you know. Liked to think he could design such things himself. He was always inviting locksmiths – to show off their newest device. Used to send the Queen insane with boredom; the King and his toys.' Roland smiled benignly at the idea. 'He had the ridiculous affectation of being somehow sympathetic with the heart of the artisan.' He shook his head. 'A foolish world, now happily passed.'

He left.

'You were hasty, Guilbert!' Fouché was immediately back into their conversation. His obsession with the palace and the steward was feeling like a foolishness itself. 'He were better alive. Now he can give us nothing.'

Guilbert was impassive. *Monsieur has come round to torture fast enough.* 'Regrettably it is not always possible, Monsieur.'

Fouché was circling the table. 'The great British spy, the centre of all of their recent ga-'

'There is some confusion, Monsieur. It seems this is not the man Kinnaird. This is Benjamin.'

Fouché stopped. 'Benjamin? I seem to know the name.'

'One of the circle of the woman Lavalier. Sir Raphael Benjamin. A gambler. A philanderer. A *flaneur*.'

'A spy?'

'A ten-sou adventurer. A scoundrel only. Certainly not the man we wanted.'

Fouché was standing still, looking through Guilbert. 'This Kinnaird. He grows more mysterious. More elusive. A wizard, truly.'

———— ◆ ————

'I'm no one, Lucie, truly. And I have no idea what's happening around me.' Kinnaird shifted his back against the tree trunk. A beetle considered his outstretched boot, and then began to climb over it. 'And I've nothing to hide.'

'Nothing to hide? No one believes that, Monsieur. Everyone has something to hide.'

'I'm innocent of all they believe.'

'That's the weakest defence of all.' She was pacing the ground, as usual.

They were in the glade by the river. The sun was playing pale among the branches again, but the branches were barer now, and it was much cooler than when Lucie had first brought him here.

Kinnaird considered the faint sense of damp under his backside, and shook his head. 'It's madness. By association with Hal Greene I am assumed to be complicit in whatever he was doing. And by continuing to exist in France, just by living from day to day, I am complicit in mysteries and plots I know nothing about.'

Lucie stopped pacing. 'There's an answer.' Kinnaird looked up. He wondered at her. She never seemed to settle in this place, however pleasant. 'Simple. Leave France.' Perhaps it was freedom, not restlessness, that kept her moving. 'Or cease to exist.'

He smiled. 'There's a third answer.' She frowned. 'Find out the mysteries and the plots.'

She growled and spun away. Then immediately she was back, coming for him and dropping into the leaves beside him. 'Monsieur, you're a fool. You're . . . you're like a child here. You play a game you don't understand, and you'll get hurt.'

He nodded. 'I'm also Scottish, Lucie. And we're the worst fools of all. We will not – will not – be told. Tell me to run; I stay. Make a game of me, with plots and tricks, and I will defeat you.'

Now Lucie looked rather scared.

———— ◆ ————

In an attic flat in Les Halles district, on the mattress which was the only furniture, Edward Pinsent slumped and drank.

The loneliest man in Europe, he thought.

'The loneliest man in Europe,' he said out loud.

'Fuck Europe,' he said. And took another mouthful from the bottle.

Keith Kinnaird didn't have to knock. He pushed cautiously at the door, remembering suspicions and a loaded pistol.

The opening door revealed the bare boards, then the mattress, and then the body of Pinsent. Pinsent took a moment to focus. When he realized who it was, he closed his eyes. Eventually – he didn't know if it was a second or an hour – he opened them again. The Scotsman was still standing in the doorway.

Edward Pinsent laughed. It was a Falstaff laugh, old and dirty and world-battered. 'How is it,' he said, apparently holding his head up with difficulty, 'that whenever I am in the shit – whenever and wherever the shit is shittiest, wherever I run – the door opens, and you have come to pay a social call?'

'It's easy, Mr Pinsent. I follow the smell of shit.'

He stepped in, and closed the door. 'Or perhaps I'm your one true hope.' Slowly, the door swung open again. It was warped, and the catch hadn't engaged. Kinnaird pushed it back firmly with his heel and this time it stuck. 'And you've just never noticed.'

'How in hell did you find me?' Pinsent looked like a sulky child.

The clumsiness, Kinnaird thought. *The stink, even.*

'You cut rather a distinctive figure, Mr Pinsent. Not to belittle your skills of deception, but you don't pass easily for a Frenchman.'

Pinsent chuckled. 'Perhaps I don't, at that.' He fought a skirmish with his own limbs and scrambled upright from the mattress. By some extraordinary feat of self-possession, some deep-buried decorum, he became controlled and almost sober. 'My dear fellow,' he said with resonance. 'My manners. Please to come in.' He reached up a large hand, and at the second attempt gripped Kinnaird's shoulder. 'This might surprise you as much as it does me, but I'm genuinely glad to see you. Friendly face.' He opened a sweeping arm. 'I'd offer you a chair, but ... '

Other than the mattress, the room was bare. The mattress, a sprawling bag in one corner that appeared to contain Pinsent's limited wardrobe, and – against the ripped and damp grey wallpaper over the mantelpiece – the drawing of two girls.

Kinnaird said, 'But the chair was stolen?'

'Furniture stolen, linen in the laundry, and I've pawned the silver to fund the revolutionary army. You're welcome to the mattress, but I confess my fear that it has prior occupants who bite.' His face twisted. Kinnaird saw that it was real anger. 'Look,' he said, and bent and gathered the clothes back into the bag, and pushed it into the form of a large cushion. 'Settle yourself on that. Everything I have is yours.'

Kinnaird did so. It was surprisingly comfortable. Pinsent returned to his mattress.

'Do you know, Mr Pinsent, this is probably the first time in all my weeks in France that someone's genuinely made me welcome?'

In a Paris slum attic, two worn and hunted men laughed.

Kinnaird overcame it first. 'Oh, pardon me,' he said. 'I had come firstly to offer you my condolences. For the death of your companion.'

Pinsent grunted. 'Thank you.' A heavy nod of approval. 'Courteous of you. Hell of a way for a man to go – murdered by those vermin. But perhaps he was happier blazing out – in action, you know? Not some dribbling old beggar, as the rest of us will surely end. Still, one's sorry – '

'Actually not, Mr Pinsent.' Pinsent frowned. 'I was thinking of you.'

'I'd rather you didn't, Kinnaird. I may be a washed-up fool and fraud, but you'll kindly allow me my pride.'

'Not him, at any rate.' The frown still watching him. 'Since I have the strong impression that he was trying to get me killed that night, you'll forgive me if I don't spend too much time regretting him.'

'Ah.'

Kinnaird waited. Pinsent was considering him.

Eventually he seemed to come to a resolution. Delicately he placed the bottle on the floor, and pulled himself straighter and folded his hands in a kind of formality, the best he could manage on the lousy mattress. 'Mr Kinnaird, I don't rightly know what he was doing that night, as he left me out of it.' He leaned forwards and made sure he was looking straight at Kinnaird. 'But I shouldn't be at all surprised.'

'Thank – ' Kinnaird stopped, and shifted his weight. He reached under his thigh and into Pinsent's bag and pulled out the pistol. He placed it on the floorboards next to the bag. 'Thank you for your candour.'

Pinsent rolled forwards, grabbed the neck of the bottle, and brandished it at his guest.

Kinnaird shook his head. 'No, I thank you.' Pinsent took a swig. 'That was the second reason I called, in fact.' Pinsent, bottle halfway to mouth, stopped and watched him. Kinnaird was taking his time. Eventually Pinsent lowered the bottle again. 'Pinsent, I have spent these weeks the dupe and prey of every man. I tell you this clear: I am fed to the teeth of it, and am resolved on a different role.'

It was quiet, and steady, and Pinsent listened the more carefully.

'You would oblige me by confirming everything you know about Hal Greene's work, and what happened to him; and what deceptions were practised with my name.' Pinsent pulled back into the wall. 'I may say that I know he was involved to some degree in espionage work, that I know he sometimes worked with you, and that I know you and Benjamin conspired to use me as cover when the attention of the Revolution turned in your direction.' Pinsent watched him, bleak. 'I may further say that we, you and I, might even find occasion to work together in the future; or that I, knowing what I do, could have you in the hands of the Revolution within an hour, and this time you wouldn't come back.'

For a full minute: silence.

Then Pinsent spoke. 'You've had a hell of a time of it, haven't you?' Kinnaird gazed back at him. Once again, Pinsent pulled himself straighter, and folded his hands in front of him. 'Greene had connections in London. He would do errands for them. Hide behind a curtain here. Hold up a coach there. I think they paid him for it. He pulled in Raph and me, time by time. Didn't pay us directly, but he was rather a liberal sort of fellow, and we did well enough by him.' He felt his own dignity pricking him. 'A scandalized and ruined by-blow of the rustic gentry must survive as he can, you hear me?' He took in a great breath, swallowing his anger at his world. 'So much for Hal.'

'Did you kill him?'

Pinsent was startled.

'Pinsent, there is decency and dignity in you. But there's no honour among thieves, and less among spies. Did you – or Benjamin – kill my friend?'

'No, Kinnaird, we did . . . I did not.' He smiled without warmth. 'If we're being so honest, I may say that I cannot formally speak for Raph on the point. But I cannot think why he would have killed Hal, and I cannot find it in his character. I saw them squabble over a bet sometimes, over a woman almost nightly, and even once or twice over politics . . . I cannot find it in his character.'

'Very well. And your games with me?'

'Distraction. The massacres started. Lavalier was questioned. Hal had disappeared. A couple of Englishmen on the lam, done a few dirty deeds in our time here, we were vulnerable. We needed someone to play the part of British troublemaker.' He settled back against the wall again. 'And you, Kinnaird, you've been trouble ever since you first walked through my door.'

'The meeting at the Galerie Marillac. The note and the map half-hidden in my rooms for the police to find.'

'Us. Raph used your name a few times. And he spread some stories, faked up some reports, making you the grand man of British skulduggery.'

Again, there was silence.

Eventually Kinnaird said, 'Thank you.' Then he stood.

Pinsent also stood, more deftly this time. He stepped forwards, and very slowly offered his hand. 'Sorry,' he said.

Kinnaird considered the hand for a long time. Then, surprised by himself, he took it. 'Well, an apology's a start I – '

'Not for the deceptions. All's fair in you know what.' Pinsent kept a grip of Kinnaird's hand. 'You were damn' fool enough to come to France and stick your nose in, and to run around like the village idiot with a turnip up his arse. You were going to get into trouble with the traps regardless, and we did what we had to do to survive. No . . . ' The grip eased, and then strengthened, and he shook the hand and finally released it. 'No, I'm sorry for how we spoke. Behaved like blackguards. Not courteous.'

Kinnaird nodded. 'Mr Pinsent, I confess I found the manner a little ripe and the instincts a little trivial. But whatever your spirit and motives, you executed feats of daring as easily as most men take luncheon.'

Pinsent considered him. 'You're a good fellow, Kinnaird.' He reflected, lugubrious with the wine again. 'When life seems to have lost its worth, one's apt to risk it more blithely.'

'You seem to have wandered Paris at will.'

Pinsent's hand came up and clutched his arm with surprising speed and considerable force. 'It's not easy, Kinnaird! It's not a bloody game. Every time, the . . . the doubt – the – the fear. It never ends. And time by time your stock of nerve is used up.' His hand eased, and his voice drifted. 'Used up. Until there's nothing left.'

'You survived La Force, I was told.'

Pinsent shifted uncomfortable. 'Nothing to speak of. No great elegance to it.' A smile flickered on the sour face. 'Raph walked in there once. Twice, indeed, for we went back the next night. And came out with a prisoner each time – Royal ladies-in-waiting, or something.' A sudden inspiration on his face. 'Here. Souvenir for you, as you're interested.' From the pocket of his coat he pulled out a crumpled paper. 'Found it in there again yesterday. Didn't know I still had it. Raph's *aide memoire* – he'd got a message from Greene, and he destroyed it as a precaution, but he took note of the names he needed.'

Kinnaird smoothed out the paper in his palm. It was an etching of a priest and a nun enjoying a distinct and wild kind of communion.

A moment's confusion, Kinnaird's uncertainty and Pinsent's discomfort, and then Kinnaird looked at the back of the paper. There were two lines written in pencil.

Delambre SD.
Tourzels LF.

'Hal would send written messages?'

'Occasionally. If he was travelling. Via that servant girl – the pretty one. She brought the last – Raph made that note of it – and so that night I must buy drinks for an army of peasants to get them warmed up to disrupt some French government bod on the road while Raph was stirring 'em up on the spot.' Heavy smile. 'Still remember him turning up at Lavalier's afterwards. More alive than any man. In his element, you know?' Pinsent seemed to wriggle. 'He . . . He sent for my things. When he got me out of clink, he also sent for some of my things, from my room. That's how the coat came back, with the paper.' He glanced at the drawing on the mantelpiece. 'And my girls. He could be thoughtful, you understand?'

'He just walked into La Force?'

Now Pinsent smiled. It hung heavy in his jowls. 'Oh, getting in's easy enough; as a former prisoner, I should know better than most. Getting out's harder. And getting out with something or someone you're not supposed to, that's the hardest of all.' He pulled his shoulders up. 'Lessons of a life ill-lived, Kinnaird.'

'I'll bear it in mind.'

'Do.' He slumped again, the air seeping out of a bladder. 'Worldly advice.' An indifferent snort. 'Only worth it if you've got someone to pass it on to.' His eyes wandered the room. 'Burbling it through drink, to some odd little Scotchman. In a room that smells of the privy. Oh. No offence, my dear fellow; nothing against you, nothing against the Scots; ingenious fellows, aren't you? Trade, and so on.'

Kinnaird's expression offered gracious acceptance of this grand compliment. Pinsent wasn't looking at him. 'I had, but . . . no more.' He was staring at the two girls in the picture on the mantelpiece. 'I don't even know how old they are now. I will surely be damned for that, wouldn't you say?' He didn't wait for agreement. 'Lovely, ain't they? Virginia and Charlotte. Ain't they lovely?' Kinnaird mumbled something. Pinsent wasn't listening. 'I don't belong any more . . . I don't deserve . . .'

Edward Pinsent's face was shaking, with big wine-hot breaths. He turned. 'He came back for me, Mr Kinnaird! That's the thing, d'you see? And I'm not sure I'd have done the same.'

He wanted reassurance, or absolution, and Keith Kinnaird had none to give.

------ ◆ ------

A man was standing on Pieter Marinus's doorstep. Marinus saw him from his first floor window, first indifferent and then concerned. It was becoming dangerous to have visitors; to have connections; to be known.

Head bent, clothes tattered. A beggar, hoping for a coin or a mouthful of wine to warm the early evening.

Marinus's face twisted in discomfort. *The forgotten victims.* Then he shook his head at himself and turned his face away from the window.

The man knocked.

Marinus ignored it.

A minute later, the knock again.

Why hadn't the servant – ? The servant had left a quarter-hour before. A final glance out of the window – still the bent head, the ragged shoulders – and Marinus was walking wearily for the stairs.

The eyes, when he opened the door to the man, were more alert than he'd expected. It was immediately an alarm. The rags and the smears of dirt on the face confirmed his beggary, but the eyes belied it.

Still Marinus held out a coin: 'Here my friend – '

'Your name is Marinus.' The words came in *English*. 'My name is Kinnaird, Mr Marinus, and these days I come cheaper than that.'

Instinct told Marinus it was all wrong. Already he was closing the door. 'I have no notion – '

'We were both invited to a meeting.' Hesitation. 'By Henry Greene. I went. You didn't. I – Close the door and I will have your name all over town, Mr Marinus! I will implicate you in everything!'

Marinus had gasped, held his breath. Now he let it go with a burst. And shook his head. 'This is nonsense. Good night!' and the door starting to close again.

But the man's boot was in the way.

'The Galerie Marillac, Mr Marinus. You were too shrewd to come, and that tells me something about you.'

'What goes there?' A shout from along the street. Marinus's head darted up: a National Guardsman. The beggar man's dropped. 'What trouble?'

Marinus, desperate for this all to go away, started to speak but he didn't even know to whom. 'I respect you for a man of discretion, Mr Marinus. But I can shatter that discretion tonight, for ever.' The guard coming nearer. 'You thought me a beggar and you let me in for a moment. You can tell I am no robber. Letting me in, you have nothing to lose. In an argument on your doorstep . . .'

'What goes?'

'Nothing, Monsieur, I thank you!' And he was letting Kinnaird past him into the hall, and the door was closed, and Marinus had the uneasy sense that it was he who had crossed a threshold.

Upstairs, the man Kinnaird refused a seat.

There was a tension in his movements; an unpredictability. Marinus watched him as he moved.

Remember Karl.

Remember yourself.

Marinus offered a slight bow. 'I bid you welcome. Will you take a glass of wine with me, Mr Kinnaird?'

The man stared. 'No, I won't. I want answers, not more theatre show.'

Marinus sat. It took some of the volatility out of the scene.

Still the man Kinnaird would not settle. He made various attempts at a relaxed or commanding stance in the centre of the room. 'I was chosen for this masquerade because I am associated with another man who is associated with disreputable and secret dealings in this country. Why were you chosen, Mr Marinus?'

The face of Marinus was open. Blank. Innocent. Faintly, he shrugged.

'You have no such association? You were pulled into this affair by some staggering coincidence, picked off the street by chance?'

Marinus frowned.

'Why don't you answer, damn you? In the whole of France, is there no – ?'

Still the frown. It wasn't anger, or worry. It was ... irritation. It was distaste.

And Kinnaird saw himself. A great sigh, and a scowl at it all.

He smiled sadly. 'I owe you an apology, sir. Whatever you are, you are a man of prudence, and you will do nothing for bluster.'

Something at Marinus's lips. And he seemed to relax. The frown eased.

'I think, Mr Marinus, that I will take that glass of wine with you.'

Marinus smiled, and it seemed sincere. 'You would honour me.'

Kinnaird sat. He kept silent until the wine was poured. He made to speak, and then stopped again.

Marinus raised his own glass, and nodded slightly, in toast.

Kinnaird reciprocated.

He sipped at the wine.

'Most pleasant,' he said. 'May I ask whether you buy here or you import?'

'This I buy in Paris. Despite the late disquiets, there is still an adequate trade. My man has only a small concern, but he takes his pick of the French vineyards and imports according to his own instincts and the preferences of his private clients. Are you a connoisseur of wine, Mr Kinnaird?'

'No, sir. But I'm fascinated by trade. Would you allow me, Mr Marinus, to rephrase my earlier question?'

Marinus sat back, the wine glass held close to his chest. 'I would encourage it, Mr Kinnaird.'

'I thank you. In that case, begging of you no more intimacy than you would share with a stranger in the street, might I ask your occupation or interest?'

'Why ever not? As a citizen of the Low Countries, Mr Kinnaird, I am the inheritor of three worthy traditions: humanist scholarship, painting, and trade. I dabble a little in each. It's a dilettante interest, in truth, but I am not too proud to say that I earn money, and it enables me to offer an acquaintance a pleasant Chenin of Touraine rather than a flask brought up from the inn. Were you ever in Amsterdam, Mr Kinnaird?'

'Once. A trading visit merely, and speculative. A most tidy city, Mr Marinus, and the most steady driving men of affairs I ever met. It's no flattery, sir, yet I could give no greater praise.'

'We have been fortunate. A climate for moderation, and we have tried to avoid the fevers of religion and politics.'

They both nodded, silently, at the prudence of this, and sipped their wine.

'And now,' Marinus said mildly, 'you find you have come to France.'

Kinnaird took a moment to answer. A breath.

'Yes.' Now he looked up. 'And I don't claim it my shrewdest decision.' Marinus smiled. 'A former business acquaintance, Mr Henry Greene, invited me with the promise of trading opportunity. I found him disappeared. And my attempts to investigate where he might have gone only attracted hostility and suspicion.' He saw Marinus's expression. 'Which I should surely have expected, in these times.' Marinus looked sympathetic. 'Among the more peculiar incidents was a message, apparently from Hal – from Greene – inviting me to a rendezvous. I learned there that you were also expected.' He looked at Marinus again. 'I have traced you today, I should say at this moment, most discreetly and without linking you in any way with my true name or any of the recent incidents.' Marinus nodded, courtesy returned. 'Yet you were shrewder than I, for some reason – hardly difficult to be less shrewd. I escaped by a window when my instincts told me of my predicament. The National Guard then came to arrest me, and I hardly escaped. Greene is confirmed dead, and somehow I am more embroiled. I have been in hiding, well away from Paris.'

'And now you have returned.'

Kinnaird nodded. 'I have been caught up in I know not what. I fancy I have been made a dupe, or grossly misrepresented or misunderstood. I am done with stumbling and with hiding.'

Marinus watched him, now more soberly. He took a sip of wine, and continued to watch, and to consider.

'What, may I ask, is your purpose?'

'My purpose?'

'If you seek answers, I would ask whether the questions are worth the risk. If you seek revenge, I would urge you to fly to the coast immediately and not to be so foolish.'

Kinnaird considered it. 'I own a stubborn unwillingness to be pushed off.' Marinus winced. 'And since some things are clearly being kept from me, I am the more determined to find out what they are.'

'I can't pretend it is the wisest course, Mr – '

'Sir, each man must be who he is. I find that I have not been myself as well as I could. If you will pardon an allusion more familiar to us both: I have found in trade that a man should not let it become known that he is easy to cheat.'

Marinus smiled; nodded.

He seemed to gather himself. 'Allow me, Mr Kinnaird, to offer such context as I may. Perhaps because of my affairs and my contacts, you have speculated that I am likewise linked to irregular dealings involving foreign citizens. I own nothing of the kind. Because of the coincidence of our invitations, you speculate that I must in some way have an equivalence with you. I acknowledge the logical possibility, but I do not own the fact. Yet as a man active and connected in some of the circles of interest to you, I make the following points.' His hands were crossed on his folded legs. Now he opened one palm, and began to count out. 'Point the first: this is a world in ferment. In fever. Point the second: it is a marketplace, in which all habits and restraints have been removed. Grand prices may be secured for a bale of cloth or a barrel of powder; royal fortunes for a paper. But a man may as easily get his throat cut. Point the third: the normal possibilities of exchange between foreigners – men who gain their margin by the relative scarcity of that powder or that paper – are much magnified by the politics of the nations. Point the fourth: at the same time, and it is hardly to be wondered at, the world of the foreigners, and the intricacies of such trade, attract the greatest suspicions from our hosts.'

He paused. Kinnaird waited.

At last Marinus's right index finger touched his left thumb, and now he lifted the thumb, and waggled it at Kinnaird. 'Point the fifth, Mr Kinnaird: your acquaintance Mr Greene was a grand specimen of the phenomenon. I would not own any familiarity with him, but, as I have told the authorities, when they interrogated me after that affair at the Galerie – not all of us, Mr Kinnaird, are as fast out of a window, and some of us find it less obtrusive not to try – but, as I say, I own and owned to having met him in semi-public once or twice. It seemed that he enjoyed an occasional grand trade. It seemed, from his manner, that he did not care how licit the cargo. By character and by context he was the kind of man to benefit maximally from the times. And he was likewise the most dangerous and vulnerable. You will have been suspect merely as a foreigner, Mr Kinnaird. You will have been doubly suspect by association. And trebly suspect by your insistence on asking questions.' He refolded his hands. 'As you will know as well as I, it does not do to spread doubt in the market.'

Kinnaird absorbed it all. He nodded, slowly, sincerely.

Then he smiled. 'And you, Mr Marinus? Might I ask with whom you habitually trade?'

Hand on heart. 'I would prefer you not to oblige of me a discourteous answer.'

They both smiled.

'Mr Kinnaird . . . If I – If I should wish to transact some business with you, how may I find you?'

'I am staying – ' He hesitated. Marinus affected to examine his glass. 'I fancy we are men of the same cloth, Mr Marinus, and I fancy we have ways enough to dish each other. I'll tell you how to find me, although you still won't find me unless I wish it.' Marinus nodded. 'I am sheltering with some acquaintances I met on the road. I am living in Maudi'ville.'

Marinus frowned at the name. 'I don't know it.'

'Except when it wishes to,' – Kinnaird smiled – 'it doesn't exist.'

------------◆------------

Later – an hour unknown, a day unknown – Edward Pinsent sat slumped against the wall, the mattress rucking up beneath him.

He was staring at the picture of his two girls.

He had memories of them. Memories of himself with them – holding them, playing with them; in these memories, the girls were happy and he was smiling benign.

He heard them giggling.

It was possible the memories were dreams.

He was supposed to be replaying his life: recalling, searching. But each time he happened to glimpse something that he thought might be true, it made him wince. Discomforts, and embarrassments, and losses, and betrayals, and shame. He couldn't see a single smile.

Raph. He thought he could recall Raph smiling.

Raph was dead.

He flexed his hand.

He looked at the picture again. He was sure he could hear them giggling.

He raised his hand.

The picture seemed misty. He couldn't see his girls clearly. Somehow, he heard them.

Downstairs, they heard the pistol shot: alarm, and immediately they were waiting for something else, something worse, a knock at their own door. Gradually the alarm subsided. They did not investigate. These are terrible times, and terrible things happen. It's best to leave strangers alone.

------------◆------------

Strange heralds

Sir,

Welsh Williams continues popular here; and why should he not? For if they know not what he can do, it seems they know he can do no harm. Not to France, at any rate. He continues to heat up the matrons of the salons, while bustling between the political offices trying to convince them of the peaceableness of a more refined element in British society, and spread the spirit of fraternal love. I don't say the ministry couldn't do with a dose, but in these days their preoccupations are otherwise, and it were as well to try to pacify a tiger by offering him a titmouse. Interior Minister Roland has had Williams made a citizen of France. (Little Matthews, one fears, had to be content with one of the lithographs of Danton being hawked on the Embankment.) Perhaps he thinks this shall save him at the last trump; myself I shall trust to a closed coach and a well-fed four. Of more interest, he has had two meetings with Lebrun, at that time temporarily Minister for War. Perhaps he thinks it fittest to take his message of peace to the cradle of belligerence; more likely he had introductions to Lebrun, for Lebrun is of the faction of the Gironde, and these gentler fellows – such also is Brissot – seem to be Williams's acquaintances in France.

He may find that he has come too late, though, for the growing military success and warlike spirit in Paris is matched by the eclipsing of the Girondins, and the man who inclines to peace and to pacific souls may find himself soon out of fashion.

I must also report a meeting with the elusive Kinnaird – for I confide it was he, though he was most delicate to obscure the point. It is my habit to take a turn in the Gardens before supper, and he contrived to greet me there most discreetly, at dusk, such that we might not either of us be embarrassed by the encounter. (I have had fellows turning up at my very door,

which is rank amateurism and damned ill manners with it.)
He confirmed who I was, and gave his name as Mackay, or
McCorkadale, or it may have been Louis-the-King for all the
credit I gave it. At the end of our encounter I asked him to
repeat his name, saying that I had forgot it quite, for it seemed
a name as did not quite suit him, and if he was in earnest was
there not some other name that might not do him as well, and
he said that no, there was not, not that a man such as I would
want to be obliged to own to having met, or to be put to the
trouble of denying, which I call prudent and most courteous.
But I hazard that this was the mysterious Kinnaird, for there
are surely few Scotsmen, peculiar race though they may be,
loitering in the public gardens of Paris under tomfool names
on errands of intrigue, especially not now the evenings are
become much cooler.

Our conversation was the prettiest exchange of discretions
that two gentlemen could wish for. He made no crass
assertions of my status, inclinations or activities, merely
confided that he had understood me to be a man who interested
himself discreetly in trade and in public affairs, and that my
nationality gave me a nice distinction in the current ferment;
he owned himself, in a small way, a man likewise interested
in the affairs of the moment, and was no more bold than to
suggest that should occasions make our acquaintance more
easy, we might the both find it congenial to exchange data of
interest. I thought this all most becoming, and told him that
should he ever find himself able to present himself openly at
my door without risk of discomfiture he'd be my honoured
guest at supper, and that for the meantime he should feel at
liberty to accost me in the twilight whensoever the mood
took him. He took it all most courteously, and withdrew as
prudently as he had come.

This, then, I take to be Kinnaird, who seems to feature
ever larger in the imaginations of the police, or so I understand
from my acquaintances privy to their preoccupations. A lean

fellow, with a good steady bearing; his eye clear and watchful. And above all a man apparently born to discretion, and that's a treasure in these boisterous times.

E. E.

[SS F/24/152 (DECYPHERED)]

———————◆———————

Fouché watched Emma Lavalier for a long time.

He was invisible to her, behind her in the shadows, and it gave him leisure to contemplate her body, and her reactions, without the unsettling scrutiny of those eyes.

She gleamed like the moon in the night, down here in this Paris cellar.

He considered her back: stiff, tight-bound, and distilling itself into the neck that swept up under the dark curls. It had been her back and her neck he had glimpsed that night at Roland's, the guest of Madame Roland.

He tried to read her reaction to the body on the boards in front of her. There had been no physical reaction, but he waited for something in the tilt of the head, or even just the breathing. He hoped to catch something of an expression, even though her face was away from him. But she was absolutely still.

Death had no interest for Fouché. Humans were meat, and dead bodies were how they all ended. But he was fascinated by the reaction of others to death.

The man on the boards had been her lover; so the rumours said. What does a woman feel, when the body that has been warmth and life to her is laid out cold and dead? Does she remember him warm, and deny the death? Or does she wonder how she could ever have mistaken the wax statue for life?

Emma Lavalier was silent, and still.

Fouché had wondered if she might throw herself on the body of Sir Raphael Benjamin, in grief and in passion. At least a touch, a tremulous hand outstretched – to what was lost; to what awaited her as much as anyone.

But nothing.

A servant lurked in the darkness at the other end of the body – a shadowed, shuffling figure who'd followed in a few paces behind the lady, presumably to help carry the dead Englishman out. She wouldn't want to show emotion in front of a servant, naturally. But tonight, alone, what might she cry into the night? When that bodice was untightened, and she was alone.

Fouché stepped forwards. He saw the sudden tightness, in the tendons in her neck and the muscles in her jaw.

Emma had assumed Fouché would be there. Another triumph over his enemies. A triumph over her. He would wish to enjoy it. He would wish to take advantage.

'Your invitations are surprisingly irresistible, Monsieur Fouché,' she said without turning.

She didn't see his reaction; half smile, half wince.

There were various things he could have said: that she kept suspicious friends; that she and the dead man had been lovers. Instead he said: 'You'd said he had been of your circle. I thought that . . . his friends; or his people.'

Now she faced him. 'Thank you,' she said; and meant it.

Fouché stepped away from her, and accordingly she felt her breaths easing. But it was only a couple of steps, and he was knocking at a long plain box which she hadn't noticed in the gloom. A closed box up on trestles; a coffin.

Having knocked, he cocked his head as if listening for reply, and his eyes shone at her in some mad delight. It was such a ludicrous performance, and she knew it utterly unlike him, and wondered how much he had rehearsed it; wondered at the odd obsessions in this stiff pale man.

'That one you may take,' he said. 'This one' – he pointed at the box beside him – 'we will keep a little longer.' She felt her breath coming out in a hiss. 'Another foreign friend. Mr Greene.'

She merely nodded.

'We are not yet satisfied with the story of this one. There may yet be signs, from his clothes. He seemed to attract trouble, this one. We will keep him a little longer, and we will see what he attracts.'

She was suddenly aware of her position relative to these men; to all men.

Standing between the dead bodies of two lovers; strange and in their way exotic foreigners, who had brought something of their different world and had promised a new world of amusement and had not been strong enough to survive the experiment. Benjamin and Greene had been pleasure, and possibility, and that door had closed. Now they were a stained past she would have trouble escaping; they were vulnerability.

And closer to her Fouché, the new world not of romance and escape, but of endless accusation and threat, of the remorseless scrutiny of her actions and even her thoughts. An unknown, unstable future. And there was another man in the cellar, the attendant: there was always, of course, someone watching silently from the shadows.

'If this carries on, Monsieur Fouché, there'll be none of my salon left to invite; and then I suppose it'll have to be you, won't it?'

Fouché was startled. Not the words, but the tone. She hadn't spoken bitterly, or in sorrow. It had been a mild pleasantry, and utterly controlled. Suddenly he saw her as she was: not some gilded court adornment, but someone who knew about scuffling to get a foot in the door; someone calculating. She wasn't a victim, or an obstacle, but . . . a fellow-player?

Or a rival?

'Any deed would be worth that honour, Madame.'

'You could have just asked.'

'Yes; I suspect I could.' He realized that he could, and it came as another lesson about her.

'Marie-Jeanne Roland has a much more notable circle,' she said. 'But I'm sure you'd find mine more interesting.'

'I have no doubt of it.' Fouché was uncomfortable in the pleasantries now. He nodded towards the silent attendant in the shadows. 'I shall send a man to help your servant with the body.'

Emma glanced at the attendant, as if noticing him for the first time, and nodded. Then she turned to Fouché and nodded more formally. 'Thank you.'

Fouché left, a scratch of bootsteps disappearing down the damp passage.

Silence, and stillness, and then at last Emma Lavalier came close to the body on the boards, to the frozen features, and bowed her head.

'And you, Mr Kinnaird?' she said softly without looking up. 'If you're wanting an invitation to my salon, you've an even stranger way of going about it than that creature.'

The face of the attendant lifted, and the shadows on it shifted, and a half-closed eye opened and the head pulled out of its hunch and Keith Kinnaird glanced intently around the cellar. 'I'm a sight more desperate than he, I should say.'

She repeated his checking of the cellar, and the entrance to the passage, still grappling with his wholly uncharacteristic boldness. 'And rather more enterprising, it seems. I didn't see you coming in with me.'

'I came up behind you as you entered, and they assumed me with you. No one notices servants, even in revolutionary France.' His lip curled, and she heard the scorn against himself. 'A foolish dare to myself, perhaps, and I fancied it might prove useful to know the rhythms and weaknesses of this building.'

She saw the calculating man, and remembered his calm in her salon when he'd visited after her first interrogation. 'You risk becoming permanently acquainted with it. The ministry is easier entered than departed.'

'The last weeks have taught me to measure risk anew.' He stepped quickly to the coffin at the side of the cellar. For a moment he let his palm run over the rough timber. Then he took a breath and lifted the lid, keeping the opening away from Emma.

His face revolted at the sight, but he forced his glance. The contents were as advertised. The late Henry Greene, getting later all the time. Kinnaird tried to find the face he remembered. But his memories were elusive now.

The side of the head was misshapen. Greene had been hit there: something rough; something fatal.

They'd tossed some powder over the body, presumably to contain the stench; it wasn't doing much for the stench, and only made the man more strange than ever, part statue part ghost.

Then Kinnaird was glancing around the cellar: its arches and deeper shadows, an ancient rotting barrel and, against one wall, an empty coffin – ready for Benjamin. He saw her watching him, and stopped a moment. She was still; poised; composed. 'You were magnificent,' he said, nodding towards where Fouché had left. 'He's not comfortable about you, but he's getting used to you.'

'That,' she said, looking into the darkness of the passageway, 'is now France. It is no longer a matter of supporting or resisting; of liking or repelling. One must accommodate.' He nodded, watching her face, trying not to let his admiration distract him. 'And this one?' she asked, nodding down at the body of Sir Raphael Benjamin.

She saw it herself. Remembered his hungry vitality. Remembered his touch. She wished she could feel something.

Kinnaird stepped forwards, and looked once along the length of the man.

'Cheap boots,' he said.

Their eyes met over the body, and they each wondered at the other, hunted the weaknesses; and the eyes held steady.

Footsteps tramped damply towards them. 'Place him in the coffin and carry him carefully,' Emma said louder, and in French. 'He deserves respect.' Kinnaird bowed his head, and it stayed bowed as a guard appeared from the passageway.

Raph Benjamin was not a small body, and Kinnaird and the guard made heavy work of carrying the coffin. Emma Lavalier walked ahead of them. She wanted to hurry. She wanted to be free of this place. She wanted to escape the ghastly box that was following her, like a terrible memory she couldn't forget. But she knew that Kinnaird was safer in her entourage, and for some uncomfortable reason that seemed important now. She also knew that haste would attract attention.

She walked on, steady, feeling the tension in her thighs and her belly.

The passageways stretched out for an eternity, dank and grey and hopeless. Still she walked. Still the box trudged indefatigable behind her, still the memory keeping pace with her.

She could hear the men's breaths, heavy behind her.

At last a turn – more discomfort for the men carrying the coffin – and another turn – a thump and a curse and she thought briefly of the live Benjamin, and how his elegance did not deserve this mauling – and then light ahead.

'One moment!'

Fouché's voice from somewhere behind her shoulder, a doorway she'd not seen.

She walked on.

'Our trade, Madame, makes it probable that we shall continue to meet.' She slowed. 'I shall hope that more civilized excuses for an invitation will prove more congenial.'

It broke her stride, and she hesitated.

It was true. France was changing, and she must change, and she must continue to meet Fouché and men like him.

She nodded. And walked on.

———— ◆ ————

The National Convention is brittle. Fouché likes to sit on one of the higher benches, and from this perspective he can see the divisions developing and shifting and firming across the chamber, like cracks racing across ice. He knows that sometime soon the ice will break. It's becoming important to know where you stand.

'He must die, now! End the danger! End the myth!'

'Louis is our greatest asset. While he lives, the world is reminded of his weaknesses and his failures and his treacheries. While he lives, they will fear what could happen to him.'

'To make a king a hostage? We are become kidnappers now?'

'Enough of these mediaeval fancies!'

Roland is becoming more uncomfortable. Fouché sees it in his thinness, in the eyes that won't rest, in the weariness. Roland does not like chaos. Roland does not like extremes. But the ice is thinnest in the centre.

'Try him, now.'

'Try a king? For what? You make the Revolution a puppet-show.'

And Danton? Fouché thinks. *Where does Danton stand?* Danton is a big man. If you're standing next to Danton, you want to be sure the ice is firm.

'On what charge? What point of law? His whole existence is a crime. What would be the purpose of identifying one incident from a life of obscenity? What would be the purpose of remarking one smudge in a sea of excrement?'

Sometimes Fouché's mind wanders. He revises documents in his head. He reviews the inter-relationship of documents.

What would be the purpose of identifying one incident from a life of obscenity?

Louis's bizarre gilded life. Ludicrousness and luxury while his nation starved. Games with locksmiths.

Locksmiths were always being invited.

So why is the visit of one locksmith remarked in the steward's book, when none of the others is?

———————— ◆ ————————

Emma Lavalier was sprawled on the divan in her parlour, eyes heavy, a pamphlet in her lap that would not be read however hard she came at it, when she heard the knock.

The knock came from the door to the functional parts of the house – to where Colette was presumably doing whatever she did in the afternoons. Colette usually passed through the door without knocking. Or she would knock and enter.

Lavalier came fully awake.

Again the knock.

'Colette?' she said, voice louder and echoing. She disliked raising her voice.

Which was precisely why Colette knew that – unless Madame was obviously not to be disturbed – she was expected to move silently through the house.

Again the knock.

Lavalier stood. It was not supposed to be like this. It was wrong.

She walked to the door, feeling her loneliness in the house. Where was Colette?

She couldn't remember ever having gone through the door. It was plain; barely visible within the panelling. Beside it, a vase of late roses, frail and pale. Was there even a handle on her side of the door?

She felt that she ought to knock.

An unobtrusive brass handle. She pulled at it. 'Colette?'

A face was immediately in front of her. A young woman, staring back at her – but not Colette. It was the apothecary's girl . . . It was Lucie Gérard.

'How did you – ?'

'Benoit the policeman has his afternoon off today; you usually sleep at this hour; so this is when Colette goes out to play with him. Easy to slip in the back door, and it's close to the trees.'

Lavalier was angry and amused by it. 'Truly you know everything, Mademoiselle Gérard.'

'I'm probably not the only one. You should watch your jewels, Madame. Or do you also keep them – ?' she nodded towards Lavalier's cleavage.

'I'll bear it in mind.' She opened the door further. 'And are you after my jewels, Lucie, or why – ?'

The opening door revealed the man standing behind Lucie.

Kinnaird bowed his head. 'Madame.'

'Mr Kinnaird,' she said, politely, 'of course. Have you once, in all your time in France, entered somewhere by invitation?'

'I've a standing invitation to La Force, I understand; but it's the one I don't choose to accept.'

'Naturally. You are,' Emma said, 'a most contrary man.'

'It used to be a bad habit. It turns out to be the one thing keeping me alive.'

'Mm. I refuse to lurk in a kitchen. If you're so anxious for my company, you can enjoy it in the salon.'

She saw them installed on chairs close to her divan. Kinnaird said, 'Madame, I – '

'First of all and most importantly, Lucie: should I fear that Colette may be in trouble?'

Lucie shook her head. 'She's not obliging Benoit yet.'

'Is she not? Truly the Revolution has changed things.'

'When she starts stealing your perfume you should worry.'

'I will have it in mind. Dear Lucie, your sense of poise is charming. But not the stiffness. You have the height – you certainly have the legs – to lie back a little. It suggests control, and will emphasize the features of your lovely young body.'

Lucie folded her arms. 'I don't play other people's games, Madame.'

Lavalier smiled. 'Lord, but you're a wild beauty, aren't you? Have you fucked this one?' Hardly a nod towards Kinnaird. 'Has he tried?'

Lucie shook her head, and shrugged. 'I thought maybe he was the other sort.'

'No . . .' Lavalier reviewed it. 'No, he's not that. One learns to tell. But he's choosy, this one. Stubborn. Difficult. It's rather frustrating; removes one's greatest power of control. There's one like him in the Ministry of the Interior.'

'Madame' – Kinnaird, at last – 'you disappoint me if the extent of your brilliance relies on men wanting to bed you.'

Emma Lavalier sat up, neck high and head proud. 'Monsieur Kinnaird, no man has understood more than one hundredth of my brilliance. You have not seen more than a candle's glimmer.' She relaxed against the divan again, laid an arm along a cushion. 'It's a matter of courtesy, really. To desire one's hostess a little is no more than good manners.'

Kinnaird smiled. 'As you've no doubt observed, Madame, I have no manners. You're certainly the most beautiful woman I've ever met. But that's God and your mother. Much more impressively, you are without doubt the most controlled, the most certain being I've ever met. At the same time abandoned and wholly in command, of yourself and your world. Self-contained and yet wholly unbounded.'

'Well, that's a bit better. And still you wouldn't deign to throw yourself at me?'

'I'm not so young any more, Madame. My time of chasing dreams is passed. In your embrace a man might find the enchantment of a sorceress or a knife in the back. He certainly would not escape unchanged.'

'What about poor Lucie, then?'

'She's got trouble enough without my embraces, the poor child.'

'Chi-'

'Monsieur Kinnaird . . . Do you really mean to say that you're a good man? No wonder you're so lonely in France.'

'That's what I came to ask you, Madame. A conversation we've twice not been able to finish. I once had pretensions to being a good man. Now the general opinion seems to be so much to the contrary that I'm beginning to doubt it myself.' He sat forwards. 'I am hunted, Madame. The National Guard; the police. I must find ways to counter this. You know these men, Madame; they have talked to you of the foreigners of St-Denis, I'm sure.

I am forced to live in a gypsy camp. Why?'

'You are the focus of the greatest suspicion, because of your association with Henry Greene, and thereby with the theft of the royal jewels, and with all the other things he might have been involved in, and with his peculiar death. And you have been directly reported in a series of compromising encounters with royalists and anti-revolutionaries. There are documents in the ministry that show all this, and much else.'

'Fictions, created by – '

'You are hunted by a man named Fouché – you met him there, in the cellar, when we brought out Raph. He is the brightest most active mind in the ministry, with increasing influence over the minister, with full control of the police and the National Guard, and with the most inhuman relentlessness.'

'Would it surprise you to know that I have done approximately none of the things I'm apparently blamed for?'

'Monsieur Kinnaird, in what used to be the most civilized city on earth, there are now massacres in the streets and British spies breaking into ladies' kitchens. What should surprise me any more?'

'How could I disprove the lies?'

'You cannot, and it would not matter.' She saw his uncertainty. 'You are an enemy of the Revolution now. The Revolution needs enemies; it needs victims. It has no use for innocent men.'

Kinnaird and Lucie took their leave at the door to the kitchen. He looked into Lavalier's eyes; it was the closest he'd ever been to her. 'What happened to Henry Greene, Madame?'

'Exactly what is happening to you, now.' Her head came back, and she considered him with greater perspective. 'And yet . . . Your predicament is not different to his; but you are different to him. I wonder at you, Monsieur Kinnaird.' She glanced down, and pulled one of the rose stems out of the vase. Holding it between finger and thumb, she held her other palm against the last blossom of the year, and then crushed it. 'Beautiful things are dying for ever. I . . . I fear you, because you may, in your stubborn ill-dressed implacable way, be the man of the age. You – like the creature in the ministry – may be the future.' She gazed into him. 'I wonder whether one of you must also be my future.'

His eyes were in hers. 'We've a pretty rough magic in Scotland, but I'll promise you no knife in the back.'

She seemed to consider this. A nod, a polite smile.

He offered her his hand. She took it, and Kinnaird saw too late that she was still holding the rose stem, with its broken flower. Eyes locked on his, she squeezed, and they both winced as the thorns bit.

Her eyes opened wider, and her lips. 'Try to feel, Monsieur Kinnaird.'

He nodded. 'In your service, Madame. Always.'

In the end he broke her gaze, with a nod of courtesy, and turned away. Lucie made to follow him. 'Lucie.' She turned.

'You don't have to be poor to be a whore, Lucie. What matters is the price you get for it.'

'I'm just trying to survive, Madame. That's all there is.'

'There must be more.'

'Easier for you, Madame.'

Lavalier cupped her hand around Lucie's jaw, and kissed her on the lips. 'We have to live life, Lucie. Otherwise there's no point in it.'

———— ◆ ————

In a laundry in Argenteuil, two men watched each other's outline through steam.

'It's all there! It must be! The pompous idiot Louis would have kept everything.'

Karl Arnim nodded soberly. 'Uncomfortable for you.'

The face loomed out of the steam close to his. 'Uncomfortable for you! All of the correspondence between Berlin and Paris, he'll have kept that. And God knows what Mirabeau will have written.'

'We're already at war.'

'The mob hasn't toppled your King yet. Those letters could do it.'

Arnim's nose wrinkled. It had been a pleasant ride here, through woods, along the river, placid out of the city. But the laundry was humid, a fog of mysterious vats with ghostly bundles floating in them, a white inferno of steam, and the poisonous sting of lye in his nostrils.

In his mind, he was recalling the latest letter from the Duke of

Brunswick's camp. The letter was ashes now; there'd been nothing in its rather overwrought words that might prove useful in the future.

Brunswick would not move against France again this year; it was essential that Prussia's correspondence with France be secured or destroyed.

'So you must find them.' Arnim's voice came more insistent than he had intended. He tempered it: 'The rewards will be great.'

'Damn your rewards. You're too late.'

Arnim's voice came harsher again. 'Meaning?'

'The shit Fouché. He's discovered something new; decisive, he thinks. God knows; he's probably sacrificing chickens in that office of his and reading the entrails. If there was a concealed hiding-place in the Tuileries, only two people would be guaranteed to know it: Louis himself, and the man who helped him conceal it.' The face loomed out of the steam again. 'Fouché's found the locksmith.'

'Found him?'

'Identified him, from palace records. Man named Gamain. François Gamain. He'll not martyr himself for the Capets, not a locksmith. Fouché's police are searching for him now – secretly – no proclamations this time – and as soon as they find him he'll lead them to the trove.'

'There is still time then.'

'To do what? Burn the Tuileries to the ground?'

Arnim considered. He considered the possibility of burning the Tuileries to the ground, to which he had no great objection except that it was hard to do the thing decisively. Mainly he considered that the conversation – and the relationship – was becoming obnoxious.

He needed Marinus. 'There is still time.'

———— ◆ ————

Alone again in her salon, Emma Lavalier heard again snatches of the conversation.

It had been a grand performance. She had dazzled her audience.

So why, when they left, did she feel they were escaping her – leaving her behind?

Wholly in command, of myself and my world. Kinnaird's words, and she gloried in their truth.

Except they weren't true any more.

Lucie, just trying to survive. *That's all there is.*

That wonderful wild girl had something to teach her. To live indifferent to the world and its changes, and to survive.

Because if she had to live in the world, Lavalier would have to choose.

And her first choice had to be about Kinnaird.

A man's indifference to the world's conventions was the most beautiful thing about him. Once, that indifference had been a statement of morality: a refusal to be limited by social conventions. By that measure, Kinnaird was as boring a man as ever lived.

But with murder in the streets, a government forced to compete in bloodthirstiness with its mob, indifference was become a statement of existence. A refusal to be limited by France's new rules, its reality; its chaos.

By that measure, the lean resilient Britisher was become the most beautiful of men. It was a hidden beauty, sufficient to itself: the strength of the mountain's age, the force of the river's flow.

He offered Emma Lavalier the most glorious example of how to treat the world of the Revolution.

But Kinnaird's was a solitary path. His survival depended on his own luck and genius, but also on the trust of the few people he must have contact with. And their own survival, in revolutionary France and confronted with an enemy of France, might lie on a very different path.

Lavalier had got thus far in her reflections when there was a knock at the front door: a messenger, bringing a summons from Fouché.

Keith Kinnaird sat anonymous in a crowded tavern, and imagined the room empty, and found a single figure filling his mind.

He had learned that crowds were the best place to hide. He had come to recognize that one of his great strengths was his indistinction. This was the lesson of Sir Raphael Benjamin. Individuality was best preserved not in distinction, but in anonymity.

So the fugitive Britisher knocked shoulders with dozens of Frenchmen who would have enjoyed his guillotining, and they did not see him.

He didn't see them either. He only saw Emma Lavalier.

Now that he had come to recognize her extraordinary strength of character – her resilience – he had come to recognize her beauty. She was an organism perfectly adapted and adaptable to her environment, and he found this wonderful. She was human nature at its most magnificent, and this thrilled him.

And might it be me that destroys her?

He had to assume – and recent experience seemed to teach – that he was watched far more than he could realize. He had to assume that she – so glamorous, so notorious – was watched. He had to assume that, by one or both means, their contact was known. And it was not merely an incidental contact, such as her acquaintance with Benjamin or with Hal Greene before they became controversial; he had to assume that it was known that she had met him long after he was a publicly declared fugitive.

She is guilty by association with me. She is tainted because she has touched me.

Should he change his behaviour? Could he – could he somehow distance himself from her, so that she was freed of the association? It was too late.

He had been declared a spy when he was not, and hunted accordingly. Now, it seemed, he was becoming one. He had striven to match his reputation to his real self. He had failed, and now he was changing himself to match his reputation.

This change is no danger to me, because I was already hunted. But to those who know me? Those who are once seen with me?

Once he would have looked on a woman like Lavalier as the most advanced in sin. Now she seemed the most innocent creature in France. In truth, she had done nothing against her country, but now her country would punish her. Her pleasures, and her sins, once the outrage of society, now seemed sadly harmless. It was not her dalliances with the men of exoticism and glamour that would destroy her; it was her acquaintance with one dull Scot. *And surely she must know.*

It was too late for Emma Lavalier.

------- ◆ -------

Fouché now inhabited a world made entirely of paper. What was once his office was now a forest of documents, underfoot and sprouting over what might once have been furniture, and from hints of shelves like branches more documents seemed to hang overhead. As if, in some brilliant new chemical process that cut through the old industry, trees were now sprouting paper directly. And these leaves were already written, too. Scraps with a few words. Bundles tied with string. Thick dossiers in card folders. Piles – puddles – of paper. The ministry building, the office, had fallen away – they had been a temporary structure while Fouché made his nest of documents, and now the documents were strong enough to stand alone.

Emma Lavalier watched him at the heart of it, as she would a wasp's nest in a tree or a fungus sprouting under the eaves, some unsettling parasitic creature that had made its habitat in a once familiar place.

His summons had been elegant, and unavoidable. *Our shared interest. Your certain loyalty.* They were assertions impossible to refuse now.

And it had been a summons. The creature was grown bold. She watched his eyes watching her, shining out of the courteous bow. He had found an advantage, he had reinforced it in the cellar, and now he was making his play.

She recalled her journey through Paris this morning: there were more soldiers now, scruffy and edgy and muskets held loose, at corners and blocking doorways and falling out of taverns; a rash of pamphlets and proclamations disfigured windows and walls, nailed and glued carelessly, warning and telling and celebrating and banning; crossing the entrance to the Place du Carrousel, she had glimpsed the machine; in the rue de Castiglione a smear of blood scarred the pavement. And it all led to this office.

'You honour me, Ma-'

'Have you read all of this?'

She'd blurted it instinctively, but it played to his vanity nicely enough. 'All of it,' he said; an unexceptional fact.

'You . . . you can recall it all?'

This he considered. 'It is not some exterior reality – a name, or a list – to be recalled. This totality of information, and my mind, are as one. They reflect and remind each other.' It was unremarkable to him, despite the little pride. He didn't think himself inhuman, and that was the most inhuman thing of all. 'Do please sit, Madame Lavalier.'

There was a chair for her: a temporary and alien phenomenon amid the paper.

She sat. She checked first that she wasn't sitting on a paper. 'You have . . . collaborators? Assistants?'

'I tried a pair of clerks, but they were dull men, and their insistence on tidying was merely a crutch for their own weak minds, and an interference with the more natural arrangements of my own.'

She touched one palm to her chest, opened her eyes wide, and said, 'I see that this is where France is truly governed'. And she meant it. It was the revelation she had felt watching the watcher in the street, the night of Raph Benjamin's death. This was the Revolution: everything would be known; everything would be controlled; everything would be judged.

'You flatter me, Madame.'

'I think we are both beyond such poses, Monsieur.' She sat back, breathed in deep.

He smiled; nodded. He was still standing, and his hand roved over the papers in front of him. 'It's all here,' he said, picking up a card folder and slapping it down in front of her. A name she didn't recognize was on the cover. Then he touched his forehead with one shaking finger. 'And here.' Then another folder slapped down. 'The Prussians.' Another slap. 'The British.' Another slap. She hadn't caught one of the titles; the other had been *Abbeys*. 'Greene. Benjamin. Kinnaird.' Slap. Slap. Slap. One of the folders, as Emma's eyes flicked up and down between Fouché's face and the growing pile, did indeed have Kinnaird's name on it. Another was *Stockpiling*. Another had been a Spanish name she didn't recognize. Slap. She missed the name.

She kept her eyes on Fouché's face now. Slap. 'And me, I presume.'

Fouché stopped. He thought for a moment, then waved a dismissive hand, and its fingers flickered towards the papers around him. 'De Guichy. Martineau. Baron Holheim. Your acquaintance with the woman La Motte, who had contrived the scandal of the Queen's necklace. A house in Tours. Your late husband's position as secretary to the commission on the charlatan Mesmer.' He shrugged, sneered. 'These are trivia, Madame. These are not you, nor your true status. I am indifferent.' He had deliberately not mentioned that he knew that the Friends of Magnetism continued to circulate correspondence through the apothecary in St-Denis. 'As you rightly say, we are beyond such poses.'

But they are me, and they are mine. She smiled at Fouché, let her tongue hesitate on her lip. Inside, she felt as if those flickering fingers had made to touch her. *Tours . . .* And inside, every muscle recoiled. *Everything is known. Everything is controlled. Everything is judged.*

The clarity came out in a sigh of satisfaction. 'You put it very sensibly, Monsieur. And beyond the poses, where are we?'

'*What* are we, Madame? *Who* are we? Let us start by confirming this. I invite you here to . . . to offer you a picture of a reality. I invite you to accede to it.'

'By all means.' *This is violation.*

'The period of compromise – of negotiation, of ambivalence and ambiguity – this period is passing. The Revolution is predominant, sure, and absolute.'

My life has been a glorious orgy of ambiguity. I have bathed in ambiguity like Cleopatra in milk and blossoms.

'There can be no more wavering. No slipperiness; no shadows. You are a loyal citizen of the Revolution, or you are an enemy and you are destroyed.'

Martineau and I seduced each other over three months, and we exploded like the sun.

Fouché's fingers flickered towards her. 'Your prominence, Madame, it gives you a certain vulnerability in these times.' *Wake up, Emma.* 'And yet, once you are surely committed to the Revolution, your distinction and your abilities will give you new influence and new rewards.'

There can be no Tours, not any more. 'The argument becomes irresistible, Monsieur.'

He leaned forwards. 'It were wise to decide fast. The crisis is imminent.' She tried to make alarm look like polite interest. 'I am convinced that the former King left behind him a trove of secret correspondence. There is a man called Gamain, Madame; a locksmith who has become a key. I will have him imminently, and he will unlock all of Louis's secrets. The royal duplicity. The trove will be substantial, I am sure; I already have ample lodging set aside for it – down next to your friend Greene, indeed. From what we already know, I expect that these documents will shame Berlin, and they will shame London, and most of all they will shame Louis who was King. His credibility will be destroyed for ever. Europe will shake, and most of all Paris will shake.'

Fouché could see her pleasure. He could see that she loved the sense of knowledge, of influence, and he knew that this was why he had won her.

A woman can feign pleasure more habitually than anything. Luxuriant smile. 'You long ago recognized me for a practical woman, Monsieur; and you appeal to practicality. At the same time I am . . . attracted by strength. The Revolution is the great force of the age. We are obliged – we are drawn – to contribute to its power, and in doing so we are empowered.'

'Indeed. I knew in the end you would make a just calculation.'

'Yet I am uneasy, Monsieur Fouché.' *I must be more than passive.* She saw his eyes narrow. *Careful, Emma.* 'I am, as you know, familiar with diverse figures of the Revolution. What if I find that some of them lack the . . . the necessary certainty?'

He was nodding; smiling. 'In the end, and soon, all will be found loyal or disloyal. There is a line, Madame; a line as fine as the guillotine's blade.' She nodded, sombre. 'We should develop the habit of confiding in each other.' Now she produced a little smile.

Fouché was still talking. 'I said that Paris will shake at the secret documents; I said that Louis's credibility will be destroyed.' He nodded to one side, to the half-open door. Perversely, Roland's office had become the ante-room to Fouché's, and Lavalier had been escorted in accordingly, her warm greeting to the minister as she passed reciprocated uncomfortably. 'I strongly suspect, Madame' – Fouché was looking at the door, seeing the minister beyond it – 'that the credibility of the compromisers and the corrupt ones will be destroyed by the King's correspondence too.' And he was seeing others beyond Roland.

His face came round to hers. She smiled.

A knock at the connecting door. A clerk. Monsieur Fouché sought by the President of the Convention. For a moment Emma wondered if he'd contrived the summons to increase his importance, but his irritation seemed genuine. He stood – courteous regret – and she with him. He pulled fully open the door to Roland's office. 'I may have the honour of escorting you out, Madame?'

'I have not had the pleasure of greeting the minister.' Roland looked up from his desk. 'I will remain here a moment.'

Fouché nodded and, his back to Roland, he smiled. 'We should develop the habit of confiding in each other, Madame.'

She smiled at him; faintest nod, shared secret. 'It is beginning, Monsieur.'

His instinct to solitude and his limited tolerance for over-cooked squirrel had led Kinnaird to the habit of finding his supper in an inn a mile or so from the gypsy camp. Today, it was a natural break in his journey home.

The landlord recognized him – Kinnaird realized that this was probably unhealthy, felt a twinge of his old naivety – and nodded at his request for food, and started to usher him to a back room. Kinnaird hadn't been in it before; but the landlord seemed insistent and, saddle-weary, he let himself be ushered, and the door closed behind him.

There was a man sitting in one of the chairs, looking up at him.

Kinnaird took a deep breath, steadied himself. The man stared at him silently. Kinnaird watched him for a moment longer, looked slowly around the room, stuck his head out of the door and looked, then came in again with a knife in his fist. The man was still considering him.

'1769: the young Keith Kinnaird is before the Musselburgh Bailie as one of a group of apprentices charged with riotous assembly. 1775, your name is recorded as one of the acolytes of Harrison, the pamphleteer.' The voice was low, businesslike. The voice was also, clearly, English. '1784, you sailed a little close to the wind in the repackaging and selling on of a certain shipment from Lisbon. You were sailing in a storm as soon as you set up with Henry Greene, and you tacked back into it when you came to Paris at his invitation.'

Kinnaird said, 'Did my mother send you? You'd impress me more if you told me something I don't know.' The man just smiled. 'Such as what happened to Hal Greene, and why I'm hunted for the crimes of other men.'

The man nodded. 'Rather a childish bit of bluster, I'm afraid. But it's all

I have. The aim was to make you aware of how much we know of you. To impress you with the omniscience of the department I represent.'

'You may consider me aware but unimpressed. I've spent the last weeks trying to avoid a knife in the back or the guillotine; old John Cochran of the Musselburgh bench seems less of a threat than he used to. Who are you and what do you want?'

'I am the representative of a department of the British Crown. I decline to give you my name. I apologize for the discourtesy. If I gave a name it would be false, and I can only hope that you take this as the greater sincerity.'

'I'm overwhelmed. What department?'

The man watched him gravely. Then he said, 'Would you consider putting away the blade? We are among the very few people in Europe who at present do not wish you harm.' Kinnaird didn't move. 'It's rather an uncomfortable pose, and I'm hoping for an extended and earnest conversation with you.'

Kinnaird pulled another chair forwards, and sat down in front of the man. 'Well?'

The man took a breath. 'We are the Comptrollerate-General for Scrutiny and Survey.'

'I've never heard of it.'

'We're not in the news-sheets, Mr Kinnaird.' Then the cheeriness died. The man spoke lower, more intent. 'We are the shadow in the darkness. We are responsible for the most secret British espionage work in France, and everywhere else. We are older than the present British system of government. We were old when Walsingham thought he was new. I will not give you the details of our covenant, because I don't know them and you don't need to. The endurance of peace and relative stability in Britain is our greatest achievement and our enduring duty.'

'You'll get few thanks from a Scot.'

'That's fair. But you'll own we've been successful enough.'

'What do you want of me?'

A shrug. 'To make you aware of us, which is something granted to few men. To invite you to align your interests and intentions with something greater.'

Kinnaird looked at him with distaste. After a moment he said, 'Greater? I've seen the British here: salon games.' He stood, and strode to the table and grabbed up a bottle and a glass. Halfway through pouring he glanced at the man. He continued to pour, and handed over the glass. He poured another for himself, and sat again.

The man watched him. 'Mm. You mean Madame Lavalier and her circle. That time is passed, I think.'

Kinnaird took a gulp. 'So easy? In her own way, that woman's the truest thing I've seen in this country. And there's a strength – '

'She would work with anyone. Sleep with anyone. Say anything to anyone. She has seemed to work in concert with us, and we know she's been talking to the French authorities – naturally – and we're fairly sure she's dealt with the agents of at least one other power.'

'You sound like a jealous husband.'

'Grow up, Kinnaird. Soon she'll work out that her only hope is to work exclusively for the Revolution. Or she'll be dead by Christmas. Drop her.'

'I've never held her.' Kinnaird took another mouthful. 'You were inviting me to align my interests with yours, or some such flannel. You want me to work for you? To spy for you?'

The man considered this. Then he said: 'Yes.'

'You're not going to . . . to threaten me, somehow?'

The smile was pleasant, the surprise apparently sincere. 'What would be the need, Mr Kinnaird? You're the most wanted man in France. Your chance of surviving a week is one in a hundred.'

'Again I'm led to wonder then: why me?'

'It has been the habit of the department to deploy – or, better, to identify – men of resolve and resource in France. We begin to find that you are such a man.'

Kinnaird shook his head, weary. 'Why does everyone think me what I am not?'

'Why do you continue to think yourself not what you are?'

'As you say, I may not last a week.'

'Indeed. But, ah, but then the Comptrollerate-General doesn't really have anything to lose, does it?'

Kinnaird looked at him, cold. 'Thank you so much.' His head came back and he considered the man afresh. 'The dandy. Benjamin. That's why you want me. Benjamin was your man, and now you've lost him, and you're running out of men to trap in a corner.'

'Sir Raphael Benjamin worked for us on occasion. Though to be honest he was a secondary figure, an occasional servant and not wittingly.'

Kinnaird considered this doubtfully. Then: 'Greene, of course. Hal was a much shrewder man than Benjamin.'

The man nodded. 'Indeed. Henry Greene was exactly what he seemed to be, and exactly what you knew him: a merchant, an adventurer, and a bit of a rogue. He also did worthy service for London on the side, and we guided him when we needed and ensured certain business benefits by way of reward.'

Kinnaird thought again about Henry Greene. Thought again about his insistence that he join him in France. Thought again about the consequences of that ill-considered journey. 'I – I ain't like Benjamin. I'm not really like Hal Greene, either.'

'You're alive, ain't you? That puts you one up on both of them.' The man leaned forwards. 'London is scared, Kinnaird; or they should be. We've radicalism enough at home – Tom Paine wrote the script for the Americans and now he's here – and half of British society, from Rotherhithe Docks to the Royal Mile, thinks itself sympathetic to the Revolution.'

'I was one of them.'

'Yes, Kinnaird. You were. I don't wish to sound malicious, but how's your radical sympathy after a few weeks hiding in a ditch to escape the guillotine?'

'My radicalism is fine. I still don't trust governments.' He knew it was a lie. France was a betrayal of everything he might have believed in politically, and an endless threat to the good order on which he had built his world.

'How lucky for you that despite your scruples there's one government, at least, prepared to continue to offer you a stability in which to prosper.' The man sat back. 'There's more. Somewhere in Paris is the greatest trove of secret diplomatic information in European history.' Kinnaird's eyes widened. 'Louis the King's correspondence, his schemes and his deals with every regime. The French want it, because it will destroy the King and give them untold influence over the neighbours. The Prussians are hunting it, and they have their best man – a legend, and ruthless – in the field. And I want it.'

'Of course you do.'

'It might save a King's life.' A shrug. 'And there are certain . . . embarrassments that we would also be anxious to avoid.'

'And, in passing, all that influence would be London's instead.'

A smile. 'I've no moral argument to put to you, Mr Kinnaird, for working for me. But it might save your life.'

'I'd the impression that London's activities here were all lace cuffs and larking about.'

The man smiled. '*Touché*, Mr Kinnaird. There has been – perhaps it was appropriate to the time – an . . . amateurishness, to British activities in Paris. As if our national interests might be managed as some sort of recreational diversion in the margins of the Grand Tour.'

'I ain't no gentleman.'

'You been in the Place du Carrousel of late, Mr Kinnaird?' Kinnaird grunted. 'Gentility may no longer be enough. You're different, somehow. You fit the times. Your name has got around. It even cropped up in reports about an escapade of ours in which I know you weren't involved – pretty sure you weren't, anyway. Either you've claimed the deed falsely, which would be imprudent, or you're enough of a devil for it to be the sort of thing you might do.'

'I'm hardly anonymous.'

'If everyone thinks you work for us anyway, we might as well try to get some benefit from you.'

Kinnaird leaned forward and refilled the man's cup. 'And – you'll excuse the instincts of a Scots merchant rather than a London gallant – what do I get from you?'

'It's a fair question, sir.' A sip; a consideration of the wine. 'The answer: precious little.'

'That's poor trade.'

'You're a poor investment. Oh, we'll see you well enough. It's not a salaried post, but a man who makes himself useful to the Crown may pick up a little pension, and you'll find that trade becomes a lot more successful when the right people are giving you the right contracts and the right information.'

'Pension? I'm worried about surviving to Sunday. And I'm perfectly capable of profitable trading as soon as everyone stops trying to kill me.' He scowled at the man. 'How do we – how do we communicate with each other?'

'We will communicate with you when we need.'

'How?'

A pause. 'Discreetly. Effectively.'

'And if I don't reply? If I ignore you?'

The man smiled, and shrugged. 'London has bigger things to worry about. And so do you.'

'Can I contact you?'

'You catch the eye, Mr Kinnaird, but you're still a pretty queer fish for London.' He hesitated. 'Please pardon an insolent comment, but even if you know who your real parents were, and which side they were on in '45, we don't. Loyalty's a funny thing, Mr Kinnaird.'

'For a Scotch subject of the British Empire on the run in France, loyalty's a damned hilarious thing.'

'Quite.' Kinnaird waited silently. 'If you accept the proposition, you will chalk a cross and a circle on the post marking this end of the ferry service to Bezons. I will give you details of three or four places where you may leave a message, such that it will be received by other trusted hands and read rapidly, and neither you nor the intermediary need meet. I will give you instructions for one or two ways of seeking urgent assistance.'

'But London's damned far away, and here there's a police agent on the nearest corner.'

'Indeed.' The man leaned forwards. 'You could have run, Mr Kinnaird. As soon as you found Greene gone and things getting uncomfortable. Made for the coast, and bought a passage home. Autumn in London, at the moment, and it's rather pleasant. Cosy evenings, you know? Pleasant to trot in the park in the afternoons, or take some punch in Pall Mall in the dusk. Roasted chestnuts, Mr Kinnaird! Pretty girl beside you and you don't even mind when some little sod lifts your purse. Safe and pleasant in London. But you stuck, Kinnaird. You pushed. You learned, and you endured.' He sat back again, folded his hands on his stomach. Not much stomach; he was a lean man, Kinnaird saw. 'Something kept you here. Some stubbornness, some determination, some goal. We want some of that, Mr Kinnaird.'

Then he shut up. They watched each other for a minute.

Kinnaird said, 'I was only in Pall Mall once. Never found a place so damned smug. I'll take Paris.'

The man smiled, sober. 'Mr Kinnaird, I rather think you might.' A nod. He shifted in the chair, made to stand.

'That's it? No final plea? No patriotic exhortation?'

'Happy to do it if you want, Kinnaird; "Greensleeves" and "God Save the King". But we're both rather beyond that sort of thing, aren't we?' Kinnaird smiled. 'Mr Kinnaird, one final word: proof of my sincerity, if not my generosity. You asked two questions: what happened to Greene, and why you're hunted for the crimes of other men. First, Henry Greene got tangled in every possible thread of intrigue and opportunity in this place, and we liked him for it, and he'd have done it for his own devilment regardless, but in the end he got those threads twisted around his neck. I saw him early on the morning of the fourth of September, on the Pontoise road. I told him to tighten his habits and put a bit of distance from his friends in St-Denis for a time, and I gave him instructions for two activities: the removal of Madame and Mademoiselle Tourzel from La Force prison, and the disruption of French efforts to survey the meridian north and south of Paris; I fancy he was going to try to interfere with the southward expedition himself, but I've had no report that he managed it.'

Sir Raphael Benjamin's note, of Hal Greene's instructions: *Delambre SD. Tourzels LF.* 'You don't know who killed him?' *A British Government agent is the last man to admit to seeing Hal alive.*

'I don't know. Could have been the French. Could have been the Prussians. Could even have been the Americans, though I – '

'Could have been the English.'

A sniff, and a nod. 'Yes, Mr Kinnaird; it could have been the English.' The man gazed at Kinnaird without discomfort. 'And secondly: you're hunted for the crimes of other men because until now the other men have been cleverer than you. We judge that that balance is shifting. You're on the front foot. You're fighting. Twice now your death has been conjectured, yet other men have died in your stead. You're lucky, and you're alive.' He stood, picked up his hat. 'Keep it up, eh?'

---- ◆ ----

Arnim said, 'I don't like this place.'

'It is an idyllic place!' Marinus seemed genuinely upset. 'It is a . . . a dream, far from the city and far from the chaos we inhabit.'

'It is too open, and we are too distinctive.'

The river looped in from Paris to the left and looped away to the right, towards the vast emptiness of the sea and the rest of the world. The water sat flat, as if the world had stopped.

Marinus had chosen the place for the possibility of concealment: in the trees that fringed close to the river, in the stretch of reed grass nearer the bank, and in the network of paths that crossed them.

He said, 'You're right, of course.'

'Nothing is far from the chaos, dear Pieter.'

They sat on a fallen tree trunk. Marinus passed Arnim a goblet of wine, and then the bottle. 'Corton? My dear fellow, this is excellent. One would think there was no Revolution at all.'

Marinus smiled gently at the big Prussian. 'Are we not trying to overcome the chaos? To resist?'

Arnim breathed in deep, as if by some vast effort he could pull the Seine into his lungs. When his bulk was full, he turned to Marinus, and nodded sombrely. 'It is well put. But first we must recognize the chaos, and learn how to survive in it, and then how to triumph.' Marinus tried the wine himself; savoured it on his tongue, saw the sun on the reeds and the water, closed his eyes. 'And today the chaos is a locksmith.'

Marinus opened his eyes, and looked the question. Arnim told him.

Marinus nodded. He took another sip of wine. He considered the Seine once again. Still looking over it, he said, 'It seems that we are – pardon me, dear sir – less subtle in our methods. Hitherto we concerned ourselves with information, and perhaps misinformation. We listened. Very occasionally we influenced. We were not wont to run around . . . This crudeness, this – this brutality.'

Arnim was a growl. 'You think I like it?'

Marinus hesitated. 'I think, perhaps, that you do.'

And, in the middle of the chaos, Karl Arnim laughed; and the laugh rolled across the water and the water seemed to ripple. 'Well, perhaps I do a little at that.'

They sat in silence a moment, each a smile.

Marinus said to his goblet, 'I have a suggestion. A proposal.'

'I long to hear it.'

'In the chaos, I find that we have an ally.' Immediately, he sensed Arnim stiffening beside him. 'The Britisher, Kinnaird. A man –'

'Strategically, our interests may be opposed.'

'I begin to doubt that. And anyway, I leave strategy for the men who have the great privilege of existing outwith the borders of France. Within those borders, we are alone and vulnerable and we find it very hard to act with the energy that you now seek. This Kinnaird is a man of great discretion and restraint, a man –'

'I don't like it.'

'Of course you don't.'

'If he is as good as he is reputed, every one of our problems is an opportunity for him to gain the greatest advantage over us. London getting those documents would be more of a disaster than Paris getting them.'

'He doesn't have to get them or even to know of them. But he might help us survive.'

There was danger in Arnim's voice again. 'I fancy you begin to doubt me, dear Pieter. I fancy that you find our partnership –'

'You are the greatest man in Europe.' Marinus spoke without emotion. 'But that does not make you invulnerable. You are great enough – wise enough – to take additional advantage when you see it. Today, the British are that advantage.'

Arnim watched him. Marinus, uncomfortable, took another sip of wine.

Arnim growled: a bear digesting, or readying to strike. 'It's pretty flattery, dear friend. It may even be good sense.' He took a mouthful of wine. 'Well then, I'll let you have your Britisher. But not for the documents, Marinus. You may meet him, you may discuss our mutual advantage, but you make no mention to him of the documents, or the locksmith.'

Marinus nodded. Arnim gazed out across the river, and contemplated the possibilities of another British corpse.

———— ♦ ————

The arrival of a closed carriage at the house of Madame Lavalier in St-Denis was noted, because everything is noted in these times, but hardly noteworthy. Carriages – though of late they'd rarely been this smart – were always coming and going at the house of Madame Lavalier. That it was two men who got out of the carriage first was typical of Madame Lavalier. So many of her guests were male. Reports were more vague about a woman travelling with the two men. Nothing was certain about women at Madame Lavalier's, anything was possible, and everything was believed.

They were American, these visitors. This became known later, as the news started to spread, to become more detailed and more elaborate. Again, it was hardly unusual. *More foreign visitors than Havre docks, and more unsavoury.* The exotic and the erotic have a lot in common.

It was shortly after the American visitors had first gone into the house that it became clear that today was unusual, with hasty movements seen at windows and urgent messages rushing out of the house. *The woman more in evidence at that point? Would be, when there was panicking to be done.* And the alarm and the attention it received accelerated rapidly, and soon all of St-Denis knew what the Americans had found.

Distress is private and builds slow. Scandal is public and spreads like disease.

———— ♦ ————

Trade is sacred, and well-kept tools are oily, and so as usual the locksmith Gamain waits before opening the letter addressed to *François Gamain, locksmith*. Madame Gamain has put the letter aside for him and, knowing that it awaits, she is more prompt with his bowl of warm water. Eyes on the envelope, he washes his hands carefully, and dries them likewise, then sits formally. It is a commission, and even after all his years of steady prosperity it still feels like reassurance; like his first independent request after he completed his apprenticeship. And it has been such a worry, during the late upheavals, that trade might suffer, or cash payments be fewer, so perhaps it is not so strange that a new commission should still feel like reassurance. He has obligations to meet; a dignity to maintain. He wants to provide properly for Madame Gamain.

Immediately Madame Gamain starts to complain: what new demand is this? Why does he not pass on the lesser work to Lasalle, or Dominguez? It will take him away from her, no doubt.

And indeed this will take him away from her. The magistrate in Chantilly is moving into new offices, and naturally they require new locks and the greatest quality and reliability, and Maitre Gamain has been commended to them. Recognizing the distance and the scale of the work, the commission notes that this might well be a labour of two full days; accordingly, the magistrate will pay for Gamain's lodging in the Peacock in Chantilly, for two or as many nights as is appropriate, on top of his fee.

Gamain finds that very fair, and appreciates the respect for the intricacy of his craft – *fitting a lock of quality isn't hammering in a nail, sir, though many men seem to think so* – and for his dignity. Nice to deal with serious people. Reassuring to find them, in these times. Discussion some two months back in his circle: *will a fairer society give more respect to the craftsmen?*

But they need him now. The magistrate's offices must function, and he will naturally understand that they cannot be left unprotected. His fee will reflect the urgency. As it happens, he can set off immediately – the commitment at a house in the rue Honoré can be passed to Dominguez. It will delay him starting at the Desmarets saltpetre works by a day or two, and that's another big commission and he doesn't want to disappoint them. But they were flexible. The parts will all come together very neatly: a complex week, but it will work nicely.

Madame Gamain will protest at the impositions of Gamain's trade, and at his obligations despite his seniority within it. Her voice will rise with alarm at the threats to her, a woman of property, left alone in Paris at this time, and is Gamain not paying attention to what's happening in the streets, and did he not hear what she told him of what Madame Fouilly told her, and hasn't he seen that the cobbles in the Place du Carrousel are actually red with blood, and what's the point of living with a locksmith when houses aren't safe any more? She will scold him to the stairs, and then clutch his arm with desperate pleas that he return safe, and avoid meals he hasn't seen cooked properly, and remember that customers are paying for his courtesy as well as his skill so he shouldn't get so caught up in the mechanism that he forgets to make dignified pleasantries.

And Gamain will for the second time open his bag and unroll the cloth-wrapped set of tools, and touch and count them each, and re-roll the bundle and settle it snug in the bag and close the bag and swing it over his shoulder. Then he will catch Madame Gamain's hand wherever he finds it in flight, and bend over it and place a delicate kiss on the knuckles. Then, still holding her hand, he will step forward and kiss her full on the lips, and with her little squeak rising up the stairs after him the locksmith Gamain will step out of his workshop and into the chaos of revolutionary Paris.

<hr>

The gypsy camp sprawled over the hillside like the residue left by a receding tide. Marinus felt exposed as he approached it, along an unhedged track through bare fields, though others were making the same journey and he was not conspicuous.

Arnim had stopped at the last village a mile back. Less risky for both of them, if Arnim did not travel on with him, and a sign of the Prussian's trust.

The camp was a smear across the low hill. Well before Marinus was among the first huts and tents he could smell it, the smell of cooking and humans and horses somehow as dark as the camp. The gypsies would stay on the hill another week at least, depending on the weather and the trickle of trade coming in from the nearby villages. Particularly in the evenings there would be visitors from Paris too, wine-warmed young men daring each other to risk a wager on the dice or a tumble with one of the devil's daughters.

Maudi'ville. The town of the accursed.

He was among the first shelters now, tight-strung shanties of poles and cloths and mysterious folding panels, that looked as if they'd been there for years, but could disappear in an hour. A cross-eyed man was sitting on a log, under the neck of a horse, sewing a saddle cloth. Behind him, a young woman sat on the ground with a baby clamped to one breast.

The saddle cloth looked richer than any of their clothes. Marinus stopped a courteous couple of yards from the man. The man stopped sewing, one of his eyes glaring at Marinus, the needle held like a knife. The woman looked at him openly, blankly. The baby had better things to think about.

'Good afternoon,' Marinus said. 'I seek Jean the Dog. We have some business to transact.'

In this place where they'd cut his throat to steal his neckcloth, Marinus knew that courtesy was respected and that a trade was sacred.

The man blinked twice. Marinus tried to focus on the one good eye. 'Middle row,' the man said, pointing with the needle, 'halfway along; he is marked.' And with the needle he mimicked parallel scars on his cheek.

The real scars were where they'd been described, and so was the man who wore them. Though even after Marinus had spent a polite minute inspecting his rough-carved wooden tools, a performance in which the man showed no interest as he continued to test the fit of a hammer-head on its haft, he still could not imagine why Jean the Dog had his name.

When he was alone at the stall, Marinus said, 'I seek an Englishman'.

Jean the Dog didn't look up. Instead he clouted the hammer twice against a post, the noise suddenly vast after the murmured words, and the head was tight on the haft. 'Who seeks an Englishman?'

'A man of no particular place. A man who travels as he does.'

Still Jean the Dog did not look up. 'Wait,' he said.

Marinus waited.

Jean the Dog didn't move. Instead he began to consider the head of the hammer, and the wedge he would use to secure it in its new place.

After half a minute, Marinus said, 'Monsieur?'

'Wait.'

Marinus waited.

Out of the silence, and the cloth wall behind Jean the Dog, someone coughed twice.

Jean the Dog looked up. 'Walk back to the end of this row, go to the next, and walk down it halfway. Blood-red cloth in the door.'

Two minutes later Marinus was contemplating a rough shack of boards and cloths, the doorway hung with a dark red cloth. He glanced around himself once again, crossed the path and reached for the cloth.

It pulled away in front of him. Kinnaird welcomed him in. 'My dear sir. I give you welcome; you honour me with your visit.'

'The honour is mine. You are truly an Englishman?'

'I am anything on earth before that. But everyone keeps calling me so, and if I'm to be a fugitive and a criminal I'll go the whole way and be a damned English one.'

A candle helped Marinus see around the single space: a palliasse, on twigs to try to keep it dry; books and maps spread on a cloth. 'And to complete your damnation you take refuge among these, the most cursed people in France – the outcasts of Europe.'

'I'm an outcast.' Kinnaird smiled. 'In France I've met every nationality, I've met aristocrats and revolutionaries, diplomats and dandies, and I've learned I can't trust a one. These? These are trading men, sir. These are my people.'

Marinus nodded at the point. 'How wonderful it would be: a world governed entirely by trade, and not by these political factions and fevers.'

Kinnaird blinked a few times, considered it. 'For our trade we rely on relative differences of value. No factions and fevers: no differences between men: no trade.'

'I have a proposal for you.' Kinnaird's eyes were immediately blank. 'A proposal between men of differences, who may yet find useful matter for exchange.'

'Whom do you represent?'

'Myself; I.'

Kinnaird blinked once. 'And?'

'And one other party.'

'May I meet the man or men?'

'He is a man of excessive prudence, and he has cause to be. You may equally feel that it serves both of your interests to remain anonymous.'

'I understand.' Kinnaird considered it, and Marinus stayed silent. 'Given your own character and background, and certain political realities, I think I may hazard a presumption.'

'I hoped so.'

'But as you say, it would be unnecessarily indiscreet to haggle with names.'

'Quite.'

'The proposal?'

'That in these disrupted times, your individual and potentially rival interests are less important than your shared interest that France spread as little instability as possible beyond her borders.'

Kinnaird considered it, and nodded. 'Do you require a definite answer on the point, or any particular token of commitment?'

'No. The offer remains open for as long as the politics of your respective interests render it relevant. I shall remain at your disposal as intermediary.'

'I am glad of it.'

Marinus made to go; hesitated. 'Something more; proof of good faith, if you will. You are still interested in the circumstances of the death of your friend Mr Greene?' Kinnaird nodded. 'I think he was involved in some little act of provocation or obstruction around the time of his death.'

'The surveyors of the meridian, yes.'

'Indeed. I was walking in St-Denis the day that the expedition was passing through, and I understand that they had greater difficulties that evening.'

'But Hal was going for the southern party; not the northern party passing St-Denis.'

'I could not say what he was doing that night. But I can tell you where he spent the previous night.'

In the doorway, their handshake still clasped, Kinnaird said, 'You were followed here.'

'I took pains to avoid it. I saw no one here who had been near me earlier in the journey.'

'In the camp at least, you were watched: soldier's coat, bandage over one eye, bent-backed.'

'I would be most embarrassed if I had caused you any inconvenience.'

'Think nothing of it. In this place they would not risk anything even if they had a regiment.' The handshake ended. Kinnaird started to turn, but then said, 'I hear he is a titan, this partner of yours. If my presumption of his nationality is the right one. For a long time the most hunted man in France, and still the most brilliant agent of espionage.'

Marinus smiled. 'He is indeed a phenomenon, sir. A man truly to be wondered at. By the sheer brilliance of his mind, and the certainty of a suicide draught on his finger, he scorns any possible threat they may offer, and rules supreme over himself. The complete man, and you have his reputation rightly.'

Kinnaird considered it. 'He has the character that I am only rumoured to have. I hope that one day circumstances allow us to overcome our prudence and meet.' A slight bow. 'I give you good-day, sir.'

The soldier did not follow Marinus away, and nor did anyone else. Kinnaird let the cloth fall back over the doorway, and returned to his books and his maps.

Karl Arnim – his soldier coat in a knapsack, the bandage become a neckcloth, and a hat low over his eyes – watched Marinus disappear round the corner, and looked back to the blood-red cloth, and began to consider an alternative vantage point from which to observe the movements of the Britisher.

———— ◆ ————

At this time, the workshop of François Gamain, locksmith, is easily found. Today the Revolution has found it.

Two policemen in the street in front. Two policemen in the alley behind. A thumping on the door and it's only just opened in time before a musket butt does the job.

In the lodging downstairs, Madame Gamain stands in her cramped parlour, at bay. It's a terrible assault on all the laws of privacy and decency – the mechanism smashed – and she's told them so. She's boiling angry, and the policemen can see it. She's afraid, and they can see that too.

She's told them about the letter he received – nothing unusual – a sudden commission. No, he didn't say where. Yes, that was typical. He'd had her pack a bag for him, which meant the possibility of a night or two away. Yes, often he might be a night or two away. *He's a craftsman of distinction* – as always, she repeats his practised phrase with care – *and people who value quality and discretion summon him considerable distances.* Within her fear, a brief warm flicker of pride. *Once, the Count of –*

She's cut off, by a single raised hand.

She's always said she wants to move somewhere where they don't have to hide, a home befitting his supposed success. Now, more than ever, home broken open, she wants to move.

In the centre of the room, gently turning himself on the stool, foot by foot, one man sits silent. His hand falls to his lap again.

Guilbert is aware of Madame Gamain, but only as much as he's aware of the tidiness of the kitchen space, of the discreet prosperity of the craftsman's parlour, of the absence of any disorder in the few rooms.

Gamain has slipped him today; but it's not flight. The locksmith will be back.

* ◆ *

Kinnaird's grasp of Lucie Gérard had changed and grown over the weeks. He understood better now her resourcefulness. He appreciated that behind her blank facade there could be wit and, occasionally, just possibly, sympathy. He had started to see the factors and experiences that had nurtured her inhuman indifference to life.

So her face now, as she hurried in, was a surprise.

Her eyes were wide. They engaged with him; they wanted something; for once they actually looked. Her mouth was struggling to expel something.

Lucie Gérard was showing emotion. 'She's – she's dead. Madame. Madame Emma. She's dead, M'sieur.'

Already rattled by her distress, Kinnaird felt it like a punch.

This could not be. The essence of Emma Lavalier – the meaning of her – was that there could be a kind of life greater than the mob's madness.

A kind of hatred began to burn in Kinnaird, a hatred he had not previously felt despite all that had been inflicted on him in these mad weeks.

He sat. Slowly, and stiffly, and poised, he sat.

'Tell me,' he said.

He felt something dying in one part of him, and becoming rekindled elsewhere as the hate.

'She – she killed herself.'

Kinnaird's eyes closed, clenched. 'Tell me.'

'She had invited guests. Two men – Americans. No – two men and a woman. They were seen arriving – and leaving. When they arrived, they knocked but got no answer. No servants. The door was open and they went in. And they found her. They say she took poison.'

It was so understandable, that Emma Lavalier of all creatures should have found life under the Revolution impossible; and still Kinnaird hated it. 'The funeral. I must be there.' Why was he so sentimental? Surely he wasn't –

'No. You shouldn't. And you can't. It's done. It was done – it was done' – she started to lose control of her lips – 'cheaply.' Now the tears came.

Kinnaird growled. 'Look at us, Lucie. Look what she has made us.' He took a breath. 'This damned age. The greatest souls are drowning in it. With her, something truly beautiful, something . . . defiant, goes out of the world. She was something too splendid for this mayhem, and I'd have hoped that she endured rather than it.'

He remembered his conversation with the London man. *And I have in some way betrayed her.*

'It was all a dream, M'sieur. The house wasn't even hers any more. Rented, from some old widow.' The tears were thick under her eyes and she was angry. 'Some vicious grasping old crone in Rouen named Philemon; it all goes back to her and her daughter. That's what they say; ugly, grasping women.' Amusement flickered in Kinnaird – wonder even – at Lucie's spite. 'In the end Madame Emma had nothing herself at all.'

With a mighty sniff, Lucie sucked all of the emotion back inside her.

She made to leave. He had been allowed to glimpse another Lucie, and Lucie wanted to leave that other one behind.

'Oh. There's this. Left at the house for me, but it's marked for you.' Two-handed, she held out a cloth-wrapped package.

She heaved in a wavering breath. 'She had nothing herself at all!'

'But Lucie – ' Kinnaird reached for her, gripped her hand, and she winced. 'Emma Lavalier had herself. And that was more extraordinary than anything.'

To Fouché, the news of Emma Lavalier's death came as a shock. He was not emotionally disturbed by it in the least; another unreliable human more or less. But it was . . . a surprise. He had not expected it.

More irritating was the paper that reached him shortly after the news of the death. A coincidence, and ill-timed. It had been intercepted as part of the selective watch on correspondence at the apothecary's in St-Denis. As had been ordered, the original had been resealed and replaced, so that it should be harder for the correspondents to know of interruption. But the need to make a copy had further delayed its journey to Fouché. At least a day or two old now, and he wondered if he could have altered events had it somehow reached him sooner.

The letter had been sent using the old arrangement of the Friends of Magnetism, but to one member of the circle only.

> To the office of Franklin, United States of America
>
> I find that the power of the Revolution grows unstoppable, and I can no longer endure it. Monsieur Fouché is all-seeing, and grows all-powerful. He has by the heels one Gamain, a locksmith, and Gamain will reveal the secret correspondence of the King. It is predicted that the King's credibility will be destroyed, and that Paris and all Europe shall shake.
>
> Unaided, I find no way out of my own predicament, and it seems that Europe's troubles are too great to afford a moment to care for mine. I wonder, would you find an hour during the afternoon of tomorrow, the 15., when two or three persons of your legation might call at the house of Lavalier? The servants shall be absent for the day. And pray, if it is possible let them be someones of my acquaintance. They shall serve fitly enough to see what this life has done to me, and why it is become impossible.

Such was the nearest thing to a suicide note that Lavalier had produced. In the end, rather a pathetic acknowledgement of the new realities of life. He had thought, from the interview, that she aspired to a kind of collaboration with him. Instead he had proved too imposing, and she had broken.

And so the Americans had called at the house, and found her dead. The letter's melancholy became, with hindsight, clear intent. He wondered what poison she had used. He assumed poison. Or . . . Lavalier might have been strong enough for a knife.

Of course, the letter would not have gone immediately to Franklin himself, across the Atlantic; and she must have known this. Some official in the American entourage in Paris had received it first – such, presumably, were the current arrangements according to the Friends of Magnetism – and it had been acted on in Paris; the original, perhaps then forwarded to Philadelphia.

Had she corresponded with the Americans before? Fouché found the idea disappointing. If she was going to turn servant of espionage, why should she not do it for France? For him?

Ironic, perhaps, that after all the suspicions of her intimacies with the European powers, it should be the Americans chosen as her mourners. Another sign of the emptiness of her life by the end. All the superficial attachments fallen away, and only strangers left.

But her death was a convenience, in many ways. She was unreliable in the extreme: too inter-connected, too unpredictable. With her death, there was a small but significant simplification. It was neat.

Only one irritation; one concern. By the note, someone else knew about the hunt for Gamain. Guilbert must work faster. That was the significance of the letter; and the little human melodrama, one more over-fragile animal, fell away.

Still, the news of Lavalier's death was a kind of shock to Fouché. Somehow, he had miscalculated her.

———————◆———————

Kinnaird waited until Lucie had left, before he unwrapped the cloth package.

He was still trying to understand why Emma Lavalier's death had affected him.

The package felt solid, but slightly flexible. The cloth fell away to reveal a card folder, filled with papers.

His name was on the cover.

Sitting on his palliasse in the gypsy hut, he held the folder a moment. Emma Lavalier had been the one clearly impressive thing he had seen in France. She had shown that it was possible for control to defeat chaos.

He opened the folder.

Except that she hadn't.

Dear Kinnaird,

I address you thus as an equal, and that revelation is the last and greatest of many surprises that recent times have shown me.

You entered my life as the personification of strangeness. Perhaps it is natural that my own alienation from this world should have started at the same moment. We thought you ridiculous. But your discordance only showed how out of harmony we were with the times.

You were a better man than any of them. Not morally better — of that I know little and care less — but more capable. I came to understand why it is natural that you should survive Raph Benjamin and the rest. I begin to understand that it is natural that you should survive me.

You have the strength of the tree that bends in the wind and does not break. You learn; you adapt; you endure.

I have prided myself that I have some of the certainty and force of a man. You will endure because you have the flexibility and resilience of a woman.

With your stubbornness and your funny prickly wisdom you gained something of my affection; but that was always cheap won. Much rarer, you gained my respect. It would honour and amuse me if you would have some such regard for me after I am gone.

I did not at first give you the courtesy your qualities deserve, and I have played games with your character for petty advantages. My gift to you now is not an apology, for that means little to either of us, but it is the tribute that I owe for not recognizing your qualities and for not recognizing that you are the future rather than I.

I give you you.

I give you you as ~~France~~ knows you; the Kinnaird of the Revolution.

~~Enclosed~~ is the private dossier of ~~Fouché~~, embodiment of all that is most dangerous and vile about the new ~~France~~, on Keith Kinnaird. You will find much that is unfamiliar in here, for this is the Kinnaird that has been created by ~~Fouché~~'s cross-referencing and speculating, and by the games that Ralph Benjamin — and I — played, and by the chaos of recent times. Depriving ~~Fouché~~ of the few truths in here may give you some advantage; showing you the many falsehoods may give you more.

Perhaps it is a credit to you that yours is one of the thickest of ~~Fouché~~'s many dossiers. When he left me in the company of his minister I had but a moment, via the pretence of a lost glove, to re-enter his office and snatch up the dossier. But men understand so little of women's show, and the modern fashion allows a looser bodice than it used to. Thus I smuggled the more exotic Kinnaird out of the ministry, clasped to my bosom as neither of us would, I think, have expected.

~~Fouché~~ is everything and everywhere. Soon he will have the royal documents, secure in a cell next to poor Hal.

I have all my life thrived on ambiguity. Now I am pushed instead for a slave's certainty, and even that may not save me.

I reject this mean life utterly. Rather than submit a false self to this life, I shall take my true self out of it quite.

Breathe life back into my flower. In your pinching calculating scheming, try once a little flamboyance, will you? Try the impossible and do it. Think the unthinkable, and think of me.

You cannot fight the chaos. Instead you must learn to thrive in it. Kinnaird, you must become part of the chaos.

Lavalier

'Do you know what loyalty means, little girl?' In truth, Arnim despised women, and trusted little and cared less about their loyalty. They were useful only as points of vulnerability in a man's defence of his knowledge or his dignity; or sometimes an alternative to money as a temptation. But so much effort to manage, and in the end it was always cheaper to rely on money. A man's relationship with money was always more simple than his relationship with a woman; more dependable.

The blank fear of the child in front of him – she was twenty or more, surely, but such a frail little mammal – did not give the impression that she knew what anything was any more.

She said nothing. Didn't move her head. In the dumbness of these creatures was their only defence. Some animal instinct, perhaps, had taught her that to say nothing diminished the chance of a provocative mistake.

It hardly mattered that she was in contact with the British. Indeed, at times it had been a decided advantage. If this child was to play a minor and yet positive role in his operations, he needed to know whom else she knew and contacted. And if the British were to remain his rivals on this field, better that they operated through couriers whom Arnim controlled.

And this girl – really, she was smaller than suppers he had eaten – he controlled. Her weaknesses had only made her more vulnerable to him, and so more useful.

Arnim said: 'You have been seen visiting the British, Kinnaird.'

A faint adjustment around her eyes – as she tried to control her alarm, he fancied.

'I visit many men, Monsieur.'

'And you are expected to tell me, or tell my intermediary.'

'I always answer any question, Monsieur.'

Gods, it was wearying. Arnim could not contemplate anything so ghastly as having children of his own, but these games of dumbness would surely be typical. 'That answer is not clever enough, girl.'

Lucie Gérard gazed up at the Prussian. *What does he want, this monster? What answer will satisfy?* Normally he avoided meeting her.

'You were not always as honest as you should have been about your dealings with the man Greene. And look what that got you. You said your contact with this Kinnaird was incidental, and yet you are visiting him in his hiding place. What is the objective of this man? What does he intend?'

Lucie thought. Shrugged. 'Survival,' she said to the Prussian's chest. 'And he wants to understand what he is caught in.'

She looked up. *He doesn't care for the answer.* He was watching her, some mighty contemplation going on behind the vast face. *He doesn't care for any answer.*

His eyes grew, and the face loomed larger over her.

Oh. He wants fear.

She clutched her hands defensively across her breasts.

Men.

'How do messages reach him? Through you?'

'Some. But not all.'

'Delivered how?'

'The ones I bring come to our house in St-Denis. Others I don't know.'

Arnim growled, over her head. 'Of course.' He rarely bothered looking at her unless he wanted particularly to intimidate. 'That apothecary shop is become a second Amsterdam. Does Kinnaird visit himself?'

'Not any more; not since he is hunted.'

'Do the ministry still watch it?'

'Sometimes. There is sometimes a man there. Maybe there are others but I don't know them.'

'Do they intervene? Do they check messages? Read letters?'

'Sometimes. They are quite open.'

'Very well. These are your instructions. In two hours a letter will arrive at the shop for your Kinnaird. You will then wait until you are sure there is a police agent there, and you will ask loudly if there are any messages for Kinnaird. When you hear that there is one, you will explain that you will return to collect it in a further hour, after you have completed other errands. However stupid the policeman, he will be prompted to act quickly. You will collect the letter as promised, and then you will destroy it. Do you understand?'

She nodded.

'Now go. Pray that I do not have cause to speak to you directly again.'

She nodded more urgently, and saw that he was satisfied.

Arnim considered her. It was not ideal to meet her directly, of course.

Normally it was one of the many benefits of Marinus. But once or twice it was necessary, under carefully managed conditions, to remind her of her predicament. She could tell no one anything useful about him, and she could not lead anyone to him.

She didn't even want to look at him. She was trying unobtrusively to slip past him.

His hand came up fast in front of her, palm open. It was as large as her head and filled her vision. She stared into it. 'There is no disloyalty you can contrive that will affect me, little girl. If you wish, you may disobey me and not destroy the letter. You may tell your Kinnaird exactly what I have done.' He suspected that she wouldn't. The man Kinnaird would feel more fragile about her loyalty than Arnim. 'That is the sophistication of my plan. You cannot know what I intend. You cannot imagine what I need from you.'

Now she looked up into his face, and her eyes opened wide, and she shook her head. 'No, Monsieur.'

Men.

* * *

Kinnaird kept the horse at a trot as he approached Chambourcy.

In truth it was a day for lethargy, a thick-skied heavy-headed day; Hal Greene was in his mind. But so was anger. His first reaction to the news of Emma Lavalier's death had been to mourn the futility of it; of the death, and of the changed life that had caused it. Now, though, he felt the world crowding in on him: before her death Lavalier had been summoned to the ministry, which meant that the police might be even closer to him; someone had been watching Marinus at the camp; London's spies had found him and had plans for him. So the horse clopped brisk along the road.

The Comptrollerate-General for Scrutiny and Survey. What could he know of it? When so much was pretended to be true, what to make of something that pretended not to be true? He did not intend to be their puppet or their decoy. But their games might suit his own interest.

The loss of Lavalier showed that it was no longer a world of romantic life; it was a shabbier world, a world of little calculations and transactions, and she had told him that he must make it his and thrive in it.

The younger Kinnaird, intrigued and even excited by the promise of the Revolution, was a world away; the other side of death and chaos.

On the outskirts of Chambourcy, he found the house that Pieter Marinus had named, in connection with Hal. A house standing on its own, small and pretty and well-kept. It seemed an unlikely thing, under the slab of a sky and against the landscape of threats.

Lavalier had written that he must become part of the chaos. And for that he must recognize it for what it was. As he had sailed down the coast, he had dreamed of what the world of equality would mean for the nameless son of a dispossessed race who had had to make his own way in the world. And he had arrived to find that it meant an immediate and unending danger. The Revolution had betrayed its own promise of new order and rationality, and betrayed it savagely.

He tied his horse to a tree, and walked up the path to the door.

The Revolution was not the answer to his hopes of an unimpeded path in the world; it was yet another obstacle. And so among the murderers and spies he would have to find his way.

As soon as the door opened he knew it all: the woman in front of him was so clearly a woman that Hal would have fallen in love with. Pretty and wide-eyed and demure, and big gallant Hal would instinctively have swept her up with his energy and charm; and steady and quiet, and strong in the bones of her cheeks and jaw, and restless world-weary Hal would have longed to find shelter here.

'Your pardon, Madame. I think you are Madame Emilie Violet. My name is Kinnaird; I am a friend of Henry Greene.'

The colour flushed in her cheeks, and after a moment she nodded and let him in.

Kinnaird remembered an eldest daughter in Galashiels, and a widow of Berwick. *Hal Greene; the most susceptible cynic there ever was.*

They sat in her parlour, as neat as the house itself; simple well-scrubbed prosperity. 'Madame, I assume . . . I assume that you have heard the news of Hal – of Henry.'

Her jaw clenched. 'From the news-sheets. From the gossips.'

'I express my sympathies, Madame; for that indignity on top of the loss.'

She smiled. It was a woman's smile, not a girl's: world-used and sensible. 'Do you know, Monsieur Kinnaird, I think that he truly believed he would settle here?'

'I believe he might have, Madame.'

She shook her head. 'But that never seemed likely, I'm afraid. I knew that one day – after a week, after a year – he would go and not return. A fall from a horse, a fight in a tavern, a policeman, or a woman.' Again the smile. 'I knew there had been other women. It was not a spirit to settle.'

'You had been acquainted for long?'

'For five months.' She stared into Kinnaird. He realized that he was sitting where Hal would probably have sat. 'I suspect that when he was younger he would poke with a stick the wasp's nest.' He smiled. 'What was he like?'

Bizarrely, Kinnaird found himself amusing her with stories of their earlier exploits as Hal would have done, and prompting with his honesty about Hal's flaws the same maturity and care that the man himself had aroused.

She knew nothing of his political activities.

At the door, Kinnaird asked, 'When he arrived that night, Madame, did Hal seem as normal; did he say anything to the contrary?'

She shook her head. 'Like a boy. Like a very tired boy.' She looked into his eyes. 'He was happy, Monsieur.'

Kinnaird nodded. 'And when he left the next morning, Madame, had he a particular objective?'

'To meet a man, was all he would say.' Kinnaird nodded. She had confirmed Marinus's assertion: Hal Greene had passed the night, what seemed to have been his last, in this pretty house away from the world.

'Pardon an indelicate question, Madame: are you . . . satisfactorily settled?'

'I have a little money from my late husband, and I support myself comfortably as a seamstress.' Margaret Mackay had part-owned a mill. The Quinn girl had had an annuity. Neither had had eyes as beautiful as this one. *Oh, Hal: why did you not stay abed for once, and leave the world to its own devices?*

Instead, Hal Greene had ridden off to meet a British agent, and then to disappear from the world.

Kinnaird kept the horse at a trot again as he headed back eastwards. The world was crowding in, and he needed to be alert to it and not lost in nostalgia. He went no nearer Paris than St-Denis, and no nearer the centre of St-Denis than the glade by the river.

Once again he stood in the centre of the glade, and turned a slow circle. He tramped, head down and thoughtful, around it and through the undergrowth. He was looking for Hal Greene still, but the rustles in the undergrowth were foreign spies and encroaching National Guardsmen and lost royal documents.

Hal had been here, but he had gone. Keith Kinnaird must look to himself.

The real Hal Greene had eluded him again. All that was left was an unrecognizable corpse in a ministry cellar. But Kinnaird was beginning to perceive the journey it had taken to get there.

———— ◆ ————

Dear K,

His Grace the D. of B. is with all his usual energy making preparations for his new assault, and now that the French are grown more complacent, so much the easier shall his assault be. While the agents of police do chase shadow-men and shadow-papers, a most substantial Prussian army becomes daily more substantial. Of your borrowed diamonds the most effective use is being made: the path of the army of our Prussian allies will be bought not won, for the French farmers are willing to sell provender, and prominent officials are willing to sell their disloyalty and idleness yet more cheaply. If you will open the gates of Paris, you will find us soon outside.

I hope that you are well enough among your gypsy friends. If my travels take me across the Pont de Neuilly, perhaps you might sell me some ribbons, or sell me Paris!

Brutus

Another letter intercepted in St-Denis, and it seemed warm in Fouché's fingers.

The implication that the ministry – that he – was being successfully deceived burned. The allusion to shadow-men and shadow-papers: what did this mean for the locksmith, and the secret royal correspondence? Once again, the faint sick sense that he had been impetuous.

And yet – this the more pleasing warmth – once again his control of information had served him well. There might be foreign attempts at deception – of course; of course there were foreign attempts at deception – but he was aware of them because he read what was not to be read; he knew what was not to be known. This gave him the advantage. They – Guilbert – need not sit waiting for the locksmith to drop from the heavens, nor wander Paris dreaming of documents. The wizard Kinnaird was the heart of it all, and following him would unlock the rest.

A summons, called snappish through the open door to the corridor. Guilbert, to be found immediately. He felt a pang for his documents. But Brunswick and the military threat to France should be the priority, naturally.

This Kinnaird . . . He should review the dossier. This new transcription would need to be added to it.

The dossier on Kinnaird was not where his hand sought it, where his mind led. A flicker of disruption in the smooth working of his mind.

And then a memory, creeping in . . . The woman Lavalier. He had moved the folder when he had been convincing her where reason should rightly lead her. The folder would be in the pile on his desk.

'Dear Fouché, how do you?'

'Well, Minister. Well enough.' Roland drifting uncertain in the doorway. Fouché's fingers brushed the paper in front of him. 'A new report, from one of my operations. The pre-eminence of the man Kinnaird is confirmed. British involvement in the theft of the royal jewels is confirmed. And they will buy the advance of the Prussian army.'

Roland's vague presence was immediately solidified: he gripped the door and his head came forwards and the voice sharpened. 'But Fouché, this is surely new!'

'A new synthesis, Minister.'

'The Prussian army – that's . . . that's a matter of the safety of the Revolution. This is no longer an affair of individuals, of conspiracies. No longer mere speculations.' Fouché felt his irritation rasping in him. 'This is national strategy. National survival, Fouché.'

'Indeed, Minister. For that reason I am devoting all of our efforts to counter the enemy arrangements. Thanks to my arrangements, we now know where the man Kinnaird is. He will be hunted, and destroyed, and the British and Prussian schemes will be blocked.'

Roland was drifting again, distressed. 'The Prussian army . . .'

'The Prussian army, if it crosses our borders again, is the affair of General Dumouriez and our soldiers. We have to give the Ministry of War something to do.'

'All of our efforts, Fouché. No distractions.'

Fists clenched over the paper. 'There are no distractions, Minister. Everything is connected. In my mind, at least.'

On the morning of 19th November, Jean the Dog found that a departing customer – he presumed it had been a customer; he had seen nothing – had slipped a folded paper among his tools. It was a note, enclosing another folded paper. The note read, *'If you do not have a British neighbour, do not give him this.'*

Kinnaird got both the cover note and the enclosure, Jean wanting as little to do with the affair as possible.

Kinnaird liked the style. Deniability; discretion.

This, then, is how the Comptrollerate-General for Scrutiny and Survey does business.

The enclosure was more impressive. A hint. A possibility. The Comptrollerate-General was close on the track of its trove of European secrets.

I am still on a journey through a forest. I must follow the paths that open to me.

He would set off immediately. His neighbours would lend him the necessary tools for a disguise.

No name at the top, no name at the bottom, and little in the middle to implicate anyone. Deniability. Discretion.

But now he'd have to stick his neck out.

———— ◆ ————

Workshops of the Olympeans

The Revolutionary authorities are finding it hard to get credit, one of the misfortunes of men given explicitly to upheaval being that it is hard to give reassurance to men who prize predictability. Yet they find ways enough to force finance. And the necessities of their war and their administration are, by some immutable law of nature, obliging the manufactures of essential goods to work as hard as ever and to trust to providence and General Dumouriez for their eventual reward.

Thus, although some of the artisans do suffer – the cutlers gone to bayonet-making or the wall, the turners of fine furniture turned to making rough benches for the spectators at the tribunals – industry is hale enough, if it can make itself useful. The great cotton house at Jouy prints fewer fine cloths for the ladies, but has plenty of soldiers to clothe. The regime is a great engine of administration, and the paper-makers must supply the fuel for it.

Most of all, those who supply the fuel for the revolutionary war do thrive and must daily contrive new improvements to increase their productivity. Thanks to the inspirations of the great Lavoisier, now out of favour and position and hoping that his services to the revolutionaries' muskets do overcompensate for his former exactions on their pockets, the production of saltpeter has left forever the farm shed and taken residence in vast new premises that produce the stuff on a gargantuan scale. Every road out of Paris now has a saltpeter factory on it, and

Lavoisier's new process has multiplied the output.

The newest is at Joinville, and the building was not yet quite complete before it was functional in its essentials and turning out its incendiary powder by the cartload. It is a mighty edifice, a forge such as Hephaestus must have used, in dimension and yield built for Titans. Its main chamber is the size of a church, and the alchemy that on the farm was practised in barrels here transpires in vast vats. The choleric fluid produced in the process comes out not in drips, but flows by an elaborate system of piping, and the further drying and crystallizing of the saltpeter occurs on a like scale.

The yield is massive – I will continue discreetly to enquire after figures – it may surely be measured in the suffering of Prussian soldiers. And yet by concentrating the production of this essential military substance the Revolution may be thought to have left itself vulnerable to individual incidents of misfortune or malice.

E.E.

[SS F/24/149 (DECYPHERED)]

———— ◆ ————

When working at the premises of a customer and staying away from home, Gamain the locksmith was obliged to forego the fortifying routine of Madame Gamain's midday soup and depend on the creativity and kindness of a landlady. Today a loaf of bread and a block of cheese, and he'd paid extra for them. The cheese was fresh – come in from one of the farms hereabouts, where the countryside came close to the city's edge. He worried that it would prove too heavy a meal and render him dull-witted for the afternoon.

He sat on a stool, in unconscious recreation of Madame Gamain's kitchen. The saltpetre factory of Desmarets soared above him. The window over his shoulder was three or even four times his own height. The vat in front of him was approximately the same: the image and proportions of a copper kettle, if he were a mouse at its foot. There were four such in this chamber, in a measured line. Above them, running along the line of them, a wooden gantry.

He'd watched the movements of the workers all morning, when not bent over his work. The men fed the machines; served them. They wheeled barrows along the gantry and emptied them into the vats and moved away. Their movements were monitored and guided by a foreman. To avoid a jam, the men moved at a steady interval – ten paces between them, Gamain reckoned it.

He did not consider the men much. They weren't craftsmen, clearly. Peasants, governed by something much more regular than the weather or their wills. They were part of a mechanism as much as his watch-springs.

The fatness of the cheese felt luxurious. He could feel his stomach filling.

A perplexing time. So far he and his business had not suffered from the chaos, but he realized that he was perpetually tense, waiting for disruption. His stomach always felt tense; an overwound spring. (Or perhaps that was the cheese.) The letter commissioning him to fit a new set of locks to the magistrate's offices in Chantilly had been most specific. Yet when he'd reached Chantilly, after fully a day travelling, they insisted that they had sent no such letter. They didn't even want any locks; indeed, they were most discourteous on the point, even though it was surely he who had been put to inconvenience.

So an unnecessary night in an inn, and an unnecessary day of travel back towards Paris, to Joinville. At least the Commission at the Desmarets factory had been as stated. Two days of work, and most courteous methodical people.

Gamain considered the pipes leading out from under the vat; he wondered at the valve mechanism.

———— ◆ ————

He leaves discreetly, among the bustle of other men. He looks about him once, an unobtrusive review of the faces around him. His hand feels to check that the cloth has recovered the doorway. His hands flex. They rise, and they touch his lapel, and his neckcloth. They drop to his sides, and flex again. One hand comes back up to his pocket, pats it, and drops again. He turns to the right. He seems to disappear for a moment between the huts, but reappears almost immediately. Again he looks about him. Then two – three – steps. He stoops and untethers a horse. He leads the horse along the alley between the huts. His face disappears and reappears among others. He mounts without elegance.

Guilbert sees it all.

He notices things. *The horse is near enough for flight, but not too near to betray the exact hut where he shelters.* A careful man, this. *He does not mount immediately, but hides himself among the movements of others.*

Guilbert has been practising the man's name. It is still uncomfortable. *Ki-* as the French 'qui', and then the tortured vowels: *-nnaird.*

The Monsieur is becoming obsessed by this Kinnaird. Guilbert doesn't think about him too much. Guilbert watches. Guilbert sees.

This Kinnaird has chosen his sanctuary in the gypsy camp to be able to spot people approaching. It means that he can be spotted leaving.

He sets off along the track, the horse at a walk. Unobtrusive. He is followed.

Guilbert waits until he's confident his prey is not returning, checks again that his two men are following but not too close, then stands to his full height. He puts his hat on, and starts to walk. The hat is the signal, and as he walks his other two men converge on him. They reach the door at the same time, and Guilbert pulls the red cloth aside.

One man waits outside the door. Guilbert and the other enter. The single room is searched quickly enough. The palliasse. Under a blanket, two maps: Paris; and northern France. A cloth bag hangs on a nail, to keep valuables dry and away from rats, but it's empty now. Guilbert's head is empty; he lives only through his eyes.

Down in the dirt, beside one of the timbers holding the roof up, is a tiny coil of string. Guilbert kneels quickly, and finger-and-thumb takes one end and very slowly begins to pull. The string disappears into the dirt, and as he pulls more firmly, it strains and straightens and something is shifting under the dirt.

In an oilcloth packet hidden under the dirt, there's a letter.

From outside the door, a squawk. Guilbert only half hears it.

'Pinon?'

The sentry outside the door doesn't reply.

Guilbert stands, the other man with him. Standing away from it, Guilbert reaches out and pulls the red cloth aside. He sees three men through the doorway – gypsies, by their faces and their layers of rags. He sees two knives and one smith's hammer.

He considers the weapons. He looks up at the faces again. He realizes that they can't see him clearly. He shifts slightly to the side. Pinon is no longer by the door. He steps forwards, one careful step. He sees the three men tense. He sees Pinon now, to one side, slumped on the ground and still.

The gypsy in the middle says: 'You didn't knock.'

Guilbert's finger touches the red cloth. 'There's no door.'

The gypsy smiles. 'You come uninvited in the house of our friend; you are a stranger and a thief.'

Guilbert shakes his head once. 'Ministry of the Interior. I am authority. I am law.'

The man hesitates. 'Not here you're not.'

'Your friend is an enemy of France. An outlaw.'

'In this place, we all are.'

'I can burn this place.'

'It'll save us packing up.'

'I can erase you from the earth.'

The man steps forwards. 'We are the earth, and when I or my sons have visited you in the night and cut your throat we'll still be the earth.'

Guilbert considers this, nods, and steps forwards through the doorway, his companion keeping close behind him in hope of safety. 'I have no business with you or your people. Look and see: I have damaged nothing, and done you no harm.' He holds up the letter between finger and thumb. 'I take nothing. I borrow this. Anyone who wants it can come to the office of the Minister of the Interior and collect it.' He shakes his head again. 'Your friend isn't coming back again.' He glances down at the body of Pinon, then up. 'Don't suppose any of your lads wants to be a policeman, does he?'

At this time, the saltpetre factory of Desmarets dominated the village of Joinville and the landscape around it. The meandering of the Marne brings the river almost back on itself at Joinville, and the land was mostly meadow.

The only other building of any eminence was the Musketeer Inn. Karl Arnim had taken a room at the Musketeer, on the first floor, and from its window he could watch Joinville, and the Paris road that ran through it, and the factory.

The factory stared back at him across the valley, a bland unadorned face with its big windows, out of place in the mediaeval fields.

Arnim had lately taken an interest in the new method of saltpetre production, with the same wary intellect he would have devoted to learning Chinese. Instinctively he considered technical things the province of artisans – paid servants – and therefore far beneath a man of quality. Factories were, in their way, even worse: commerce was even less dignified than manual skill.

But he found himself to be a modern intelligence, untrammelled and *au courant*. Increasingly – and however distressing it might seem – commerce was influence; commerce was power. Commerce preoccupied Berlin, and accordingly Karl Arnim had stirred himself to understand it enough to maintain his pre-eminence, and even – discreetly, of course, through agents – to spread his money into certain prudent investments.

Saltpetre was power too; and before they'd let the mob take over, the finer minds of France had developed new ways to produce it in quantities that were a proper concern to the chief agent of France's enemy. So he sat in a first-floor window of the Musketeer and contemplated the factory of Desmarets as a general might a battlefield, or a cat a mouse.

Today, though, his affair was not the factory but one particular man working in it: the locksmith Gamain. The Revolution sought him, but Arnim had found him; found him, distracted him away from the authorities with the spurious commission to Chantilly, and now come to Joinville to collect him. He had given the Ministry of the Interior a conspiracy to delight them for days, and he had given them the man Kinnaird, and the police could follow Kinnaird round and round Paris and at this critical time Joinville, and Gamain the royal locksmith, were in Prussian hands. Marinus, dear steady careful Marinus, would call at the factory shortly, and Gamain would be invited discreetly away, and then the Revolution's vital witness in the hunt for the royal correspondence would disappear.

Once the correspondence was secure and preferably destroyed – saving such pieces as Arnim might find useful for his own ends – he could return to Joinville and renew his study of the factory.

Saltpetre production was hardly a sophisticated process, in any case: essentially the passing of water over excrement. He did it himself every day at a fixed hour. Trust the French to make a science and a trade out of it.

————◆————

Guilbert had set off in one direction, catching up with the men following Kinnaird. The letter he had found in Kinnaird's hut he sent in the other direction, with a fast rider and the instruction that it be delivered immediately into Fouché's hand.

Guilbert smiled a little at that. The Monsieur would have his document. Guilbert would have the man.

At the Ministry of the Interior an hour later, the reaction was all Guilbert might have hoped. The knowledge that Kinnaird was found and tracked brought a sigh of pleasure from Fouché, and the document was snatched from the courier's hand and immediately in the centre of Fouché's desk.

Sir, we learn that the Revolution attaches surprising importance to a locksmith named Gamain. Surprising, although the man was at least once commissioned by the Crown, and there is speculation at the international secrets he helped to hide, reckoned likely to destroy the credibility of the King and shake Europe as well as Paris. The importance you may gauge from the prominence given to the point by a lady in her last hour. Those disposed against the Revolution might calculate the advantage should its agents be delayed or defeated in their hunt. Should more recent information emerge, and should you care for it, it will be available at the rendezvous of the wasp.

Fouché admired the brevity. He re-read it. Then he read between its lines.

Point the first: the man Kinnaird is active, and engaged in the affairs that most concern me.

Point the second: a familiar phrase – a discredited King and a shaken Paris; a familiar phrase repeated for the second time. *My phrase.* This information has also come via Lavalier.

Point the third: but it has not come directly from Lavalier. This correspondence is aware of Lavalier's message to the Americans, but it is not the product of that relationship.

Fouché felt his blood warming at the implications, and with clenched teeth and clutching fingers he urged Guilbert onwards.

--------- ◆ ---------

Marinus was enjoying his visit to the Desmarets factory. His letter of introduction to the manager had been waved aside, the interest of a foreign visitor credential enough. The manager was enthusiastic, and expert, and part of Marinus's mind drifted into warm contentment at the company of another careful enquiring mind.

And with each new figure they saw in the place, Marinus's mind would kick at him, and he would check to see whether the figure was noticeably a locksmith.

' – things about capacity,' the manager was saying as he ushered Marinus out of the main factory building and the sunlight glared at them, 'is that we seem to have reached a natural limit. Temporary at least. Not the volumes that may be put through the vessels, but the way we can have the men service them.'

They both stood still a moment, blinking hard and waiting for their eyes to adjust to the day.

'Which would imply,' Marinus said carefully, 'an adjustment to the habits of the men or of the relationship between the men and the equipment.'

'Indeed! Indeed.'

The yard outside the main building was a large rectangular space, paved with brick, and the two of them had just stepped into one end of it. Along the right-hand side the brick gave way to grass, sloping briefly up then dropping to the Marne and Joinville itself, a shadow in the sunlit landscape. A wall ran along the left-hand side of the yard, where the factory had been built into the side of the hill to keep the ground level; the wall was perhaps ten feet high, with a low parapet along the top of it. At the far end of the yard was another building: two-storey, but substantially smaller than the factory behind them. Offices, perhaps, or stores.

The yard was forty or fifty yards long, but Marinus could clearly see a man kneeling at the door to that other building, tools spread out on a blanket beside him, apparently working at the handle or the lock.

They started to walk along the yard, and Marinus felt his heart hammering, the double beats matching his footsteps exactly and thumping in his chest.

'The latter would mean a rearrangement of the whole plant, of course,' the manager was saying, and Marinus heard the words distantly, like a lost innocence.

From the direction of the river a man stepped onto the brick surface of the yard. He had something hung from a strap around his neck; a simple knife-sharpening wheel. He looked around himself, presumably seeking custom.

' – and that's frankly impossible for another year at least.' Still the two of them walked, footsteps on brick, heartbeats.

With each step, the man on his knees at the lock became nearer and more distinct.

From behind the locksmith, a cart rumbled off a track and into the yard, the sound of its wheels changing immediately it moved from earth to brick.

The man with the knife-sharpener turned towards the locksmith.

'Hey!' the manager called, and the man hesitated. The manager started to stride towards him, Marinus following. To Marinus: ' – have to control those fellows. They interrupt the rhythms of the place, do you see?'

The knife-sharpener watched them warily. The cart continued towards them, iron-shod wheels sharp on the bricks, rolling beside the high wall with a load of dung for the factory. Uncomfortably, the man with the knife-wheel pulled the strap over his head and set the device on the ground beside him. It was as if he was readying for a fight, Marinus thought. 'Not without permission!' the manager was calling out as they walked.

The locksmith was a blur at the end of Marinus's vision. He refocused on the knife-sharpener, as they came close at last.

It was Kinnaird.

'You?' Marinus hissed. 'But you should not be here!'

'Since my first hour in France people have been saying that to me.'

'Kinnaird, I urge you – '

'Stand fast!' Guilbert striding into the yard, arm thrust towards them; beside him a policeman with musket level, two more men behind, more men coming in from beyond the building. To one of his men: 'Get the locksmith!'

Kinnaird was twisting in confusion. Marinus stared at him. 'Betrayal. You have brought the police to me.'

'I didn't kn-' Now Kinnaird saw it. 'Only because you brought them to me.' Guilbert and his men were a loose circle around them, the manager stumbling backwards bewildered.

'I would not dream – ' And now Marinus saw it too. Saw it all, and behind it all saw Arnim, capable of a perspective and a calculation greater than any individual care.

He nodded. Sad smile. 'All life is betrayal.' And then, behind it all, he really did see Arnim, standing on the parapet, staring down bleak at the scene in the yard, grasping how his scheme for the police and Kinnaird had coincided so catastrophically with his scheme for the locksmith.

Marinus gazed up at him. His eyes did not move as he said quietly to Kinnaird, 'His name is Karl Arnim. He is the greatest mind in Europe.' A faint smile. 'Today, alas, he seems to have shown a human fallibility.' Still he gazed up.

Oblivious to the tension between the men in the yard, the dung-cart continued its progress beside the wall towards the factory building. None saw it. Kinnaird was looking up at Arnim, and Guilbert's eyes had followed, and now everyone was looking in the same direction. So none of them except Arnim himself – so shockingly, so distastefully, exposed for the first time – saw Marinus reach into his coat and pull out a pistol.

They only saw it when it was pointing at Kinnaird's chest. 'Hold!' from Guilbert; the lead policeman's musket level and firm.

Now Marinus was looking at Kinnaird. 'At the end of any relationship there must be sacrifice,' he said, 'and one party is sure to suffer. I regret that we must have the parting before we had a chance at the partnership.' Still quiet: 'In different circumstances ...'

The pistol was fixed to Kinnaird's chest. Marinus looked up at Arnim again; he placed his left hand on his heart, and bowed. 'God speed you, Mr Kinnaird,' he said, and swung the pistol round and shot the man with the musket.

Guilbert was already moving and in an instant he was driving into Marinus, hand to collar and knife up. A roar of pain, from Arnim, and the valley of the Marne echoed to it, and Kinnaird knew this heartbeat had to be his. With Guilbert still entwined with Marinus, and every other eye on Arnim's pain, Kinnaird took half a dozen thumping steps and scrambled up the side of the cart, hands on its side and feet scrabbling at the wheel as it continued to turn. Then he was over and wallowing through the dung, pulling himself up onto the other side of the cart and reaching for the parapet and swinging himself up onto it with feet kicking against the bricks and then he was over and staggering upright and running hard for the trees.

In the yard, Guilbert was yelling orders and policemen were running. Still on his knees, the locksmith Gamain watched uncomprehending the chaos of noise and running men, and bent to gather his tools to safety.

The body of Pieter Marinus dropped tired to the bricks. Arnim, face ghastly, watched it drop. And then he dragged his head around and strode for his horse. Marinus's eyelids flickered, tried to understand the distant green, and the sun, and why they were supposed to be looking for someone, and then they closed.

5

Dawn

My dear Bellamy,

the tone of our exchanges has always been most congenial, and this has been a charm to me. Your somewhat stony intellect, if I may so describe it, for its cool and hard and unpolished aspects, has proved an unexpectedly engaging prompt to my own suppler continental fancies. And though I have only a few years on you, you have borne most courteously my lamentable habit of talking de haut en bas, and most correctly my resilience in the face of your official entreaties. It is in the spirit of our exchanges that I condescend now to a brusquer tone than you will have heard from me ere now. Bluntly: I write seeking help, and offering advice.

By divers sources, not all of them English, I have been immediately apprised of the latest calamity in Paris, and surely the greatest. This news may be death to several great men at least, and permanent exile for many more. I must avoid the former, and I fear that the latter may be my fate. In which case I am more dependent that ever on your good offices with your Government.

Entreat of them, I beg you, to suffer my continued residence here, with the facade of the continued consideration of my embassy. I dare not risk a return to Paris at this moment (nor the dark corners of London should it become known that my mission is in vain). We shall serve each other well, by protecting each other's indiscretions.

And so to my advice to you, which might well be heard throughout your Government, but which is first of all offered to you personally, in gratitude for your unflinching courtesies to this old French tergiversateur. The tide turns, my friend. It is a new dawn, a spring the like of which has never been seen. A new age; a harder age. An age in which the mob must be counted a constant threat. An age in which only the coolest calculation of advantage may protect the established social order, and the interests of men of discernment, from chaos. The men who rule in Paris, they have seen this — so I now understand. I suspect that this will not save them from the chaos that they have created, but they may have taught a valuable lesson to stronger men who will come after them. A few others — most particularly, it seems from my correspondence, your errant compatriots in your former Atlantic colonies — they have seen it too.

British society has not seen it. If your society does not see the danger to the established order, then it will be overwhelmed by disorder. Even if it does so fail, individual men of fortitude and flexibility may yet float on the waters to a new safety. I would advise you, my dear friend, to learn to swim.

I yet remain,

Yours faithfully,

Charles Maurice de Talleyrand-Périgord, Bishop

[SS G/66/97]

362

'I am advised to ask for you help, in the name of Master Philippe and the Lady Sybille.'

Absurd thing to say. Kinnaird knew it. The landlord's understandable stare at these words was like a punch in the face. It had been hours ago, but the smell of dung from the factory cart seemed to clutch at him. Behind him Kinnaird felt the screaming attention of everyone else in the place. There were no choices left.

He was no horseman, and he'd galloped away like a madman from the chaos at the Desmarets saltpetre factory. He was barely clinging on to the horse, and he was trying to duck to avoid the trees and still the branches whipped at him. Face stinging and clothes wrenched and still the beast hurtled on, cleverer than he was at this speed, and he'd lost all control. When they'd come clear of the trees Kinnaird had recaptured sense, pulling the horse to a canter and then, as the next village came closer, to a trot. He had to seem calm, he had to be inconspicuous; but he was not calm, and the police and the National Guard were close behind him.

The madness. Somehow Marinus had led the police to him at the gypsy camp; and then he had led the police to the saltpetre factory and to Marinus and now another decent man was dead.

He had not dreamed the police could be so close on his trail; they had had him in their hand, and only chosen not to take him because they wanted him to lead them. And he had led them. And Marinus had died, and the police had the locksmith, and the greatest secrets in Europe were about to be revealed.

In the village, the tavern. Down from the horse, a heart-pounding pose of calm, instructions to the ostler to stable the beast, in and ask for a room, order some wine sent up, and at the first moment of inattention away out the back door and through shadows to the trees. In the trees he took a breath, looked back at the tavern, and set off again, on foot now, the highlander's jog-trot through the wood and to the next village. There he walked again, caught his breath, came into the inn-yard knowing it would be full of his hunters waiting for him, and it was a shock when they weren't and again he forced calm and commanded another horse.

The gypsy camp was lost to him. He had to assume that everywhere he had been was now lost to him. He didn't seem to be followed, but what did he know of such things?

He needed sanctuary, but he could not know where to find it.

What was the point of it, anyway? His pose of new wisdom had been exploded in foolishness and death. He was more closely hunted than ever. The locksmith would reveal the royal correspondence to the police, and the one hope of the diplomatists was ruined, thanks in no small part to him. Hal Greene was still a corpse lying in the ministry cellar.

He had one hope left, for his own survival at least. He must depend on what he had learned.

The nonsensical Kinnaird dossier, willed to him by Lavalier, was full of administrative detail. Topographical details of places he was supposed to have stayed. Marginal references to reports by particular named junior officials. One report had happened to include the new appointment of one Trichet to a position in the prefecture of the new *département* of Eure, with its office in Évreux. A significant place, Évreux, in the history of French nobility and religion and scholarship; but the Forest of Évreux was renowned at this time for the bandits who sheltered there.

Kinnaird remembered a Trichet. And so on the 18th a letter reporting this information had arrived at an inn in Vernon, for a young man staying there; a young man once reputed a lounger and a drunkard, but now of the most sober conduct. A young man who, at his lowest ebb, had been pulled out of the gutter by a mysterious foreigner, and talked away the night with him, and found a shared pain, and exchanged a promise to maintain discreet contact.

The next morning the body of Trichet had been found in undergrowth on the edge of the Forest of Évreux. His hand still clutched his pistol, but he'd been unable to fire it before being slashed across the neck and stabbed to the heart by a sword.

And Keith Kinnaird had received a reply from the young man, full of names and addresses. And so, today, in his crisis he had come to the tavern of the Noble Lady near Pontoise, whose landlord was a former tenant of one of the old families of France.

'I am advised to ask for you help, in the name of Master Philippe and the Lady Sybille.' The landlord stared at him, and then over his shoulder to check that no one else was paying attention, and then he was hurrying Kinnaird through a door to his own quarters and locking it behind him.

—————— ◆ ——————

Once more, the royal palace of the Tuileries is the scene of a procession. There are uniforms, and muskets held erect, and the regular tramp of feet across the marble.

Up the grand staircase, the enormous mirror still staring down in approval of the dignity of the proceeding, and the procession maintains its steady pace, and the precise arrangement of the persons within it.

Corridor by corridor, indifferent both to the vestiges of grandeur that gleam and hang from walls and prominences and to the vestiges of skirmish smeared and gouged across the walls and floor, the procession continues left and right and tramp tramp tramp ahead. A procession is a mechanism, regulated and sure of itself, guided by an unseen consciousness.

Pairs of doors swing open in front of it, and tramp tramp tramp, and doors swing open, and tramp tramp tramp, and now with due awe the procession is entering the royal apartments within the Tuileries.

But there's something awry, a discordance in the ceremony, a knocking fault in the mechanism. Amongst other things, only the four uniformed men can maintain a steady pace. The other men haven't thought of this. Or, uncomfortably, they've only become aware that there's a rhythm because their own steps are breaking it and then, guiltily and ineffectually, they're trying to catch it.

Tramp tramp and stumble-double-step and tramp.

Two soldiers bracket the front of the procession.

Two soldiers march at the rear. Neatness, protection, and the suggestion that no one from the procession may be allowed to drop behind or wander off.

Second to last, two men in the recognized attire of new-made officials, coats fashionable but cheap and neck-stocks too tight, one from the Ministry of Justice and one from the Ministry of the Interior. It's their first time in the Tuileries and they're trying hard to be sombre, and they don't quite know what's going on but it's fine to feel important.

In front of them, the heart of the procession, because this is a matter of the security of the Revolution and the stability of the state: Minister of the Interior Roland, with cramped forced steps because it's hard to walk easily in the bunched heart of a procession and because he's teeth-fist-arse-clenchingly tight-wound. At his shoulder, former Minister of Justice Danton, feet striding wild and impatient and damn the rhythm because he's trying to rediscover the Revolution and has the lurching sense that time is running out. For these men, each footstep is a heart-beat, a worry.

At the head marches Fouché, aide to the Minister of the Interior, clean shirt and eyes bright. And at his side is another man, pale-faced and dressed for work and carrying a bag. It is the locksmith Gamain, the only one of the civilians to understand the rhythm of the mechanism, and the only man who knows where he's going.

These two are between the front pair of soldiers.

Another door. Ivory white panels; the details and decoration in gold. This time the front pair of soldiers stops. It might actually be gold. The soldiers know – they all know, all France knows – that this door has never been opened from outside, and never been opened without permission from inside.

Smears of dust have collected on the gold.

The soldiers glance inwards. Fouché hesitates, unknowing. Roland and Danton have bunched up behind him; they've been through this door before, and it's always trouble.

Only the face of the locksmith is untroubled. Pale, intent, sure, he nods the way forwards.

The holy of holies is opened at the command of a craftsman. This is the Revolution.

———— ◆ ————

Revelations and Lamentations

The Minister of the Interior found his locksmith, and the locksmith showed the Minister the secret closet within the royal apartments in the Tuileries, and within the secret closet was a substantial cache of royal correspondence. And all indications thus far suggest that the results will be as tumultuous as the hunters had hoped and as we had feared.

I have this from more than one source connected to the authorities, and I could get most of it from the boy on the corner, for the Revolution – and in this we may perceive the triumphant Fouché, rather than his more wary minister – has elected to make a public spectacle of the development. This has two implications of the greatest moment. The first is the content of the correspondence. I need not rehearse the significance, and this has never been doubted. The only question had been whether in some unprecedented urge of prudence the King had had the documents destroyed, during two years of instability or during the last hours of his residence in the palace, with the mob at the gate and discovery certain. Alas, Louis ran true to form, for hesitation and dullness, his privy correspondence went unburned, and now the most private dealings of several European monarchies and dozens of prominent persons are made most public.

The second implication comes from the prominence given to the episode by the revolutionary authorities. The hunt for the locksmith having been conducted in secret, and the opening of the cache tight-managed, they could have kept the existence and matter of the correspondence unpublic, and used it for influence and pressure, diplomatic and individual. Instead they are clearly resolved to make a show of it, to shame the monarchies of Europe that have challenged the Revolution, and most of all to shame Louis. For the monarchies this may herald some discomfort; for Louis it may herald destruction.

The cache was broken open this morning, with Minister Roland himself present. It is reported that the cache was in point of fact an iron cupboard, concealed within a wooden compartment, hidden behind a panel in the royal apartments and all protected by the most elegant conformity of decoration with the rest of the apartments and by the most cunning of locks. In conjecturing the existence of the cache, and then in recognizing the significance of the craftsman who had installed it, and then in identifying and locating the craftsman, and thus in revealing France's greatest secrets with the turning of a single spring, the Revolution showed great perspicacity, and an unusual instinct for intricate skill rather than brute force.

The documents, close-guarded, have been carried to some fastness in the Ministry of the Interior, where they may be perused and their contents used as their new possessors may wish. And truly, at the minute of the opening, some great hourglass turned and the sands are running for courts and great men across Europe. All this for want of a tinder-box and a moment's resolve.

The Ministry will I trust excuse my incontinent use of the express channel of communication, for I judge that the importance and implications of this development so merit.
E. E.

[SS F/24/153 (DECYPHERED)]

———◆———

The Kinnaird dossier – the mad collection of coincidences, half-truths, and wild products of Sir Raphael Benjamin's imagination that Lavalier had brought out of Fouché's lair – has shown him this place.

The dossier is an encyclopaedia of counter-revolutionary activity. More importantly, it is a gazeteer of it. The places Kinnaird has really been that happened to have royalist connections; the places Benjamin had been or heard of and knew to have such connections, and where he has accordingly placed Kinnaird in his confected documents. All illuminated by Fouché's marginal notes commenting on suspicious elements linked to such places and people.

Accordingly, Kinnaird's documented association with the establishment of Pelletier in the rue Honoré is nonsense.

Except now it won't be.

He assumes that to Benjamin's mind the association would have seemed spicier if it was based on something vaguely true about Pelletier.

Nonetheless he must grip, and fast.

'Good day to you, sir. My name is Kinnaird, and I have two things to say to you. Firstly, you are suspected by the Ministry of the Interior of harbouring escaped prisoners, passing royalist messages and supplying suspicious persons with goods on generous terms. If that's true I strongly urge you to find a way to disprove it or fly. Secondly, noting that – whatever the truth is about either of us – I am obviously sympathetic to you, and that I seem to know enough about you, I would be much obliged by your help this night.'

It's a risk, revealing himself like this in Paris. He has to trust to Pelletier's sympathy or his fear.

Either way, Kinnaird has connected himself to this place now.

Bizarrely, he is proving the insane dossier true.

———— ◆ ————

Lots of things have kept Saint-Jean Guilbert alive: amongst others luck, a strong stomach, a discriminating taste in whores, a complete indifference to dignity and honour and thus the willingness to hide in a dung heap and stab a man in the back if it's faster than the front, the refusal to gamble or drink too much, and a knife or pistol about him at all times; preferably both.

And silence. Guilbert does not speak except when he needs to. Words are dangerous, and he doesn't trust them.

The Monsieur's face shows that it's one of those times. Fouché is stamping up the corridor like an angry five-year-old, and his face is the most extraordinary colour. Even a man who didn't know him as Guilbert does would see that he is *steaming* furious.

Fouché's been getting gradually more powerful – and after the discovery in the palace he has got dramatically more powerful. Guilbert tracks such changes – it's another one of the things that keeps him alive. Fouché's anger gets people demoted, dismissed, sent to the war. Right now, Guilbert thinks, given that face the anger could get a man struck by lightning.

By the time Fouché reaches him, Guilbert is standing alert, face buried in a courteous bow. Fouché leads him into the office without breaking stride.

The two men finally look at each other properly when Fouché turns and sits at his desk. The smile on his face is *terrifying*. The eyes are mad bright, and the smile is a rigid contortion of his muscles, a distorted thing; Guilbert's only seen such a thing on the corpse of the Englishman that he found in the house of the servant Bonfils.

Guilbert waits.

'In the cellar below us, Guilbert,' Fouché begins, and the strain of the voice is as bad as the face, 'is a collection of documents that will upturn Europe and possibly change the direction of the Revolution. Naturally, we want to examine these astonishing documents as rapidly as possible.'

Guilbert waits.

'Except that the minister has agreed that we shall not, Guilbert, until a commission of enquiry has been established with representatives of other relevant ministries. Another twenty-four hours at least. You know who's behind this, don't you Guilbert?'

Careful. Not to respond would be dangerously rude. To respond wrongly could be disastrous. Guilbert scowls in distaste at the shared understanding.

Fouché's face screws up, and he shakes his head. 'It's all down there, Guilbert! More or less unguarded. I could walk in there in five minutes. But . . . too many eyes in this place, and I won't jeopardize everything I've gained, in one moment of impetuousness.' Another shake of the frustrated head.

Now Guilbert speaks. Carefully. 'You're a man of honour, Monsieur. Of great profile now. Impossible that you could be seen in there. I'm none of those things. If there was anything in particular you wanted . . . '

Fouché's smile is closer to human. 'I don't know what I don't know, Guilbert. And you, for your sins, are known to be close to me.' Again the head shakes.

'A great coup nonetheless, Monsieur.'

This smile is approaching normal.

'I confounded them all, Guilbert. The Prussians, and the British, and perhaps French plotters too. Another one of their main agents dead, the locksmith secured, and his secret revealed. But the Prussians! Was I so wrong? I thought the British . . . All along it was the Prussians, it seems.'

'One of the men watching may have been the great Prussian agent of the rumours, Monsieur.'

'We didn't capture him, Guilbert.'

'We broke his scheme, Monsieur.'

'The Prussian master behind everything. Distracting us and distracting the locksmith. The boldest deceptions and manoeuvres. And still we broke them.'

'What about St-Denis, Monsieur? The dead woman Lavalier, and the British and the Americans.'

'Quite the network, is it not? She sent her last note using the copyist. It had been for the American Legation. But somehow the British were reading the correspondence, and they had noted the point about Gamain the locksmith, and had set their agent Kinnaird against him.'

'We can break this net, Monsieur; we can end their game in an afternoon.'

'No, dear Guilbert.' Guilbert was immediately watchful. It still wasn't healthy to be wrong with Fouché. 'Quite the contrary. We maintain it. Only now there will someone else scrutinizing the correspondence. I shall know what the Americans know, and what the British know.'

'You don't want to finish this, Monsieur?'

Now the smile was genuine. 'Finish? Guilbert, the game is only just beginning.'

———— ◆ ————

Dear Monsieur,

the affair of the Armoire de Fer has told us all which way the wind does blow, and we see that you soar highest on it. I don't pretend to be comfortable yet at the new climate, but there are things a man cannot change, powers greater than he, and he must set himself to conform and co-operate and keep warm as best he may.

Since your unique coup, it seems you are become the pre-eminent connoisseur and repository of documents. And I think I may presume a particular interest in documents of what we may call a political and diplomatic character, especially discreet documents pertaining to relations between great persons inside this country and out.

I am not a person of significance, but as intermediary I believe I made myself useful for a time, and my very insignificance may have appealed to certain persons whose ambitions outstepped their prudence. I find in my possession copies of certain letters that would surely be of interest to you, if you do interest yourself in where truly lies the loyalty of men who seemed to change loyalty so speedily in recent months. I expect no great reward, but I own that any generosity will help in these times, and frankly I calculate that a clear demonstration of my own loyalty would be my wisest investment at this moment.

You will understand from all this that I am not eager to enter your ministry walls, which — documents as well as men — do seem to absorb more than they release. But if you will reply, to R.B., at the Sign of the Duck in Argenteuil, giving your authority for me to call at the ministry at 12 of the clock with a sample of the correspondence to add to your trove, I shall take you at your word and I'm sure your letter of reply shall serve me with the sentries.

Respectfully, R.B.

Fouché considered it. The positive reply to R.B. was quickly written and sent. A pleasing additional benefit from his triumph. As the writer implied, the momentum was with him now – *power attracts power* – and surely more information would come to him and men would hurry to insure themselves with him.

Still the trove in the cellar awaited him. He hungered to be at it – an appetite he could never remember, not even as a boy – and at the same time he recognized in himself an austere restraint, a desire for just a moment more to prolong the anticipation.

To dream of the certainties he might find. *To dream of the men who would fall.*

Actually, it would not be a long moment. Roland would have his twenty-four hours, a last nod to his dignity as minister, a sign of Fouché's respect for the protocols of the Revolution.

In truth, Roland could not stop him – no one could stop him – plunging into the treasure at any moment. There were sentries around the ministry, but none who would stop him. Yet it was possible that Roland would find out, and something of pride told Fouché to prove his correctness even at this climax. It wouldn't do for a procedural dispute to tarnish his triumph.

Besides, he had seen enough as the dossiers had been stowed in the cellar, thousands of pages in their leather folders, to thrill him: names spilling out of the dossiers to shake France. The King. Of course the King, always the King and so indiscreet. His agents, Collenot and others. Lafayette, and Mirabeau and the Austrians, and others who had crossed too many borders. Affairs with Prussia. Affairs with England.

Fouché reached for pen and ink.

And Danton.

———————◆———————

Arnim had propped the letter up on the other side of the table, against a wine bottle; as if it were the partner in a conversation, or the subject of an interrogation.

Dear Sir,

it will I think be congenial to us both if I avoid writing your name or my own on this page. It is what one represents, and not the mask behind which one does it, that counts.

I represent a department of the new government of this country. You represent the interests of another country. I will not comment on the present relations between our countries, partly for discretion and more because I would rather focus on how relations might temporarily be between us, than on how they have generally been.

Into my possession has come a large body of private political correspondence. Within this are two dossiers relating particularly and exclusively to affairs between my country and yours. Allow me merely to hint at the deeper context behind the tales of Monsieur M. after his journey of the year '86, and of discussions related to the co-ordination of political and military positions in June of this year.

I am willing to return these documents to you, in return for the payment of 15,000 livres; knowing your repute, I am confident you may gather this money in time from banks where you have credit.

I make no assertion about any prior secret relation you may have with any figure of the revolutionary government of France, beyond suggesting that it might offer a precedent for a shared willingness to reach a trading arrangement based upon shared interest.

Both of us will hesitate to venture ourselves in a rendezvous. There is a place which might serve: the Étoile Royale, at the farthest limit of the estate of the deserted royal residence of Versailles. There we should be far enough from our fellow men for discretion, and able each to observe adequately that the other has brought no muskets. I judge that, each of us taking his desired precautions, and *coming alone, we might satisfactorily conduct our exchange without undue alarm. Tomorrow, at the hour of dawn, I shall await you there.*

Please do not trouble to reply; we have both learned that the risks of corresponding may be as great as the risks of the correspondence. I shall be at the place, and you may take advantage should you choose.

Arnim gazed into the paper. There was no signature. But he could presume the ministry in question, and he fancied he could presume the man.

Beyond the paper, as if out of focus across the table, he seemed to see Pieter Marinus. Could see the frown, hear the caution.

You entertain this? Naturally.

Of course you recognize the risk. Of course.

It is possible it is a trap. It is probable it is a trap, dear Pieter, but that does not change its positive possibilities.

You would run this greatest risk? Your own exposure? For the greatest prize, yes. The correspondence is out: Mirabeau, Brunswick, my King, and much else. If I do not succeed imminently, I lose immediately.

Is the Revolution so desperate for money? Yes, other lines of information would suggest so.

So desperate that they would sell part of their prize? So desperate that they would do business with Arnim? Perhaps they calculate a greater prize, than what perhaps is to them mere historical gossip.

Perhaps perhaps. Arnim saw Marinus's polite disapproval. *Greater prize . . .*

What greater prize might there be?

Then Arnim saw it, and having seen it he nodded his gratitude to the shade of Pieter Marinus, diligent and shrewd. '*I make no assertion about any prior secret relation you may have with any figure of the revolutionary government of France . . .* ' No assertion, but a damn great speculation.

That was the prize, for the Ministry of the Interior. Not the trivia of past conflicts, but ammunition for a conflict that was just beginning.

The moderates, the Gironde, were weakening. There was blood in the air. The differences between the revolutionary factions were becoming battle lines, and if the author of this letter could get the slightest confirmation of his speculation about past treachery it would be a devastating weapon.

Arnim considered this, Marinus's patient reflection as a model before him. He would lose or weaken one productive source of information and influence. But it was a source he had been finding less congenial of late. And the benefit would be the promotion of division in the revolutionary government.

Tactical cost; strategic gain.

Arnim raised his glass to his silent friend.

———————— ◆ ————————

Fouché had pushed the surrounding papers to the sides of his desk, so that one paper lay square and alone in the exact centre.

> Dear Sir,
>
> we may agree, as men with a particular experience and concern for discretion, and a peculiar instinct for subtlety, that our names are irrelevant to this correspondence. I know you for the ministry you represent, and as the man of the hour within the ministry. For myself, I will own to being at the least an intermediary to a country currently counted your enemy on the field of battle. We may agree, as men of rarer and longer perception, that despite that temporary condition of affairs we may nevertheless find points of agreement or, allow me to say, certain points without mutual disbenefit.
>
> I go so far as to say that I do not find disagreeable the idea of a meeting between us, given the adequate mutual assurances of security. As demonstration of my own perception of the advantages that we might identify between us, allow me from my side to propose a exchange of tokens thus:
>
> it is a principle of my conduct of my affairs that I will

never allow a servant of mine to remain in foreign hands; that, whatever befall him, he shall in the end come home. I own that the late Henry Greene, by birth English, had been before his demise in my employment for the rendering of discreet services. You would oblige me by returning his body to me, that I may pass it to his people and maintain a precedent that, however foolish some might consider it, I have found serves my principles and interests. You will please also to furnish me with the necessary authorizations to take the body beyond the borders of France;

in return, I find myself in possession of one of the jewels previously the property of your former King. Pretty enough, but one admits that it belongs in France, and I suppose that my government continues to claim to uphold the laws of property. It will serve me well enough as token of exchange.

If you are the man you are reputed, discourse with you would be the greater prize. I find that the tide in Paris begins to turn, and that men who previously rose may be swept back, and that having entrusted myself to one vessel, I might be better served with another of a different quality.

You may calculate an advantage in trying to capture me, thereby ending my activities in your country. The suggestion of the Étoile Royale, with its distance from Paris and natural isolation, offers me some protection, and meeting alone. I find greater protection in the judgement that your greater advantage as well as my own will lie in the opening of communication between us, rather than the closing, and that we may leave the generals to decide their battles. Tomorrow at dawn let it be.

Reply is indeed not necessary or desired.

Fouché considered it for a long time.

He had put himself in this position. This letter was a testament to his success – another profit from his great speculation.

But though he might have expected it, there were unexpected elements.

That the man Greene had worked for the Prussians – for this was clearly the Prussian master, the one Guilbert had glimpsed at the saltpetre factory – was an intriguing insight. He should review what he had on Greene: given this new insight, might the files tell him more about Prussian activities in Paris? And were there things he should have spotted earlier?

A fanciful notion, to seek the return of the agent even when dead.

Surely too fanciful.

Surely the Prussian would hope to get more for his jewel.

Or perhaps not: the Duke of Brunswick or the King of Prussia might prize such a thing, but they could never show it publicly except to declare that they were holding it for the French Crown. Perhaps the Prussians really did find it distasteful to seem to benefit from common theft.

Surely there's more.

Fouché smiled. There *was* more. The elliptical optimism about their communication. *Does he hope to buy* me?

Fouché didn't really consider the possibility of accepting, but it felt pleasant to be thought such a prize. Or perhaps he was being naive: the Prussian didn't want to buy him, but truly calculated that a channel of communication between two men at the heart of their respective societies might have advantages.

And so it might.

Above the clash of armies, two men might get to grips with one another: discreetly yet titanically. The battle for Europe, the games across different nations, had come to this final engagement.

And might there truly be some mutual advantage? '*I find that the tide in Paris begins to turn, and that men who previously rose may be swept back, and that having entrusted myself to one vessel, I might be better served . . .*'

Fouché felt an thrill; knew it irrational, wondered anyway. Was there a hint in the letter that his suspicions were accurate? Might the Prussian confirm things that the documents, even when he had finally absorbed them all, could only hint at? The former confederates of Prussia unmasked; Fouché's success doubled; and in some new position of brilliance in the European network of information. Mutual advantage indeed. He found his hands were fists over the letter.

Or perhaps not.

In which case there would be Guilbert and his blade, and Fouché would have completed his destruction of foreign espionage in France.

————— ✦ —————

When Lucie Gérard had wandered through the deserted dead house of Emma Lavalier, she had been looking for two things.

Souvenirs, both of them. She understood that she and Madame Emma had shared a rare moment of understanding, just once; and that had to count for something. Count for more than the old widow Philemon and her daughter, who would otherwise get all of it. And deserted houses still filled with the possessions of an elegant woman were not to be found in St-Denis every day.

In two months France has been transformed. She drifted through the house, fingers brushing its surfaces; a ghost in the tomb. In two months, *I have been transformed.* Greene, and Greene's death. Kinnaird, who was surely destined to die but had not, yet. Madame Lavalier, who had seemed destined to live for ever but had not. *These people have changed me.*

I have only dreamed of avoiding the world. But I find I cannot.

So: something useful – by which she understood sellable; and something to keep as a remembrance. The latter was an unfamiliar emotion; she didn't quite understand the latter.

The useful something was easily found: a pair of silver candlesticks, fine enough to be really useful, not too fine to have been noticed by anyone else.

For the remembrance, she had something definite in mind. Something that Emma Lavalier would certainly have had, but Lucie had never had, something feminine and intimate. This emotion really was something unfamiliar.

A piece of fine lingerie. Just a piece; something that could be adjusted. Perhaps a couple of pieces.

But when Lucie had searched through all of the beautiful clothes that Madame Emma had worn so beautifully – she put her hands up sleeves, she felt inside bodices, she tried through the texture to sense the last warmth of the woman, but the clothes were just an empty shell now, a snail's shell pecked out and left on stones – she found no fine lingerie.

And this, for a woman of practical mind trying to find her way out of the tempest, and thinking of another woman essentially the same, had been the most powerful remembrance of all.

———— ◆ ————

Midnight is an uneasy time wherever you are, an uncanny and uncertain space between worlds, a moment when strangenesses may slip in and out between the cracks. Midnight at the Ministry of the Interior is more than this, for the evil of the place turns discomfort into danger. The nights are cold now, too, no more pretence of autumn, and they feel colder at the entrance gate of the ministry. The brazier doesn't seem to burn as well as it should. The sentries are quicker to irritation and squabble. At least two ghost stories are already circulating.

Part of the strangeness, if it's your miserable lot to have to guard the door of this grim place at this eerie moment, is that it never sleeps. Just when it feels like night, and feels like everyone's asleep as any God-fearing man should be, and you're considering a bit of a doze yourself or maybe a piss round the corner or a mouth of tobacco, some unnatural wakeful thing appears. An official, leaving after working too long, or arriving after goodness knows what errand. Visitors – *at midnight, for God's sake* – which can't be good.

So the appearance of R.B., at this strangest moment of the night, with his letter from Monsieur Fouché himself inviting him to bring his documents at this hour, is no surprise.

They talk differently about Fouché now. There was always talk, right from the start, for he seemed a miserable sod and damned ill-featured. Now there's respect, and something like awe. Fouché's power has grown and continues to grow. Fouché knows things. Fouché makes things happen. Fouché's rivals – not rivals, as such, for he has no rivals, but anyone who is known to have irritated or displeased him – unfortunate things seem to happen to these people. A sentry crippled by the misfire of a musket; a beggar hit by a cart. Like the ghosts, Fouché can do things unexpected and uncanny.

———— ◆ ————

Before dawn on 21ˢᵗ November, the *Mercury* made her scheduled departure from Le Havre bound for Philadelphia, though delayed for one tide by unfavourable winds in the English Channel.

A trim vessel, the *Mercury*. She'd come close to the record for the Atlantic crossing; twenty years later she'd still have enough about her to be pressed into wartime service. A vessel for an escapade; a vessel for a tale.

There's an edgy bustle to French ports these days. Strange people arriving: radicals, idealists, mercenaries, naive tourists fancying themselves adventurous, spies, merchants who don't care for politics, dreamers who care too much. And everyone leaving is scrutinized by the National Guard. Otherwise no one looks at anyone; the coast of France is a furtive place. Customs officials have become the front line of revolutionary patriotism, and capricious tyrants with it. An official who picks his moment in the ebb and flow of fashions in contraband, and hasn't misjudged his mate, can make a spectacular prize in one discreet tavern agreement. It's a wild and freakish market that swerves and squalls like the Atlantic winds: coffee, sugar, tin, timber, Italian boots and Scottish cloth and editions of Ovid with dirty pictures, each may have their day of ludicrous value. Information is cheap, true information is expensive, and the most expensive commodity of all is silence.

A ghostly ray of light on Le Havre quay, a woman stands watchful amid the chaos of the mart. She's watching the *Mercury*; waiting for her moment. She has her ticket, fairly bought; but still . . . If for one last time she can manage not to be seen, she feels she may never be seen again.

Some of the few passengers are already aboard, hasty to be off and trying not to think about seasickness or the state of the mattresses.

The last of the harbour officials walks down the gangplank and away. The captain's eyes follow them all the way to their shack at the end of the quay. The young woman glances that way once, and then around her. She feels the currents in the crowd.

Now.

The woman calling herself the widow Philemon of Rouen, it was no secret, had sailed in the *Merveille* a few days before. So it was hardly remarkable that her daughter should follow her; the explanation had passed without question when the ticket had been bought and when her name had been checked on the passenger manifest.

Thus Lucie had reasoned, having drawn her conclusions: from what she had not found in Emma Lavalier's house; from Madame's sudden intimacy with Americans; from the convenient vagueness that seemed to surround the widow Philemon; and above all from an instinct that in this new world of chaos even death might not be what it seemed – and that she alone understood Madame's sense of the importance of life.

And so the pale young woman stepped up the gangplank in the half-light, and away from France for the New World, sustained by a pair of silver candlesticks, a kiss, and a very personal dream of liberty.

———— ◆ ————

In every *amour* there is a moment when possibility becomes intention: a moment among the glances and pleasantries and accidental touches when one or other of us says or does something that both of us knows is unequivocal. *I am serious.* The world stops, the heart hesitates, the game changes, and the tide must either ebb away or explode forwards. *I want this.* It is the moment of the greatest excitement and daring; it is the moment of the greatest vulnerability. *This is who I really am.*

Neither an experienced man nor a cautious man would wish to make that first move.

The edge of the clearing is all shadow. To perceive anything in the shadow would be fanciful.

But the hopeful heart sees fancies. And so across the clearing, among the shadow of the trees it becomes possible to see *a* shadow. And this is only possible because the shadow is seeing a shadow.

A pair of fanciful shadows on opposite sides of the clearing, shifting and strengthening. The world outside is a sudden flurry of breeze, a whirl of dry leaves, a startled bird, and silence again. In their world, the two shadows wait.

Karl Arnim: so many flirtations, so many proposals, so many exchanges, so many moonlit meetings, and every one the first and thrilling; *this moment, this now, is my whole life.*

Joseph Fouché: surely such a conventional ambition, and yet it has led by patient brilliance to this utterly unexpected climax; *this is who I am become.*

Somewhere nearby there is a splashing of water; some creature has touched the surface of the ornamental pool.

This morning, there is no one looking out from the great royal palace of Versailles over its gardens, across the expanse of the terrace, down the steps to the fountain and the intricate plant beds with their straggling dead harvest, along the avenue to the faint silvery finger of the pool; no one to stretch their gaze between the trees and beyond the length of the pool to the farthest part of the garden. Not for many mornings now, not since the royal family was chased out of their palace by the women of Paris. Even for the ghosts, the last element of the garden is more than a mile off, and the first light of dawn plays tricks. The Étoile Royale is a perfectly round clearing in the trees, reached by a symmetrical pattern of paths between them, open on one side to the distant gaze of the palace, and to the other side to the untamed landscape of unroyal France.

For Arnim: duty; his greatness, again and always.

For Fouché: the eclipse of Danton; and knowledge, always more knowledge.

The two shadows are distinct against the shadow.

Then the two shadows are distinct from the shadow. Each has stepped forwards from the treeline, though it's not clear which was first: perhaps Arnim, who expects to control, has taken the decisive step; perhaps Fouché stumbled slightly.

The shadows begin to measure each other: one is bulk; one is leanness.

Something is certainly happening. This morning there will be a consummation. Now it's about character, not concealment. Arnim takes another step forwards, because Arnim controls; Fouché takes another step forwards because he is in his own country.

Dawn catches each of their faces, and neither has expected it. Away from the trees the first of the light feels for them. It startles Fouché, who still feels that he is transgressing; it concerns Arnim, who does not like to be seen in France. Fouché's face hardens in determination. Arnim produces a comfortable smile.

They bow.

Surprising himself, Fouché speaks. 'I should welcome you to France, for I suspect no other official has done you that courtesy.'

'I thank you. You are welcome to keep it.'

'I congratulate you on the game you have played: hidden, behind everything, and supplanting your rivals.'

Arnim nods at the courtesy. 'And I you; you transcend the chaos of this land by sheer ability.' A horse whinnies; Arnim looks beyond Fouché, eyes now sharper in the gloom, up the avenue behind him. 'You came in a cart? This is disguise, or revolutionary sensibility?'

'The cart was necessary for the coffin – the body of your agent.'

'What did you say?' Arnim is attuned to the slightest anomalies; they have saved his life more than once.

'Your agent. The trade you proposed: the body of your agent Greene, in return for the royal jewel.'

'I made no proposal.' Now his senses are screaming. He begins to glance around him in the gloom, considers whether to –

'In your letter. You proposed – '

'I wrote no letter, Frenchman.' Arnim's voice is hoarse. He takes a step to one side: he's not ready to step back, for weakness could be fatal, but he must start to change the balance of the exchange. 'You wrote to me, and I came based on your proposal.'

'What? I wrote – ' The subtle night collapses in noise, scuffling and shouting in the darkness to one side of the clearing, feet scrabbling in the dust and curses and a shout of pain. Fouché is fixed on the sound; Arnim looked briefly towards it and is now gazing around the arena, considering options.

And then a shot.

Both men stare into the empty gloom.

A figure appears out of the night, staggering, lost. It is Theodor, Arnim's man.

Theodor whispers '*Meister* . . .', and drops, shirt scarlet, eyes now as dead as his ears.

Arnim's face is cold.

Another figure walks clumsily out of the night. Guilbert's left arm is a mess of blood, and there's a cut across his cheek starting to bleed. He's repriming the pistol as he walks. He's grimacing, but then the pistol is up in his right hand and pointing at Arnim.

'If you please, Monsieur.' Eyes on Arnim, he hands the pistol to Fouché. Fouché is still bewildered, but Guilbert is reassuring, and clearly they're in control, and he takes the pistol and keeps it pointing at Arnim with wide-eyed concentration. Guilbert puts his fingers to his cheek, examines them, and then pulls off his coat with a hiss of discomfort and focuses on his arm. He rips at his shirt sleeve, and most of it comes away; there's a wound across his upper arm, and he spits on it and dabs once with the sleeve and gives another great hiss of pain. Now, one-handed, he starts to bind the sleeve tight around the wound.

'I'd hurry if I were you,' Arnim says cold. 'Your Monsieur doesn't seem too sure with that weapon, and you might lose your other arm.' Guilbert ignores it, gives the binding a last tug, gasps, and tucks in the end of the improvised bandage.

'You came with a confederate!' Fouché sounds offended. Arnim considers him disdainfully. Fouché sees the irony, and smiles. 'At least mine is competent.'

'He appears to have had the greatest difficulty in assaulting an old deaf man. I don't find much to trouble the army of Prussia.'

Guilbert has pulled on his coat again, disappears into the darkness for a moment, and returns with a satchel. He opens it, considers the contents, finds a bottle and drops the rest. He pulls out the cork, takes a swig, replaces the cork and slips the bottle into the pocket of his coat.

Arnim has been considering him. 'You murdered my dearest friend. You have murdered my servant. And now you're stealing my wine. I do not concern myself with peasants, but I'm seriously considering dirtying my hands with you.'

Guilbert looks at him again. 'Big man,' he says. 'More to cut. More to scream.' He takes the pistol back from Fouché, and says to him, 'Prussian was playing tricks with you, Monsieur. I thought it was time to get his attention. His old man slowed me down some, but here we are again. Over to you, Monsieur.'

Fouché nods. It's all very comfortable now. First there was uncertainty and risk, then there was crisis, and now there is dominance. 'Some answers,

I think,' he says. 'You wrote to me offering to meet at this place. You wanted back the body of the Britisher Henry Greene, who was your agent, in return for one of the French royal jewels, which you had stolen.'

Karl Arnim doesn't care about words any more. Everything is uncertain; everything is ambiguous. But everything is always uncertain and ambiguous. There is only life, and death.

The fingers of his left hand flicker against the ring. 'Every single element of that statement is untrue,' he says. 'In its way a triumph of the French language.'

'Monsieur, let – '

'Wait, Guilbert.' Fouché considers the Prussian. 'I cannot find any reason in logic why you would deny it now. Surely you can't hope to pretend that . . . that what? That you are an innocent traveller in France, who happens to be Prussian and happens to come to this place at this time?' He shakes his head. 'Amuse me. Offer me an alternative truth.'

'You wrote to me, Monsieur Fouché. You offered to sell me documents of the secret royal correspondence relating to Prussia.' Something flickers across Guilbert's face, and Arnim sees it. 'You might want to watch your servant now. He's wondering if you've sold him out. No honour among thieves.'

'Or perhaps he's just interested to know you have money with you.' But Fouché's voice is distant; he's still confused. 'I wrote no such letter. I don't understand . . . ' He shakes his head. Then he remembers that Guilbert still has the pistol pointing at Arnim. He smiles. 'One of us must be lying.'

'Or both!' A new voice, and three heads veer round.

Fouché and Arnim have each expected the possibility of a Guilbert or a Theodor appearing, but no one has expected another voice, and no one has expected anything else to emerge from the darkness of the trees. But now a pistol thrusts out of the shadow, and then an arm. It points at Arnim, and then at Fouché, and then settles on Guilbert between them. 'It would be no surprise if the both of you were lying.'

Now the pistol and the arm lead a man into the clearing. A lean man, and unremarkable.

'But what if you're both telling the truth?' A cold, hard face. 'What would that imply?'

And now it smiles without humour. 'That would imply . . . me.'

Still the three men stare at him.

'My name is Keith Kinnaird.' He makes a little bow, but his eyes and his pistol are fixed. 'And at last this damn' country will know me.'

Guilbert has survived the slums and sins of Paris this long by being sensible. He knows that he's the most vulnerable because he's the one holding the pistol, and so he's not moving at all. His eyes watch Kinnaird intently. They wait. He glimpses Fouché near him, startled and angry. Without looking round, Guilbert nods. 'It's him, Monsieur.'

Kinnaird comes forwards another step. 'You: lay the pistol on the ground and step away from it.' Guilbert's mind is fast in the fray. He's looking at the distance and looking at the Britisher and reckoning from eye and arm that he hasn't fired many pistols in his time. But there's still a good chance – half a dozen paces now – that the Britisher will wound him bad enough. And even if he could shoot the Britisher he'd then have an empty pistol and a big angry Prussian.

Also he calculates that, as soon as he isn't holding the pistol, he's the least important and the least vulnerable. Already, by the end of this calculation, the pistol is gleaming in the dirt, and Guilbert is a step back towards the shadow.

Kinnaird relaxes a fraction. To the Prussian: 'We more or less met, sir, at the factory, but too brisk to be introduced. You're Arnim, I think.' Arnim produces a deep bow. It's courtesy, respect, and the beginning of a calculation that the game may be turning. 'Mr Marinus spoke most highly of you. I wish I'd had more time to learn from him.'

'He was too good for this world.' A glance at Fouché; Guilbert is beneath his contempt. 'I find that I only erred when I ignored his advice, and perhaps my greatest error was to ignore his advice that we should work with you.'

'You may have missed the boat there, old lad.' Now Kinnaird turns to Fouché. 'We've not been introduced, Monsieur, but I fancy I've felt you at my heels these two months. You're Fouché. You're the new France.'

Fouché bows stiffly, determined to match the Prussian's courtesy.

Rationally it seems inconceivable that the solitary Britisher – one man with one pistol – can finally survive. But Fouché's never had a pistol pointed at him before.

'I've spent the last two months playing your game, gentlemen. Politics. Deception. Now you're playing my game.' Again the dead smile. 'Trade. But you didn't know what you're trading, and I did; because I wrote both of the letters.' His eyes shift between them, pistol still steady. 'I came to France for one reason only: for Hal Greene. So let's go and get him, shall we? Mr Arnim, I'll have that other pistol, and we'll escort the gentlemen to their cart.'

Still for Fouché the confusion: *what can this man hope to achieve?* And still the fear, now that he finds himself captured in the night by a stranger with a pistol. He glances at Guilbert, but Guilbert is impassive, and Fouché finds the limits of loyalty. He turns slowly and begins to walk up one of the paths towards the cart, and he learns that a pistol is even bigger and more alarming when it's pointing at your spine.

Still for Guilbert the simple calculation that, the way things are going, he's going to come through the night alive. And that's always the priority.

Within a few minutes the two Frenchmen are stumbling back into the clearing with the coffin swaying between them. On their cart, Kinnaird has also found a lantern, and given it to Arnim. Three faces are clear and wild in its light. Kinnaird a few steps behind is in gloom, and Arnim and Guilbert at least know that it strengthens his advantage. Kinnaird gestures them on into the dawn, out of the clearing again into the landscape beyond the estate, onto a track and a second cart. The Frenchmen return to the clearing breathing hard.

'And the authorizations for transit?'

Fouché hesitates, then reaches into his coat and pulls out two papers. Kinnaird takes them, a glance at Fouché's face and otherwise watching Guilbert. 'Thank you. I have people who will ensure the body reaches the coast safely.' He steps back. 'You, see, Monsieur, our game is only beginning. I plan to stay in France a while. I have work to do here.' Fouché's eyes widen. And out of his confusion and frustration comes a determination, and he smiles Kinnaird's cold smile. 'Now, Arnim doesn't have your jewel, I'm afraid. But he does have fifteen thousand livres. One third I'll need for my expenses, for France is hellish pricey for a fugitive. One third he keeps: call it professional courtesy, Mr Arnim. And one third, Messieurs, you may take; call it payment for your inconvenience this evening.'

Arnim is watchful, trying to decypher Kinnaird. 'Their inconvenience?' he says.

One of the two pistols swings to Arnim. 'If you please. Frankly I'm interested to see if one of them cuts the other's throat. Whatever happens, the story that two servants of the state took payment from a Prussian and a British spy will serve me handily.'

Arnim places the lantern on the ground. Now all of their faces glow satanic from the light at their feet. He pulls a wad of *assignat* notes from inside his coat. The distance between him and the Frenchmen is three paces. He takes an approximate third of the wad, and steps forwards two paces. He holds out the money – between them; watching their faces.

Fouché hesitates. Guilbert doesn't, not for more than the second it takes to register Fouché's uncertainty, and then he's snatched the money and it disappears from the lantern-light.

'Don't worry, Fouché,' Kinnaird says, taking his third from Arnim. 'Reckon he'll work out during the journey that he's no alternative but to split it with you.'

'Journey?'

'Oh aye, it's back to Paris for you. I'm no assassin, and no kidnapper. I've got all I wanted: the body of a friend, who deserves better than a pauper's grave in Paris, and the chance to look you in the eye.' He steps closer. 'I've seen you, Fouché, and I've measured you. And know this: I'll be watching your every deceit; whatever you do with your Revolution, however high you rise, this is the face that will haunt you.'

He steps back again. 'I watched you coming: you've no policemen within five miles. Plenty of time for me to get away with old Hal. And I checked you've no weapons in your cart. I don't want to shoot you, gentlemen, but if I see you again tonight I will.'

Arnim takes a step forwards, and reaches down and pulls the wine bottle out of Guilbert's pocket. He takes a swig. 'A toast for a man who would have appreciated it.' He takes another. 'Anything more for them, Mr Kinnaird?'

The faces turn to Kinnaird. He shakes his head. 'A safe journey, gentlemen. Strange people abroad tonight.'

The two Frenchmen hesitate, and Arnim steps forwards again still gripping the bottle and Guilbert snatches it instinctively.

Arnim's smile is deathly in the wild light. 'Remember me, little man. Remember me at your last, because it will be I who has hunted you to your destruction.'

Guilbert has no answer for the face. He contrives a shrug, and turns away. For a moment Fouché finds himself alone with his British and Prussian rivals, and then he hurries after.

Now Kinnaird is watchful: of Arnim, of the darkness.

Soon they hear the clumsy roll of the wheels, and then the cart looms into the lantern-light, but it's turning, Guilbert at the reins and Fouché grim and uncomfortable beside him, and Arnim and Kinnaird watch it into the gloom again. They listen as its sound dwindles.

Silence. The leaves again, a swirl in the gloom and then gone.

Arnim and Kinnaird watch each other, Arnim impassive and gazing down at Kinnaird, watching him alert.

Eventually, Arnim smiles.

'That was bold,' he says.

'You would know.' Kinnaird breathes out. 'I wasn't sure you'd respond to the letter.'

'You do yourself an injustice, Mr Kinnaird. Your invitations are most intriguing.' He glances down at the pistol. 'You have me at a disadvantage still.'

'That's the idea. Now come; we haven't much time.'

'Where are we going?'

'I don't give a damn where you go, and I don't propose to tell you where I go. But our business isn't done. Quickly – to my cart.'

Kinnaird leaves Arnim standing on the ground, glowing in the glare of his lantern, while he himself climbs into the cart and squats beside the coffin. The lantern-light shows the coarseness of its planks. It shudders slightly with Kinnaird's movement, and as the grass-munching horse strains at the shafts.

'This extraordinary gambit,' Arnim says, 'just to recover the body of your friend.'

'Not quite.' Kinnaird glances down at his pistol, and up at Arnim, the vast head glowing in the darkness. 'Mr Arnim, you're a calculating man.

I'm about to put down my pistol. It is my assertion that if you don't use my temporary distraction for any foolishness, you will profit from it.'

Arnim considers the dim figure looming over him. 'You too are a calculating man, Mr Kinnaird. A fair trade, as you would say.'

Kinnaird lays the pistol down beside him in the cart. He looks up quickly.

Arnim's face is impassive. Then he smiles.

Kinnaird's lip twists up, and he bends again and finds a hammer and chisel and begins to work at the coffin lid. The Frenchmen haven't wasted many nails on it, and inside half a minute it's wrenched up and aside. 'Now hold the lantern higher.' Arnim does so. 'You see, I wrote a third letter. An anonymous source offering Fouché more documents if he would receive me in his ministry. He agreed. I visited, but at twelve of the clock last night, not midday. An acquaintance of mine, a man named Pinsent, gave me the idea. I carried documents, consistent with Fouché's reply, and this satisfied the sentries.' He's rummaging in the coffin now. 'Documents of my own preparation: rather misleading of course, for Fouché. Easy to get in; harder to get out.'

He has something in his hand.

'You see, Arnim, I spent an hour last night in Fouché's cellar, in his trove of documents – the royal correspondence.'

Arnim's eyes widen in the light.

'Would take a week just to catalogue the dossiers properly. But I had time enough to find a few essentials. A handful of dossiers, of particular concern to Britain. And I put them in here, under Hal's body. Old Greene, in this cheap box, for all he ain't turning into any nosegay, he's the most precious thing in the whole of Europe. Fouché has just smuggled the best of his own secret correspondence out of his own ministry.'

His hand comes forwards, and closer to the lantern a leather dossier is more clearly visible. Its skin seems to glisten yellow in the light.

'My calculation, Arnim; and my trade. I'm no diplomatist, but I judge that the interests of our countries are becoming more closely aligned. Call it a . . . a down payment on future co-operation. Call it a debt that I might one day have to reclaim.' Arnim's hand closes on the dossier. 'Less certain documents that I found of particular curiosity, this is the King's secret file – Fouché's secret file – on Prussia. Try not to lose it again, eh?'

Arnim has put the lantern down on the edge of the cart, and now he has the folder two-handed. A glance inside, then he looks up at Kinnaird. And bows deeply.

'A pleasure doing business with you, Mr Kinnaird,' he says. 'And it would be my pleasure to do so again.'

'Aye, well, I'm sure we'll both want to keep it to a minimum, but one never knows when one might need a friend in a foreign field.'

'A friend in a foreign field,' Arnim repeats. 'A friend in a foreign field. I shall remember it, sir.' He looks around them. 'And now what?'

'Now you skedaddle,' Kinnaird says, 'in any direction you choose as long as it's not anywhere near me and my cart.'

The lantern goes out. 'Perhaps I shall see you around Paris.'

'I think we both rather hope not.' Arnim chuckles in the dawn gloom. He bows again, and takes a step backwards, boots rustling in the leaves.

'Arnim, there's something else.' Arnim stops, wary. 'Fouché brought me information, and I'm hoping that you did too.'

Silence.

'I came to France to find my friend. The man here in this box. Eventually I found that he was dead. And I've been wondering who might have killed him.'

Silence still.

'There were so many men he might have crossed. He was playing games for the British government; so the French might cheerfully have killed him. But they'd more likely have made something public of it, and the way his body turned up – together with the death of the royal servant Bonfils – didn't seem to involve them. I thought it very possible that one of the British might have done it: some silly little betrayal or other, some cynical game. But again, the way his body turned up drew attention very dramatically and deliberately to the British community, and so I couldn't make that work either.'

Arnim's face is shadows, the greys and blues of dawn, and nothing shows that he is listening.

'I fancy that you know, don't you, Arnim?'

Kinnaird waits.

'I know.'

'You killed the servant Bonfils, didn't you? To stop Fouché finding out whatever he knew.'

'I killed the servant.'

'And you – you and Marinus – you thought that it would be handy to add to the confusion; to shift attention onto the British. That was in your interests more than anyone's. So you put Hal's body into the servant's house.'

A pause. 'We did.'

'Which made it rather obvious that it must have been you who killed him. Poor Marinus mentioned that he'd been in St-Denis that day – the day I think Hal died.'

Silence.

'Except that you didn't kill Hal, did you?'

Still silence.

'At that point you had no interest in killing a British agent: he was little threat to you, surely. More importantly, you had found a way to get the information he sometimes passed. So why take the risk of murder, drawing attention to yourself, perhaps drawing revenge from the British, and cutting off the flow of information?'

Arnim is a hulk in the pale light.

'And yet you knew he was dead and could lay your hands on his body. How was that possible? How was it possible, unless you or Marinus knew the murderer and knew the crime? You didn't want Greene dead, but he was dead, and then for some reason it was in your interests to collude in the mystery of his disappearance.'

Is Arnim *smiling*?

'Why might that have been? Because this way you gained new power over the murderer. More importantly, it bought their silence. *Her* silence. It was her, wasn't it? The last thing you wanted was her in front of the Tribunal telling all about Marinus, Marinus whom she passed information to, and about the terrifying foreigner she'd met once or twice. You'd forced her to work for you, to help you watch the foreigners of St-Denis. She was ideal, with all those messages coming to and fro her father's shop. Marinus was coming to meet her that day, and he must have found her just after she'd killed Hal, and he helped her bury him in the undergrowth at the edge of that glade – I think I found the trace of it – and that's how you knew where to dig him up again.'

Arnim shifts. 'It's a splendid speculation, Mr Kinnaird.' His face is still in shadow.

'Lie number one: she claimed that Greene had broken their appointment that day – the 4th of September, if I'm right – but it's clear from the timing that the message he wanted her to carry was a British request for the disruption of the meridian surveyor in St-Denis, and I know from the recipient that she passed that message. Lie number two: she can't have seen Greene in the carriage, near the Garde-Meuble, that night of the theft of the royal jewels, because he was long dead.' Kinnaird leans forwards. 'It was you in the carriage, wasn't it Arnim? She saw you. You weren't robbing the Garde-Meuble yourself. But had someone promised you some of the loot? You were keeping an eye on your investment. By a most unfortunate coincidence you were seen, by one of the very few people in France who knew you for what you are. But you could force her to lie even to the Tribunal, because you knew her a murderess. She was instructed to name Greene instead; again, shift the attention from the Prussian to the British.' A pause. 'It must have been you, Arnim. And it must have been her.'

Kinnaird's voice drops. 'Lucie Gérard. The girl Lucie killed Henry Greene, Arnim. Yes or no?'

'Yes.'

Kinnaird breathes out, a long sigh.

Arnim turns away.

'Arnim.' Arnim stops. 'One more thing. A point of curiosity, if I may. I understood that you carried a poison dose – in a ring. Tonight you came to the crisis. You weren't tempted to use it?'

Silence a moment. Arnim doesn't turn around. 'Oh but I did use it, Mr Kinnaird.'

———— ◆ ————

Joseph Fouché left Paris with a dead man in his cart, and he returns with another, Guilbert's corpse slumped back beside him. He has had to watch violent death for the first time, to watch Guilbert's brief confusion, the wine bottle still clutched in his hand, and his shock, and his contortions and his fear and one final moment of realization of how he has been hunted and destroyed.

And it is only the first of Fouché's disappointments, and the first flame of his anger.

———————◆———————

'Keith Kinnaird, I cry you the damndest, deviousest rogue north of the Forth!'

'If you say so, Hal.'

'Look at you! Gravedigger face. Quiet as a fucking rabbit. I swear at one point you looked like you were praying. They must have thought you the weediest little puritan in Scotland, and didn't they think themselves smart?'

'If you say so, Hal.'

'Not so fucking smart now, are they?'

'We didn't actually lie to them or break a law, Hal.'

'Course we didn't! Not us. Not innocent Kinny! Not Saint Keith. That'll teach 'em. Couple of scheming Merseyside pimps thinking they can best Hal Greene in the trade. Reckon they'll not try that again, will they?'

'No, Hal. Might come for us anyhow, Hal.'

'They'll get their arms broken then.'

'Might send them a little something anyway. Misunderstanding; professional courtesy. Keep them sweet.'

'The hell . . . Whatever you think right, old lad.'

'Yes, Hal.'

'Kinny, you're the devil. I mean to say, you might actually be. Old Nick himself, in last year's coat and bright-polished boots.'

'If you say so, Hal.'

'George Rentoul's talking about putting fifty guineas in. But he's not the man for me, I reckon.'

'Your decision, Hal, but you know I've always been cautious of spreading too –'

'You miss my point completely, you silly sod. Rentoul's a good fellow and an old friend. Men like him – him, and Mackay and Ross – they're the closest *friends I have. All the sport a man could want, and Mackay has a cousin who may be the most gorgeous creature I've ever seen and I'm half determined to ruin myself over her. But I still think that of all men on earth, Kinny, the one I would depend on for anything, the one I would trust for my life, is you.'*

'If you say so, Hal.'

———— ◆ ————

Kinnaird, alone again, risked a moment longer staring down at the cloth-wrapped corpse of Hal Greene.

Against his chest he still had the letter. *'I need you, Kinny . . .'*

Perhaps you did, Hal. But I wasn't fast enough, and for that I am truly sorry.

'If I have so surely found the darkness here in France, damn me if I don't secure an equal measure of light.'

Did you find it, Hal? It didn't seem so: not for this rotting flesh, rude-buried and ruder-unburied, dragged in and out of Paris cellars, coarse-wrapped and boxed, and now out into the night on a cart.

'it is a very paradise . . .' Perhaps it was after all. Hal Greene had lived and loved as he always had: wildly and completely. And at the last, his eyes had seen only a charming scene and a pretty girl. How ridiculous it was, that a man who'd risked death from the agents of three or four countries should be knocked on the head with a stone by a jealous young woman.

Lie number three. Lucie's insistence that Monsieur had always been so correct with her, so gentlemanly. *The least credible thing of all.* You'd dallied with her, hadn't you, Hal? Of course you had, with all the instinct of a mob scenting blood. And that drowsy afternoon you said something that exploded the fairytales; she found out where you'd spent the night, and she understood that you truly loved, and it was a betrayal worse than any inflicted on France or Britain or Prussia these past weeks. And Lucie Gérard – Lucie of the horse and Lucie of the glade and Lucie of the forest, who was so wary of the world that she had found a way to live entirely in its gaps, who had dared just once to feel something full – Lucie would never be innocent again.

A summer's afternoon, and the scream of a passionate woman. Hal didn't know or care about the mad games that had followed his death.

But then Hal had never cared about anything – except, frequently and briefly, a woman. Hal Greene – and Raph Benjamin, and even Ned Pinsent – swaggering glorious around France, somehow oblivious to the dying of their world.

'And believe me as ever, unfaithfully yours . . . '

What have you done to me, Hal? You died as you had lived, and a part of me envies the life and envies the death. For I am not you. Surely I am what Emma Lavalier and Lucie Gérard called me: an unremarkable thing.

Yet I am changed. From being the cheapest life in France, suddenly I am the most valuable. I have made myself the guardian of the greatest secrets of Europe, in these dossiers in your coffin. And then there is the dossier of Kinnaird: the invented Kinnaird, and now the Kinnaird who has reinvented himself. The core of a network of escape and espionage to confound the Revolution. I have remade myself, and at last I have made myself a life worth saving.

'yours, H. Greene'.

You were no one's, ever. Were you, Hal?

He beckoned to the trees, and two men emerged, silent acquaintances from the camp of the outcasts, men whose whole ancestry had lived below the regard of other men, and moved unnoticed.

But one last time, Hal, we may pretend.

Together, and with the care of men who live closer to the earth and what is in it, they buried the body once again.

H. GREENE. Back on the cart, Kinnaird looked down at the now empty coffin. Efficient to the last, the Ministry of the Interior had scrawled the name in pencil on the lid. The man had gone, and in truth the reality of him had long become a thing to be rumoured, and doubted.

The dawn was fully come. Kinnaird patted his pockets to check he had what he needed, and settled back with the rough timber close at his shoulders, and gazed at the sky, and nodded.

For one last time, Henry Greene – or, more precisely, the absence of Henry Greene – would serve the strange dreams of other men. In his coffin, Keith Kinnaird adjusted to the swaying, wondered at the faces that would visit him in the darkness, and began the journey home.

Author's Note

The great spring of history can be turned by the smallest pinion, if the mechanism is of the right quality. After playing his part in helping to destroy the French monarchy, the locksmith Gamain returned to obscurity, and we may only speculate as to whether he prospered in accordance with his diligence and skill, and whether Madame Gamain ever moved into a satisfactory home.

As well as the secret archive of the Comptrollerate-General for Scrutiny and Survey, there is substantial publicly available material recording much of the detail of the incidents of autumn 1792, including the stories of the Garde-Meuble and the Armoire de Fer. The memoirs of Mademoiselle Tourzel and Madame Campan are excellent sources for the last years and the last days of royal government, and give some indication of the bewildering business of the royal documents. The published memoirs of Talleyrand are an excellent source for Talleyrand's view of his own greatness. Various British travellers in France published their accounts of what it was like to be a foreigner on the ground at this time, even as their government contemplated war. Generally, their reaction to the strangeness and distastefulness of what was going on sounds like that of most British travellers to France over the last couple of centuries.*

The robbery of the Garde-Meuble was, in terms of the haul and the sheer bravado of the deed, one of the most remarkable in history. The thieves used great daring, the chaos of the times, and surely some inside

---

* The story of two in particular is an extraordinary insight on contemporary politics, scientific enquiry, medicine and espionage, and links diverse elements of *Treason's Spring* in the most curious way. The radical Williams, mentioned in some of the intelligence reports included in this book, was supplanted by his companion Matthews. Despite initial progress in his apparently private attempt to negotiate with the revolutionary government, Matthews was imprisoned because of his association with the moderates. Released as a lunatic, he returned to England and, confined to Bedlam, displayed with increasing passion the signs of what would now be recognized as paranoid schizophrenia. As well as stating that he had been involved in espionage work for the British government but then abandoned by them, he declared that a gang of spies was torturing him using magnetism. He kept his own clinical notes on the man whose diagnosis was preventing him from leaving Bedlam, leading to the man's eventual dismissal. Just because you're paranoid doesn't mean that the Comptrollerate-General isn't out to get you.

information to spirit away enormous wealth in the course of their five-night escapade. Most were rapidly caught. Strangely, two of the most prominent, Joseph Douligny and Jean-Jacques Chambon, had their death sentences suspended, were given new names, and disappeared to enjoy what are said to have been long and peaceful lives.

The story of the most prominent of the jewels is itself as extraordinary as their robbery, with all of the required romance and melodrama of stories about legendary diamonds. The Regency soon reappeared, though until now it had not been clear what had happened to it between its theft and its rediscovery by the French authorities. For more than a century it has been on public display in the Louvre, though the public can only dream of holding it as close as did Raph Benjamin. (Some, of course, may envy the jewel its proximity to the man.) The Sancy disappeared for a time; there has been reasoned speculation that Danton used one of the great jewels to bribe the Duke of Brunswick to retreat. The French Blue was always thought to have been carried to England; few journeys across the Channel can have been as pleasant as that afforded by Mademoiselle de Charette. In England, it disappeared forever. In 1812 a blue jewel that would become known as the Hope Diamond was recorded. Only recently has scientific analysis confirmed that it was cut from the French Blue, and we can but guess at the motives of policy, economy, or sheer deviousness that led the Comptrollerate-General for Scrutiny and Survey to manage things thus.

Raph Benjamin's hooliganism in St-Denis on the night of 4th September was only the first of the misadventures of the surveyors Delambre and Méchain. Their triangulation of the meridian – and thus the establishment of the new 'metre' – continued to be obstructed by war, revolution and imprisonment. The measurements were eventually completed in 1798. They were very slightly out.

The commission of worthies appointed by Louis XVI to examine the claims of Mesmer looks even more impressive in hindsight. Rarely can such intellectual greatness have been applied to such a dubious question; at least they took the opportunity, as Fouché found, to move forwards the very concept of scientific enquiry. Benjamin Franklin was already a legendary statesman, scientist and inventor when he went to France, having contributed to the American Declaration of Independence; he returned to contribute to the new nation's constitution. Dr Joseph-Ignace Guillotin did not, of course, invent the guillotine (Kinnaird might have pointed out that there'd been a similar machine in Edinburgh in the sixteenth century); nor did he die on it. But his enthusiastic advocacy of what he saw as its more humane method of execution gave the machine his name for ever. Imprisoned for sheltering royalist fugitives, he survived to become an early supporter of vaccination. Jean Sylvain Bailly, astronomer and later mayor of Paris, had helped to launch the early, moderate phase of the Revolution and then tried to obstruct its more extreme turn. Already fled from Paris by the time of the events of *Treason's Spring*, he was tried and guillotined in late 1793. One of the great figures of the history of science, Antoine-Laurent de Lavoisier failed in his attempt to lie low and conform to the new order: eventually he was arrested with the other tax farmers, denounced by Robespierre as a traitor, and executed in 1794. 'It took only an instant to cut off his head,' Lagrange observed, 'and one hundred years might not suffice to produce its like.'

The secrets exposed when Gamain revealed to the Minister of the Interior the location of the Armoire de Fer had as much impact as the spies of France, Prussia, America and Britain had anticipated. Above all, they destroyed Louis XVI. The revelations of his dealings domestic and foreign turned rumour into fact, and within weeks he was on trial for treason. After he was overwhelmingly found guilty, 360 deputies of the National Convention voted against the death penalty or for a delay; 361 voted for immediate execution, and the King was guillotined on 21st January 1793.

At the same time, it became clear that there were strange gaps in the royal archive. Although Talleyrand and other high-profile figures were badly tarnished, the story began to circulate that some even more significant and embarrassing material had been destroyed. This may have been true, in part: Danton was left surprisingly untainted. Or we may perceive the work of Fouché, anxious to cover up his humiliation in a royal garden at dawn; certainly his zeal about the opening of the trove served him well.

And so the Revolution entered its most notorious phase, as successive factions tried to sustain themselves by feeding others to the mob. Interior Minister Roland found himself increasingly at odds with the bloodthirstiness of Paris and radical leaders such as Robespierre. The alleged destruction of the more embarrassing political material from the Armoire de Fer was blamed on him; he may have come to regret his caution around its opening, as well as his patronage of Fouché. After the King's execution he resigned and fled Paris.

His brilliant young wife did not go with him. Manon Roland assisted her husband's escape then stayed in Paris to defend their principles, despite her increasing unpopularity and vulnerability. She and other Girondin moderates were arrested in June 1793. Still she refused to compromise, writing her memoirs in prison until she went to the guillotine in November of that year. Truly, she had been essential to her husband. Two days later Roland burned the last of his papers and, sitting against a tree in a country lane near Rouen, pinned a note to his chest: 'Whoever finds me lying here, respect my remains: they are those of a man who died as he lived, virtuous and honourable . . . I came out of hiding as soon as I learned that they were going to slaughter my wife; I would no longer remain in a world awash with crimes.' Then he stabbed himself to death with a sword.

Whatever the exact details of Danton's dealings with the Prussians and others in 1792, they saved neither the Revolution nor himself. He helped to drive the overthrow of the Girondins in 1793, and became the elder statesman of the Revolution, shaping the new system of government while remaining aloof. Increasingly embattled by the disagreements over the direction of the Revolution and by the jostling for power within its structures, at last his prominence and style worked against him. In spring 1794 he was accused of large-scale corruption, including insider trading and the taking of enormous bribes. Fearing his enduring rhetorical power over the mob, Robespierre and his confederates rushed the trial, suppressed the right of defence, threatened jurors and had Danton executed immediately after sentence.

Fouquier-Tinville was formally named public prosecutor for the new Revolutionary Tribunal in March 1793, and became one of the most ruthless and notorious servants of the Terror. (In *The Scarlet Pimpernel*, it's Fouquier-Tinville who receives messages describing the hero's exploits, signed only with a flower; see Kinnaird and the network *de la fleur* below.) He survived the initial reaction against the Terror, but was soon denounced. His defence – essentially an early outing for the claim that the servant of a vicious regime was only following orders – did not save him.

Talleyrand's caution – and perhaps certain arrangements with the British authorities – saved him. He stayed in England for a time, and then went to America, continuing throughout his life to combine grand diplomacy, corruption and womanizing. He returned to France in 1797 as foreign minister, and facilitated the rise of Napoleon. He continued to shape the affairs of Europe, and though not always appreciated – Napoleon once called him 'a shit in a silk stocking' – he survived the Emperor too.

We may doubt that the widow Philemon of Rouen and her daughter really sailed from Le Havre in the November of '92; we can be sure, from American records, that they never arrived in Philadelphia. History has not recorded what happened to Emma Lavalier and Lucie Gérard; but with two women so brilliantly determined to live outside the conventional patterns of history, that's hardly surprising.

With rare prudence – perhaps for one last time he heard the voice of Pieter Marinus – High Counsellor Karl Arnim was safely beyond the borders of France by the end of November 1792. Publicly he resumed the profile and activities expected of one of his rank. That he came out of France with his reputation intact or even enhanced, and maintained his status and presumably his shadowy influence on Prussian policy for at least two decades more, is an indication of the significance of the dossier he got from Kinnaird. As he had promised, he lived to see Paris fall.

Perhaps Fouché was as much affected by that mad autumn as Kinnaird. His biographers have remarked a curious change of attitude near the end of 1792: a diligent moderate at the inauguration of the Convention back in September, when invited to give his verdict on the fate of the King he stood and, to the surprise of many who knew him, delivered a cold vote for death. Perhaps, having seen into the archive of the Comptrollerate-General, we can understand his vindictiveness. But what he really learned was survival. Having become notorious for the atrocities he ordered when suppressing rebels in Lyon, he fell out dramatically with Robespierre, who denounced him. On what could have become the last night of his life, Fouché criss-crossed Paris, warning, cajoling – perhaps threatening; perhaps this night was the true triumph of his meticulous intelligence work. And when the next day Robespierre delivered a long speech in the

Convention condemning the excesses of men like Fouché and warning of a conspiracy, he was met with silence. He went to the guillotine two days later. Remarkably for a man so prominent in the worst excesses of the Revolution, Fouché endured.

We saw Keith Kinnaird in the half-light, at the edge of the royal ghostland of Versailles. He never really emerged. No history of British espionage at the end of the eighteenth century and the beginning of the nineteenth could be complete without him; which is perhaps precisely why no published history mentions him. He can be glimpsed – a bony finger, a cold eye, the turned back that was Lucie's first sight of him – throughout this section of the Comptrollerate-General archive. He developed a web of spies and supporters out of the infamous dossier, his way of inhabiting the chaos and a masterpiece of espionage management: the network *de la fleur*. His exploits in 1805, when Britain was within hours of invasion and defeat by Napoleon (presented as part of the material in *Treason's Tide*, which also reveals the paths of certain others from this volume, including the Pinsent family), suggest that he had grown willing to try the impossible and do it, as Emma had demanded; to think the unthinkable – and to think of her.